ANN ARBOR DISTRICT LIBRARY

3162101114510

W9-ALM-085

WITHDRAWN

The Sisters from Hardscrabble Bay

BEVERLY JENSEN

The Sisters from Hardscrabble Bay

VIKING

VIKING
Published by the Penguin Group
Penguin Group (USA) Inc., 375 Hudson Street, New York, New York 10014, U.S.A.
Penguin Group (Canada), 90 Eglinton Avenue East, Suite 700,
Toronto, Ontario, Canada M4P 2Y3 (a division of Pearson Penguin Canada Inc.)
Penguin Books Ltd, 80 Strand, London WC2R 0RL, England
Penguin Ireland, 25 St. Stephen's Green, Dublin 2, Ireland
(a division of Penguin Books Ltd)
Penguin Books Australia Ltd, 250 Camberwell Road, Camberwell,
Victoria 3124, Australia (a division of Pearson Australia Group Pty Ltd)
Penguin Books India Pvt Ltd, 11 Community Centre,
Panchsheel Park, New Delhi–110 017, India
Penguin Group (NZ), 67 Apollo Drive, Rosedale, North Shore 0632,
New Zealand (a division of Pearson New Zealand Ltd)
Penguin Books (South Africa) (Pty) Ltd, 24 Sturdee Avenue,
Rosebank, Johannesburg 2196, South Africa

Penguin Books Ltd, Registered Offices: 80 Strand, London WC2R 0RL, England

First published in 2010 by Viking Penguin, a member of Penguin Group (USA) Inc.

1 3 5 7 9 10 8 6 4 2

Copyright © Jay Silverman, Executor of the Estate of Beverly Jensen, 2010
All rights reserved

"Wake," "Gone," and "Panfried" first appeared in *New England Review.* "Idella's Dress"
first appeared in *Sisters: An Anthology* edited by Jan Freeman, Emily Wojcik, and Debo-
rah Bull (Paris Press, 2009). "Wake" was also published in *The Best American Short
Stories 2007,* edited by Stephen King (Houghton Mifflin Harcourt).

Publisher's Note: This is a work of fiction. Names, characters, places, and incidents either
are the product of the author's imagination or are used fictitiously, and any resemblance
to actual persons, living or dead, business establishments, events, or locales is entirely
coincidental.

LIBRARY OF CONGRESS CATALOGING IN PUBLICATION DATA
Jensen, Beverly, 1953–2003.
The sisters from Hardscrabble Bay / Beverly Jensen.
p. cm.
ISBN 978-0-670-02166-6
1. Sisters—Fiction. 2. City and town life—Fiction. 3. New England—Fiction.
4. New Brunswick—Fiction. I. Title.
PS3610.E5625S57 2010
813'.6—dc22   2009049272

Printed in the United States of America   Set in Adobe Garamond

Without limiting the rights under copyright reserved above, no part of this publication
may be reproduced, stored in or introduced into a retrieval system, or transmitted, in
any form or by any means (electronic, mechanical, photocopying, recording or other-
wise), without the prior written permission of both the copyright owner and the above
publisher of this book.

The scanning, uploading, and distribution of this book via the Internet or via any
other means without the permission of the publisher is illegal and punishable by law.
Please purchase only authorized electronic editions and do not participate in or encour-
age electronic piracy of copyrightable materials. Your support of the author's rights is
appreciated.

To Noah and Hannah

CONTENTS

Part One

Gone

Bay Chaleur, New Brunswick
April 1916

They had strung their shoes by the laces from a solitary elm before entering the woods edging the back field. Both girls were glad to shed them, to feel the cool slap of spring mud against their bare soles. Over the long Canadian winter, their feet had grown. The shoes, hand-me-downs from distant cousins, still molded by the shapes of other feet, cramped their toes.

"How much farther in are we going, Della? My feet are cold."

"You want to find mayflowers for Mother, don't you?"

"Yeah." Avis had plunked herself down on a rotting log, her knees splayed before her like grasshopper legs.

"Then come on." Idella lifted a stray raspberry cane from in front of her face and kept walking.

"I'm stuck all over with damn burrs."

Idella turned back. "Jesus, you look like a porcupine." She started pulling the thorny clusters from the folds of Avis's dress.

The dress, too, had been worn by some cousin—probably one of Aunt Eva's girls from down in Maine. Avis twisted her skirt all in front of her like a washrag to get at the spines jabbing her skinny legs. "I got enough on me to fill a bucket."

"You got some in your hair, even."

"How come there's none on you?"

"I look where I'm going." Idella glanced ahead. "Come on. It's near suppertime."

"Is Mother going to get much bigger?"

"I don't think she can. The baby's due to come now."

"I won't be the baby anymore," Avis said.

"You're almost six. That's not a baby."

They walked along together, lifting back scruffy bushes, stepping over roots and fallen trees and patches of squelchy mud ripe with the smell of spring, until they entered a small clearing. Avis leaned against a large, moss-covered rock. Idella scooched down searching for bits of green beneath the crackly remnants of last year's growth.

"Mother said to look for them on the edge of clearings."

Avis squinched up her nose. "Something died around here. Something stinks."

"Your feet. You stepped in something."

Avis stuck her foot under her nose and laughed. "Yep. It's me. You want a whiff?" She pointed it toward Idella.

"Quit it!" Idella scanned the clearing. Raspberry canes took up most of it. She circled the edge, to what looked like blueberry bushes between the low rocks. Then she saw the small white blossoms. "There's mayflowers!"

Avis ran up behind her. "Where? Where are you looking?"

Both girls crouched over the small patch of flowers that flitted like tiny moths among the vines. "Mother said if they find a little sun, they can be open for May Day. They're closed up now 'cause the light's gone." Idella lightly fingered a blossom. "Little white bits of things."

Avis reached out to snap a stem. "Let's pick 'em."

"No!" Idella grabbed her hand. "They'll wilt. We'll get them in the morning. That's May Day."

"What if they're gone? What if they get picked?"

"Who's going to pick 'em?" Idella stood. "And don't step on them. There's not many."

"What do you think I am, a horse?"

"Sometimes I wonder."

Avis laughed, raised a foot over the flowers, and held her leg out wider. "Pissssss!"

"Avis!" Idella giggled and picked up her skirt bottom. She galloped ahead. "Or maybe just the horse's ass!"

Avis snorted. When she got laughing about something, it came out like that. Dad called them "nose farts," and when he said it, Avis snorted all the more.

"Come on!" Idella called behind her. "We're late for supper."

Breathless and laughing, pinching and poking and calling each other the names they'd heard the men use—"horseshit," "jackass," "goddamned Frenchie"—the girls emerged triumphantly from the woods. The sky was a milky expanse. It was dusk. Light drained from the clouds, leaving soft gray streaks and smudges of blacky blue. The girls scurried to get home before the dark set in. They found their cast-off shoes, dangling like drunken crows from their laces, and ran across the flat, scratchy fields, on home to supper.

"Where the hell did you two run off to?" Dad was standing in the middle of the kitchen, tall and straight as a pitchfork. They were good and late. "Five more minutes of waiting on you two and you'd have no goddamned supper at all."

"Let them be, Bill." Mother was slowly carrying plates to the table. Her belly was so big that she had to hold them way out in front of her. "Della, finish setting the table."

Mother's voice was tired sounding. Dad sat down at the table. Dalton, the oldest at twelve and the only boy, was already at his place, staring down at it, with nothing in front of him. No one said anything. There was a strong feeling not to. Still breathing hard from running, Idella set up all the plates and sat in her chair. Mother, standing in front of the stove, turned to Dad. "Bring this kettle to the table for me, Bill."

Then she walked into her pantry, an alcove off the main room, and came back with Dad's big knife. "Here's your damn knife." She placed it in front of him. "Now, hand me your plate, Della—Avis's, too." Idella handed Mother the plates, and one by one she ladled stew from the pot onto them and handed them back. It was chicken stew with carrots and potatoes. That was special, to kill a chicken. "Now, Dalton, give me yours."

Dad grabbed the plate as it passed in front of him. "I work all god-damned day, sweating my arse off, and I have to wait like a damn dog? You'd feed that lazy bastard before you give me a pot to piss in."

"Don't worry, you're not likely to starve." There had been fighting going on. Mother took Dalton's plate from Dad and heaped it with stew. Idella was afraid their being late to supper had started things off.

"Now give me your plate, Bill." She spooned ladle after ladle of food onto Dad's plate. "You damned fool."

They ate without talking. The only sounds were Dad and Dalton chewing and scraping their forks up against the plates.

"Eat your food, Della," Mother said quietly.

Idella forked a piece of carrot. She never could eat much when Dad was in one of his black moods. She tried mostly not to do anything.

"Where the hell were you two?"

"Don't start something, Bill." Mother's voice was weary.

"I'm just asking them what in Christ's name they were doing while we sat here waiting on them." Dad turned to Idella. "Where were you, Della?"

"We were walking. In the woods." The longer Dad looked at her, the more she felt she had to keep talking. "We were . . . we were looking for something."

"It's a secret," Avis said, her mouth full of stew that she hadn't dared to chew since Dad started in. "It's a secret."

"A secret?" Dad turned to Avis. "What kind of secret?" Idella thought that Dad might be teasing now, but she could never tell. That's what made it so hard. Avis could pull him from out of his black moods more than anyone. "Who's this secret from?"

Mother stood up. "Let them be, Bill. If they've got a secret, let them have it. Lord knows they've little enough as it is." She walked into her pantry and returned with a loaf of bread.

Suddenly her face changed; she made a startled noise. She slowly put the bread down, took off her apron, folded it, and laid it across her chair. She looked at Dad, her hand resting atop her swollen middle. "Bill, my water's broke." She turned to Idella. "Della, hon, you and Avis finish supper and then get up to bed. The baby'll be coming." Idella nodded. Mother went into the bedroom and closed the door. Idella could see a puddle of clear liquid where Mother had been standing and a trickle of wetness following her. She was leaking. Somewhere there was a bag of waters, and it just broke. Dad got up and followed Mother in and closed the door.

"It won't be long now. Another mouth to feed." Dalton reached over and took the bread. He tore off a large piece.

Dad came out of the bedroom. "Dalton, go get Elsie. Tell her the baby's coming. I'll go for Mrs. Jaegel." For once Dalton ran to do Dad's bidding. Dad went out to harness the horse to the wagon and go get the midwife. Mrs. Jaegel lived just up the road.

The sisters sat at the table, not daring to move from their chairs. Mrs. Doncaster, who lived the next farm over, came running back with Dalton. Her arms were full of rags and sheets. The bottoms of old dresses and torn work shirts were all rolled together across her wide front. She looked like she was carrying laundry, but Idella knew it was for the baby. For the waters.

Mrs. Doncaster was smiling. "I just get one baby to sleep and I have to take care of another." Her baby, Austin, was three months old. Mother'd gone over in the middle of the night and helped deliver him.

Mrs. Doncaster saw the puddle Mother'd left on the floor. "Della, honey, take this rag and wipe that up. That's a big girl." She dropped a rag onto the floor and took the rest of her bundle into the bedroom.

The waters soaked the rag a pale yellow. There was still a warmth to it, and a kind of sweet smell.

"What's that water for?" Avis asked, still seated at the table.

"I don't know." Idella mopped the thin trail that led to the bedroom. "Maybe it was for the baby to drink."

"It looks like pee." Avis laughed. "Like it was drinking pee."

Mrs. Doncaster came out of the bedroom. "We'll have a new baby by midnight." She stooped and took the rag from Idella. "Now, you girls eat up your supper. Your ma's goin' to be busy. Probably the last proper meal you'll have for a while, if I know your father." She put all the used rags in the tin dishpan and rolled up her sleeves.

"I can cook." Idella sat back at the table. "I can make Parker House rolls."

"I should say." Mrs. Doncaster was busy at the kitchen pump. She filled the pan with water, then started scrubbing her hands with the lye soap.

"I'll be eight in July. I'm more eight now than seven."

"Well, you're skinny as blades of grass, so you girls eat that supper." They watched as she scrubbed her arms all the way up to the elbows and then disappeared into the bedroom. Her hearty voice came right through the closed door.

No one ate another mouthful. It was too exciting.

The wagon drew up to the house. Dad came in, followed by Mrs. Jaegel. She was a short, squarish woman. She had a black suitcase with her, the same shape as she was, only smaller. Mrs. Jaegel went directly into the bedroom, nodding to Mrs. Doncaster, who had returned to the kitchen.

"She's doing fine, Bill." Mrs. Doncaster smiled at Dad.

"You're a godsend, Elsie." Dad walked over to the table and picked up his plate and stood till he finished his stew. "Damn baby's interfering with my meals right off. I'll probably lose sleep tonight, too." He tore off a hunk of bread and headed for the door. "You know where I'll be."

"Not yet you don't, sir. Get the washtubs filled and going on the fire. You ought to be some help."

"Now, Elsie, let me get the hell out to the barn. You women take care of it best yourselves."

"Jesus, Bill, fourth time around and you're still useless."

"I get things started pretty good." They both laughed.

"You do know that much. Now, get my water going and then get out to the barn."

Dad came in with the big tin tub they used to take baths in and a bucket they used for washing floors and such. He put the tub up on the stove, added wood down below, and got the fire going strong. Then he went to the sink pump and started filling up the bucket and pouring it into the washtub till it was mostly full.

"You girls get on upstairs. Della, get Avis to bed. Do what your mother does. Don't come running down bothering the ladies." A sharp cry came from out of the bedroom. "Go on," Dad said. "Get!"

There was no lagging when he gave an order. The girls ran up the stairs and into their bedroom. They heard the door slam as Dad went out to the barn.

"It hurts to have a baby." Avis rolled on the bed from side to side with her knees up, making moaning sounds.

Idella sat down on the bed beside her. "Quit that, Avis."

"I'm going to listen." Avis sneaked out of the room and crouched at the top of the stairs.

With the door open, Idella could hear Mrs. Doncaster moving about the stove. Suddenly she heard the rapid click of footsteps. "I seen a mouse, I swear it." Mrs. Doncaster stood at the bottom of the stairs. Avis came flying in and closed the door.

"You'll get us in trouble."

Avis plopped back onto the bed.

"Come here," Idella said, "I'll brush your hair."

Avis sat still. Idella brushed her chestnut hair, the same color as Mother's.

"I have an idea of what we could name it," Idella said. "If it's a girl."

"What do you mean?"

"Mother said that I could maybe help with the naming." Avis turned and stared at her in that squinty-eyed way she got when she was mad about something. "If it's born tomorrow, on May Day—" Idella stopped and smiled shyly. "I thought, maybe . . . Daisy May! Like May Day backwards."

Avis puckered her mouth into a tight wad of wrinkles. "Daisy May! That's stupid! That sounds like a cow name."

"Well, what would *you* call it?"

"Cow Patty!" Avis cackled.

"Be serious. And quit picking the straw out of the mattress."

"If it's a girl," Avis asked, lying back and dangling her legs over the bed, "will she have to sleep in here with us?"

"She won't get a room of her own!"

"Three in one room." Avis groaned. "I think Dalton should share with whatever it is."

Idella climbed into bed. The girls stilled their bodies and listened for any sounds from down below.

"Della," Avis asked, "do you think the baby will get in the way?"

"Of what?"

"Of giving her the basket. What if she don't notice it on the doorknob?"

"She'll notice." Idella rolled toward the window. "I think she will. Now, go to sleep."

She was tired. Avis kept shifting around and rousing her from near sleep, whispering, "Are you asleep, Della?" She didn't answer and pretended to be. Soon enough she really was.

"Della! Wake up!" Avis was tugging on her. "It's here! I heard the baby cry. I been awake the whole time." Avis ran to the door and opened it.

Idella roused herself from the bed and stood in the doorway behind her. There it was! A thin little cry barely made its way up the stairs.

"It sounds like a lamb. Baaaaaa," Avis whispered.

The bedroom door opened downstairs. "I'll go tell Bill he's got another girl." It was Mrs. Jaegel's voice. "He must be in the barn."

"He'd best be sober," Mrs. Doncaster said. "He was wanting a boy. Go tell him. And Dalton, too, if you see him. Funny kid."

Mrs. Doncaster came to the bottom of the steps carrying a lamp and looked up at the two girls. "I thought you scamps was moving up there. Come on down, then. Mother wants her girls to see their new baby sister. Be quick, mind, and be quiet."

"What day is it, Mrs. Doncaster?" Idella asked. "What's her birthday?"

"Well, that baby'd be born on the first of May, Della. Just after midnight." Mrs. Doncaster held her lamp up for them as they tiptoed down the steps. It made their shadows slide along the wall beside them. Mrs. Doncaster waited with a cautioning finger pressed to her lips.

"Your mother's very tired. It come easy, but it still takes a lot out of a body."

The girls followed Mrs. Doncaster into the bedroom. The lamp by the bed was turned to a soft flicker. Mother sat propped on a pillow, her hair hanging loose down her back. She was holding the baby across her front. But it was so bundled that they couldn't see anything of it to speak of.

"Here's all my girls. Together for the first time." Mother smiled. You could see her smile, Idella thought, no matter how dim the light. The girls leaned as far as they could toward the baby to see what it looked like. Its tiny hands were pressed against Mother. Its face was closed up. "It looks like a walnut," Idella said.

"Oh, Della." Mother smiled again. "I can't even wake her up for long. She's sleeping the sleep of the newborn."

"Can I touch her?" Idella couldn't take her eyes off the tiny knots with fingers.

"You can each touch her gently. Just don't push on me, sweetie. Don't touch my belly."

Idella brushed one finger on the baby's cheek. It felt soft as warm butter. Avis laid her palm lightly over the top of the little head and then pulled it away quickly. "It's wet!" she said.

"That's right." Mother gave her a hug as best she could. "Now, it's high time everyone got back to bed."

Mrs. Doncaster came forward. "Come, girls, I'll take you up."

"Where's Bill?" Mother asked as Mrs. Doncaster was closing the door. "Elsie, get Bill. He should be here."

"Mrs. Jaegel's gone to tell him, dear." She paused. "You all right down here?"

Mother nodded. "Just so tired all of a sudden." She gave a little wave with her hand and blew them a kiss, then lay back on the pillow and closed her eyes.

"That father of yours." Mrs. Doncaster shook her head as she ushered Avis and Idella up the stairs. She was whispering under her breath as she came up behind them, but Idella could make out what she was saying. "Damn fool if he's drunk." She watched the girls climb into bed. "Now, I don't want to hear a peep from this room till morning," she warned, and she softly closed the bedroom door.

Avis and Idella lay staring up at the ceiling. "Do you think he's drunk?" Avis asked.

"Could be."

"Do you think it's 'cause it's a girl?"

"Maybe."

"Maybe he didn't want one more baby."

"Too late. It's here." Idella turned toward the window and pulled the blanket up over her shoulder.

"Quit hogging." Avis pulled it back. "I'm here, too, you know."

The door opened downstairs. The girls listened. Dad's footsteps crossed the kitchen. The steps of a man sound different, Idella thought. They land so heavy on the floor.

"He's going into the bedroom," Avis said, lying flat again.

"If he's drunk, at least he's not roaring," Idella whispered.

"I hope he ain't." Avis kicked out from under the blanket entirely. "It's kind of funny looking, don't you think?"

"I couldn't see much face to it." Idella had been alarmed by the puckeriness of the face. She knew that sometimes babies didn't come out right.

"Are you sleepy?" Avis was sitting up.

"Maybe." Idella pulled herself tighter into a ball.

"I'm not," Avis said. But she lay down, and soon enough Idella heard the familiar sounds of slow, steady breathing.

Idella couldn't make her thoughts stop, even when she kept her eyes closed for a long time. She opened them and stared at the window. The sweep of the trees made soft sounds outside, their branches studded now with tiny buds. She could feel how full up the house was. It felt heavy with people. And there was the new baby.

It seemed to her that they had plenty of people in the family already. Where was the need? "You take what you get," she'd heard Mother say once to Aunt Francie. Idella wasn't sure if they'd been talking about babies. She'd just heard that phrase, and it stuck with her.

Another time Mother told Aunt Francie that they were "always scraping." Idella thought that was a funny thing to say. She thought about all the scraping she did: scraping the dishes, scraping the floor, especially where the mud got dried all over from the men's boots, scraping the potatoes from out of the field. That was a lot of scraping. It was like the rows of potatoes would never end. And they scraped the fish insides. Guts, the men called them. She didn't do that scraping. But she held up the lantern so the men could, when they came in off the water at dawn.

Oh, and she helped Mother scrape wallpaper. That was fun. They got the water real hot and took big rags, sopping-wet ones, and rubbed them all up and down the walls in Mother and Dad's bedroom. Then they put up the new. Lovely blue cornflowers all over the walls. Mother had ordered it from a catalog, and it came on the train from down in Portland, where she grew up. Dad said he felt like a "goddamned mealy bug going to sleep with all them flowers." Idella'd felt bad when he said that, but Mother had laughed and said it wasn't the first field of flowers he'd laid down in.

When Mother had first said, "Idella, we're going to have a new baby come spring," Idella'd looked at her for a long time and then finally asked, "Does Dad know?" "Oh, yes, Dad knows." Mother had laughed in that warm way she did. "He's my rooster, and you're my little chick."

Mother called them lots of funny things when she was happy. They were her sweet peas or her toadstools or field mice. She called them things like that, and then she'd chase them around the kitchen and tickle them. Avis would get wild with giggling. Then Mother would march them out of the house. They would scatter like bees in a frenzy until she gathered them in. "Come back, come back!" she'd call across the yard or up into the hayloft, where they sometimes hid. "It's time to do something useful." And they'd come. Together they'd set about cleaning something . . . or patching a quilt . . . or shelling those endless beans . . . or peeling . . . or scraping.

Idella turned her face into the pillow and fell asleep.

There was a sound. Idella could hear it, strange, dragging at her from outside of sleep. She turned restlessly. It's the baby, she thought, remembering. The baby's crying. But it didn't sound like a baby. Idella stiffened. A scream shot through her whole body. But it wasn't her scream. It came from down below. "Oh, God, the pain! The pain! It's going right through me!" It was Mother.

Idella listened hard. The house had changed. There were footsteps, both men's and women's. She could hear men's voices outside. Dad was there. She sat up and looked out her window. It was still nighttime, but she could see shapes. Blackie was out there, Dad's horse. He was jumpy, and someone was holding him steady. "Change 'im at Mulligan's, Bill. They've got good horses, and they're 'bout halfway." Dad swung up onto Blackie in one motion and took off fast. No wagon, just the horse, pounding down the road in the darkness.

"Della?" Avis was whispering beside her. "Why is she crying? The baby's come already."

"I don't know, Avis. Dad just took off on the horse."

Idella went to the door and opened it a crack. The kitchen lamps were full on. She could hear Mrs. Doncaster at the stove. "We need more rags. Fred, go over the house and get more rags. Bring the sheets and blankets if you've got to. We'll tear 'em up. These are black with it. And bring our kettle for clean water. I'll stay here till the doctor comes, and then I'll take the baby." Idella heard Mr. Doncaster's heavy footsteps leave before Mrs. Doncaster had finished talking.

She crawled out into the hall. She could see Mrs. Doncaster stirring things in the big washtub. There were ugly dark splotches across the front of her dress, on her skirt, and up her arms. It was blood. Black blood was coming from out of Mother, soaking up all the rags. And Dad had gone twenty miles for the doctor on horseback in the night.

The bedroom door opened. Mrs. Pettigrew, from down the road, came out holding the baby. "You'd best take her now, Elsie. The poor thing needs to suck. I'll take over here. Lord help us get through this night."

Mrs. Doncaster was wiping blood off her arm with her apron. "Give it to me. I'd take it on home, but I don't want to leave Emma." She put her hand carefully under the baby's head. "Any letup?"

"Not to speak of." Mrs. Pettigrew moved to the stove and looked into the steaming kettle of rags. "Lord, how quick these have all been gone through. And she keeps on so about the pain. Straight from her heart, she says, straight through her."

Idella lay flat on the floor and pushed her fist tight against her mouth. She wanted Mother. She wanted to run down the stairs and send all those people home and take care of her. She wanted the pain and the bleeding to stop. So much blood was flowing that it made everything black.

A sharp cry came from the bedroom. "Go on in to her, Petty, and do what you can." Mrs. Doncaster stood holding the baby, rocking it, with her pinkie finger up against the corner of its mouth. The baby turned to it and began to suck.

"What's going on? Who's down there?" Avis was whispering through the cracked door.

Idella motioned Avis back into the bedroom and then crawled in after her. "Mother's sick," she whispered, pulling the door to. "I'm going down there."

"You can't go down, Della. We ain't s'posed to. Dad said." Avis took hold of Idella's nightgown. "Mrs. Doncaster said, too. Please, Della, don't go down and leave me up here."

"I've got to, Avis! Mother's not right. They got the doctor coming. Let go!" Idella pried Avis's fist from her nightie. "You stay here." She was not going to tell Avis about the blood.

She returned to the hall and peered down. No one was there. All the voices were coming from the bedroom, and the door was closed. She had to get down there. She pressed close to the banister, slunk to the bottom of the stairs, then slipped onto the narrow plank bench tucked away behind the stove, where they put their socks and mittens to dry in the winter. It was dark back there. No one would take notice of the bench or of Idella on it.

She pressed her knees and feet together and looked out into what she could see of the kitchen. The table had been pushed over closer to the stove. She could see last night's supper, plates of stew stacked right into each other. Part of the loaf of bread was sitting where Dalton had torn into it. The big knife was gone.

The bedroom door opened. Idella pulled herself closer in behind the stove. "I've never seen anything like it." It was Mrs. Pettigrew. "She was healthy as a horse."

"I thought the blood was going to drain right out of her. It's let up some." Mrs. Doncaster was huddled with her next to the outside door. She was holding the baby up tight against her and seemed not even to notice she had it.

"In the name of God, I wish that doctor would come." Mrs. Pettigrew opened the door and looked out into the night. "We give her them after-birth pills, for the pain, but it don't help. She's crying for more. We can't give her but what they say."

"No, I don't think . . . The doctor'll know about that. Leave it open, Petty. Fred's coming right back." Mrs. Pettigrew nodded, and both women stepped into the open doorway. "The air feels good," Mrs. Doncaster said, and sighed. "Will this night ever end?"

"Her color's gone so bad." Mrs. Pettigrew lowered her voice to a hissing whisper. Idella strained to hear. "I never seen anyone turn that color."

"Gone black, I swear to God." Mrs. Doncaster lowered her voice, too. The women stood silent for a minute, looking out.

A loud scream came from the bedroom.

"Mother of God, I'll try to help Mrs. Jaegel." Mrs. Pettigrew rushed back into the bedroom.

Mr. Doncaster came in carrying more sheets and another big kettle. Mrs. Doncaster looked at her husband and shook her head. "You get that kettle filled and on the stove. We need clean water. Then take the infant back to the house. Tell Lilly to keep an eye on it. Maybe it'll stay sleeping for a while now." She stood holding the baby until Mr. Doncaster had hoisted the second kettle up onto the stove and poured buckets of water from the pump like Dad had done. Then she handed him the bundled baby and took the armful of sheets into the bedroom. Mr. Doncaster carried the baby out of the house. It seemed swallowed up against his red plaid shirt.

The women stayed in the bedroom a long time with Mother. It got quiet. Every once in a while, the door would open and Mrs. Pettigrew or Mrs. Doncaster would slip out, the door swooshing softly behind them. They'd check the water on the stove or go to the window, looking out toward the road for the doctor to come.

The whole while, hours, Idella sat on the wooden bench. The rough edge of it rubbed under her knees. The warmth from the fire pressed on her face, like someone breathing close up against her cheeks and forehead. Wisps of hair stuck against the side of her cheek. But her bare feet were cold. If she put them against the stove, someone might see her. She put one on top of the other and tried to rub them warm. She could see out the window from here. She couldn't see the road, where the doctor'd be coming from, but she could see out over the field.

It must be getting on toward dawn, Idella thought. The light had gradually changed. Morning fog had pushed up from out of the bay, hovering gray outside the windows. It'd swirl around your feet like smoke when you walked on the fields. Mother said it was like walking through the clouds, only better, because it smelled of the sea.

Idella had been up this early before. There were times she and Avis and Mother would hold up the lanterns for the men after they'd been out fishing all night. The men would clean the fish and set them on racks to dry in the sun. Herring. Some would be kept for winter, and some would get barreled and pickled and sold to people all over the world. Idella's arm would grow achy trying to hold the lantern just right. Mother told her to concentrate on the coming and going of the fog, to listen to the birds and the sounds of the water from the bay. That made it a little easier, and Idella knew that what they were doing was important, but she always wished she was back in bed.

Her back felt awfully tired. There was nothing she could lean up against. She dared not move from her spot on the bench, not even a little. She knew that she should do like Mother said, concentrate on the fog and the coming of the day. Birds were starting up. She heard the cows. Dalton must be out in the barn, seeing that they were milked. He hadn't come in at all. Idella wondered what he knew.

The bedroom door opened. Idella drew back. Mrs. Doncaster went to the bottom of the stairs and looked up toward the girls' bedroom, listening. Idella thought she heard the door close up there. Avis. Then Mrs.

Doncaster went to the window by the door. She stood for a long time. Idella could see her plain. Mr. Doncaster came into the house. He put his arm around her, and she leaned up against him. Idella'd never seen anything like that between them. "She's awful weak," Mrs. Doncaster whispered, "awful weak."

"The infant's crying. I come to get you. Lilly don't know what else to do with it." He brushed her hair out of her eyes.

She nodded. "The best I can help her now is to feed her baby." Mr. Doncaster kept his arm around her and helped her out the door.

Idella was trembling. Mrs. Doncaster was going to feed Mother's baby. It didn't have a name. No one was even thinking about giving it a name. Idella pressed her knees tighter and tighter till they hurt. She started rocking back and forth, hugging her whole self with her arms.

Suddenly Mr. Doncaster ran back. "They're coming! They're riding full out!" Idella forced her body to be still. Mrs. Jaegel came out of the bedroom. Idella could hear Mother's groans when the door opened. She listened as Mrs. Jaegel filled a bowl with hot water and rushed back in.

The bench trembled beneath Idella as the horses approached. "Is she here? Is she still here?" Dad shouted as he rode up.

"I'll take the horses, Bill!" Mr. Doncaster was shouting, too.

Dad and the doctor rushed through the kitchen and into the bedroom, closing the door behind them. They didn't even wipe the mud off their boots. The muffled sounds of the men talking were low and thick. Idella strained to listen. Sometimes she heard Mrs. Pettigrew's voice, or Mrs. Jaegel's, but barely.

Someone came out of the bedroom. It was the doctor. Idella pulled herself back. He walked right up to the stove. Idella could hear his breath, still coming hard from the ride. The stove door opened and shut. Then he went back into the bedroom as quickly as he'd come out.

Idella sat on the bench, alone in the kitchen, not daring to move, for a long, long time. She watched as the room grew lighter. It was morning now. Avis must be awake, afraid to come down, lying up there with the door cracked, listening. Idella placed her hands on her stomach. She realized that she was hungry. She wished she could reach out and grab a piece of the bread from off the table. Mother had made it just yesterday. How could she be hungry with something so bad happening?

Suddenly the voices got louder. "Emma! Emma!" Dad was calling

Mother's name. Something made a loud noise, like a crash, something heavy hitting the floor. There was commotion. Then everything stopped all at once and got quiet. There weren't even whispers. She listened and listened, pressing her whole body down so that nothing would move, but there was still no sound.

Finally the bedroom door opened, and Mrs. Jaegel came out carrying the bowl of hot water, holding it with both hands. Steam was still rising from it. The water droplets slid down her face. She stood in the middle of the room and said aloud, quiet but clear, "She's gone."

Mrs. Pettigrew came behind her, like a drunk person. She reached out to keep from falling over and collapsed into a chair, flinging her head and arms down over her knees. She was crying. Idella could see her body shaking.

Idella's mouth was dry, her tongue thick and heavy. Everything was far-off-sounding, as though the fog had come into the house and filled it up.

"Them pills." Mrs. Jaegel walked slowly to the table and put down the bowl. She bent over next to Mrs. Pettigrew and whispered. "He threw them pills into the fire. He took one look at her, and he took that packet and come out here and threw the whole thing into the fire. You seen it as well as me."

Mrs. Pettigrew sat up in the chair. "Do you think . . . ?"

"He walked right up and threw them in." Mrs. Jaegel gestured toward the stove. "She was healthy as a horse. You know it. That baby come out easy. Then we give her them pills he give her for the after-birth pain. That's when the trouble started. And she kept asking for more."

"But we've all took them pills when it was our time."

"He took one look at her, and he took them pills and threw them into the fire. Just like that." Mrs. Jaegel made a quick throwing motion.

Mrs. Pettigrew looked over at the closed bedroom door and then back up into Mrs. Jaegel's face, which had come to life with a thick rage. She wiped her eyes with her skirt. "Holy Mother of God. Did Bill see it?"

"He took no notice. He was on his knees to her, poor man."

"It won't do no good to tell him. It won't bring her back. He'd kill him with his bare hands."

Dad came out of the bedroom. The women stopped talking. He stood in the doorway, staring out at the room. Then he crossed the kitchen and went out onto the porch. "That bitch! That goddamned Christly bitch!" Dad's fist, his boot, something, was hitting hard up against the side of the house. "That goddamned bitch!" Idella could feel the vibrations as he kicked and kicked and kicked at the porch posts.

"He'll hurt himself," Mrs. Pettigrew whispered. "He'll break a window."

"Leave him be," Mrs. Jaegel said. "Leave the poor man be."

Gone. Idella heard the word over and over in her head. Gone, she thought. Mother was gone. Idella crumpled over onto the bench. The cries that she had held off for so long came shuddering through her.

"Holy Mother of God!" Mrs. Jaegel was standing over her, trying to lift her. "Come, child. Come on out from there." Idella clung to the bench, her fingers grinding into the rough grain of the wood. "Get her upstairs. Dear God, let's get the child upstairs."

"Della, honey, Della, hang on to me now. Let Mrs. Pettigrew get ahold of you." Mrs. Pettigrew was picking at her, poking at the back of Idella's neck, grabbing at her wrists.

"What's going on?" It was the doctor's voice, dark and low. "Poor child. Let me help. How long has this child been here?"

"We just found her. She's been hiding."

Idella felt the doctor's large hands take hold of her shoulders. He lifted her out and up into his arms with a strength she could not resist. He smelled of something strong and burning. "No!" Idella cried. "No, no, no! Let go of me!" She beat her fists against his shoulders.

"This child is hysterical. Let me give her something to calm her."

"No!" Idella was wild. She thrashed and tried to escape. "No pills! No pills!"

"I'll take her." It was Dad, suddenly standing in front of them. Idella reached for him and grabbed him and pulled herself over into his arms. Dad lifted her chin and looked down at her. His face was tired and loose and strange. "Come, Della, come sit with me." He carried her over to a kitchen chair and sat with her on his lap. He put his hand on the back of her head and stroked her hair. Idella rubbed her face against his red woolen shirt, feeling its worn softness. She grabbed onto the front with both her hands and pulled it to her. It smelled of the barn, of hay and the horses.

"Now, now," Dad said, his hand taking up the whole back of her head, gently, like it was a teacup, and pressing her softly up against him. "She's better off, Della." He whispered it. "Your mother is better off away from here."

"I want to go with her," Idella sobbed.

"Me, too," Dad whispered. "I want to go with her, too."

All the rest of the day, the girls got put in one place or another, herded upstairs and downstairs, then up again. Different people, Mrs. Pettigrew or Mrs. Doncaster mostly, announced what they thought would be best. The girls obeyed, sitting quietly out of the way, on chairs pushed back against the kitchen wall, allowing neighbors—who started showing up as word got out and spread through the farms—to kiss their cheeks, to take their hands, to pat them on the head and say how sorry they were. They were told to be brave, what their mother would and wouldn't have wanted them to do. They were told to help their dad.

The girls nodded shyly to everything and kept their eyes on the bedroom door, where Mother was being tended to by a small, dark-dressed man named Mr. Beeny. He'd come out from town in late afternoon, sent on by the doctor. He'd come alone in a black wagon with a long wooden box behind him for a load. Dad had flared up as soon as they'd started to unload it. "Goddamn, I wanted green oak. Take the damned thing back and bring me what I wanted. I won't have her lying in some plain pine box." Idella could hear the slow, deliberate voice of the undertaker talking to Dad, and the voices of the other men gathered round. In the end Mr. Beeny had come in, nodding without words to the women, and passed directly into the bedroom.

Uncle Sam took off in Mr. Beeny's wagon, promising Dad he'd bring him what he wanted, what Emma deserved. Idella watched Dad's brother riding high up on the seat. He was riding out with that pine box a lot faster than it had arrived with Mr. Beeny.

While the undertaker was in there with Mother, Idella kept wondering what he might be doing, what was in the black bag, and what it could mean to take her under. She kept a watch on the door, in case he set about to take her anywhere.

Toward evening Mrs. Pettigrew came over to where they were sitting. "Such sad little faces, such poor little things. Come, my dears, I'll help you up to bed. You've been watching what no children should ever have to see." She pulled Idella and Avis to their feet and ushered them up the stairs.

"Idella, you've got to eat a little something. You know your mumma would want you girls to eat." Idella shook her head no and lay down. How did *she* know what Mother would want? She just lived down the road, was all. Idella put the blanket over her head and curled up under it.

"I'm going to put some corn bread Mrs. Adams baked right here on the dresser." Mrs. Pettigrew was tapping her shoulder, her fingers picking through the blanket like bird's feet. "Della, honey, you eat something. You're the oldest. You show your sister what's best."

Idella closed her eyes. She had kept inside her the secret—that the doctor gave Mother the wrong pills and then threw them into the fire. The secret was balled up so tight inside her it was like she'd swallowed a stone.

Avis was crying in the corner. Idella could hear her ragged, sniffled breathing. I don't have the strength to comfort her, she thought. I just don't. She felt her moist breath push back into her face beneath the blanket. Mother's breath had stopped. Idella blinked, feeling the soft scrape of her lashes against the blanket, then pressed her eyes closed. Against her will to see and hear everything, she fell into a long and tangled sleep that took her right into the next day.

She woke early to the sounds of other people moving about the kitchen. She lay quietly, not knowing how to start up into this terrible day. Mother was going to be buried in the ground. Idella heard footsteps coming up the stairs. Mrs. Pettigrew stuck her head in.

"Why, Della, dear, how long have you been awake? Let's get you dressed. People will be arriving soon."

Idella numbly submitted as Mrs. Pettigrew fussed and fiddled, combing her hair into braids. Idella knew to put on her best dress. Her only shoes would have to do. Avis was awake now, watching silently from the bed.

"You should be bathed proper, but there's no time nor place for it. You go on downstairs now, sweetheart, and have some breakfast. I'll get your sister ready."

Slowly, cautiously, Idella went down the stairs. The kitchen felt strange and quiet. Baskets of food covered the table. Neighbor women were in the bedroom with Mother, shuffling and moving about.

Idella stood in front of the closed door and looked through the keyhole. She could see Mother lying on the bed. But her feet were on the wrong end. Her head was at the foot. Her long hair was combed out over the end of the bed and hung all the way to the floor. That's all she could see, her chestnut-colored hair touching the floor and a little bit of a lacy sleeve from Mother's blouse. Her arm was hanging down.

Idella knocked softly on the door. Mrs. Doncaster opened it a crack. "Oh, Della, honey, she's not ready yet. We'll let you see her when she's all ready. We're waiting on your aunt Francie to do up her hair. You get yourself something to eat now. Your dad will bring you to see her when it's time." Then the door softly closed.

Alone in the kitchen, Idella chose a chair, pushed it against the wall, and sat, her hands in her lap, waiting. Dad came quietly in. Without seeing Idella, he walked into Mother's pantry off of the kitchen. Idella watched him slowly run his fingers over surfaces, touching things.

Everything in it was Mother's doing: the rows of jars and barrels, the special teacups carefully wrapped, the Sunday tablecloth ironed and folded square. Mother's jar of honey was in there on a high shelf. Dad had bought it for her from a man who kept his own bees. "Wild clover honey," Dad said when he gave it to her, and she laughed like he'd made a joke and hugged him. Mother would take whole spoonfuls of the honey, lapping them slowly off the spoon, while she sat in her chair under the window and looked out at the field.

Now Dad stood looking out that pantry window for a long time. Then he turned away and saw the laundry basket that had been sitting, untouched, for two days. He looked up and saw Idella watching him. He came over and bent down. "Have you got enough dresses?" He looked so serious and worried. "Do you girls have enough dresses?" Idella nodded. She'd have said yes to whatever he asked of her. "Good."

Avis came down with Mrs. Pettigrew, dressed, combed, and silent. She sat next to Idella up against the wall.

Dalton came in from outside. He stood in front of the closed bedroom door, his arms pressed straight to his sides. Dad came up behind him, opened the door for him, and spoke to the women. "Let him see her alone for a while." They nodded and swept from the room. Dalton spent a long time alone in the bedroom with Mother. No one said a word. When the bedroom door opened, he walked straight out with his head bent down. So people can't see his face, Idella thought. She saw that his fingers were curled tight into his hands. He walked through the kitchen and out the door.

Neighbors arrived all morning, a constant flow, bringing food in covered bundles, like they were coming to a dance. Only they were so sad, so stunned, so shocked. Over and over, Idella heard people whispering how healthy Mother'd been, how strong, how easy that baby'd come.

Horses and wagons were all about the yard. Idella had never seen so many people in their house. Dalton had been sent more than once to the train station to pick up more people.

When each of Mother's sisters came—Aunt Martha, Aunt Linda, Aunt Ida, Aunt May, and finally Aunt Francie—there was crying and hugging all over again, like a storm passing through the house. Then it'd die down to whispers and women holding on quietly to each other, not saying much.

The whole time the two sisters kept their hands in their laps, staring out at the terrible comings and goings, afraid to speak even to each other.

Idella watched Mrs. Pettigrew pulling women into the corner of the kitchen and whispering. Idella knew it was about those pills.

"Nothing on this God's earth can change it."

"Not a thing."

"And what help would it be to Bill? What help to send him tearing off into town after the doctor?"

"None."

"And then what would become of his girls?"

"Lord knows as it is."

Idella could feel the eyes of the women on both of them as she stared down at the tangle her hands made in her lap.

Dad wandered about the house. People let him be. He'd sit, then stand, then go into the bedroom to be alone with mother, causing the women who were tending her to come rushing out like spooked chickens. Finally he walked out of the house and headed for the barn. Everyone watched him go. Mrs. Pettigrew said she hoped he wasn't doing anything foolish, anything he'd regret, anything to do with whiskey. Idella hoped that, too.

When Aunt Francie came out of the bedroom and gave a nod, Dad hadn't returned. Idella watched as people started to file quietly into the bedroom. The men held their hats in their hands; the women clutched their shawls around them as if they were going into a cold place. Idella was afraid to get up. Mrs. Doncaster said Dad would take them in, but he wasn't back yet. She could see Avis looking over at her. She really wanted for all the people to leave. She wanted Mother to be alone with her girls, even the baby, like they'd been that one time.

Suddenly Dad was standing in the middle of the kitchen wearing his suit. His hair was slicked and combed, and he was freshly shaved. He was handsome. He beckoned to Idella. She could smell the soap still on his cheeks when he bent down to whisper. "You look pretty, Della. You do." She could tell by his way that he wasn't drunk. Crouching, he reached open his arms. "Where's my girl?" Avis came running up to him. Dad's arms closed around her, and Avis pressed her head against his shoulder. She was like a puppy, Idella thought, while she herself felt stiff and awkward standing in the crook of his arm. She was too tall to fit right against him.

"It's time to say good-bye to your mother." Dad's voice was serious and low. "I don't want you girls at the cemetery. You see her here in her home, where she looks so beautiful. You remember her that way."

None of the adults said a word. The men that weren't already out there stepped onto the porch. Idella could hear them clumping their boots on the steps, waiting. She could feel their discomfort. The women seemed to push back against the walls like pillows, soft and quiet as goose down in their church dresses.

Dad stood, Avis still clinging to him, and turned. "Francie, we'll each take a girl in, one by one. Della, you're older. You wait and come with me."

"Come, Avis, sweetheart, come with Francie."

Idella stood and waited beside Dad. Her hands were wet. She rubbed them in the folds of her dress. Aunt Francie was saying something to Avis; she could hear through the bedroom door. There was no other talking.

Idella knew that as long as she was waiting, as long as the door was closed, it was *before*. There was still time for her to be with Mother. But once the box was shut, there would be no more time to see her mouth or her hair or even her hands. Idella wanted it to be *before* forever. But the door finally opened, and Avis came out with Aunt Francie. Her face was red and splotched. She went right up to Dad. "I want to go to the cemetery. I want to go, too."

"No, Avis." Dad's voice was firm. "You stay here with your sister."

"I won't!" Avis cried. "I won't stay stuffed in the house!" She yanked her hand from Aunt Francie's grasp and ran to the front door. "She's not sleeping!" She raced out into the yard, past all the horses and people waiting for the procession to the cemetery. "She's not sleeping!" she yelled, heading out toward the pastures. "She's dead!"

Everyone stood silent. Then Dad took a step toward the door. "Leave her be, Bill." Mrs. Doncaster put a hand on his shoulder. "She's been cooped up with all of this for too long. Let her run off now by herself."

Dad nodded. "She's a Hillock, that one." He turned to Idella. "Come now, Della. Come with me." He reached down and took her hand. They stepped cautiously into the bedroom.

There was Mother, in the box. Idella stepped close, feeling the edge of the bed against her legs. Mother's eyes were closed. Her head was on a little pillow all rimmed with lace. Aunt Francie had done her hair up beautifully. She'd put a black velvet twist of ribbon in it and let it fall soft and shiny beside her pale face. All around the edges of her hair, like an angel's halo, there were tiny white mayflowers. Someone had found some, maybe the same ones as for the May basket, and Francie'd placed them carefully.

The box lay down the middle of the bed. Idella had been worried that it would be too small, that Mother wouldn't fit. There was room at the top, her shoulders weren't cramped, but at the bottom her skirt was bunched around her sides. It didn't get to be full out, like a skirt should be.

She had on a beautiful white blouse. Lace ran all up and down the sleeves and around the wrists, arranged and folded back so as not to cover her hands. Mother's hands were folded together across her waist. They were strong hands. Mother had said so herself, "strong hands for a woman." They weren't as soft as you might expect if you were to look at just her pretty face. Idella knew the feel of them. She reached over to touch them. "No, Della." Dad stopped her, quickly grabbing her fingers as they reached out. "They're cold. You don't want to feel how cold. Remember them warm."

Idella put her own hands down straight to her sides. She was suddenly afraid. Cold. Mother had gone all cold. They stood for several minutes, looking down at her face. Already Mother was so far away.

"It's getting on time to go, Bill." Mr. Doncaster talked low to Dad through the door. "Whenever you're ready, of course. The wagon's pulled up."

"Della, the time's come. You remember, we had us the best." Dad spoke behind Idella. "You go on now," he said. "Leave me here alone. Then we'll have to take her out." He gave Idella a gentle push toward the door. "You're a good girl. You're both good girls. God help me, I'll try."

Idella walked out of the room. She felt empty, as though something important had been forgotten. Mr. Doncaster and Uncle Sam and Uncle Guy and several other men were all lined up behind each other in the kitchen, grim and awkward in their Sunday suits. None of them looked at Idella for more than a flicker. They were lined up to carry Mother out in the box. Idella could see through the open doorway that the horse and wagon had been backed up against the porch. Mr. Pettigrew was holding on to the horse, keeping it steady.

Dalton was standing off to himself on the porch. He had on somebody else's suit. He didn't own one, never'd wear one, didn't go to church.

"Della, dear, come sit with me." Idella went willingly to Mrs. Doncaster. She nestled up against her. She could smell the sweetish-sourish scent from all the milk she was making, feeding two babies. It had leaked out in dark, spreading splotches.

Sometimes Idella forgot there was a baby. They'd named her Emma, after Mother, because Dad had said to. They'd been keeping her next door at the Doncasters'. Relatives were probably going to take the baby, she'd heard. Aunt Beth, over near Bathurst, had always wanted a girl. They'd be taking a cow, too, the best milker, because the baby needed milk to live.

Dad opened the door. He nodded to the row of men. "Let's bring her out." Everyone in the room stood up, like at church when it's time for a hymn. Solemnly the men marched in. Dad must have closed the box alone in there once he'd said good-bye. This was *after*. Suddenly Idella wished that she'd touched Mother's hair. That would not have been cold, but soft and lovely and normal. But it was too late. She couldn't go back. She started to cry.

The men were coming out now. They were trying to carry the box on their shoulders, dignified, for Mother, but they had to put it down on the floor and shove it to get it through the narrow bedroom door. Dad was leading. When they'd gotten it through, the men stooped to pick it up again and carried it on out of the house. Idella watched as they stepped onto the porch and lowered it into the wagon. The men who weren't helping had their hats in their hands.

Dad turned to Dalton. "We'll take her out together." Dad climbed up onto the seat and took the reins from Mr. Pettigrew. Dalton climbed up next to him. "No sense waiting any longer." Dad gave a shake to the reins, and the wagon started to pull forward. Suddenly the horse bucked, jerking the wagon backward. The box with Mother in it slid and hit against the porch post with a terrible whacking sound.

"Steady, boy, steady." Mr. Pettigrew grabbed the reins to quiet the horse. Dad stayed on the wagon. Mr. Doncaster and some others pushed the box back in. This time the horse went forward, slowly dragging the wagon away and up the road. The women walked out to join their husbands, and the string of wagons haltingly started for the cemetery.

Idella stood in the doorway watching. "Why don't you go upstairs now, Della." Mrs. Doncaster was wiping at her eyes. "I'll be next door if you need me. I have to feed the babies. You come running over now, honey, if you need something." Idella hardly heard the words. She watched the wagon with Mother in back for as long as she could. Then she ran through the kitchen and up the stairs to her bedroom window so she could watch it more.

As she watched, she saw a lone figure come running across the fields from out of the woods. It was Avis. She was running, running, like a wild creature—her dress pulled up, barefooted, hair all undone—running up onto the road, toward the cemetery, way behind the long row of wagons. Idella could see that she was clutching something. Part of it fell at her feet, and she scooped it up and kept on running, leaving some behind. The mayflowers. Avis had gone and picked them all. She was going to get them to Mother. Idella smiled. Avis would get there. Idella stood with her forehead pressed against the window, feeling the flat coolness against her skin, and watched until the scraggly, frantic figure disappeared over the hill to where the wagons had gone.

Idella knew that when she moved away from the window, her different life would begin. Already there was so much to be done.

Pomme de Terre

March 1918

"Will you look at this one coming down the road now? What do you suppose?" Elsie Doncaster muttered to herself as she flung a wet union suit over her clothesline and secured it with wooden pins at the shoulders. The breezes swooping off the bay pushed against her back, flapped and whipped at the long, empty trouser legs that so often held her husband, Fred. She stood and watched the figure of a girl or a woman, she couldn't tell which, lumber slowly along the edge of the rock-riddled horse path they all called "the road."

She was French. Elsie knew it. They had a different way about them, the French, something about the walk, using their whole bodies, not just their legs. Walking steady and alone, the girl got close enough for Elsie to see that she was clutching something up against her, a cloth bundle of some sort, and a pair of men's boots. What looked to be a piece of paper was gripped in the other hand, flapping at the corners.

By then Tippie had run out barking, and Elsie had to call her off. The girl stopped and looked up at Elsie looking back. Long brown hair blew in a tangle around the girl's face, but Elsie could see the large, soft features now—round and firm with youth, not the second-time-around saggy fullness like she was getting herself. The girl had breasts, though, two plump loaves fresh from the oven. She could see their ampleness across the front of her dress—which was tight under the arms, pinning her breasts in position. She'd been growing of late, that girl, and no one was paying enough attention to get her new clothes.

The girl raised the hand with the paper. Elsie waved back and stood waiting. The girl started toward her, across the piece of field that was the backyard.

"Bonjour." The girl did not smile. She was intent. *"Pardon,"* she said when she stood in front of Elsie. The clothesline hung overhead between

them, Fred's long johns licking at the girl like cold, wet tongues. "Is there soon a . . ." She hesitated and spoke carefully, "H . . . Hillock?"

"Oh, there's lots of Hillocks around, honey." Elsie reached up and grabbed the wet clothes to stillness. "You've got to be more specific."

The girl looked down at the paper she was holding. "With girls."

Elsie looked at the paper and smiled. "You mean Bill. He's got girls, all right. Three of 'em. And a boy."

The sun was behind the girl, so it was hard for Elsie to see her face. She raised a hand to shield off the glare.

"He's down to two girls living there, but the two left are a handful. Plus the boy. Plus Bill. I'd say them four are a straight set of Hillocks." She laughed. "You would make five. A full house."

The girl looked at her, squinting in concentration as though trying to squeeze in the information.

"You get that paper down to Salmon Beach?" Elsie pointed at the wrinkled handwritten notice, the likes of which she had seen before. Bill kept putting up signs at the general store for someone to help take care of the housework and the kids. And he kept coming up with French girls that didn't last long. There were plenty of reasons for them not to last.

"Which house, please?"

Elsie turned and pointed. "You can see it from here, dear. Next one down. That little gray house on the cliff edge. See?"

There was no way not to see. It stood alone against the morning sky, a ways off from the little barn. A strip of blue deeper than the sky was just beyond it, like a ribbon. That was the Bay Chaleur.

"*Merci, madame.*"

"Oh, you're welcome, dear. And you can take the shortcut here." She pointed toward her field. "They've beaten a path, those kids, right up to my door." She laughed. "Don't let 'em scare you. They're good kids. It's just that they've had all Bill and no Emma now for almost two years." She shook her head. "God bless her dear loving soul."

Elsie knew the truth was that Avis and Idella—and Dalton—were not interested in having anyone else living with them and trying to help. They thought they got along just fine by themselves. They went to bed when they were ready and ate when they pleased. They didn't fuss about having a certain day for washing—either the clothes or themselves. And they did get around to washing and cutting toenails and beating the rugs and airing the quilts. They just didn't like being told to. She'd learned that early on and had taken a watchful seat in the shadows.

It was the memory of their mother, of Emeline, of wanting to please her still, that got them to fill the tub with hot water and take a bath, or to make stew like she used to, or to wash all the curtains come spring. For their mother they'd do anything.

Elsie watched as the girl—must be fifteen, she thought—made her way to Bill's house with a slow, steady gait. She didn't pause or look about as she crossed Bill's yard and stepped up to the house. Must be the boots she was wearing, Elsie thought, that make her walk like that. Like a cow coming in from the fields—weary, deliberate, ready to be milked and put in her stall. Poor dear.

The girl stood on the slanted porch, knocked once, and waited a long time till someone happened to open the door to go out.

"Monsieur Hillock?" she asked. It was Dalton who confronted her. He stood, tall for his fourteen years, gazing down at her. His hair, un-combed, had the appearance of a thatched roof left exposed to foul weather.

"I ain't no monsieur." He laughed. "Though I'm stuck being a Hill-ock." He lifted his head and called out from the sagging front porch across the barren yard to the open barn door. "Dad, a new Frenchie has showed up!" Then he took the girl's hand and shook it. She still held on to the paper, the blanketed bundle, and the boots clutched up against her. "Good luck," he said, and walked off toward the ladder protruding from the edge of the cliff. "I'm going out to set my lobster traps."

"Bonne chance." The girl smiled when he turned back and cocked his head. "Good luck to you also. With the fishing."

Dalton smiled and started down.

She stood on the porch and watched him slowly disappear. She could hear the lapping of the bay down below, and she could smell it. She walked to the edge of the porch and stood looking about. There were no trees to speak of near the house. The few there grew as though bent from the waist, away from the winds that must blow fierce come winter. For there was no shelter from the winds. The fields that stretched beyond the barn were broad and flat. She knew from looking that there were as many rocks as potatoes to dig.

"How long you think this one'll last?" Idella peered from behind the kitchen curtain.

"Not long, I hope." Avis was crouched before the window, her eyes just over the cracked wooden sill.

"Do you see her feet?" Idella whispered. "She's wearing boots as big as barn doors."

"I bet she's got toenails like old shingles," Avis said. The two sisters started giggling. Avis peeked over the sill again. "She's like a moose from behind."

"A big old pumpkin," Idella said, "gone all rotten in the dirt."

"Or a fish gone belly up and staring—with flies coming in and out its mouth."

"That's enough, Avis. Jesus. She is human."

"I guess."

"Come back to the table, or she'll see us watching." Idella reached down and tugged at Avis's sleeve. "And she'll hear you."

"How come Dad keeps getting French girls to look after us?"

"They're all that'll come." Idella sat at the kitchen table, where she'd put out biscuits and molasses for breakfast. "To them our life seems pretty good. A step up."

"From what?"

"From living way down country."

"You couldn't pay me enough to take care of us."

"Of you, you mean." Idella laughed. "I'm no trouble."

Avis poured a large pool of molasses onto her plate and dragged her fingers through it. "I wish she wasn't sleeping in our room. There isn't room to fart in there as it is."

"You manage."

They both started giggling.

Bill Hillock came from the barn, but not till he'd finished shoveling out the horse stall. He ambled up to the porch step, wiping his hands down the front of his overalls. "You come on soon enough, by God." The girl held out the paper with his hand-scrawled job announcement. He nodded. "Put it up yesterday." He leaned an arm against the porch rail and looked down at her. "It don't pay much. But you get the roof, see." He looked up, then paused. "While it holds." The girl followed his gaze. A weathered shingle had loosened at the edge and was dangling like a drip of water ready to plop. "I'll get Dalton to fix that." He reached up and grabbed it off the eave.

"And you get food." He gestured to the flat fields. "We got enough potatoes this year to feed every cow and human ten miles square. If you like potatoes every which way but raw, with a herring along or under or on top, you'll be happy with the food." The girl smiled shyly, looking down at her worn boots.

"Well, if you can get something hot on the table and keep the chickens and the cow happy and clean the clothes and the house and whatnot, the job is yours. We've been running through you ladies like bonbons, but I'll give you a try." He nodded toward the house. "They've had the run of the place. No mother going on two years." He paused and looked toward the cliffs. He shook his head and then looked back at her. "It's damn cold come winter. You interested?"

The girl smiled up at him. "*Oui.* Please."

"Better get used to the English here. We don't speak a lick of the French."

"Yes." She nodded her head slowly, like a sunflower heavy with seeds.

"You got a name?"

"Madeleine."

"Well, we'll call you Maddie. That okay?"

"Maddie."

"You met Dalton?" Bill pointed toward the ladder. She smiled and nodded. "You won't see too much of him. Mealtimes. He's got a boat he made and spends most of his time out in it pulling lobsters—unless I drag him out to the field with me." He glanced down at her. "Kind of young, aren't you?"

Maddie shrugged and looked away.

Bill stood staring at her another long moment. He reached out to take her blanket bundle, but she pulled it closer. He reached for her extra boots then, and she shook her head no in that slow-moving way she had.

"Well, then, Maddie," he said, his hand on the door, "let's go meet them girls."

Avis and Idella were back at the table. Only their eyes moved when Bill pushed open the door and Maddie walked behind him into the house. They'd been listening to every word. They sat in front of half-eaten biscuits, their legs swinging back and forth beneath the table.

"Girls, this is Maddie. She'll be helping us. Della, you show her where she'll sleep and the drawer to put her things in."

The girls eyed her without greeting.

"She won't fit in our room," Avis said after a pause. "I'll have to stick some of me out the window if we're all s'posed to sleep in there."

Bill laughed. "Stick your head out, then. That'll save space." He turned and walked out. Maddie stood looking down, hunching her broad shoulders as if she were cold.

"Come on, then." Idella stood and started walking up the stairs. Maddie didn't move or raise her head. Idella stopped and turned around. "Come on, I said. What's the matter with you?"

Avis had stayed in her seat watching. Maddie raised her head and turned toward Idella on the stairs.

"You don't speak English?" Idella asked.

"Not so good when I am new."

"All I said was come on. Jesus."

"This here is your drawer." Avis had scampered up after them. She pulled open the bottom drawer of the one dresser in the room. It was empty.

"This is your bed. It's pretty small—I don't think you can fit on it." Idella was annoyed and didn't know why. She felt tall and stiff looking down at this new one, crouched in front of the bed, sticking the extra pair of men's boots under it. Then she sat on the bed with her bundle in her lap. She did fill up most of it with her broad bottom.

"*Très bon.*" She smiled at them tentatively. "Good." She corrected herself and patted the bed.

Idella and Avis watched as she slowly untied the knot and unfolded the blanket. Her hands were large, the fingers like a man's, her fingernails broad and thick.

Carefully she took a few clothes from out of the blanket and placed them in the drawer. There was another dress, as sacklike and shapeless as the one she was wearing, some underwear, and one other pair of long stockings. But something was left in the folds of Maddie's old blanket, a lump still in there. Both sisters noticed. Maddie tied the blanket again around the lump and kept it on her lap.

Idella stood in the corner, looking out the window. She didn't have the strength to be nice to this one, didn't want to be bothered. They all left, the girls. What was the point?

"You walk the whole way from Salmon Beach?" Avis was so nosy.

"Oui." Idella looked over at Maddie impatiently. "Yes," Maddie said. "It was Salmon Beach."

"They tease Dad about them notices at Wheeler's Store," Avis said. "Mr. Wheeler said he should charge Dad a nickel for every one he puts up, and he'd be rolling in it."

"Avis, get your feet off the bed with them shoes." Idella reached down and brushed dried clods of field off the patchwork spread. She'd worked hard getting that clean.

"Did you sleep somewheres?" Avis ignored her sister and leaned over toward Maddie eagerly, her behind barely lighting on the edge. "You come so early this morning."

"In a barn."

"They know you was in there?"

"The horses." Maddie smiled. "And the cow. I drank milk."

"From the cow?" Avis laughed. "You put your mouth right up over her tittie?"

"Avis!"

Maddie laughed. "I spray." Maddie made a noise like something squirting. "It is good. Warm."

"Why'd you come here?" Idella turned from the window and snapped the question across the room.

Maddie looked at her. "Here I get air. Not like the lobster factory."

"You work there?" Avis asked.

Maddie nodded. "I hate it."

"Me and Idella watch the girls walk up and down on their lunch break. We can see them from our back field."

Idella could see, even from this distance, that Maddie's fingers were covered with ragged cracks. They looked red and sore.

"What you got in there?" Avis pointed at the bundle.

"Avis! That's none of your business! Quit picking at her. You're going at her like *she* was a lobster. Pick, pick, pick."

Maddie looked down at her large hands and shrugged her broad shoulders.

All that first day, Maddie moved slowly about the house, taking things in. She was nervous, fidgety at the beginning. Avis followed her like a fly. Idella stood off to the side more and watched. Maddie studied everything. She went into Mother's pantry and shook and lifted all the bags and barrels. She pulled the tops off all of Mother's spice jars and put her nose close down into them to smell the precious contents. She put her hands on everything.

"What is this?" Maddie reached high up and took the jar of honey from the top shelf.

"You can't touch. It was Mother's special honey." Idella grabbed it. "It was from Dad."

Maddie looked at Idella. "*Pardon.* I did not know."

"Honey keeps forever." Idella placed the jar back exactly where it had been. "I'm keeping it forever where she put it. You French girls touch everything."

There was the sound of a wagon approaching. Maddie turned quickly from the window and put her head down, as though trying to disappear.

"Hello there, you Hillocks!" The man in the wagon was yelling. "Need anything in Salmon Beach today?"

"That's just Mr. Pettigrew," Avis said. "He always calls that when he goes by. He's nice enough." She ran to the door. "No thanks, Mr. Pettigrew. Not today."

"Just asking." He kept his wagon moving. "Tell your dad not to work too hard!" He laughed as he said it. "Tell him I said so."

"Do many people go on the road?" Maddie asked.

"Nah. The Pettigrews, 'cause they live farther up. The Doncaster boys go tearing by. They're always cursing at each other, so you know it's them. Then Mrs. Doncaster yells after them from her porch. Come on out to the barn." Avis took Maddie's hand and pulled her out into the yard. Idella followed at a distance.

Maddie looked at every chicken, like one was different from the other. She came up behind them as they scattered about the yard, felt them, put her hand down around their bodies, and laughed when they pecked her.

She put her hand on the muzzle of Tater, the cow, who turned her big head heavily in Maddie's direction. "You have a nice cow," she said as they stood in the doorway of the barn watching her.

"Idella saved that cow's life," Avis said. "She got a chunk of potato stuck in her throat, and that cow was going to choke to death."

"Let me tell her, Avis—it was me that done it. Dad was yelling for me from the barn, see, and I didn't know what he wanted, but I knew he wanted it bad! He said, 'You've got to get that potato. We can't get our arms down there.' So I did his bidding. Dad and Dalton held her mouth open, and I reached my arm in—I stuck it way down in, through the mouth and beyond—and I felt around, and then I come to it—I got my fingers around it, and I pulled my hand out all along the way with that piece of potato. Dad told me I'd saved the day. He used them words."

"That's why we call her Tater," Avis said. "We used to have two cows, but the best milker went with Baby Emma."

"Who is Baby Emma?"

"Our sister." Avis picked up bunches of loose hay and scattered them over her head, twirling about. "She's two on May Day. She lives ten miles away, and she needed the cow for her milk. Mother died having her."

"Avis!"

"Well, she did." Avis stopped her spinning and stood. "So Dad give her to Aunt Beth. She wanted a girl, and Dad had two already."

Maddie stood with her hand on the cow and looked at Avis and then Idella. *"C'est triste,"* she finally said, then caught herself. "Sad. So sad."

"She was beautiful," Idella said, returning Maddie's sorry gaze with narrowed eyes. "Our mother was beautiful. She was a lady. She wasn't anything like you."

"Non." Maddie shook her head, her fingers still splayed heavily on the back of the cow. *"Non.* Not like me." She spoke softly. "I am sorry, Idella. I did not know what happened to your mother. I did not have a mother for long."

"Did she die?" Idella asked.

"She left me."

"Left you? By dying?" Avis asked.

"By going in a wagon and not taking me. She left me with my father."

Avis persisted. "He nice to you?"

Maddie looked at Avis. "There was no jar with honey."

"Dad got that honey for Mother special from the man with bees," Idella said.

"I am sorry I moved the jar. Don't be mad, Idella. Please."

Idella ran up to the pile of hay and kicked her leg through it, scattering stiff bits in a prickly flurry. She turned and ran into the house, jumping over the porch step and slamming the door.

"What bit her on the ass?" Avis said, staring after her.

Maddie turned and smiled at Avis. "Such talk, Petite Avie. She is sad. And angry."

"Petite Avie?" Avis laughed. "Is that French for 'Pretty Avis'?"

Maddie reached over and pulled bits of straw from Avis's hair. "Pretty Avis. *Oui.* Sad Idella."

Maddie did not go to sleep when the girls did. She said that she would just sit on her bed and look out the window. She slept very little, she said, and never before midnight or one.

"Well, you'd better get to sleep sooner than that to get up in time to do stuff," Idella said, sitting stiffly on her bed in her nightgown.

"Ah, *oui,* I am up at dawn. I shake the rooster."

"Why don't you go downstairs with Dad?" Avis asked.

"Ah, *non. Non,* I belong here with you girls."

"Well, I think this is weird," Idella said.

"Shut up, Idella, and go to sleep." Avis was under the covers. "Then you won't know she's here."

Idella did think it odd. She could feel Maddie's heavy presence. She was such a poor hulk of a thing. Her cheeks were rough and reddish, as if she rubbed at her face a lot. Idella pulled the blanket up over her eyes. Still, her smile had a sweetness. It came and went so quick, like a rabbit skirting out of the tall grass and then freezing up again.

"Good night, Maddie," Avis said finally, in a voice that had lost its vinegar. "I'm glad you're here." She was soon asleep.

Idella lay there longer, feeling the new presence in the room, smelling her body smells. There was dirt and milk and salt about her. Idella turned her face to the wall and fell asleep.

Avis sat up in bed the next morning and looked over at the small cot. The brown woolen blanket Maddie had brought was carefully spread over it. The lump was gone, and she was gone. "Where's Maddie?"

"Look out the window, why don't you?" Idella, who'd been lying awake, pointed toward the cliffs.

Maddie was standing at the top of the cliff ladder looking out to the bay.

"She better not go over the cliffside," Idella said, joining Avis at the window. "Dad'd be mad as hell."

Avis turned to Idella. "Let's go through her things. I want to find her treasure."

"No, Avis. That's not nice. And she's coming back now."

"Maddie's not very pretty, is she?" Avis said, watching again from behind the curtain.

"Well, no. I don't guess she is," Idella said.

They got themselves dressed and down the stairs. It was much earlier than usual for them, but they were interested. Maddie was now in the kitchen standing at the stove over the black iron fry pan. There was nothing in the pan yet. The blue tin pot on the stove had steam still coming out the spout; the smell of coffee was strong. Bill's door was closed.

Maddie looked up when the girls came in. *"Bonjour."* Her smile stayed a little longer than yesterday. *"Café?"*

"You think too much French in the morning," Avis said. "You've got to switch to English before Dad gets up. He hates not knowing the words."

"Coffee?" Maddie repeated. "Sweet?"

"Sure!"

"Avis! We don't drink coffee yet."

"I'm ready. Nobody offered it up before." Avis got herself a cup off the shelf and held it under the pot. Maddie looked at Idella, who shrugged and went to get down her own cup. Maddie nodded and half filled Avis's cup.

"Looks like spring mud," Avis said.

Maddie pursed her lips and frowned. "Too strong you think I make it?"

"Oh, no. I wouldn't say." Avis took the cup from her. "Where's the sweet?" Maddie pointed to the sugar bowl.

The bedroom door opened with a scrape. Bill came walking out, tousled and unshaven and blinking back the light of morning. "That's the best smell of coffee I've woke to in about all my life, Maddie. It smells so strong I don't even need to drink it. If you keep smells like that in the house, I'll have to marry you."

Idella saw Maddie turn red and her head go down. Her hair, still wild and windblown, fell forward and hid her face.

Dad pulled his suspenders up over each shoulder as he walked to the table. "You two are up early. Going fishing?"

"Dalton, he has gone." Maddie placed a full cup of coffee in front of him and hurried back to the stove.

"He does everything alone." Dad picked up the mug and held it under his nose. "This here is like a bed of roses to me, Maddie. To wake up and smell coffee. Not since Emma." Idella watched as Dad took a cautious sip. "Jesus H. Christ!" His eyes sprang open. "Holy Mother of Jesus!" His voice boomed. All three girls froze as they watched him. "Did you add water?" He turned sharply and looked at Maddie. Then he threw back his head and laughed full out so that they could see the buttons of his long underwear rippling up and down like waves coming and going. "Is there new hair on my head?" he asked when he was able. "Did that sip do anything to me yet?"

Slowly, cautiously, the three girls shook their heads. None of them dared go beyond a smile yet.

"You make damn strong coffee, Maddie!" He took a larger swallow. "And it's damned good!" They all started laughing then, happy and relieved.

There got to be a pattern to things pretty soon. Every morning when the girls woke early, they'd know to look out the window if they wanted to find Maddie. There were a few mornings when they could hear voices together out in the front yard. When they looked out, they saw Dalton talking to Maddie before he went down the ladder. Once they saw Maddie clap her hands and laugh at something Dalton said. Another time he was showing her how to do something, but they couldn't figure out what it was. It might have been something to do with being in the boat, by the look of things, or with fishing. Dalton didn't get excited by too many other subjects.

The coffee continued strong and hot. Dad got so he asked for a second cup before he'd finished the first and said he didn't know how he'd gotten on drinking that watered-down piddle piss he used to call coffee. Maddie blushed.

For breakfast she cooked potatoes and then fried eggs in the black pan. Every day. The potatoes were hot and brown and crisp and the eggs all cooked through till the yolks were a crumbly light yellow and the whites mottled brown at the edges. Everyone ate them as she presented them, sliding onto the plate with a slap.

Dinner was potatoes and dried salted fish from the barrels. Supper was beans and salt pork and potatoes.

"Maddie, how come we eat the same thing every day for every meal?" Avis asked one morning after Dalton and Dad had left the table. "We ever gonna have something different?"

Maddie pursed her lips and kept scrubbing a plate. "You like what I cook?"

"It's good," Avis said, "but it's sort of tiring to have the same thing every day."

"Your father, he is complaining?"

"Not to me."

"I'm getting awful tired of it," Idella said, looking up from her plate. "I don't think you know how to cook anything else."

The girls soon learned there were things Maddie would not talk about, would not even finish listening to the question about—mostly about where she came from, what her folks were like, who her people were. It was as if she came out of nowhere.

"How come you never wear them boots you brought?" Avis asked her one morning. "You walked in here carrying 'em and hardly nothing else. Whose are they? They're awful big."

"They're mine."

Even Avis knew not to keep asking after that.

As she got more comfortable in the house, Maddie loved to question the girls—about growing things, about how things were done in the house with their mother. How was a table set properly? How was a hem sewn on a skirt? These were things that Idella, at ten, knew way too much about and that Maddie, at fifteen, should have known a lot more about than she did.

Hardly any sounds at all came out of her when she was around Bill. She would answer a question when asked—never more than a word or two—or just nod. She looked down at her feet when she finished her answer.

So far Avis had learned the most. Maddie had no brothers or sisters that she knew of. French was what she spoke when she was young, but she'd had to learn the English more when her mother left her. She once had a cat named Nuage, which meant cloud, but he got lost in the woods and probably eaten by something.

She had no middle name.

"Didn't your mother give you one?"

"She never told me."

Avis liked being called "Petite Avie" and started asking for words in French. This amused Maddie, and she would point to things and tell Avis the word: *la fourchette, le cheval, la tasse, il pleut.*

Avis made Maddie laugh out loud at breakfast one morning when she asked if she could pass her "an oaf." *"Oeuf!"* Maddie laughed. "Not 'oaf.'"

"What is an oaf anyway?" Avis asked.

"Well, that'd be someone like me," Dad said, laughing, too. "Right, Maddie?"

"Non." Her laughter stopped. *"Mon père,"* Maddie replied. *"Mon père est un* 'oaf.' "

Maddie wore the one dress over and over. It was gray wool, more like a blanket than a dress, tight over her breasts and under her arms. She'd worn it so much that it was soft and thin in places, like at the elbows. One day the girls noticed that she'd done something to the dress to make it fit across her front better. She'd taken strips of fabric from her brown blanket and sewn them into the side seams under the arms like panels. It looked funny, but the dress didn't pull on her so. Her breasts were looser, not so bound. Idella and Avis chose to not say anything out loud about the changes, though they both noticed and discussed it between themselves.

There was a lot of brown to Maddie. Idella thought her hair and her eyes were the light color of leaves that've been on the ground the whole winter and crumble when you pick them up. An earthy brown.

But all of her color came out when she sang. The whole first week she was there, she didn't sing a note. She was serious all the time. Then one day she started in singing while washing the windows. It was a clear, bright, windy day, and suddenly Maddie started singing a French song. It started soft and sort of hummy, then got louder as each window got cleaner, as if the more light she let in, the more sound she let out. It was like a bird singing in the house, Idella thought, listening from the bedroom.

One day Dalton came into the house unexpectedly for some lunch. He was quiet, as he heard Maddie singing upstairs. He stood in the kitchen and listened until she tumbled down the stairs, quilts to be aired in her arms. She stopped still upon seeing him.

"Go on, Maddie."

"Oh, I thought no one was here."

"No one was. Now I am." He smiled. "I'd be glad for you to sing. Mother sang in the house, too."

Maddie blushed and smiled. But she did not sing anymore. She went out to hang the quilts from the line. She shook them busily, snapping them from the corners, until she saw Dalton come off the porch. Sandwich in hand, he waved and walked on into the barn.

"She wears things," Avis said one morning as they watched Maddie standing at the cliff edge.

"What are you talking about?" Idella turned away and slipped out of her cotton nightie.

"She wears things in her clothes. There's a lump that moves around." Avis stood on the bed to get a better look at Maddie. "Sometimes I think it's stuck down her boobies." Avis demonstrated, her hand under her nightdress across her flat little chest. "Sometimes I think it's under her skirt." Avis waggled her fanny.

"You're crazy."

"You ever seen her undress?"

"No. But I'd like to see *you* get dressed." Idella tossed Avis her clothes.

"She waits till we're sleeping before she gets into bed." Avis wrenched her nightie over her head carelessly. "And she's up before us."

"Why would anyone hide things in their clothes?" Idella carefully pulled on her stockings and stuck her feet into her shoes.

"Nowhere else to, I guess." Avis pulled her dress on.

"We give her a drawer."

"That's not much."

"You ever been into it?" Idella looked over at the closed bottom drawer.

"Yeah. Nothing in there but a few old clothes."

"Goddamn if these boots are going to walk me through another goddamned day." Bill was bent over in a kitchen chair examining his booted feet. His suspenders strained at the sharp curves of his shoulders, and his long woolen underwear rose up out of his trousers. He tugged off a boot and sat up with it in his hand. "Cracked like a broken chimney all along one side here. Salt water does it. Eats at it." He held it up and looked into the worn old boot. "Surprised I can't see light coming in."

"Church don't smell like them boots." Avis laughed.

"Well," Bill said, "that might depend on what you think of church."

"I think church smells like pine boughs," Idella said, watching Maddie milling about the stove. She was making griddle cakes of various shapes and sizes. Some were coming along a lot better than others, it looked like, by the agitated way she was turning and scraping them around in the pan. When all the batter had been poured and fried, she put the biggest and best of them on Dad's plate. Then she chose the best ones she could for Avis and Idella. Dalton had taken bread and dried fish and was already out checking his lobster pots.

"Well, I wondered what you were cooking up over there, Maddie." Bill looked down at the large, misshapen griddle cakes. "Better hand me the syrup and a new cup of coffee."

Avis held hers up. "I'm still wondering what she was cooking. This one looks like the map of Canada at school."

"Well, now, maybe I can use any extras to put in the bottom of my boots. If I can cut that one down to size, it might do the trick." Idella watched Maddie walk quietly from the kitchen while Avis and Bill were laughing. He poured syrup all over his plate.

"Avis, put your food down." Idella looked over at her. "You've hurt Maddie's feelings. She's gone upstairs. What's the matter with you?"

Everyone got quiet and set about to eat what was in front of them.

"These are damn tasty!" Bill called out loudly. "I hope you can whip me up a few more, Maddie, before I set out."

"I love 'em!" Avis called up the stairs. "I want more!"

Idella attempted to eat the one she'd been given. It was awfully burned on one side and still gooey on the other. There was no in-between to it. "Pass me the syrup, Avis."

Maddie returned to the kitchen from upstairs. She stood in front of Bill for a moment—and then took from behind her back the new pair of men's boots she'd come in the door holding when she'd first arrived. She placed the boots at his feet, without looking up, and said, so softly they could barely hear it, "*Pour vous.* These boots. They are yours if they fit you."

Everyone stopped their chewing and looked at Maddie.

"Where in hell did these come from?" He picked up the boots and examined them. "These are a fine pair of boots. They're special made. Look at that double stitching they got around the edges there. And this heel could flatten a mule if you stepped on it. Where'd you get them, Maddie?"

Maddie shook her head. "They belong to me. I don't want them."

Bill looked at Maddie hard. Idella knew that look, so intense it felt like your bones might get holes in 'em. Finally he pursed his lips and squinted up his eyes. The girls knew this to be a signal that he'd made a decision of some sort. "All right, then. They don't do any good sitting upstairs. They're a fine pair of work boots, and I've got work that needs doing." He removed his old boots and slowly slid his feet, one and then the other, down into the new boots. "They went in, by God." He stood up. "With room to spare. I can manage spare room. It's the too-tight I can't handle." He walked around the kitchen, up to the door and back. All eyes were on his new boots.

"Well, thank you, Maddie. You bring unexpected gifts." He smiled at her.

Maddie's face took on a light they hadn't seen before. "It is good, then? You don't need pancakes at the bottom?"

Bill laughed full out. "No pancakes."

"You will wear them?" She smiled.

"I'll wear them and I'll dance in them, Maddie." He lifted his feet high, one and then the other in a prancing step. Grabbing her hands, he pulled her about the room in small circles, laughing. Avis and Idella laughed, too.

Avis got up and grabbed their hands and got herself in on the circle. "Round and round the mulberry bush!" she started singing, and they all joined in, laughing and spinning. "The monkey chased the weasel." When it got to the "pop," Bill lifted by the waist—not Avis, who was expecting it—but Maddie, who was startled and shy. It was a small lift, for Maddie was not a small girl, but it was enough of a lift for everyone to take notice. The song ended, and they stopped.

"The fields are lying in wait. I'll go stomp them." Bill grabbed his hat off the hook by the door and strode out of the house.

Maddie, clearing dishes, was humming and smiling. Avis and Idella looked from the door to the old boots still on the floor to Maddie breezing about the table.

Mrs. Doncaster came over one afternoon soon after that. She brought an apple pie for them, as she was near dying of curiosity. She'd been observing as much as she could from all her windows. But it was time for a closer view.

"Bill," she said, after watching Maddie brew a pot of coffee—a sip of which very nearly threw her to the floor—and serve it up to all of them, including Avis, "you got a woman-child on your hands here. What the hell are you doing adding fish to the kettle?"

"She come along and jumped in. Hell, she showed up on the doorstep like a sorry old dog. You saw the state she was in. And goddamn it, Elsie, I need someone to cook and help with the girls if I'm to keep 'em. I'm about run out since Emma died. Life isn't life no more. It's work and then some."

"You be careful about the 'and then some,' Bill Hillock."

"Get on back to your window, Elsie." Bill laughed at her. "You see things better from a distance."

*   *   *

That night, as on most nights, Bill sat down at the worn maplewood table with his bottle of whiskey. He'd gotten the table from his brothers for a wedding present. John and Sam had cut down the tree and made it with their own hands.

He sat in the flickering lamplight with a tumbler of whiskey and ran his hand over the surface of the wood. It wasn't smooth. But it was sturdy and well oiled and familiar. Emma had loved it, so he did. Her hands had been all over it.

It was two years now since Emma had died. It had hit him hard—two little girls, a son who'd hardly speak, and a baby girl to boot. Four children. He took a sip of whiskey and moved the lamp, watching the shadows lurch across the walls.

The girls were upstairs now, where Maddie'd taken them. Someone was still walking about, though, creaking the floorboards. He had a feeling it was Maddie. She was a strange one. He hoped she'd work out. Elsie was barking up the wrong tree, looking for trouble where it wasn't.

He needed someone to help. It was wrong to expect as much as he had from Idella. She was going on ten now. At eight, Avis was her helper. Them girls needed a woman around to help them and tell them things that he wasn't so sure he understood fully himself, when it came to that— concerning female situations and skills. He'd never paid heed. Christ, he had all a man could do—plowing and planting, hunting when he could, and fishing in season for herring and lobster. It was hardscrabble land and a hardscrabble bay—not easy to get a living out of. He'd heard that out west at harvesttime there was good money to be made harvesting wheat. He'd like to get on out there if he could and make some cash. He'd been talking about it with Sam. But what to do with the kids sprouting under his lone roof?

He topped up his whiskey and held the glass against the lamplight. The whiskey glowed shimmery and gold. Emma's hair was like that when she'd been in the sun, the gold color of whiskey. He'd smother his face in her loosened hair and tell her he was drinking his fill and it still wasn't enough.

When she died, Emma's smell was still with him. He went to bed and felt the touch of her hair on his face so strong that he sometimes reached up to brush it away in his tormented sleep. He'd been near out of his mind with grief.

His mother had come to stay with them and try to help. But she was seventy-three years old. Her kids had gone through her and out and into the world, and she was spent, worn to the shape of a gnarled tree. "Them kids is too much for me, Bill," she said. She lasted three weeks, the final week only because Bill had begged her to give him time to get a girl in.

So he'd set out to get the only help he knew he could afford—he hired a French girl from way down country to come and live with them and take care of things in exchange for room and board and not much else but a little dab of money he scraped into a pile at the end of each month.

"You get what you pay for," he said out loud, and took a swig. He laughed to himself. That sure as hell seemed the truth.

He got more than he paid for in some cases, though, less in others. There was the one who shit on the rug. That was the funniest damn thing. She blamed Idella flat out. Said Idella did it in the night and rolled up the rug to hide it. He'd never seen Idella so mad. It beat anything Avis ever done to her.

He teased Idella about it. He knew he shouldn't, but sometimes she needed a little teasing. She was forlorn and sad so much of the time. He didn't know how to help her. Avis was different. She'd have laughed out loud if the girl'd accused her. Or went along for the fun of it. But Idella was wounded by it.

It was just as well that one girl was gone after that rug business. She was the pretty one. Too pretty to have on hand. He knew it. He'd noticed more about her than he should or wanted to. It wasn't just her curly black hair or her black eyes that snapped up at him in a knowing way. It was her breasts. He had more than once stopped his hand from reaching over to squeeze them. And one time he'd done it. She was bending over him to take his plate from off the table. He was sitting alone there with his pipe and his whiskey. The kids had all run off into the fields. And he'd touched her.

She'd stopped and looked at him. She looked right into his eyes while she held that plate half covered with beans and his hand pressed against that breast, and he didn't take it off. Till her eyes narrowed and she spat at him, hit him full in the face—hot, wet spittle. Then he'd taken up his whiskey and no words were spoken. That was the night she shit on the rug. He didn't know if it was from fear of him that she didn't use the outhouse or purposeful spite. He did know he had something to do with it. The next day she was gone. But not till she'd accused Idella. And not till he'd paid her.

Bill reached into his pocket and pulled out his pipe and tobacco pouch.

So this one, this Maddie, who looked like a horse and cooked about like one, too . . . well, she was the last hope. If she didn't work out, he'd about decided to ship Avis and Idella on down to Maine to stay with John and Martha and get more schooling. John and Martha had seven boys. Christ. He pressed the tobacco into the bowl of his pipe and sat for a long time before lighting it. Well, they'd offered.

One afternoon all three girls had baths in the tin tub in the kitchen—for the men were mostly gone during the day. They were sitting upstairs on the beds untangling strands of wet hair with their fingers and passing the one comb between them. Suddenly Maddie looked up at the two girls, her eyes wide. "I want to look more . . ." They sat and waited for the next word, but it never came.

"Pretty?" Avis asked finally. "You mean you want to look more pretty?" Maddie nodded, barely moving her head.

"You want us to cut your hair for you, me and Idella?" Avis was excited.

"You could do that?"

"I guess." Idella shrugged.

Avis ran down the stairs, came back with Mother's best scissors, and handed them to Idella, who was already combing and making a part down the middle of Maddie's hair.

"Hold still," Idella said. "You've got to put your head up, not down, Maddie, or I can't see which way the hair falls." She carefully set about to trim the ragged edges of Maddie's hair into as even a line as she could. "This will certainly be an improvement."

"Your mother," Maddie asked, keeping her head still. "Was her hair very beautiful?"

"Oh, yes." Avis talked while Idella concentrated on her snips. "She had long, long hair, and she wore it up on her head with ribbon. You should wear your hair up, Maddie."

"I don't know how to do that."

"Don't look at Avis." Idella was bent in concentration.

"There's a special top drawer where Dad keeps Mother's things." Avis scooched in front of Maddie so that she could talk to her. "Sometimes me and Idella go in there and look at them. Her clothes and her brushes and hair things."

"Mother's hair was a lovely light brown." Idella put down the scissors and started to gently comb. "When the sun was on it, there were streaks of blond. She'd wash it from the rain-barrel water and then let it dry in the sun. We'd all put our faces in her hair to smell it. Dad, too. He came out of the barn once and saw us laughing 'cause Mother would tickle us by brushing her hair soft across our faces. He walked right up to us and said he wanted a turn. And he got one. A long one."

"They kissed with us right there in front of them." Avis stood up suddenly. "Aunt Francie made a fancy braid of Mother's hair when she died, and we all got a piece of it. Do you want to see mine?"

"I don't think you should," Idella said.

"Why not? It's my piece."

Avis went to her drawer and pulled out a cigar box. Dad had given them each one for their birthday for treasures. Idella knew what was in Avis's. Dried flowers from Mother's grave, as there were in her own box, and shells and rocks they'd found down on the beach—mostly little bits of nothing.

Idella's box had truly valuable things. Besides her own lock of Mother's hair, there was a handkerchief that had been Mother's, and sewing scraps from one of her dresses, and beautiful buttons Mother had cut off an old blouse and given to Idella. There were eight of them, and they were blue. She planned to use them someday on a special dress, maybe even her wedding dress.

Avis riffled through her box and removed a carefully folded handkerchief. She laid it on the bed. Slowly she took from the folds a thin braid of soft brown hair. It was clipped at each end with a tiny knot of velvet ribbon. "When you hold it to the light, you can see the blond of it."

"Can I touch it?" Maddie asked.

"If your hands are clean."

Maddie rubbed her hands into the folds of her skirt and then placed the tip of her thick, rough finger onto the lock of hair. "It's so soft," she murmured.

"Avis, put that away. There'll never be another strand of Mother's hair. Never." Idella turned away and stared hard out the window.

"Let's go do something, Maddie," Avis said. "Let's get out of here." She put her braid back into the handkerchief and carefully returned the box to her drawer.

"I have to work now. I can't play with you all of the time." Maddie stood up and shook out her hair. "Thank you, Idella, for the haircut." Idella nodded but did not return her look.

"I'll help you work," Avis said.

Maddie laughed. "You want to peel the potatoes for the supper with me? Then come."

"Will you teach me more French words?" Avis asked.

"Oui." Maddie laughed. *"Bien sûr."*

"What's potato?"

"La pomme de terre. 'The apple of the ground,' it says."

"Apple of the ground! Dad calls me the apple of his eye."

"He called Mother that." Idella turned sharply and glared at Avis.

"He calls me that, too. When you're not around being prissy."

Avis went crashing down the stairs. Maddie looked at Idella, whose back was again turned. She paused but did not speak and quietly closed the bedroom door behind her. "Apple of the ground," Idella whispered. She thought of Maddie, shapeless in her woolen folds. "Yes. Potato."

Maddie went into the downstairs bedroom. She went in slowly. She'd waited all morning till Avis and Idella went off to find fiddleheads. Dalton and Bill were both out working. She was alone in the house.

It was dark in the room. The bed was all undone and tousled. There was a dresser with a mirror on top that must be where Emeline had done up her hair. Where he shaved now. She picked up the lathering brush. It was slippery on the handle and smelled sweet, still damp from his morning shave. She set the brush back and smelled her fingers. The soap smelled of him at breakfast, when she leaned down to put the plate of eggs in front of him. She loved that smell.

She looked down at the dresser. The top drawer would have been for Emeline. Maddie pulled it open, making a quiet, shuffling sound; the smell of dried lavender floated up to her. Sachets tied with purple ribbon lay on top of neatly folded clothes. There was lace, and velvet ribbon curled into a corner—and a handkerchief with lovely blue embroidery. Maddie reached down and touched the soft blue knots gathered into flower shapes at the corner edges. Linen. And soft cotton. There were hair combs and barrettes made of tortoiseshell. She ran her fingers along their sharp prongs. Closing her hand around a barrette, she couldn't help herself—she quickly put it into her pocket.

There were blouses with lace collars and cuffs, and a camisole with tiny stitches and gathers, real womanly things, white and very delicate. Emeline must have made them herself, her special clothes. Maddie fingered the folded fabrics and lifted a blouse up into her hands. Underneath was something dark. It startled her. Coiled and tied with a ribbon on each end was a long, thick braid of hair. It had been given to him, she thought, touching it with a fingertip, after the funeral. It was for him to hold and smell and put his lips to as he did when she was living, when he had a wife.

But he didn't have a wife now. She was gone. There was no woman living here who would wear these clothes for him. Maddie lifted up the coil by one end and let it dangle. What long hair she'd had.

She held the braid up against her own hair to see its full length. She walked over to the window and tried holding it against what light there was. Even in death it had shine.

Without pausing, Maddie took the braid and went out to the kitchen and reached up to the sewing basket. She took the scissors and cut off a few inches of hair, retying the ribbon around the new end. Then she put the snipped length into her skirt pocket. She went quickly back into the bedroom, carefully curled the remaining portion of the braid back into a coil, and placed it under the blouse where she'd found it. She closed the drawer and looked for a moment at her reflection, dark and shadowy in the half-light. Then she walked out and shut the door. She went upstairs before anyone got back, and she put that braid end into her pillow. She would sew it on later. At night, when she did things.

*   *   *

The next morning, before the girls were even up, Maddie's hair was piled and twisted on top of her head. She stood at the stove frying eggs. Bill's eyes were on the hot, black liquid when she poured out his strong first coffee. "I'm in need of it, Maddie. Slept like a horse with fleas last night. Feel worse off than when I started. Goddamned field needs plowing, though. It don't wait for beauty."

Dalton walked in the front door, poured out a cup of black coffee, and sat at the table.

"Where the hell you been?" Bill asked.

"Mending the nets."

"I need you on dry land today."

"I'm here."

"I'm not one to do a two-man job by myself."

Maddie moved back to the stove. "Eggs also, Dalton?" He smiled and nodded, holding up his cracked mug. "Good coffee."

"You never make it here for Maddie's breakfast." Bill winked at Maddie. "She's a master with an egg in a pan."

Maddie smiled and cracked six eggs into the waiting black skillet.

"Your hair looks different, Maddie." Dalton took a big swallow of coffee.

Bill turned and looked at her from behind. "You got it all up on top of your head." Maddie nodded and kept her eyes on the eggs sizzling in front of her. Bill and Dalton both watched her, drinking their coffee, till she served them.

They ate quickly and without comment. Standing to put on his hat and hitch up his suspenders, Bill turned back. "You look older that way, Maddie. Took me by surprise."

"Maddie, when is your birthday?" Dalton watched her from the table, where he sat scraping up his eggs with biscuit.

Maddie looked down at the stove top. "It is the twenty-third of June."

"That's last week." Bill looked up.

Maddie nodded.

"Well, you should get a present," Dalton said.

"Shit. Goddamned. Maddie, we didn't know it was your birthday. Look at your cheeks now. Red as a boiled lobster." Maddie turned to face the stove. "Here, now, why don't you take today off? Go look at the ocean all day—you're always looking at the water. Idella can do the cooking. Right, Idella?"

Avis and Idella were just now pounding down the stairs. They stopped on the bottom step and took in the scene.

"Maddie's got her hair up!" Avis was delighted.

Dalton, pouring out the last dregs of coffee from the pot, looked over at Maddie. "You want to come with me on the boat tomorrow? Whyn't you come along on the morning rounds?"

"Me, too! Me three!" Avis was jumping at his legs like a flea.

"You like the sound of that, Maddie?" Bill asked. "You want to go in the boat?"

Maddie smiled and nodded.

"Can I come, too?" Avis was pulling on her brother's pant leg.

"If you help me row." Dalton reached down and tickled Avis under the arm. "I can't be hauling the whole load of you."

"You okay 'bout this, Della?" Bill looked at her. "There'd be no room in the boat for you."

"I don't want to go in the boat. I don't like the feel of it."

"Maybe we can have a little celebration. We can kill a chicken, since the lady of the house don't like lobsters." Dad was smiling all around. "And a birthday cake. You want to bake her a cake, Idella?"

Idella nodded. She was looking at Maddie's hair piled on her head and wondering how it was staying up there.

"Well, hello, stranger." Mrs. Doncaster had heard Tippie barking and seen Idella walking along the path to her house. "Come sit awhile. Catch me up."

"I'm sorry, Mrs. Doncaster, I can't visit. I come to borrow some vanilla. We're out."

"Course you can have some. Come up on the porch at least. I'll go get it."

Idella stepped onto the porch and looked over at their house. It looked so small from here, against the blank blue sky. Dad and Dalton were in the field already. She could just make them out, dragging along behind the plow. Avis was off in the woods to find a treasure for Maddie's birthday. Course what Avis took as treasure, anyone could guess. She might show up with a bone or a dried-out wasp nest and think she was giving her something. Idella was going to show them all how good a cake she could make. She was a much better cook than Maddie.

"Here you are, dear. Are you going to bake something?"

"A cake. For Maddie. It was her birthday."

"Well, how old was she?"

Idella shrugged. "She didn't say."

"Things working out with this one?"

"She's all right. Avis likes her."

"Well, that's a hurdle." Mrs. Doncaster laughed. "If Avis doesn't like you, you know about it."

"And Dalton's taking her in his boat tomorrow. And Dad likes her coffee."

"Well, that's four or five hurdles."

Idella smiled.

"That leaves you, dear. What do you think of having her there?"

Idella shrugged. "She's all right, I guess." She held up the vanilla. "Thanks, Mrs. Doncaster." She turned and started back along the path.

"Got enough sugar?"

"Oh, yes," Idella called over her shoulder, and started to run.

Mrs. Doncaster watched her run all the way back, then stood looking for a few moments longer. The kettle's on the boil, she thought. Something is brewing over there. Poor Bill. He thinks it's just strong coffee.

"Maddie!" Idella called as she ran into the house with the vanilla. "You in here?" She stood at the bottom of the stairs. "You up there?"

There was a sound from Dad's room. Idella went to the door and pushed it back till she could see in. Maddie was standing there, frozen, in front of Mother's mirror. She was wearing the long white gloves that Mother wore to church. Mother's white blouse, with a black velvet ribbon she would tie into a bow at the neck, was draped across Maddie's front. Idella pushed the door open all the way. A long black skirt was pulled up over Maddie's shapeless gray dress. It gaped open in the back. Maddie was too broad, too hulking, to button it closed. She was clutching at the blouse with her big hands, crushing the soft folds that Mother had worn so gracefully.

"No! You take them off! You aren't ever to touch her things!" Idella rushed up to Maddie and grabbed at a gloved hand. "You are too dirty to touch them!" She pulled and scratched. "You get out of here!" The glove wouldn't slide from Maddie's swollen fingers. It had to be dragged and peeled and wrenched from the hand. "If I tell Dad, he'll kill you. He'll send you the hell out of here."

Maddie was sobbing. "I wanted to feel like a lady."

"You're not a lady!" Idella screamed. "You're a French girl from way down country! You belong in the lobster factory. We don't need you!"

"Please, Idella. I am begging you. I don't want to go back. I don't want to leave here." Her shoulders were shaking. She crushed the blouse in her desperate fist. "You don't know, Idella. My father, he will kill me. Or worse than kill me. Much worse." Maddie was on her knees, the beautiful skirt crumpled on the floor beneath her weight. Idella held the one glove, baggy and misshapen from her own frantic pulling. She stood, stilled to silence, and watched the sobbing figure.

Then she laid the glove at Maddie's feet and quietly walked from the room, closing the door behind her. She went directly upstairs and curled into a ball on the corner of her bed. She felt as though someone had poured a hot, heavy liquid over her, into her.

She must have slept. When she opened her eyes, the room had the feel of lateness; the light had moved, and shadows darkened it. Someone had covered her with a blanket and closed the bedroom door. Moving slowly, unfurling her groggy body, she went to the window and looked toward the water. Maddie stood there, holding the top of the ladder with one hand, looking out to the bay. Her gray dress blew out behind her.

Idella turned away from the window and glanced over at Maddie's bed. It was made up, as always. Idella walked to it and sat. She reached down and opened Maddie's drawer. She felt with her hands all through the scraps of clothing Maddie had folded so carefully. Nothing was hidden. She closed the drawer and looked about the room. Nothing.

She put her legs up, lay down on the little bed, and put her head on the pillow. Something was under the pillow, stuffed into the casing. Cautiously Idella felt the edges of the hidden object. It was soft and lumpy. She slid her hand into the casing and pulled it out. She gasped. It was a doll, a grimy little rag doll with no shoes and a crudely sewn dress made out of sacking. It had no face to speak of. It had a black button nose and a thin line of stitches for a mouth. Some of them were pulled out. There were holes where eyes must once have been sewn on. It had no hair or hat or ribbon of any sort. A sad little thing. Idella did not want to see it. She slipped it under the pillow again and got off the bed, smoothing everything back into place. Maddie had a doll, and she slept with it. She hid it from them all and was ashamed. Maddie wasn't that old, Idella thought, or as grown as she let on.

When Maddie came back into the house, with Avis trailing her like a wake, Idella had already put the cake in the oven. She'd just gone on ahead and made it, using the cookbook she'd ordered from the flour company.

Maddie didn't look at her.

"Did you save the bowl for me?" Avis said as soon as she came through the door. "Did you leave me some batter?"

"No," Idella said. "I didn't."

"Yes you did," Avis said, coming over to the table. "It's here waiting for me."

"It's Maddie's cake. I saved the batter for her."

"Oh!" Maddie looked up. "Oh, Idella."

Idella looked her in the eye and nodded, then looked quickly away.

"Oh, Idella." Maddie rushed up to her. "Thank you." She put her hands out as though to hug her and then turned away, confused.

"Well, it's not that great, licking the bowl." Avis laughed.

"Come, Petite Avie, let us all three lick at the bowl with our fingers." Maddie was suddenly aflutter.

"You go on," Idella said, smiling weakly. "I had quite a lot already."

"Well, that was a birthday meal fit for a queen. You're the queen, Maddie." Bill pushed his chair back from the table. "Damn good cake you made, Idella."

Idella smiled. "I just followed the recipe."

"Who killed the chicken?" Bill asked.

"I did," Dalton said.

"It was Dalton had to kill it, or we'd be eating a live chicken," Avis said, laughing. "Maddie didn't know a thing about chopping off their heads."

"I could have done it," Idella said. "I could have. But I made the cake."

"You've never chopped off the head of a chicken, Maddie?"

"No. Never."

"She's never cleaned one either," Idella said. "She don't know how. Dalton did that for her, too."

"Well, weren't you the helpful one, doing the woman's work?" Bill looked at Dalton. "I wondered what the hell happened to you."

"Why should she kill her own birthday chicken?"

"I will never be able to kill a chicken," Maddie said seriously.

"You never should have named them," Idella said. "That was stupid."

"Named them?" Bill laughed. "Who'd we eat tonight?"

Maddie's cheeks flushed, and she shook her head.

Bill grabbed a bone from his plate. "Come now, whose leg have I got here?"

"Don't tease her." Dalton glared at his father. "She don't need to be teased about it."

"I'm just having a little fun, is all. Don't get your cock feathers up. I never knew the name of a bird I've had for supper. I was interested."

"They've got French names," Avis piped up. "Maddie was naming them to teach me words."

"Is that so?" Bill looked at Avis. "You learnin' French?"

"Some." Avis smiled. "We ate Nuage Gris. Gray Cloud. 'Cause it was gray like a rain cloud. And it was the easiest to catch."

"Gray Cloud sounds more like an Indian's name than a chicken's." Bill laughed.

"I think we should forget about the chicken," Dalton said.

"Do you?" Bill turned sharply to Dalton and slammed his fist on the table. "I think I'll talk about what I damn well please at my own goddamned table, by the Christ."

Idella clasped her hands in her lap and watched her father and brother looking straight across the table at each other.

"I want to thank Idella for the beautiful cake." Maddie spoke softly, breaking the silence. "I never had such cake."

"I have a present for Maddie!" Avis pulled out from behind her chair a piece of blue sea glass.

"That's from your treasure box!" Idella said. "We found that with Mother."

"I know it. I couldn't find anything nicer." Avis handed it to Maddie. "I want you to have it."

"*Merci,* Avie."

"Petite Avie," Avis corrected.

"*Oui.*" Maddie smiled. "Petite Avie. I will have it forever."

"She's not that small," Idella said. "She's almost eight."

"I've got a present for her, too." Dalton spoke. "It's for cooking with." He pulled from out of his pants pocket a hand-carved wooden spoon and handed it to Maddie. "It's maple. I was making it for you to cook with. Then it was your birthday, so I hurried up and finished it."

Everyone stared at Dalton. Avis was openmouthed. "I didn't know you could make stuff like that."

"Well, isn't that nice, Dalton." Bill eyed the spoon with interest. "I guess that explains why the light in the barn's been burning so late. I started to wonder about nighttime visitors of some kind." Dalton blushed. "Just teasing you, boy." He reached over and took the spoon from Maddie. "Now you can stir up trouble in style."

"Thank you, Dalton." Maddie took the spoon back. She reached over and touched his hand. "*Merci.*"

"Well, if you're all going boating in the morning, I want your asses up to bed." Bill pushed his chair back from the table with a loud scrape.

"I'm not going in the boat," Idella protested.

"But you're going to town with me." He winked at her. "We've got some business to take care of at the store, I'm thinking."

"It's full moon tonight," Avis said. "I want to watch the gold light on the water."

"You'll see the full sun tomorrow. Now, do the dishes and up to bed with all of you ladies."

Long after the girls had been prodded up the stairs, Bill poured his nightly glass of whiskey. The house was awash in a moony haze, and he poured it tall, for he felt an uncommon need of it. On nights like this, he missed Emma. She loved the moonlight on the cliffs and would drag him out at all hours to watch its jagged slash of yellow-white stagger across the bay.

He stood listening to the swoosh of wind nudging the shingles from below till they creaked, ruffling the curtains. He stepped into the pattern of moonlight glowing across the floor and looked down at his new boots. Their luster was heightened in the strange light. He lifted his foot and set it down with a dull thud. New boots. Emma'd always made him shine the old ones. "They're shitkickers," he'd say. "It's no use." And every Saturday night she'd give him a soapy bucket and the rag with polish and push him out onto the porch. "They're also your Sunday best," she'd call out to him. She'd be dragging him off to church in the morning. Church gave her pleasure. Going every Sunday was one of the few things she asked of him—so he cleaned the boots and went. He even enjoyed the singing, though he never said as much, or she'd be trying to get him into the goddamned choir.

He took a long drink from his glass and then went to the table and poured out more. He could hardly feel the burn of it. It was like water with no kick, no hum. If he lost that hum, what'd be left for him? He carried the bottle and the glass outside and onto the porch step. It creaked, always, under his weight. Emma would hear the creak of the porch and the clump of his boots when he dragged his ass back from a day of hauling some goddamn thing—traps or potatoes or piles of manure—and he knew that she'd smile to know he was soon coming through the door. She'd be standing in the kitchen with the table set, the food all ready, and the smile would be there when she saw him. He shook his head at the thought. His need to touch her sometimes made his fingers move on their own, clutching the air as though reaching for some part of her, any part— hair or blouse or the soft slope of her hip. His whole hand could mold itself over the curve of that hip. He sat on the step and drank, then poured more from the bottle.

These days he knew that the sound of his boots was a different thing. There was some poor French girl on hand to hear them. Or Idella and Avis, poor mutts, in there trying to scrape something together for his supper. He scared them all. He couldn't help himself. It was seeing them scurry around the table trying to put food out, afraid to look at him for fear he'd light into them, that brought it on—the temper, the hurt, the anger at the goddamned world that had taken Emma away and left him alone. It wasn't them he'd be mad at. But it was them that got the brunt.

He saw a light flickering under the barn door. Dalton was in there still, in his own world. Funny kid, carving Maddie a spoon like that of his own accord. Dalton would've done things like that for Emma if she'd lived, he supposed. He would have made her things on the quiet. He forgot sometimes that Dalton, too, had lost his mother. He was more conscious of it with the girls. Their needs for Emma were clear. His help-lessness with them was so strong that it ate at him like a crow picking at an ear of corn, up one row and down the other. Bill let the whiskey pool onto his tongue and behind his teeth, feeling its rusty warmth. He watched the soft glow of the lamp's light spill under the crack of the barn door. Then, as quickly as it came, the lamp went out and the barn was dark again. Bill shook his head. It felt suddenly heavy—with worry or whiskey, he couldn't be sure. He emptied the bottle into his glass. Hold-ing the glass carefully against his chest, he got up and walked slowly out into the yard.

The air was swollen with moonlight, drenched in a grayish glow. He went over to the cliff edge and looked down at the beach. The water was out, the pale sand exposed and bright. Waves, skimmed with a sheen like a sheer layer of ice you could crack with a finger, lapped at the beach below. He took a sip. Emma's voice was in his ear. She would put her arms about his middle and pull him to the cliff edge to watch the water and the light. The air would lift her hair as it hung loose about her shoul-ders. She'd hold out her arms to it and let the breezes fill her long sleeves till he could watch it no more and grabbed her back again, not letting the wind have her for long.

He looked back at the house. Even it, gray and ragtag and solitary as it was, had an unearthly glow. Emma had died in there. He'd never be able to leave it without her. This godforsaken mound of nothing was his, and he'd be living off it till the end.

A sound drew him back. A sliver of song floated up from the beach, its clarity muted by the slushing of the waves. Someone was singing. He trained his eyes down onto the beach and saw, now, that there was a fig-ure sitting in Dalton's beached boat. A cloud skimmed across the moon, blotting the light. He focused on the dark shape till the cloud passed. It was Maddie, singing in French as she huddled in Dalton's boat.

"Maddie, what the hell you doing down there?" He held on to the top of the ladder to steady himself.

"Oh!" She turned and looked up. He could make out the white of her face amid a tangle of darker hair.

He emptied his glass and dropped it to the ground, then lowered one foot onto the ladder. His body felt thick. His feet seemed twice as heavy in the big boots. "Goddamn, Maddie." He lowered himself slowly. "This goddamned ladder is hard going on a clear day." He lurched for the next step and tentatively tried his weight, clinging wobbly to the sides. "One of these goddamned steps waggles like a cow's behind."

"The one almost to the last!" Maddie called.

With a deliberate step, he lowered himself down, cursing. When his boots were finally on the sand, he looked over at Maddie. "Goddamn it, Maddie. I told you never to go down that ladder alone, never mind at night, for Christ's sakes."

"I was watching the light on the water. I am so excited to be going in the boat."

"Come on. Get up and get over here. I'm responsible, God help us all."

"Some minutes, please. Look at the water."

Bill looked about him. "Well. It is something. It don't seem real." His boots crunched as he stepped across clusters of mussel shells to reach the boat.

"I can't sleep," Maddie whispered. She sat huddled on the plank seat and looked up at him. "I don't sleep much in the night."

"Like a raccoon, then? Or a fox?"

She looked away. "Too many things happen in the dark. I keep my eyes open."

"You are a mystery, Maddie. You've got secrets, I think."

She shrugged and looked out over the water.

"I ain't interested in knowing your secrets. You keep 'em. I got some of my own, I guess. Hell. We all do." He put his head back and looked at the moon. "Whoa. With the up and down and whiskey and light, my head's spinning."

"Sit." Maddie patted the seat beside her. "It's my practice ride."

Holding on to the sides of the boat with outstretched arms, he sat across from her. "It's bright as hell down here. I'd say we've got double-barrel moonlight tonight, Maddie."

"*Oui.*" She smiled. "It is so beautiful. I love it here."

"'Cause you're looking at it in moonlight."

"I have seen it in all kinds of light, even rain. I still think it is beautiful to live here."

"You ain't tried winter yet. It's a rough go trying to live off land that don't much want to be bothered. I just about push every goddamned potato through the ground with my bare hands. Rocks grow during the night. They go at it like rabbits." He laughed. "They're probably up there making more rocks right now for me to find in the morning. But my other seeds and plants go rotten or freeze or get done for by salt and wind and whatever else God cooks up in his wisdom." He shook his head and sighed. "Potatoes keep us alive."

"I love potatoes."

"Glad to hear it. You must have some Irish in there with the French."

Maddie looked down at her hands. "Maybe."

Bill lifted a piece of torn net from the boat bottom. "And the herring runs, of course. We eat them little bastards the livelong year." He pulled a tangle of seaweed from the weaving and tossed it overboard. "You ain't been here long enough for that treat. We're gone all night sometimes, the men. Whenever them fish are running, we're running right along with them. We come back in early morning, before the sun." He fingered the net. "The girls hold the lamps up. Right over there." He pointed to a high place on the shore. "They scramble down that ladder, still warm from their little beds, and come to hold up the lamps. It'll be dark yet, see, but we need to clean and salt and lay every damn one of 'em out to dry as soon as we land 'em. Supper or breakfast or both have to wait." He looked over at her, holding up a portion of the net. "My girls' arms are 'bout as thick as this here rope. But I need their help. Their little hands."

Maddie sat silently and watched him.

"But I love it, too. This place. Who's to explain? It's the challenge of it. I'm stubborn, see, mule-assed. And when there's something good here it's like no other." He stood and took a deep breath. "It's like breathing in cold water when the wind blows across the bay."

"I want to eat it!" Maddie said, opening her mouth wide. "Ahhhhhhhh."

Bill laughed and straddled the plank. He faced the open water. "Going out in the boat, you know, with the lobster traps, in summer—that's a prize God gave me on some days. To feel the water under me and the air about and to pull them damn ugly things up out of the water that people pay for down in the States. It makes me laugh. We sell 'em, you know, to the lobster factory."

"I know about the factory. Too much."

Bill nodded. He leaned over and grabbed a handful of stones. One by one he threw them into the water. They listened to each distant plunk until all the stones were tossed and his hands empty. For a long time then, they sat staring out at the water and the shimmery light coating its surface. Finally Bill turned to her.

"It's hard for my girls up here. I see the sadness in their faces, looking up at me, waiting for something I can't give 'em. And I lose my god-damned temper. It whips through me. You ain't seen that yet." He spoke quietly, looking at the shifting moonlit water.

"You miss her so much, your wife?"

Bill reached down and grabbed a stone and threw it hard. It cut through the air till it hit a rock and bounced. "What kind of God likes all them pretty songs on Sunday and then takes away Emma, leaving behind her babies? What kind of God would that be?" He looked down at her. "It don't leave you," he whispered, "that kind of hurt."

"No." Maddie shook her head. "No. It does not leave you."

"I had me the best." Bill sat, his head lowered. Maddie watched him till he spoke again. "If I'd stopped at three. Three kids." She could hardly hear him. "Emma, we called the baby, to carry the name." He looked up at Maddie. "She reminds me, the baby—when I see her. It's all together—her being born and losing Emeline." He paused, then laughed softly and hit his hand flat on the wooden plank. "Christ. The damn drink is gone." He looked at Maddie. "So I give the baby to Beth to bring up. How could I take care of a baby, never mind the rest?" He stared out for a long time at the water. "I hurt what I love the most. I kill what I love."

"No," Maddie whispered, shaking her head. "No. This is not true, what you say."

"As true as there's rats in the barn, Maddie." He stood. "Come. Time for sleep. Tomorrow you take to the high seas." He stepped out of the boat and then reached down and grabbed her hands to pull her to stand-ing. "Jesus," he said, not letting go of her hands. "You got a pair of hands on you that'd make a mule skinner proud. These are work hands." She pulled her hands away and buried them in her skirt. "Christ, I'm sorry. I meant it as a good thing. It come out wrong. Christ." He gently took hold of her elbow, coaxing her from the boat. "Come on, now." Maddie smiled. "That's not much, but I'll take it." He laughed. Smiling now, Maddie let him guide her out of the boat and onto the rocky sand. She lifted up her skirt and walked over to the bottom of the ladder, then turned to wait for him.

"You go on up and get to bed, Maddie. I've got to let out some of that whiskey I drunk before I climb any more ladders. I'll add my drops of gold to the bay after you've gone. Good night."

"Bonne nuit."

"Bun nwee." He watched her climb, her skirt hoisted, till she reached the top, waved down at him, and disappeared. Then he stumbled across the rocks to the water's edge and relieved himself in a long and satisfying arc. "Pissin' in the wind," he muttered. "Here I stand, on a bun nwee, pissin' in the wind." He stood for a long time staring up at the moon. It was now high and bright over the water, more white than yellow.

"'Buffalo Gal, won't you come out tonight, come out tonight, come out tonight. . . .'" He walked clumsily over to the ladder and grabbed the sides. He sang softly and cursed loudly as he clambered closer to the top and finally up over the edge. On solid ground at last, he stood with his arms open wide toward the water and the wind. "'And we'll dance to the light of the moon.'" He laughed and stepped forward as though to do a jig, accidentally kicking the empty glass that he'd left on the edge and sending it over the cliff to shatter on the rocks below. "Damn," he said, peering down and catching glimpses of moonlit shards. "There mighta been a drop left."

He turned unsteadily away from the edge, facing the barn, which was bright gray with moony light. Dalton was standing in the open doorway, mute, watching him. Bill stopped for a moment, startled, then waved but didn't speak. Dalton did not move, though Bill knew he was looking at him. He felt the eyes of his son watching all the way back up to the house and right on in. "Funny damn kid," he muttered as he fell atop his unmade bed. "I go down with my boots on."

*   *   *

The next morning Maddie roused Avis early, prodding her shoulder as she whispered, "Petite Avie. Get up now. We are going in the boat. Dalton says come."

Idella was awakened, too, by the voices, but she didn't move. She listened till they had sneaked out and down the stairs, too excited for silence. When she heard the front door close, she got up and looked out the window. Dalton was standing, tall as Dad almost, with his hand on top of the ladder.

Maddie and Avis, a basket of food between them, ran happily toward him. Their skirts blew against their legs in the windy morning. Maddie looked lighter than Idella ever thought possible, and girlish. She wasn't much more than a girl anyway. Sixteen years old, maybe. That wasn't quite a woman to her mind, and it wasn't a child. It was somewhere in the middle.

"You two stay in the boat, goddamn it, and do what Dalton says." Dad was out there, too. Idella could hear him, but she couldn't see him. "Don't you dare join the fishes, Avis!"

"We won't! We will! We won't!" Avis was laughing and jumping. Dalton took the basket and helped the girls down over the side, then slowly disappeared after them. Idella kept watching. Dad strolled up to the cliff edge now, his hands in his trouser pockets. He stood, rumpled and untucked, for a long time. Then he pulled a suspender up and walked back toward the house. Idella heard him come in.

"You up?" he called.

"Yes." Idella went to the top of the stairs.

"I been thinking maybe we could go to town, you and me. Everyone else is on holiday. Let's bring Maddie back a birthday surprise. What do you say, Idella?"

"I guess."

"You think you could pick out something she'd like? I wouldn't know what a young woman needs. We'll all get a little something. You want candy?"

"Candy'd be good."

"Pick out candy for you and Avis and then something nice for Maddie. Maybe a brush or a mirror. She's doing things with her hair."

Idella nodded. She would like a new brush herself. She wondered if Dad would think of that when it was her birthday. She felt a little old to always be picking out candy, though she did enjoy the hard red ones that came on sticks in the shapes of animals.

"Let's go, then. Let's do it. Cows are milked and chickens are fed. Get dressed, and let's get going before they need it again."

Idella noticed the tall man standing in front of the case of pipes and tobacco pouches from the time they entered the store. He looked up at the jangle of the cowbell over the door and kept watching and listening to them the whole time. What caught her eye first was the way his hat covered one ear but not the other and that as he listened he moved his chaw of tobacco from one side to the other of his mouth. He caught her eye once and smiled. After that she looked in any direction but his.

"Bill Hillock! Come to post another sign for a housemaid?" Mr. Wheeler was wiping his eyeglasses off with a dust rag, but he could tell it was Dad, probably by the way he walked into a place, so tall and straight. "I'm gonna start charging you a fee." The men always teased each other before they did business.

"We got us one that's fixing to stay on, I think. She likes the goddamned wind, if you can believe it."

"You can keep her supplied with wind, by God." Mr. Wheeler carefully put his glasses back on, bending the wires over one ear and then the other. "I don't know how you people stand it out there on that cliff come winter. It'd blow the skin off my old bones."

"What are you two going on about?" Mrs. Wheeler came from the back of the store carrying a bolt of fabric. "Hugh, give me a hand with this wool—I can't get it back up on the shelf." She looked at the man standing in front of the pipes. "Can I help you?"

The man smiled. "I'm not sure yet. I'm thinking."

Mr. Wheeler laughed. "Oh, don't be doing too much of that. I hear it can be dangerous!"

"What would you know about it?" Mrs. Wheeler shot back, smiling. She turned to the man. "Let me know if I can help you. What you see is what we've got, if you're looking for a new pipe. I'll open the case if you want. Men seem to need to hold them awhile before they make a decision."

"Watch what you're saying, there, Frieda. It's not just pipes they like to hold first." Dad made out like he was going to put his arms around her, and she brushed him away.

"You damned fool, Bill Hillock."

"That wouldn't apply to your housegirls, now, would it?" The man spoke to Dad, his one cheek still swollen with tobacco.

"What's that you said?" Dad asked.

"I say, that don't apply to your hired girls, now, does it?" The man smiled. "That you got to hold 'em before you make any decisions?"

Idella felt how abruptly the feeling of fun had changed. No one spoke. Everyone looked at the man. Finally Mrs. Wheeler turned and smiled at Idella. "Idella, dear. What brings the lady of the house to town today?"

"We've come to buy a birthday present." Idella smiled back, relieved.

"A present? For Avis? Is that why I don't see her hand in my candy jars? You leave her home so you could get her a surprise?"

"It's for the hired girl," Idella whispered. "It was her birthday. And I don't think she's ever had anything nice. I'm going to help choose."

"Let's see what you've got for hairbrushes and little mirrors." Dad put a hand on her shoulder.

Idella could tell that the strange man was listening to their conversation. She could feel him watching. As Mrs. Wheeler handed each mirror to her, she urged Idella to lift it up and get a feel for it and take a look. "You don't want one that's watery. You want a good clear reflection. And no spots on the back. Some of 'em are better than others, but I don't get much say in what they ship up here. We take what we can get."

Idella examined the one she most wanted to own herself. It was bird's-eye maple, with lovely little round marks in the soft pale wood. The mirror itself was oval and beveled at the edges. She looked shyly at her reflection, at her unsatisfactory brown eyes. When she turned the mirror slightly away from the sunlight coming through the front window, she saw the man in the hat watching her. He smiled. She put it down. "This one," she said. "This is the one."

"You want the brush, too, Bill?"

"Why the hell not?" Dad said. "Wrap them up while Idella picks out her candy."

The man with the hat suddenly walked past them and over to the store's open front door, leaned his head out, and spat hard onto the sidewalk. He made such a loud spewing noise that they all stopped what they were doing or saying. Then he stepped back in and wiped his mouth with his sleeve, his cheek still bulging. The tobacco had a sour smell that took some of the pleasure out of choosing the candy. She could smell it when he came up behind her.

"Pick enough for the lot of you," Dad said.

"Them's fine boots you got on your feet, sir." The man with the hat spoke again to Dad.

"I like 'em."

"They got made just for you, it looks like?"

"Could be. What do I owe you, Hugh?"

"Can I look closer? At the stitching?"

"You can see it pretty good from where you're standing."

"Whyn't I put it on your monthly tab, Bill. Pay the first of the month after the herring start their runs."

"Thanks, Hugh. I appreciate the kindness. It'll fall out easier in a month."

"What if the mirror cracks?"

"Excuse me?"

"What if the mirror cracks when the hired girl looks into it?"

Idella was watching the man's face keep changing. His smile got bigger but his face got meaner. He was taller than Dad, and thicker. The boots he wore were old and cracked and hardly worth putting on, by the look of them. Two colors of laces.

"I don't think that's going to happen. And it's none of your damn business if it does."

"I had me a pair of boots just like them, I think. Just like 'em. Down to the stitching. Five-dollar boots. They got stole from me. Goddamned bitch of a girl run off with my boots."

"Is that so?"

"You ain't seen her? Fat cow of a thing. Slow and stupid."

"Can't say that I have. Only cow I got's in the barn."

Something was being said between the men that wasn't in the words. Idella could feel herself clamping down, holding even her arms down close to her sides.

"You don't have a cow by the name of Madeleine round the house, now, do you, little girl?" Idella turned away from him. She was afraid. "You sure are a quiet little bird."

"Come on, Idella, pick out the candy. We'll weigh it out and go."

"I am part of the wind here!" Maddie opened her mouth wide to it. Her hair flew all about her face.

Dalton smiled across at her as he rowed. "No lobster pots to drag up, Maddie?" He pointed with an oar to one of his buoys.

"No lobsters." Maddie shook her head. "I have seen too many."

"What'd you do in there?" Avis was grabbing up bits of seaweed and throwing them at the gulls overhead. "When you worked in the lobster factory?"

"The water always boils when the lobsters are coming. More and more seawater they bring on wagons to boil. More and more lobsters they cook bright red, in the big, big pots." She opened her arms wide to show the size of the huge boiling pots. "It is so hot and so full of steam in the factory. They cook the lobster and clean and can right away or the meat goes bad."

"What'd you do?"

"I cracked back the tails." She demonstrated with a sharp twist of her wrist. "The shells are hot and sharp. The salt, it eats at the hands, and they bleed. I hated it."

"Dad throws their bodies on the fields," Avis said. "They smell way worse than cow patties."

"Forget the lobsters," Dalton said. "We'll just ride to nowhere."

"It is somewhere to me. I've never been on water before. Only land. Only ground."

"Apple of the ground!" Avis shouted. "*Pomme de terrre!* That's 'potato' in French, Dalton."

Maddie laughed. "*Très bien,* Petite Avie."

"You'll be a potato of the water if you don't stop rocking the boat."

They rowed and drifted happily. Maddie sang a song for them in French, very softly. The girls sat on the boat's bottom and closed their eyes, letting the sun warm their faces while Dalton rowed them gently across the water.

"It is so nice," Maddie whispered dreamily, "to float on the water like feathers."

"I'd be dead if I couldn't be on the water." Dalton looked out at the horizon. "I'll get to the other side someday. I'll get off the farm and out of here."

"You want to leave?" Maddie opened her eyes. "To me this is beautiful, your life."

Dalton looked at her. "You come from someplace belowground, Maddie, if this is a good life to you. I'm not staying in this nowhere all my life. I'm getting out. That's what I'm pulling up lobsters for. To sell 'em to the factory. To get the hell out."

"What about Dad?" Avis asked, squinting up at him. "Who'll help him with the farm stuff?"

"You, Avis. He'll hitch you to the plow. You're stubborn as a mule." He laughed. "You look like one, too."

"I do not!"

He pulled up the oars and let the boat drift. "Where'd you come from, Maddie, that you've never been on the water?"

"I am here today. No yesterdays. I don't want them." Maddie looked back toward shore. "The cliffs are so beautiful. The houses so small. Like sad little boxes."

Avis leaned over and wet her hand. "Feel this." She clapped it, cold and dripping across Maddie's forehead.

"Ah, c'est froid!" Maddie laughed. She held Avis's icy palm against her face, then dipped her own hand into the cold water and flicked droplets into Dalton's face and onto Avis's small brown neck. "We must eat our picnic or the birds will come down and take it. The gulls, they are watching."

They unwrapped their salt-pork sandwiches and ate, throwing scraps of bread out to the hovering gulls.

"I wish for them I had made pancakes," Maddie said, watching the birds dart and grab and gulp down the bits they were thrown. "Then they would have full bellies!"

Avis laughed. "But they wouldn't be able to fly."

"No." Maddie laughed, too. "They would drop like stones to the sea. I must have Idella teach me how to cook, I think."

"You just have to use that cookbook she got from the flour company. Just read the recipes. Cooking's nothing."

Maddie looked down at her hands. "I don't read, you know."

"You can't read, Maddie?"

"Not so good."

"You read that sign Dad put up in the store," Avis said.

Maddie shook her head. "No. The man at the store was making jokes about the need for one more housekeeper, and I took the sign down when he was not looking. I used it to ask the way to your house."

"Hell, I'll teach you to read, Maddie." Dalton smiled at her. "We just got to find some books, is all."

"I would like that." Maddie smiled back at him. "I have never been so happy, Dalton, as I am today." She leaned forward suddenly and kissed Dalton's knee. "Thank you for my ride in the boat. For being kind."

"Wooo-woooo!" Avis shouted. Maddie leaned over and kissed her on the cheek. "You, too, Petite Avie. You make me happy."

"Time to head back. The wind's shifted, and I'll have to row into it." Dalton threw a last crust of bread to a waiting gull. They watched the bird snatch it with a jerk and swallow it in one gulp. "Hungry bastard."

"We are all hungry," Maddie said, watching the circle of birds above them.

"I'm not," Avis said, patting her full belly.

"Oh, yes, Avie, you are maybe more hungry than all of us. You will see."

Dalton grasped the oars and turned the boat toward home.

"Whose horse is that?" Idella, still sitting on the seat of the buggy, turned toward the sound of slow, steady hooves approaching. Dad, leading Blackie up to the barn, glanced in the same direction.

"That goddamned fool followed me."

Idella could tell now that it was the man from the store. Just looking at him, she could smell his sour odor.

"Get down off the wagon, Idella, and go into the house."

The horse was almost upon them now. The man slowed it to a walk.

Dad stood, his horse now tied and steady, and watched him approach. Idella hovered by the front door but didn't go in.

The man removed his hat. "Sorry to bother you. Couldn't help but see which way you was going and thought I'd have a look myself, if you don't mind, at that cow of yours. Seeing I had boots like yours that got stolen and a cow girl that disappeared on the same day. Too strong not to smell a little."

"You smell plenty already," Dad said looking right up at him without blinking or moving.

The man got down off his horse and steadied it. "Mind if I look around?"

"I do."

"Well, I think I'm going to. I have a need to speak to Madeleine. That's her name, now, ain't it? Of your housegirl? She needs to come home with me. She's got a job to do, and she ain't doing it if she's living here."

"She's got a job here now, and she likes it fine, so you can just get the hell off my land. I don't care if you're her brother, father, or grandpa, too. She's not going nowhere with the likes of you."

"You don't understand. I been feeding her a lot longer than you have. She got dumped on me, and I took care of her. Now she's at an age where she can do me some good. It's lobster time, and she's a prize cracker with them big, strong hands of hers. I bet you know 'bout them hands." The man smiled at Dad, but it wasn't friendly. "I'm needin' the money she gets, to make up for what I've spent on her these three years."

There was suddenly singing coming up over the edge of the cliff. It was Avis and Maddie and even Dalton, singing as they climbed the ladder. "'Blow, ye winds, in the morning, and blow, ye winds, high-ho!'" Maddie was the first to come into view. She stopped when she saw them.

"Well, look here. A cowbird singing like a sailor."

"Keep going up, Maddie!" Avis called from below, still out of sight. "Move on up!"

Maddie climbed over the ladder, dropped the basket she'd been carrying, and came on, running and screaming at the man all in a rush. *"Non! Non! Jamais!"*

Avis and then Dalton scrambled up over the top. They stood by the barn, frozen at the scene before them. Then Avis started running after Maddie. Dalton caught her by the shoulders and held her back.

"I will not go with you! Get out! Get out!" Maddie's hands were in fists as she rushed toward the man.

"Whoa, Maddie. Whoa." Bill ran in front of her and caught her flailing wrists.

"I'll not go with you! I'll go to hell first!" Maddie screamed at the man, who stood holding the reins of his horse and laughing as Bill held her back.

"He's not taking you anywheres you don't want to go."

"Ain't this sweet? You've found yourself a little nest to crawl into, Madeleine. Don't let her fool you, mister. She's not one of the birdies like you got here flapping their little wings. She's a liar and a thief."

"Don't you call her that, you bastard." Dalton pushed Avis toward Idella, who was still watching on the porch. He grabbed the pitchfork leaning against the barn. "Get out. Get out of here."

"Well, well. She's working 'er way down the line, I see." The man climbed up onto his horse. "The little man."

"It was my money for the boots! It was mine!" Maddie pulled away from Bill's grasp. She was a wild thing, rushing about the yard clawing at the ground for handfuls of dirt she threw at the man.

"You little whore!" He backed up his horse as she ran up at him and clawed at his leg. "Get off me!" He jerked his foot upward and kicked her hard under her chin. Avis and Idella screamed from the porch steps as Maddie covered her face with her arms and sank to her knees.

"I'll kill you!" Dalton rushed at the man with the pitchfork.

Bill grabbed him by the back of his collar. "Whoa, son. Stop!"

"Let go of me!" Dalton struggled to get free. "I'll kill him if he hurts her."

Bill tightened his grip on Dalton's collar. "No one's going to kill anyone."

"You hold that boy steady now." The man backed his horse up well out of Dalton's reach. "And you listen to what I have to say. I'm doing you a favor, mister." He looked down at Maddie. "You stole at the lobster factory, didn't you, girl?" Maddie lay sobbing on the ground. "Got caught going through pockets." He looked at Bill. "She's a goddamned thief."

Idella clung to the porch post, too afraid to move. Avis stood away from her, watching intently.

"Pretty hankies and hairpins at first. I noticed things but didn't ask. Then she was caught with her hand in a pocket, holding on to some little girl's silver dollar. I begged for her, and they let her stay. 'Cause she's a good cracker." He laughed. "Good strong hands. Firm and strong, hard-working. That's my experience. Ain't that right, Madeleine?"

Maddie would not look up at him.

"I got her to pay me back for the trouble. Made me look bad. I showed her how to help me feel good." He laughed again. "Took right to it. She's a slut. Like her damn slut of a mother. Goddamned Frenchie. She showed up one night saying, 'Remember me? Well, here's Made-leine, your little daughter,' she said. 'I wanted her to meet her father.' Daughter, hell. Must be fifty men could've been that fat cow's father—and her showing up all these years after. I put them up. 'One night,' I said. 'Then you're out.' 'Fine,' she said. 'One night is good.' That bitch left in the middle of the night. Only she didn't take everything with her." He looked over at Maddie. "So I taught her to make coffee for me and fry eggs. And I got her a job in the lobster factory. Lied about her age. She owed me." He looked down at her again. "She was a slut from birth. Nothing but."

"Don't you call her a slop!" Avis suddenly grabbed the slop bucket from off the porch and ran at him from behind. "Don't you call Maddie nothing! I'll show you what a slop is." A wide arc of garbage pelted his hands and shirt. Startled, the horse turned sharply and reared.

"Avis, get away!" Bill let go of Dalton and dragged Avis, kicking and screaming, away from the horse.

"You little bitch!" The man's shirt was soaked with sour milk, potato peels, lobster bodies, fish heads. He stared at Bill. "You got sluts coming out your ears." He took hold of the reins with one hand and brushed the garbage from off his front. "You're working up a one-man whorehouse here, by the look of things." He glanced down at Dalton, who stood star-ing back. "Or maybe two, eh, boy?"

"Slops's too good for a pig like you, mister!" Avis yelled, struggling against Bill's steadying grip.

"When he's done diddling, he'll pass her on to you, boy. There's lots of nice French girls around. Don't have to stop with the one you started with." He turned his horse and looked over at Idella. "And then you got them nice little sisters."

"Get out of here before I kill you!" Bill's voice suddenly filled the air. He stood tall and straight, holding Avis around the middle with one arm, her feet dangling in midair. "You goddamned bastard, if you ever set foot near one of these girls again, I'll have your ass cooked so black the devil will throw you back."

The horse backed up. "I'm leaving you, mister, with all your baby whores." He started laughing. "Keep the boots," he called over his shoulder as he rode out. "You'll need 'em. She bites."

Dalton grabbed the pitchfork and rushed after the horse, but the man was already up to the road.

Avis chased after him, spewing out names. "Hog! Slop trot! Goddamned asshole!" When the horse was well past the Doncasters', she turned and ran back toward the house, skipping and prancing. "We showed him, by God. We got rid of him for you, Maddie!"

"Avis!" Bill stood with his hand on Dalton's shoulder. "Be still."

Maddie, her head buried beneath her arms, was a heap of tangled hair and coarse gray fabric splayed on the ground. No one spoke. Dalton still held the pitchfork upright at arm's length. Idella leaned quietly against the front of the house, in the shadow of the porch. The muffled sound of Maddie's sobs mingled with the splash of waves far below and the dull thud of now-distant hooves pounding the flat, dry ground.

Avis walked quietly up to Maddie and knelt beside her. She reached over with her small hand. "What's wrong?" She, too, began to cry. "Now Maddie can stay with us forever. She can be ours."

Idella came forward across the porch and down the steps. She joined Avis, crouching by Maddie, and put a tentative hand on her back. Maddie raised herself up. Tears smeared her swollen cheeks. "I am dirty. Covered in dirt."

"No, Maddie. No!" Dalton let go the pitchfork and came over to kneel in front of her. "You're not dirty. What that man said wasn't true."

Maddie shook her head. "I am so dirty and so bad. You don't know how bad."

Dalton reached over and brushed off the dirt still clinging to her fingers. "See? It comes right off, Maddie. It's like dirt on a potato. It comes right off."

"You'll be one of us Hillocks." Avis looked over at her father. "Right, Dad? She's one of us."

Bill stood alone, unmoving. For a minute he stared toward the water, at the flat horizon stretching like a gray thread in the distance. Finally he glanced over at the huddled figures. "Birdies," he said, shaking his head. "A nest full of birdies. Jesus help me."

He picked up the fallen pitchfork and carried it back to the haystack. He stuck it in harder than it needed and stood with his back to them, holding on to the handle.

For a long time that night, Bill sat at the table smoking his pipe. Avis and Idella, lying in their bed, went off to sleep with the familiar smell of his tobacco seeping into their room, settling on their blanket and in their hair. Maddie, who had spoken hardly a word since her father rode off on the horse, sat up on her little bed, aware of the smoke and the occasional pacing from below.

When she was sure the girls were asleep, she quietly rose, reached under her mattress, and carefully pulled out a hidden bundle of clothes. She groped through it until she felt the curves of the small bottle. Unscrewing the top, she poured perfume over a fingertip and smeared it between her breasts, on her forehead and wrists, and on the front of her neck. She ran her fingers through her hair, then replaced the top and pushed the whole bundle back under her mattress. The perfume rose up like a fog from her body. She hesitated a moment, then took the blanket off the bed, wrapped it around her shoulders like a shawl, and closed the door behind her. She knew that Dalton was in the barn. She'd seen his light flickering out.

Clutching the blanket, she stepped quietly down the stairs. She stood in the shadows till Bill looked up and saw her. "Maddie."

"I have come to see you," she whispered. "To tell you."

"There's nothing to say, Maddie. That's behind you now. You won't see him no more. I promise." He paused. "But, Maddie, you can't be stealing things no more."

She put her head down. "I was so bad. I am bad."

"You already stole what hearts there's here to take." She looked up, startled. He smiled. "You got to stop." There was a long moment of silence. Each of them was still, watching the other. Finally Bill spoke. "I'm sending you away, Maddie. I'm going to ask my Emma's folks to take you on at their farm. They've got a big place. Gramma Becky knows all about girls. She had five. You'll be better off."

"I want to stay here. With you."

"It won't be easy. There's jackass men all over. But I don't want to be one of them. I'm a good man some of the time. But I'm not a good man all of the time. I know it. I'm weak, and my needs are strong." He paused, watching as she stood frozen at the foot of the stairs.

"I can't stay here with you?"

"Oh, no. No, Maddie."

"It is you that I want to see, why I came down."

"You're looking at me."

"You know now that I am not a girl anymore. And I know . . . I know how to make a man happy. With my body. My hands. I want to make you happy. I have made you so sad." She stepped toward him as she spoke.

"Don't get so close, Maddie. I been drinking. And I'm lonely. Don't ask for nothing you shouldn't be having." He looked at her. "I'm an old man next to you, Maddie. You're more girl than woman. You just got steered wrong."

"I feel, with you, like a woman."

"Well, that's not . . . that's not like it should be. Hell, you're more Dalton's age than the grizzled old ass of me."

She smiled at him and stepped closer, opening out the blanket that she had wrapped around herself.

"Jesus H. Christ, what are you wearing? That's Emma's smell. Maddie, you're trying to kill me."

She reached up suddenly and put her arms around him, burying her face against his chest. He bent his head forward and smelled the thick, sweet perfume in her hair. He lifted a handful to his face.

Maddie tried to kiss him. He was so tall above her that she couldn't reach his mouth. She grabbed at his shirt and pulled him down to her. "Kiss me," she whispered. "Give me your mouth. I can kiss so good."

He released her hair. "No. You can't do this, Maddie." He covered her mouth with his hand. "This has gone all up for down." Her tongue was on his fingers.

The door opened. Dalton stood in the doorway. "You goddamned bastard." Maddie pulled away and wrapped the blanket tight around her. Bill stood, arms to his sides, and stared back at Dalton.

Dalton ran into the room and started pounding Bill's arms and shoulders with clenched fists. "You filthy bastard! Keep your hands off her! Can't you let anything alone that's good? Can't you let there be something in this goddamned house that doesn't turn stinking and dirty because you put your filthy hands all over it! You're no better than that bastard that kicked her!"

Maddie tried to pull him away from Bill. "I want to, you see. I want to be for him what he needs."

"God in damnation come to drag me down!" Bill roared suddenly as he pushed off Dalton and grabbed Maddie roughly by the shoulders and turned her toward him. "Maddie!" He shook her in rage and frustration. "No, Maddie! No! You are trying to kill me! You come to drag me to hell this minute!"

"Get off her." Dalton clawed and kicked at his father. "Get your filthy hands off her. You can't keep away from anything good. Like Mother! You killed her! You killed her with your goddamned stinking seed. You didn't need any more brats! But you couldn't stop. You couldn't leave her alone. You killed her!"

Bill raised his hand and struck Dalton hard across the face. "Shut your goddamned mouth! If you ever, ever, ever say that to me again, your ass will be over that cliff before you get to suck in one more breath."

The blow sent Dalton staggering. Maddie ran to him. "No, Dalton. No." He lay sprawled over the table, sobbing, pounding it with his fist.

"Maddie, you leave in the morning. First thing. I'm taking you. And it'll be too far to come back. It already is."

"No! Maddie can't leave!" Avis suddenly wailed down from the top of the stairs.

"She's leaving, all right!" Bill yelled back up the stairs. "Now, get back to bed, the two of you. You'll all be leaving soon enough, the lot of you! I can't be doing this no more. It's no place for little girls." He looked at Maddie. "No matter how growed they think they are. I can't be doing this no more!"

Avis cried miserably into her pillow until she finally went to sleep. Idella lay awake in the dark for hours. Maddie was out walking back and forth along the cliff edge. Idella could hear snatches of her singing, the French like a soft moan carried aloft on the wind. The moon was blanketed in clouds tonight, just a smudge of dim light. Idella leaned on the windowsill and stared into the blank dark. The sky had changed so, she thought, everything had changed so, from one night to the next.

When there was the grayest of pale light, like a soft smoke hovering over the beds, Maddie crept into the room. Idella, still awake, turned just enough to watch her without being seen. Maddie looked over at the girls' bed. Avis's foot stuck out from the quilt, and Maddie gently pushed it back. Idella closed her eyes as though asleep, then opened them when she heard Maddie open her bottom dresser drawer and start to pile the contents onto the blanket, the one she'd come with. She's starting to pack, Idella thought. She's getting ready to go.

She watched quietly as Maddie got down on her knees and pulled out from under the bed a second bundle of what appeared to be clothes. She fingered them carefully without unfolding them and held them up to her face. Then, with some hesitation, she put them into the bottom drawer she had just emptied. Idella could not get a good look at what she was putting into the drawer, but she suddenly had a sick feeling come crawling up out of her stomach, realizing what they must be—Mother's clothes.

She lay frozen, watching Maddie slowly move about the room, closing the drawer, pulling up the corners of her blanket so that she could bundle the contents. Maddie glanced anxiously toward the bed, and Idella flicked her eyes closed. She opened them again when she felt Maddie moving and watched as Maddie carefully reached behind her pillowcase and removed a small rag doll Idella'd found. But it looked odd. Maddie held the doll to her face, her eyes closed, and brushed it against her cheek. Then Idella saw the difference. She gasped. The doll had hair. A swatch of Mother's braid was attached to the top of its head. Idella sat up. "Maddie!" she whispered, in shock.

"Oh!" Maddie thrust the doll behind her back.

"That is Mother's hair!" Idella stared intently at her. "Give me that!"

"No! No! She is all that I have. Please." Maddie was on her knees in front of Idella, whispering so as not to wake Avis. "This is from my mother. But she had no hair. I wanted her to be beautiful, like your mother." Maddie was sobbing and reaching toward Idella. Her hand was like a claw flailing in the air.

Seeing how desperate and frightened she was, Idella started to cry. "Oh, Maddie," she said softly, and for the first time since Maddie's arrival, Idella reached out to hug her. She could say no more as Maddie engulfed her in an embrace of such force that she couldn't even raise her head. A deep feeling of sadness rose up in her. It was for Maddie and for herself, too, for all of them. She reached tighter around Maddie and squeezed back with all her might.

When they were able to pull away, Idella whispered, "May I see her?"

Maddie nodded, then slowly offered up the doll. Idella took it cautiously. The room had grown lighter, and she could see that the lock of Mother's braid was crudely sewn into the top and back of the doll's soft head. She fingered it tenderly, crying. There was the sad little mouth, the black button nose. "There are no eyes to her," she whispered. "She can't see."

"I lost them," Maddie whispered. "They fell off."

Idella gave her back. "Go to sleep, Maddie. You need to sleep now."

Maddie nodded and crawled into the little bed, clutching her doll. She was soon asleep.

Idella lay watching her for a long, long time, till the light sharpened the edges in the room and it was morning and Dad called to them to get up, by God, he had to get on the road.

Maddie made coffee one last time. "Back to the piss pot for me," Bill said when he poured out the dregs. "Time to go, Maddie. Blackie's hitched."

Dalton and the girls lined up to see them off. Maddie climbed up onto the seat next to Bill. Avis was bawling, and Dalton was standing with his hat in his hands.

"Hell, I almost forgot." Bill reached under the seat of the wagon and took out a wrapped bundle. He handed it to Maddie. "This here is for your birthday." Maddie sat clutching the package. She could not control the tears any longer, and Avis came up to her, and they started in crying together. "Goddamn it, Maddie," Bill said. "Open it and put me out of my misery."

She unwrapped the stiff paper, uncovering the brush and the little bird's-eye mirror. "Don't look in it now, 'cause we all look terrible," Bill said.

"Thank you. It is so beautiful."

"Idella, she picked it."

"Thank you, Idella." Maddie ran her fingers over the soft bristles.

Idella kept feeling that something wasn't right. Suddenly she knew. "Wait!" she called. "Wait!"

She tore into the house and up the stairs. She got on her knees and pulled out from under the bed her box of special things. Opening it with trembling fingers, she searched till she found what she needed. Without even closing the box, she rushed down the stairs and out into the yard.

"What in the hell got into you?" Dad asked.

Idella rushed up to Maddie and opened out her hand. Two shiny blue buttons, saved from the dress her mother had worn, lay in her palm.

"There, Maddie. So she can see."

Bill came back late that night. He'd gotten Maddie situated at the Smythe farm and told Gramma Becky as much as he knew about her, leaving out some details and stressing what a good worker she was. He could feel Becky's eyes going on through him, scouring his insides a few times in the telling, and he was relieved there was nothing there for her to see. There sure as hell could've been.

A week later, after telegrams had been sent and replied to, he drove Avis and Idella to the train in Bathurst and sent them down to Maine to live with John and Martha on their farm. He looked down at the two little girls huddled against each other in the wagon, not saying a word to him or to each other. He knew they'd be expected to help out a whole lot. They knew it, too. But they'd get proper schooling down in Maine. Martha was Emma's big sister. She'd see to it. And they'd have something closer to a mother—though Martha was spread pretty thin with them boys and another baby on the way. "Christ Almighty," he whispered as he watched Avis and Idella waving their little white hands to him from the train window. "They're in for it. But they'll be better off, by God. They'll be better off."

That night Bill fried up potatoes and doled them out for his and Dalton's supper. Dalton looked down at the greasy plate and then back at his father. They ate in silence.

"It's awful quiet around here," Bill said, finally, pushing his plate away. He got up and poured himself a glass of whiskey. Dalton sat watching him. Bill silently got a second glass, poured a splash into it, and handed it to Dalton. "We'll be bachelors now, son. You and me. We'll make do and get by."

Dalton took the glass and looked down into it. "I thought that's what we were doing before." He lifted it and drank a mouthful. Bill poured him one more and joined him at the table. They sat in silence for a long time, drinking whiskey, till Bill spoke.

"Two years ago I had the best wife on earth and goin' on four children." He stared into the flickering oil lamp on the table. "Now I'm down to one boy-man, an empty bed, an empty house . . . and a new pair of boots." He looked down at them. "New boots to wander."

Dalton had never seen Dad cry but the once at Ma's grave. This was the second time. He finished his whiskey, cleared his own plate from the table, and let him be.

Going Back Up

Scarborough, Maine
June 1921

Idella sat with her cheek pressed against the window of the train. She stared out at the passing Maine landscape. Farms and fields and small towns would soon give way to relentless trees as the train carried her and Avis back on up to Canada—back home to Dad and the farm.

Avis was fidgeting across from Idella, her braids coming all unraveled from constant nervous plucking. It was no use saying anything. She was miserable enough already.

Aunt Martha had sat them down at the kitchen table when it was still dark and done their hair in braids. "So you'll look like young ladies," she'd said, softly pushing from Idella's forehead the lank wisps that had already straggled out from any attempt at confinement. Then she'd stood looking down at them slumped miserably in their chairs. "You poor, motherless girls," she'd finally said. Idella had tried to absorb Aunt Martha's face in the soft light of gray dawn. Aunt Martha's face was as close to what her own mother's must have looked like as anyone's might be.

"Aunt Martha packed us chicken and biscuits," Idella said. "You hungry yet?" Avis shook her head. "Me neither."

She looked down at her lap, at her bound red copy of *Robinson Crusoe* that she'd clutched so hard the sweat of her hands had taken on some of the red dye. Seeing this, she wiped them on the seat next to her. She wanted the book on her lap—to feel its weight, the promise of its thick, dense pages. She wasn't going to read it till she got to Canada. It was for the bad times.

The book was first prize for winning the eighth-grade spelling bee on the last day of school. It had been a surprise to everyone that quiet little Idella had beaten out Arthur Davis—with a word as simple as "banister." And she wasn't even a true eighth grader.

Idella had begged to be allowed to finish out the school year before being sent back up to take care of Dad. News of his hunting accident had come down to them just two weeks earlier. He had been shot bad when the men were flushing out a deer they'd cornered, off season. The bullet had gone right through his leg. He had been in the hospital for over a month. The doctors wanted to keep him longer, but Dad kept on yelling so and cursing so and saying he wanted to get on back to the farm so, that they gave in to be rid of him. That's what the letter from Mrs. Doncaster said. She'd written to Uncle John and Aunt Martha.

Uncle John had laughed when Aunt Martha read the letter out loud at the supper table. He'd said if that wasn't just like Bill, then the barn didn't smell like cow shit.

Idella and Avis had sat quietly, not touching their food or daring to look at each other, holding their breath and hoping the letter would be over soon. But it wasn't. Bill Hillock wanted his girls to come home. Home to do his bidding.

Home. Back to the house and barn on top of the cliff overlooking the Bay Chaleur. What few trees there were about the house were all leaned over and bent from the cold, constant pressures of the winds that blew off the water. That's how the people got, Idella thought, from living up there their whole lives—bent over and gnarled and hard, rooted in one place. That wind worked on people the same as it did on trees. It howled and bit, especially in winter, and scraped away at you. There was nothing to do but buckle over and try to get where you were going, which was never very far—to the barn or the field or the buggy to New Bandon, two miles down the road.

Idella leaned back and felt the train pulling them north. There was a beauty up there, she knew—but it was a barren, lonely kind of beauty. The fields were flat and endless and the soil more full of rocks than things growing. Down in Maine, helping Aunt Martha tend her garden, Idella had found the soil dark and plush in comparison. It smelled heavy, moist. She'd roil handfuls of it in her fingers just for the feel of it, squeezing it and making lumps that clung together like a good dough.

Of course, Aunt Martha had worked on that soil. She'd tended it and nurtured it. Dad was more lopsided in his tending. He didn't have much patience for a good system. He'd throw fish all over, which smelled to high heaven, and leave them be, to work their way into the soil or get carted off by birds and animals. Idella'd seen enough of those herring to last her a lifetime—but she knew she'd not seen or eaten or cleaned her last one.

When Mrs. Elmhurst, the teacher in the one-room school at Scarborough, had learned that Idella had to go back up, she'd called her aside after school. "Idella, I heard about your having to go back to Canada, and I'm sorry." Idella had started to cry, right in front of her. She'd kept quiet about it ever since Aunt Martha had read Dad's letter aloud and shown them the money he'd sent for their train tickets.

Mrs. Elmhurst had sat her down at a desk and handed her the cotton handkerchief that was always peeking out of her dress pocket. Idella had been too ashamed to use it. She couldn't blow her nose on that beautiful handkerchief. There was embroidery on it. She'd sat there like a fool, clutching at it, her eyes and nose a shameful mess. Mrs. Elmhurst had been so kind. She had taken the handkerchief from Idella and wiped her eyes and then put it right up under her nose and said, "Blow." They had both smiled at that.

"Idella," Mrs. Elmhurst had said, "if you'd like, you may take the eighth-grade test, and if you pass it, then why don't you come and graduate with all the others?" Idella had nodded yes, too shy to say anything, and the teacher had taken the handkerchief and put it into Idella's hand. Now Idella reached into her skirt pocket till she felt the soft folds of the handkerchief. She'd keep it forever.

She had passed the test with no trouble. She'd been paying attention to whatever got put on the board all along. Nothing slipped past her.

Mrs. Elmhurst gave her a poem by Henry Wadsworth Longfellow to recite in the graduation ceremony. Idella worked on the poem nonstop. She kept going over it, moving her lips, after she'd blown out the light and gone to bed.

She closed her eyes, and the words of the poem rolled around in her head, taking on the rhythm of the train wheels.

> *Tell me not, in mournful numbers,*
> *Life is but an empty dream!*
> *For the soul is dead that slumbers,*
> *And things are not what they seem.*

"A Psalm of Life," Longfellow called it.

When the time had come for graduation—lining everyone up just right and getting them all to sing, then getting them all seated again—it had gone a little slowly. Meanwhile the sky had started to threaten. The ceremony was out on the lawn behind the school, so all the relatives could come. Avis had scooched herself down in the front row where she could make faces.

By the time they got to Idella's turn, there were little spits coming down and things were turning restless. Mrs. Elmhurst had played the musical chord of introduction on the piano—that was her sign to begin. Idella had stood up, trembling. She had looked directly at Mrs. Elmhurst and shaken her head no, ever so slightly. Mrs. Elmhurst had smiled and nodded that she understood. Idella sat down, with great relief, and Raymond Tripp stood up and began his poem from Shakespeare. He'd barely gotten anything out when it started to pour. Everyone scattered like chickens. The men rushed at the piano, practically knocking Mrs. Elmhurst over, to get it inside quick. Poor Raymond kept stopping and starting the first line over again. He never got to finish. Idella was more glad than ever that she'd passed herself by.

She sighed and looked over at Avis slumped in her seat, knees under her chin, staring out at the fields. Her eyes were red and her cheeks salty and sore. She'd been biting on her lower lip till it looked ragged. It'd bleed if she kept at it. But Idella didn't say anything. She let her be.

"Della," Avis asked, tentatively, her voice a thin thread, "Della, do you think we'll ever come back? Will we ever see Aunt Martha and Uncle John and everybody again?"

"Oh, sure," Idella soothed her. But she had been wondering the same thing as she felt the miles slip behind them, the train pushing them farther and farther toward what sure seemed like nowhere, back to Dad and the farm.

Bay Chaleur, New Brunswick
April 1921

"Go on! Go on in after 'im! Chase 'im out!" Bill Hillock called across the field to Dick Pettigrew. He was waving him around into the woods from the far side.

"I seen 'im go into them trees by the pasture, Bill." Fred Doncaster was trotting across the field, his rifle in hand. "If we get him turned in to the swamp, he won't know which way to go and we'll bag 'im for sure." He stopped and snapped the gun open. "Don't know when I've seen a buck that big."

Bill dropped a bullet into his own rifle. "Here come the rest of them. Smelling it still on the hoof."

Across the pasture loped the two Doncaster boys, Will and Donnelly. They were followed by Sam Hillock—Bill's brother—and Stu Wharton, who'd come by hoping to sell lobster traps to the Hillock brothers.

"He's got ten points on 'im." Stu was out of breath, straggling in back of the younger men. "Must weigh three hundred pounds."

"He's in that stand of trees," Bill said. "Let's fan out around the edge of them. I'll go on around to the far side."

The men scattered across the muddy fields, toting their rifles. Each took up a position at the edge of the woods. They waited and watched, staring into the spaces between the bare, gray tree trunks, among the almost-barren branches just beginning to sprout tight little buds. They waited for what seemed a long time—lifting their rifles up to their faces and slowly resting them against their shoulders, silently flexing, looking for movement in the woods.

"I'm goin' in to flush him!" Bill called. "That bastard's in there, and I'm getting him out. Get ready." Each man listened for the crack of a branch and watched for the sudden rush of antlers through the brush.

The explosions and the shout were simultaneous. "Jesus Christ, I'm shot!" Bill cried. "Mother of God, they shot me."

No one knew whose bullet it was. No one wanted to know. They all felt part of it. The stag, too, was wounded, but they paid no heed as it charged off out of the woods, trailing blood.

"Bill! Bill!" Sam dropped his gun at his feet and ran to his brother. "Get the women! Run like hell!" he shouted to the men who surfaced from all directions. Bill lay writhing on his back among the trees. "Where you hit, Bill?"

"The goddamned fools shot me! Right through the leg," Bill shouted from the ground. "Jesus Christ, the blood."

"Don't move him till we get him onto something." Stu Wharton was summoning all his strength to run and shout. "I seen McPhee's mail car a ways back. Get a horse!" The Doncaster boys were tearing for the barn.

Elsie Doncaster was flying into and across the field as fast as her two boys were leaving it. She'd heard the shots and yells and had run to pull her sheets off the line. She ran with no heed to her bulk, charging down a plowed furrow like a train. Her skirts were pulled above her knees, her arms clasped round the bundled sheets. A bottle of whiskey was in one fist and a wooden spoon in the other.

She reached the edge of the woods and stopped. "Lead me to him straight through. Get me to him." Her husband pulled her through the trees. "Get the door, Fred," she said when she saw Bill's long body lying like a pinioned snake and blood pouring onto last year's leaves. "Get the door down!" Without a word she handed Sam the whiskey bottle.

"We need the front door!" Fred Doncaster took off running, calling out to Stu Wharton.

"And rope to strap him!" Elsie shouted after him. "Blankets off the beds!" She bit into the edge of a sheet and tore down a strip with a great wrench of her arms. "You damned fools," she said, bending down next to Bill. "You goddamned foolish men!" She started wrapping the strip around Bill's thigh. "Keep tearing, Sam."

Bill cried out, "Jesus Christ, Elsie, I'm bleeding!"

"Hold still so's I can wrap it." Elsie wound the strips as quick as Sam handed them to her.

From the other direction came Cora Pettigrew. She, too, had heard the yells. She'd pulled the curtains from her windows and grabbed her good scissors. Guided by Bill's shouts, she'd headed straight into the woods.

"Lord help us, Bill, what have we done to you?" Cora knelt down in the mud and immediately started slicing through her curtains.

"Those goddamned sons of bitches shot the hell out of me! My whole backside's on fire!"

Both women started wrapping Bill's leg and thigh. The pooled blood blackened whatever it touched, smearing the hands and arms of the women.

"Sam, give me the whiskey. Ah, goddamn it, Elsie! Don't finish me off!"

"Lie still. Stop bawling." Elsie bore down with a single-minded intensity, wrapping layer upon layer of torn fabric around his leg and groin.

"Hold on, Bill," Sam said. He raised up Bill's head to let him drink. "Easy, now. Easy."

McPhee's mail car, horn blasting, came heading across the field. Sam ran to the edge of the woods, shouting, "Get the door! Where's the damned door?" The car bounced across the furrows.

"We've got it!" The three Doncaster men were lunging across the furrows with the door. "We're coming!" When they reached the woods, Sam led them to Bill, clearing away brush and snapping off branches with his bare hands. He helped Cora prepare a clearing for the men to lay down the door and put Bill onto it. McPhee was turning the car around, backing it into position, opening the doors, the motor running.

"Get me the hell out of here!" Bill's bluster was losing its edge. He tossed his head restlessly from side to side, as though trying to block out a blazing ball of sun that only he could see and feel. "It's burning. It's burning a hole right through me down there."

Sam took hold of one end of the door, ripped from its hinges, and helped to lay it down as flat as possible next to Bill. The men stood ready holding the ropes.

"We're gonna move you now, Bill," Sam cautioned. "Get ready for a ride."

Elsie placed her wooden spoon between Bill's teeth. "Bite this." But he'd already grabbed onto it, snarling through his clenched teeth. She took hold of Bill's hand and squeezed it while the men lifted him carefully onto the door.

Then four men knelt at the corners and hoisted the door above the ground. Bill's yells of pain were muted by the clenched spoon. Two other men and Cora Pettigrew started tying his arms and legs down with the rope, winding it over and around the whole frame, securing the loops around the doorknobs that still remained on top and bottom. Bill's feet jerked in anguish. Elsie kept squeezing his hand, and he kept biting down on the spoon. Her voice was low, deliberate, steady. "Hold on, now, Bill. We'll get you there."

Sam looked down at his writhing brother. "You're gonna get that fast ride in McPhee's mail car you been wantin' for years, Bill. But you ain't gonna enjoy it."

Bill heard his brother's voice through the white heat. He spoke through gritted teeth. "I sure as hell won't be drivin'."

Idella leaned back in the seat of the train and closed her eyes. While she was so happy to be in school, those men, the men she'd known all her life, were flushing out a deer off season. Now she was having to pay for it. Her life was getting changed. Going back to the same damn thing, only worse.

She'd heard how they'd put Dad on a door and carried him out of the woods and onto Mr. McPhee's back seat. Neighbors and Uncle Sam had been writing Uncle John and Aunt Martha letters. They got a new one nearly every day from someone who'd been there or seen part of it or heard all about it. Dad had nearly choked on a wooden spoon that he bit clear through on the way. It was a full fifteen miles down to Salmon Beach, where Dr. Putnam lived. A good thing they caught the doctor at home. He'd just come back from waiting on an old woman way down country and was about to have his "breakfast lunch and dinner," as he'd told it, when he heard that horn blasting nonstop, it must have been three miles away. He'd got right up from the table and gone over to his office and started getting things ready for whatever might be coming through the door. He didn't know it'd be coming *on* a door.

Before he'd even gotten sight of the car—he was standing in his office doorway, waiting, and people were coming out of their houses—before he even saw the car, he heard Dad, screaming from the back seat.

Dad was hurt bad, but he made it. He could hardly walk yet. And he wanted them home, Avis and Idella.

She knew what that meant—his girls, to take care of him. Emma, living over with Aunt Beth and Uncle Paul, was too small. Idella sighed and turned to the window. Clouds were moving in. The whole sky seemed lower. There wasn't much to see now anyway, just trees. She'd seen enough of them. God help us, Idella thought. Soon enough they'd be home.

It was getting toward twilight when the train finally pulled in to the stop near their farm—not even a station, just a place to take on water. Dalton was there, tall and lean as a post, propped up against the wagon, somberly waiting. He was squinting down at the tracks, his hands in his pockets. Even in a busy place, Dalton seemed alone.

Idella and Avis dropped their bags off the train and dragged them away from the tracks. Avis stared up at him, her arms pulled down from the weight of her suitcase. "Aren't you even going to say hello?"

Dalton looked down and smiled as much as he ever did, that queer little half smile of his. Idella always felt that he was holding back a secret, as if there were something more he wanted to say, but she never dared ask what. Her brother never talked much with anyone, and when he did, it wasn't to say much of anything.

"Well, if it ain't Avis-Mavis." He reached over, tousled her hair, and nodded at Idella. "Better give me those bags." He hoisted them up into the wagon. "I hope you got your learnin' good. 'Cause you're 'bout done with it now, I'd say."

Idella clamped her mouth tight and stared ahead at the nodding neck of Blackie pulling them home. They rode along in silence. Dalton had not been allowed to go to school in Maine. Dad needed him on the farm to help with the fish and the lobsters. He'd been to the local one-room school some off and on, and he could read well enough and do figures. Idella didn't know how Dalton felt about his sisters getting to go, because he never expressed an opinion. She clutched at the book she still carried in her hands.

"He's fiery. Get ready." Dalton didn't turn to look at them. "He can't get up yet for more'n a few minutes. Hates lying there." He pulled the reins to slow the horse over a muddy patch of road. "Been home four days. Seems longer."

Idella noted the houses of the few neighbors as they rolled past— Uncle Sam's, the Doncasters', the Pettigrews' in the distance. All the houses were slanted and gray and sparse-looking, sticking up out of the flat land like rotten teeth.

When they turned off the road toward the house, Idella smelled the sea. A deep breath filled her up. She didn't know she'd missed it. Tippie, the Doncaster dog, came up barking at the back wheels.

The farmhouse was like all the other houses along the road, with two bedrooms upstairs and a spring kitchen attached to the main house. Most had been built by the same men. Dad had built theirs himself, with Uncle Sam's help, just before Dalton was born. He had put it on the high cliff overlooking the bay that pounded and raged beneath them. Mother had wanted it there.

Idella could hear the restless water while she lay in bed or while she was cooking suppers. The house was exposed and unsheltered, perched so near the cliff. In winter the press of the winds wrapped around its corners and pushed on the walls. Steady streams of cold air whistled under the windowsills, prodding the loose shingles that Dad never got to fixing.

Mother had loved to hear the sound of the water far below, crashing over the rocks. One of the strongest memories Idella had was of standing in the middle of the kitchen during a fierce storm, with her mother crouched at her side. Idella had been afraid. "Listen, Idella, listen. Isn't that a wonderful thing—to hear the ocean? Can you hear it crashing? And the wind howling and howling. And here we are safe in our own home. Aren't we lucky!" Idella had not been so sure, even then, but she had tried to smile like her mother. She'd trailed after her the whole afternoon, one fist clutched in the folds of her skirts. Her mother didn't seem to mind. She'd sigh sometimes and pat Idella's head, but she never told her to let go.

Dad hated the wind and loved it both. He'd shake his fist and rail against it, and then he'd start talking about his dead wife, saying it was her damn fault for perching them all on the goddamned brink like that and then dying. When he was drunk one time, late on a cold winter night, Idella heard Dad talking as the wind beat mercilessly at the windows. He spoke as if her mother had come back to haunt them. It had scared her. He'd started out loud, raving. Idella had snuck to the top of the stairs to listen, thinking at first that someone else was really down there talking to him. But Dad had ended up quiet, standing in front of a window, his head pressed against the glass. She had gone back to her own bed and cried. She missed her mother, too. Everything had changed when she died, everything.

"You'd best go on in. He'll be waitin'. He raves, then he rests. You'll see." Dalton rode the wagon up close to the door, and his two sisters jumped down and got their bags. Then he clucked to Blackie and headed him over to the barn. "I'll be in for supper."

"Come on," Idella said to Avis, who was looking longingly at the open fields, still visible in the soft late light of June. "We better go in."

"I'm coming." Avis jabbed her feet into the dirt, making powdery bursts. "I just don't want to see blood."

"There won't be blood. It's all bandaged. You won't see a thing. Come on, now." Idella hoped she was right. She took her thin jacket from her shoulders and wrapped it around the red book she'd carried so carefully. She had an urge to hide the book, to keep it to herself.

She opened the front door and called tentatively. "Dad? You here?"

"Where else would I be?" Dad's voice came tearing out from his bedroom. "Get in here, you two. Let's see what Aunt Martha's done to you. Let's see how much you've grown."

They set down their bags, Idella placing her covered book on a bench under the windowsill. Then they walked cautiously across the kitchen and pushed back the half-open door to their father's room. It smelled bad. The chamber pot was on the floor beside the bed. No one had emptied it. Right in the middle of the braided rug, slopped over. Dirty clothes and empty glasses were strewn about the floor. And discarded bandages.

In the middle of the room, lying in a tangle of bedclothes, was Dad, one leg, the good leg, sticking out from the bottom of the bed, hairy and bare. The sheet was stretched across his middle and wrapped up under an armpit. One of the cotton quilts was wadded on the floor. The washbasin lay on the floor beside him, filled with old water. A rusty layer, like fine sand, had settled on the bottom. Old blood.

It was difficult, at first, to focus on him. The evening shadows were like a gray blanket draped over the entire room. Finally Idella's gaze rested on Dad's face. He was gaunt and pale. All the color seemed to have gone right out of him—except for his eyes. They were red-rimmed and fiery all around the edges. She could tell that, even in the dim light. His hair had been cut in a strange way, very short, probably by someone at the hospital. He was stubbly and unshaven.

"Damn glad you're back. I been trapped in this goddamn house like a hornet in a damned jar." They stood in front of him, Avis strangely shy, hanging behind her bigger sister. He started to rouse himself to a sitting position but was jerked back down as though by an unseen hand. "Son of a bitch." His face closed up, his eyes squeezed shut, and his breathing became slow and audible.

Idella and Avis stood before him with lowered eyes and clenched fists. Idella had never seen him weakened before or showing pain. It embarrassed her.

Finally he let out a long, slow breath and opened his eyes. "It grabs me still, like a claw." Idella and Avis nodded. His voice was tired, the blast gone out of it. "It's healing, mind you. I'll be on two feet. But it stiffens, see, and there's goddamned lightning when I try to move it." He pointed with one hand toward the bandaged mass below his torso. Again the girls stood there nodding. "It come as near to my body as it could, the doctor said, without goin' in it." He closed his eyes again. When he opened them, he whispered, "I wanted my girls back. I wanted you with me." He lay still, spent, and quietly eyed the scrawny creatures before him. He smiled and nodded. "I wanted my girls. . . ." His voice trailed off, and he closed his eyes.

Idella and Avis stood together at the foot of the bed. When a ripple of slow breathing moved down his belly, they realized he had drifted into sleep. "He don't look right," Avis whispered.

Idella said nothing. She had never seen his face like this before. His mouth was a little too open. It made her uncomfortable. "Come on," she whispered. "Let's leave him be." She and Avis tiptoed out of the dim bedroom. Idella would have to spend all of the next day making order in the house. It must have been bad even before the accident. Now it was beyond words. But that could all wait till tomorrow.

Mrs. Doncaster had baked a pot of beans and left it for them on the stove. That was a help. Avis was ready to eat the beans cold, but Idella insisted on lighting a fire and heating them through. There was nothing to go with them, but the girls didn't care. They had to gather dishes from every surface and wash them in cold water before they could even eat off them. When the beans were ready, Idella sent Avis out to the barn to get Dalton. They all three sat around the table, not saying much, till the only sound left was Dalton scraping the spoon across his plate. All Idella could feel was the heaviness of being back, like a weight that made it hard even to breathe.

Suddenly from Dad's room came a yell. "Where the hell's my supper? I brought you all the way home by train, goddamn it, and you're going to sit out there and let me rot lying in here on my backside? I smell beans."

Dalton abruptly pushed back his chair and stood. "I been taking it from him four days now. I'm 'bout done with it. I got used to bein' on my own, with him in the hospital, and I won't be goin' backwards. He can't hit me no more. Be sleeping in the barn tonight. Animals is better company than the likes and smell of him."

Tears started streaming down Idella's face. She felt all alone in this godforsaken place. She watched as Dalton walked over to the door and opened it, stepping out into the night without even a glance back. Avis sat crumpled in her seat. From the bedroom Dad's voice grew louder. "Where the hell are you? Della, bring me something to eat!"

Without a word Idella got up and scooped a plate of beans out of the warm pot. Wiping her eyes with her sleeve, she stood for a moment in front of the stove, until she was done with her crying for sure. Then she quietly walked into the bedroom with the plate of beans.

"Give me a hand, goddamn it. Help me sit up."

She propped his pillow behind him as best she could with one hand and gave him the warm plate with the other.

"Get rid of this mess, will you, Dell?" Dad waved his hand around the room, spilling a spoonful of beans across his blanket as he did it. "Having you back's goin' to make things a damn lot easier around here. Your cookin's a hell of a lot better than mine and Dalton's, or that goddamned hospital slop they threw at me."

Idella's foot touched the cold china washbasin on the floor. She bent down to pick it up and carry it out. It was so full and heavy that some of it spilled over her bare foot, cold and clammy. She stared down at the dark stain the water made on the floor. Enough had spilled to make a stream that followed the slant of the floorboards, heading out toward the kitchen. She looked into the bowl, the brown and bloody water still lapping the edges. It made her dizzy and ill. She could not breathe this stifling air, heavy with the smells of sickness.

"What're you standing there for?"

Idella lifted her head and walked unsteadily into the kitchen, past Avis, who had kept herself in the shadows as best she could.

"Let me out, Avis," Idella said, "or I'll be sick in the middle of the floor."

Avis ran over and opened the kitchen door. "Where you going, Della?" Idella walked past her without a word, out into the middle of the road that led between the house and barn. She stopped, still holding the basin of dirty water, and took a deep breath. She had to get air into her lungs. Clean air. She could hear the water sluicing between the rocks far below, at the bottom of the cliff. The tide was coming in.

She was flooded with impulses—to walk to the rocky edge and gaze down into the blackness where she knew the water was; to run, escape like a deer, through the field and into the woods.

She dragged her bare feet against the earth, feeling small rocks between her toes, scraping clammy wetness from the tops of her feet. She started circling, slowly, turning in small circles, her head bent back to the sky. Stars and clouds skittered across the moon like smoke. She started to circle faster. The stars blurred into tiny streaks. Idella held the basin away from her, at arm's length, and started spinning and spinning. Water spewed from the edges of the bowl in a scattering circle. Cold droplets spattered her arm. The ground felt gritty and wonderful. She could see, in a blur, little Avis standing in the kitchen doorway, lit from within, watching.

Idella opened her mouth. It filled with wind. A sound flowed out of her, a soft and steady gust. The water basin's weight was pulling her now, round and round and round with the sound. Suddenly the words to the poem rose up within her and poured out into the fresh, wonderful air. "'Life is real! Life is earnest! / And the grave is not its goal.'" She spun over near the edge of the cliff and released the china basin, opening her hands to the black cavern of air. The basin flew from her, a white vessel cast out into the darkness. She spun lightly away on tiptoe. Somewhere, far below, it crashed. Dalton came to the barn door and looked out. Idella saw his lean silhouette, one arm reaching overhead against the doorframe, watching her spin.

She slowed and looked up into the night sky. The sound coming out of her softened to a flutter and became the sound of her breathing. She planted her feet in a broad stance in the shaggy grass. The stars were swirling overhead, dizzy in a bright, bright sky. Idella let her knees buckle. She lowered herself clumsily backward, until she could feel the long, cool field grass down her whole length.

She lay flat on her back and looked up into the tumbling sky, then closed her eyes. The space behind her eyelids continued to spin. She ran her hands across the grass and clutched at scratchy wads of it. There was a rock under her shoulder blade, cold and hard. It had been here forever, probably, the whole time she was alive, buried in the hard-packed ground. It had been here when her mother was alive and the whole time Idella was gone down to Maine. It'd be here still after she was gone.

Idella listened hard. She could hear the water far below the dark cliff, lolling and slapping over the rocks. A cow drawled from the barn. The Doncaster dog was barking off in the woods. She was back up in Canada. Nothing much had changed, nothing the eye could see.

"Della?" Avis's wisp of a voice floated cautiously in her direction. "Della, you done?"

Idella sighed in the darkness and then called out, "I'm coming, Avis. I'm coming right back in."

Avis stood in the doorway waiting. When Idella got to the dim pool of light by the kitchen door, Avis reached out her hand. "Can we go up to bed now?"

Idella hugged her. "You go on upstairs and go to bed."

"Aren't you comin', too?"

"I'll be up in a minute. You'll be all right. Go on now. I'll check on Dad, and then I'll be up. Here, take the lamp with you and set it on the bureau. I'll get a candle." She went over to the sideboard and took a candle from its holder. Carefully lifting the glass chimney from the oil lamp on the table, she lit the candle and stuck it back into its holder. "Here now, take this." She offered Avis the lamp. "Walk slow and steady. I'll blow it out when I get up there. Good night, Avis. We've had a long day."

"G'night, Della." Avis was so tired she could barely speak. She carefully held the oil lamp with both her hands. Idella stood in the kitchen watching her wobbly steps all the way up to the top.

Idella continued to stand in the center of the kitchen, her candle flame the only light. She stared into its warm, wavery yellow, eyeing the dark veins of blue that flickered at its core. She felt peaceful, spent. Here she was, back on the farm, back in the kitchen, where she'd spend all of the next day and plenty more days after that washing and scrubbing and fetching for Dad. She'd never been down here alone like this so late at night. Dad was always around, always stayed up late. Already the little schoolhouse in Maine, the teacher, the blackboard, the books seemed long distant, more than a train ride away.

She thought of her book. It was still where she'd put it near the door. She walked over and picked it up and turned toward the stairs. There had been no sound from Dad's room. Idella went up to the half-opened door and peeked in. He was lying there, awake, staring up at the ceiling in the darkening room.

"What's that? What's that noise?"

"It's me."

"Idella?"

"Yes."

"What are you doing out there?"

"Nothing."

"Come in here. Come in. Bring the light." His voice was different, soft somehow.

Idella shyly opened the bedroom door. She had never visited him in the night before, never come to him with her nightmares or fears or illnesses. She'd been afraid. Afraid to bother him—he worked so hard and got up so early. Afraid to anger him—he was so quick-tempered. Afraid.

He looked helpless lying there under the bedclothes, long and thin. His beard was growing in all scruffy. He'd been unable to shave, and it made his face dark and shadowy as she held up the candle.

"Tell me, did you like school? Did you like going to live with your Aunt Martha?"

Idella looked down at the blackness of the floor. She felt somehow ashamed. "Yes, sir, I loved it."

"You loved it, eh?" He lay in the darkness, but she could feel his eyes upon her. "You loved it."

"More than anything." There was a long pause. She could hear his breathing. "I passed the eighth-grade test when I'm not even in that grade yet."

"Did you? Well, Della, that's good. I think that's good. Your mother would have liked to hear that. She was a great one for books, you know. You prob'ly don't remember. She used to read to me by the hour."

"No. I didn't know that."

"This is the bed where she died, you know. Right here in this spot. I should have moved the bed. She must have stared up at the ceiling there, same as me."

Idella lifted her candle till it glowed on the ceiling. Sometimes it was hard to imagine that she'd really had a mother. Her memories didn't seem real.

There was another long pause. "Idella, I need to pee, and I can't wait till morning, and I can't get to the damn pot by myself. Dalton's nowhere to be seen or heard from. I'm going to need you to help lift me out of here and get me the pot."

"Yes, sir." Idella carefully placed the book and candle on the small table next to his bed and walked over to the chamber pot in the middle of the floor. She lifted it and carried it over to her father's bed.

"Take this arm and pull me up first. . . . AHH, goddamn it." He took a long, deep breath. Idella reached down and grasped the offered arm but was afraid of what to do next. "Go on now, give it a pull. It won't come out, it'll just hurt like a son of a bitch down below. Come on now, Della. Give a pull." She pulled till he was in a sitting position, wincing with pain.

"Now get my legs out over the edge. Go slow, especially with the left there." Idella reached down and guided his legs, one at a time, over the edge. "Jesus, Mary, and the little bastard, too! Good girl, Della. Now get the damn pot. You gotta hold it right up to me, 'cause I ain't gonna stand. Put it right there and hold it. I'll do the rest."

Idella held the pot up with both her hands to where he pointed. She closed her eyes and turned her head toward the window. She could tell by the sharp intake of his breath how difficult it was. She kept her eyes closed and waited till the sound of pee splashing into the metal pot had stopped.

"Holy Mother of God, that does it. Help me back in now."

Idella placed the warm, pee-filled pot on the floor next to him and helped guide him back into bed. "Would you like something to drink, Dad?" she asked him.

"Well, now, that'd start the whole thing flowin' again. I'll wait till mornin' before I go through that goddamned rigmarole again." A faint smile crossed his wan face. "You'd best go on up to bed now. You've had a big day. Leave me a light on, will you? I'm like as not to lie here awake till morning. My leg burns so, I can't sleep."

Idella lit the lamp next to his bed with her candle and turned to go. Then she saw her book lying on the table where she'd put it. She walked over, picked it up, and held it close for a moment. Then she turned around and looked at her father, who was quietly watching.

"Would you like me to read to you, Dad? Like Mother used to? Would you like me to read from my book?" She saw his startled expression. Without waiting for an answer, she took a small cane-bottom chair from the corner of the room and pulled it over next to the oil lamp.

She sat and opened her book. "'*The Life and Strange Surprising Adventures of Robinson Crusoe.* Chapter One.'" Idella's voice was trembly and shy. "'I was born in the year 1632, in the city of York, of a good family, . . .'" Idella looked up. "Can you hear me, Dad?"

He nodded. There were tears in his eyes.

Idella continued slowly and carefully, "'. . . though not of that country, my father being a foreigner of Bremen, who settled first at Hull. . . .'"

She read for more than an hour, until he had finally drifted off into a merciful sleep. She sat watching for a while, then took from the pocket of her skirt the handkerchief Mrs. Elmhurst had given her. Laying it flat against the open page, she marked her place and put the book on the bedside table where he would be sure to see it. Then she tiptoed back up to her room.

Avis's Cow

September 1922

"Bossy! Bosssyyyyy!" Avis called up into the darkening sky and down into the already dark shadows of the woods. She had gone over every inch of the field looking for her cow. Now she felt her foot slide as she stepped down into the middle of a large cow patty at the edge of the woods. "A nice fresh one," she said out loud, grabbing a stick and scraping the bottom of her shoe. "If Bossy can't hear me, she can sure as hell smell me now. Wanderin' off where she's got no business."

Dad had given the calf to Avis four months ago. He had brought it into the house wrapped in his arms, no more than a day old. The cow was bawling the whole time. Dad had plunked it down in front of Avis as she'd sat at the table shelling peas with Idella. "Look what I found in the hay this morning," he'd said to her, "a rapscallion, like you. So I'm givin' it to you. It's yours."

He'd put the calf down on the big hooked rug and walked out, laughing, wiping his large hands on the seat of his pants. The calf had stood there, all rickety, raised up its tail, and started a stream of pee out the backside that was aimed dead center of that rug. Idella'd let out a scream to wake the dead and run around calling, "Get a bucket! Get a bucket! For God's sake, get a bucket!"

"Don't worry, Della," Avis had called, "I'll get the mud. And the shit. And the piddle. I'll get it all." Then she had taken the cow's head between her hands, kissed the white star on its snout, and led it out of the house. "Come on," she'd whispered, steadying the calf. "We'd better start moving or Della'll have our heads."

Avis knew that calf was hers. Tater was her cow mother, but Avis was her real one. She'd spent the rest of the day boiling up water and scrubbing the rug, while Idella watched and gave unwanted instructions. But

Avis didn't care. She had decided to name the cow Bossy, because that was a cow name, and she was the perfect little cow.

Now Avis stood at the edge of the field. She had already looked in the woods. She'd followed all the cow paths. Only the reedy, muck-filled swamp was left. Avis had been listening for Bossy's bell for over an hour. The other cows had been in the barn before she'd set out to get them. It got dark sooner in September, and the cows reacted. Tater was the lead cow. She'd come back early, clanging her bell, moaning to get her teats squeaked. Molly and Queenie had followed behind.

It was Avis's job to round up the cows every evening. She could hear Tater's lead bell clanging through her sleep. But it was Bossy's little tinkle of a thing—Dad had gotten her her own bell—that snuck into Avis's dreams and sometimes woke her. She'd dream that Bossy was being chased down by dogs. She'd wake up in a sweat and sneak out to the barn, past her sleeping sister, past Dad's snores. He was often asleep at the table, his head on crossed elbows, too tired or drunk to go to bed. She'd take the oil lamp from in front of him—sometimes it was still lit—and go out to the barn.

She'd find Bossy nestled on top of her hooves in the stall, breathing out that warm, musty steam breath. Avis would get down in the hay and put her head on Bossy's belly and breathe it in. "There's my girl," she'd whisper. "Safe and sound."

Bossy was the first thing in Avis's life that she'd gotten new. Everything else was handed down from Idella or sent in boxes at Christmastime from Aunt Martha and Uncle John. Idella always got the pick of the litter. She'd get the box from the mailman and open it and take the best. She denied it, but Avis knew she had a few things stuffed under her mattress. There were some girl things, a few dresses, that Idella was hoarding. Avis had caught a glimpse.

She knew that people felt sorry for them, and that's why neighbors sometimes gave them clothes. She'd see Mrs. Doncaster and Mrs. Pettigrew watching them walk across their fields. They'd be whispering and shaking their heads. Avis could tell they were talking about them, and she hated it when they'd call her over and ask her how tall she was now and how much she thought she weighed—even how old she was. She lied. "I'm going on seven," she'd say sometimes. "I'll be sixteen next month," she'd yell at them a few days later. Both neighbors had known her since she was born. They could figure out that she was twelve if they were that interested.

They'd known her mother, too, for a lot longer than Avis had. They knew what her mother's laugh sounded like and what her smile had been like. Avis had only ever seen two pictures of her mother, and she hadn't been smiling in either one. Avis remembered little flickers of sounds that might be her laugh. But she wasn't sure about her smile, her teeth. Somehow their knowing these things—women who happened to live next door—and not Avis, her own daughter, made her mad.

Avis wanted secrets. She wanted privacy. She didn't want to tell those busybodies how old she was because then they'd be wondering why she was still straight as a board with no breasts in sight. Not that she wanted breasts. She didn't. She had no use for them. They'd be a nuisance. But Idella was getting them. They weren't much to look at, not that she let anyone. Idella'd been taking her baths lately when she was sure no one else was home, but Avis had come running in yesterday and caught Idella climbing out of the big tin tub in the kitchen. Avis had been shocked to see the pink-tipped bulges before Idella covered herself quick with her arms. Avis had felt betrayed.

The neighbor women knew better after a while and stopped asking Avis for information. She'd see them calling Idella over. Idella was always so polite. They'd invite her in. She'd come home smiling, hiding a brush or a hairpin. Idella'd squirrel the things away in her side of their room. Not that Avis gave a damn.

Della's hair wasn't much better than Avis's, but it was blond. She was always washing it and fooling with it and tying it with rag ribbons. Avis wasn't going to be putting rag scraps into her hair. She'd rather have nothing than wear rags instead of ribbons.

Dad always said their mother had the most wonderful hair. Sometimes Avis took her mother's braid out of its envelope and looked at it. She felt it and smelled it and held it up to the sunlight to see the veins of reddish gold. Avis's hair was mousy next to it. She did anything she could to keep it off her face and not have to look at it.

Aunt Francie had beautiful hair like Mother's. She and Mother had grown up on that nice big farm, the one where Francie and Avis's grandparents still lived—where Maddie was. It was about thirty miles away. Sometimes, out of the blue, Dad would say, "Load up the wagon. Feed the chickens. Let's go visit your Aunt Francie." One of the Doncaster boys would milk the cows. Dad loved Aunt Francie, too. He didn't care so much for Gram and Grampa, but he loved Aunt Francie. She was stylish all the way. She must have reminded him of Mother. Everything about her was beautiful and womanish.

Avis took a step into the spongy bog. It was darker in here. Cat-o'-nine-tails towered ominously overhead, their brown tips like spears. Some were snapped over. Their seeds had burst, and fluffy bits stuck to her clothes when she brushed them away. Avis got two mosquitoes with one slap right on her cheek.

She tromped without heed through the reeds and brambles. It was slippery, and her feet kept scudding out from under her. They got sucked with a *thwop* into the oozy places like she was stepping down into molasses. "Della'll kill me when she sees me," she whispered.

Her insides were acting queer. Where was Bossy? Why couldn't Avis hear the bell? She'd been crashing around too much. Reeds were bent and pushed every which way, but it could have been Avis herself who had moved them. She didn't know what direction was what. She stopped and looked up at the sky. One star was peeping from way up there. She called one last long time, "Bosssyyyyy."

Avis didn't move. She stood, eyes closed, and listened hard. The reeds scuttled and scraped one another; the mosquitoes hung in midair around her head. She blocked them out. She clenched her teeth and slowed her breathing and concentrated. Then she heard the faintest of tinkles. Her hands knotted so tightly into fists that the nails pushed into her bones. Again. It was coming from behind, it was off to the left. Avis made herself stay and listen again. There it was.

She forced herself to walk slowly in the direction of the bell. It was dark, hard to see where to step. Sometimes she sank up to her knees. It was a bad place here. Then Avis saw what must be her. She could just make out the familiar bob of her head.

"Bossy, Bossy my girl," Avis whispered to her as she approached. She didn't want to startle the weary cow. Bossy could not get up. She had sunk into the mire. "Oh, what a pickle you're in." Avis knelt and kissed where she knew the white star to be. "You poor dear. And you're getting eaten alive." She flung her arm hopelessly into the teeming darkness. She bent down and whispered into Bossy's flicking ears, "I'm not gonna leave you. I'm not goin' nowheres. I'm here."

Avis's hands were shaking as she raked them lovingly over Bossy. She pressed her face round and round into the gnarled wetness of the muddy hide. She loved the strong, familiar smell of cow and swampy mire. "Oh, Bossy!" she cried. "Bossy, don't you go!"

It was full-out dark when Avis finally heard Dad and Dalton calling her. "Well, I'll be damned," Dad said, swinging the lantern way over his head and letting the beam fall onto their huddled figures. "A sorrier sight I've yet to see." Avis's body was pressed against the cow. The bottom halves of both creatures were sunk into the mud.

It took both men to get Avis out and all three of them to get Bossy to her feet. Dalton led the cow to higher ground and on out. Dad picked Avis up in his arms without a word and carried her toward home. Her wet legs dangled from his elbow. She rested her head against his shoulder and looked up at the stars. They were all there. Her hands clasped the back of his neck. She could feel the warmth of his chest and arms right through his shirt. Avis could tell, even in the darkness, that Dad needed a shave. Up ahead she could see the silhouette of Dalton and Bossy, the little bell still tinkling. She was afraid to look at Dad's face. He held on to her tight, she could feel the hard muscles, but he wasn't mad. She didn't think he was mad. She hoped he wasn't going to be mad.

"Best take everything off," he said, putting her down at the doorstep. "Drop 'em in a pile. Della'll clean 'em or burn 'em in the mornin', whatever seems best. I'll send her out with a blanket. We'll scrape the mud off you tonight and boil you in the morning."

"Like a potato." Avis smiled hopefully up at him.

Dad laughed. "Like a potato." He started to go into the house and then stopped, his hand on the door. "You did a good job, Avis, bringing in the cows. You saved Bossy." That was all. In he went, to have his cold supper, to pour a glass of whiskey.

Avis stood staring after him. Then she looked down at the remains of her skirt and blouse and shoes. She was as filthy as she'd ever been. And that was saying something. Jesus God, she was as filthy as a human could be on this earth.

Idella came to the door holding a lamp next to her cheek. She looked out at Avis, standing like a mangy animal in the darkness, and handed her a rag and a blanket. "Here, get off what you can and wrap that around you and come on in. It's late." Then she smiled and shook her head at her sister. "Just don't come too near me."

Avis peeled the reeking clothes from her body, scraping off the mud and muck, and wrapped the blanket around her thin shoulders. The blanket felt good. Idella held the door open.

"Dirtier than the devil on a Saturday night," Idella whispered, laughing, as Avis passed her.

"That's me," Avis answered, snickering, "in a pig's eye."

That got them going. Avis raised her foot and threatened to plant it on Idella's skirt. "Right there in the middle of your arse—now, won't that look pretty?"

"Don't you dare, Avis," Idella warned her. "Don't you get those smelly swamp feet near me." They climbed the stairs together, giggling. Idella's long, thin arm held the lamp high, leading the way to their bedroom.

Idella's Dress

Idella was the only one around the house. Dalton was in the barn, Dad had gone off somewhere—back into the field, probably—and Avis was picking blueberries. The highbushes by the edge of the pasture had ripened in these last few days of July heat, and she had set out this morning to get them before the Doncaster boys found them.

Idella would have liked to go, too. Just to get out. But she had to stay and scrub Dad's and Dalton's work clothes. They were full of those "goddamned burr things," as Dad called them. "They'd scrape the skin right off a bull's ass," he'd said, throwing them in a pile at her feet. "Here, Della, clean these damned things." Never a please. Never a thank-you.

Idella stood now at the stove, boiling up water. It was too hot to be boiling anything, let alone the likes of this. The clothes reeked of manure and mud. She'd had to pick through them, pulling out the spiny prickles and thorns. Her fingers were sore from the sharp points. She had gotten a stick from the edge of the woods out the back of the house, and she lowered the stinking mass of clothing into the big tin washtub, the one they took their baths in. When the kettle of water was boiling, she lifted it off the stove, wrapping her skirt around the hot wire handle, and held the kettle as high as she could with both her hands. Turning her face away, she poured the water down over the clothes and stirred them with the stick. Steam rose up around her and made her hair all stringy. She kept trying to brush back strands with the top of her shoulder. Her nose itched, and she gagged from the heavy smell of the steaming manure.

There was no end to it, she thought, the things to be done. She was sixteen years old next week, and she'd never gotten to be a child, not one day in her life since Mother died. Idella carried the empty kettle over to the water pump and filled it again. "This'll take half the day," she muttered. "They'll put 'em on and go right back out into it."

It was then that she heard the mailman's car come puttering down the road toward the house. Most days he kept on going past the farm, but today he was turning in. She could tell by the nearness of the sound. Maybe there was something for her. Maybe Dad got her something for her birthday. He'd given Bossy to Avis two years ago. Twelve years old and she got a cow for her birthday. Avis was always out there in the barn bothering the poor thing. A cow. That's about the last thing on this earth that Idella needed—something else to take care of.

The Sears catalog might be coming anytime now—maybe that was it. Idella could think of no better way to spend an afternoon than looking through its pages and making up orders in her head.

The mailman's car was near the house now. She put down the heavy kettle and ran to the open door. Mr. McPhee, the only mailman she'd ever known, was making a cloud of dust right up to the door with his old roadster. It was one of the few cars around, and everybody knew the sound of the motor.

"Hey there, young lady!" he called as he yanked the car to an abrupt stop, leaving the motor running. "You Hillock girls get taller and skinnier every time I see one of you. I've got a package here. It's got 'Idella Hillock' written on it. Should I send it back?"

He made this joke every time he brought something special. It might be clothes from Aunt Francie. He smiled through his open window, purposely making her wait a little. Men thought teasing was so funny.

"Well," he said finally, "if you're sure you want it." He reached to the back seat and lifted up a large brown box. "Something for the lady of the house. I got to open the door here just to get it out."

Idella walked up to the car door, wiping her hands on her skirt. She wanted to reach in and just grab the box. "Here you go, young lady."

It was Aunt Francie's beautiful script across the package, no question. Idella held the box so tightly that the corners pushed at the insides of her elbows.

"Thank you, Mr. McPhee."

"How's your dad? What's Bill Hillock been up to? No good, I suppose?"

"He's out working the field today."

"Tell him I'll see him tonight." The men played cards on Saturday nights, sitting around the table and drinking. They played at Dad's house because there was no woman to shush them and make them go home. "I'm going to whip the pants off him. Tell him to wear two pair."

"I'll tell him. Bye, Mr. McPhee."

Idella walked right past the stinking tub of work clothes, past the filled kettle of cold water she'd left on the floor. She paid no heed to the stove, its fire pouring heat into the stifling July air. She walked up the stairs and into the bedroom that she shared with Avis, closing the door behind her with a foot. A fly, embedded in the folds of a curtain, buzzed in response to the jolt. Tippie, the Doncaster dog, barked. Idella went to her open window and looked out. No one was coming in from the field or the woods. Dalton was clanging away on something in the barn. He never came into the house anyway unless it was supper.

She sat on her bed and stared at the script. Even her name, "Idella," looked pretty when Aunt Francie wrote it. Her fingers found the edge of the brown paper and pulled it off in shreds.

The box's flaps fell open. She lifted back tissue paper with her fingertips. It was something blue, a deep gray-blue. There was a collar, and tiny black buttons. Idella stood and unfurled a dress of the most wonderful material and shape and color. She held it at arm's length. It had velvet on the collar and cuffs. Black velvet! And the waistline was low, below the hips, like Idella had seen only in catalogs. And it was short! It was above the ankle, she could tell just by looking. It was beyond beautiful.

Holding the dress by her fingertips, she walked up close to the dresser that had been her mother's and stood before the mirror. She could see herself only from the waist up. A pock in the mirror distorted the line of the shoulder. Avis had done that, made that hole, flinging her shoe off one night. Always fooling around. There'd been a stone in her shoe, and it had flown out and pinged the mirror. You could never have anything nice.

"Yoo-hoo! Della!" Avis. She was coming back from picking. "Della, come help me drag these damn buckets." She was coming across the field, her mouth preceding her as usual.

"Quit your yelling!" Idella called through the open window. Then she laid the dress across her bed and carefully folded it. She placed it under the tissue paper. There was a note lying in the box, a letter from Aunt Francie that she hadn't seen. Idella slipped it into her apron pocket.

"Della! Where are you?" Avis was in the kitchen. "I left a bucket in the field. My arm's about pulled out by its roots."

"Hold your horses!" Idella opened the door enough to call down to her and then closed it again. She slid the box as far back under the bed as she could. Avis was tromping up the stairs.

She opened the door. "What the hell have you been up to?" Avis surveyed the room. She was always so suspicious, afraid she'd get left out of something. But Idella wasn't going to show her the package from Aunt Francie till she was good and ready.

"Come on," Idella said, pushing Avis out of the room with her, "let's go see what the poor little birdie picked."

Idella finished stewing the clothes and washed them out, and then she scrubbed the tub they'd been in. When she was finally finished, she walked over to the table where Avis sat sorting through the blueberries. There were more leaves and sticks and bad ones than if Idella had done the picking.

"Wouldn't those damn Doncasters love to've found these?" Avis crowed. "They'd have stood like bears on their hind legs and eaten 'em off the branches." Avis kept her head bent over the bucket. She looked up at Idella, with only her eyes moving. "I thought maybe we could make some pies with these berries. It's poker night, and I thought I could make the men some pies. As a surprise." Idella watched as Avis pursed up her lips and started speaking in her baby-doll voice. It was the only way that Avis could ask for help from anyone, by making a joke. "I could make a berry pie if Mama bird would help her poor little baby sister."

"All right." Idella sighed. She sat down next to Avis and started picking out leaves. "I'll help you make the dough. And I'll help you to measure. If I don't, you'll use all my sugar."

"I'll be good, Della. I promise." Avis reached an arm around and stuck a blueberry into Idella's ear. "Thank you, Mama bird."

"Don't call me that. Avis, so help me, if you start acting up, I won't do a thing to help you."

Avis took a handful of berries, stood up, and dropped them down the front of her dress.

"Jesus, Avis," Idella said, "you're not fit to live in a house. We should keep you tied up out in the barn with that cow."

Avis crawled under the table and rounded up the scattered berries. Idella knew that she was excited. Avis loved poker nights. She was a favorite among the men. She'd sit on Dad's lap like the cat who ate the canary and watch them play by the hour. They teased her and tried to get her to tell Dad's hands, but she had a face that revealed nothing when she didn't want it to and a mouth on her that would say anything. The men egged her on something terrible, and she was always after them to give her sips of whiskey.

Idella made herself scarce on these evenings. She'd sneak up to the bedroom as soon as she could. The men made her self-conscious. They started out nice. Most of them she'd known all her life. But the later it got, the rowdier they were.

Dad would always embarrass her. "When you going to get some meat on your bones?" he'd say to her, in front of everyone. "I've got me some goddamned stick figures for daughters." Then he'd reach over and slap her on the behind. He laughed when he said it, but it was his mean sort of laugh, his whiskey laugh. It shamed Idella something terrible.

All afternoon the two sisters worked on the pies. Idella knew she wouldn't be alone till evening. Dad and Dalton stayed out in the fields. There was much rolling of pins and flicking of aprons, but in the end there were three grand pies and a patchwork tart steaming on the windowsill in the summer heat.

When Dad came in, Idella had supper on the table as usual. He was in a good mood—he always was on poker night. "No dessert tonight," Avis announced before he'd even set down in his chair. "There was no time." It was impossible to ignore the sweet smell of blueberries and cinnamon that hung in the sticky evening air.

Avis had insisted on hiding the pies on the wooden bench behind the stove. She was going to surprise the poker players when they all got seated at the table. She didn't even want Idella to be there, she said; she wanted to do it all herself. That was fine. Idella didn't need to show anyone that she could make pies.

"Damn," Dad said, looking Avis's floury figure up and down, "I'd have sworn you were going out to pick berries. I was hoping for pie."

"Nope," Avis said. "Those damn Doncaster boys must've found 'em. There was nothing there but big footprints. Not one goddamned berry in the whole place."

"Well, that's too bad. We'll have to speak to Fred tonight when he comes. Tell him to shoot those boys." He winked at Idella.

Avis laughed. "That'd be good. Then next year *I'll* pick 'em."

"What's that smell I'm smelling? It smells like horse manure. You smell it, Idella?"

"Nope."

"How about you, Dalton? You smell it?"

Dalton kept on eating, barely lifting his head from over his plate. He was fixing to leave as soon as supper was over. He never joined Dad's poker games. "Nope," he said. "Nothing."

"Avis-Mavis, puddin' an' pie, don't you smell anything?"

"Nope." She started giggling and looked down at her hands. "Just Della's feet." She could barely get the words out for laughing—they came out in a snort.

"Jesus, Avis," Idella said, standing to clear the table. "There's no need to make fun of me."

"You're a fresh one, Avis-Mavis, puddin' an' pie." Dad always took to her foolishness, Idella thought. She got away with murder. "You just be sure that tonight you don't kiss the boys and make them cry."

Idella felt like she'd been waiting to be alone for days. "Come on, Avis, help me wash the dishes. They're going to be here soon, and I want to go upstairs and read."

Idella was alone in the bedroom. She had been standing and sitting in her beautiful blue dress for more than an hour, observing her shadow's silhouette stretch silently across the flowered wallpaper and up to the ceiling. The poker game roared below. She had combed and pinned and parted her hair in different ways. She had watched herself in the mirror and in the reflected lamplight of the bedroom window.

The men had all come. They were settled with their bottles and their glasses around the kitchen table. Avis had uncovered her pies to a roar of applause. The men had teased her mercilessly and praised her nonstop. Avis was in her element. The noise would rise up to the bedroom in walloping bursts and then settle down to the quiet shuffles and flicks of cards being dealt, of glasses being set heavily on the table. Idella could hear Avis's laugh getting louder and rowdier with the rest of them, as the evening wore on.

Idella went to the bottom of her closet and felt for her Sunday shoes. She reached down into the toes till she found the lipstick she'd been hiding since she'd discovered it going through her mother's trunk.

In the yellow light, she stood up close to the mirror and uncapped the lipstick. It had a wonderful perfume smell. The rounded end had been worn down by her mother's lips. Idella leaned in to the mirror and applied the lipstick with trembling fingers. It looked dark and uneven, but she was afraid to try to fix it. She daubed little streaks on each cheek, like she'd seen Mrs. Doncaster do, and rubbed them in with her palm.

Idella looked startling, even to herself, in the mirror. She wasn't sure if she was pretty—she couldn't say—but she did look different. The straight drop of the dress's loose bodice was broken by the small points of her breasts. She'd never worn anything before that showed them.

"Della!" Dad's voice broke her dreamy solitude. "Della, get the hell down here!" Idella's chest tightened like it had been suddenly bound. "Della! Get down here and slice us another pie. We're all of us pie-eyed!" The men laughed. She could hear Avis cackling.

"Come down here, Della!" Dad roared. "We need you to wait on Queen Avis. She can't be cutting her own pies. Get your skinny ass down here."

"I'll be there in a minute!" Idella called through the closed door. It made her so mad—that calling and yelling and loudness. There was no need for it. At the end of poker nights, he always got mean. He treated her like she was a belonging, something he owned, like a horse or a cow.

"Della, get your ass down here!" That was Avis calling. That was Avis! Her voice had an edge to it. Whiskey.

"That little bitch," Idella whispered. "I showed her how to make the goddamned pies." She went to the mirror, brushed her hair off her face, and refastened it with the barrette that Mrs. Doncaster had given her. "I won't stoop my shoulders," she said to her reflection.

"Della! Get your ass down here!" That wasn't even Dad. That was one of the men talking to her like that.

The louder they got, the more deliberately she prepared herself. "I'm coming!" she shouted, to stop their yelling. They were down there banging their glasses on the table, the bastards. Idella opened her door and stepped out into the hall. "Quit yelling. I'm coming."

She stopped at the top of the stairs. The cigarette smoke made her eyes water. The room below was hazy with it. She started to come down slowly, keeping her back straight, not sure of where to put her hands. One by one the men saw her. One by one their voices stopped.

"La-dee-da!" a loud voice called when she reached the bottom step. "Will you look at what's come down the steps?" Someone whistled. "Bill Hillock, you been holdin' out on us. Look at what you've been hiding." For a moment there was silence.

"Well, I'll be damned," Dad whispered. He put his cards facedown on the table and pushed Avis off his lap. He stood, his face flushed from whiskey, watching Idella. His voice got soft. "Don't you look pretty, Idella. Don't you look pretty. Avis, look at your pretty sister."

"She turned into a woman, Bill, when you wasn't looking."

Idella thought that was Mr. McPhee's voice. She stood frozen. The lipstick felt strange and waxy. She forced herself to look into the room, to see each face. She looked at Avis last.

"Where'd you get that dress?" Avis was staring hard. Her voice was low and queer. "Where did you get that dress?" Idella averted her eyes. She turned back to Dad's flushed face.

"I got me a princess I been raising," he said. "She's even got titties on her. Will you look at that." Idella felt her cheeks go hot.

One of the men stood up. "Let's drink to the lady," he said. "Let's drink to Bill's Idella."

All the men stood, scraping back their chairs. They raised their glasses. "To Idella," they said.

There was a loud crash. "What the hell?" Dad turned behind him. Avis stood in front of the stove. Dark gobs of pie filling were spewed across the wooden floor. Avis scooped a glossy handful and rushed at Idella. She smeared it across the front of the blue dress. "Where did you get it? Where did you get that dress?" She was clawing at Idella. "Where did you get it?"

"Damn you!" Idella cried, untangling the clutching fists. "Damn you, Avis. Leave me be!" She got hold of Avis's wrists and squeezed them hard.

"You whore!" Avis screamed. "You're nothing but a whore!" Idella thrust the writhing figure from her. Dad came up behind and pulled Avis away, kicking. "Whore!" Avis screamed.

Idella was shaking. She stood up and looked out into the room of men, her arms covering the smeared dress. Her eyes bored through the smoke to the stunned faces. "Damn you," she said in a low voice. "Damn all of you in this godforsaken place." She turned and ran up the steps into her room. She crouched behind the closed door, jamming her fists over her wretched mouth. Avis's wails, coming now in waves, pierced the floorboards. They matched Idella's own hopeless sobs.

A week later Avis's dress came. Aunt Francie's note had said it would. She'd been waiting on an order of lace. The mailman drove up with the box on the seat next to him. Aunt Francie's writing was unmistakable. Mr. McPhee didn't tease Idella when she came to get it from him. He handed it to her with a sorry smile and said that he hoped she was feeling better.

She walked listlessly back into the house and up the stairs to the bedroom. She put the box on Avis's bed and left. She slammed the door behind her, even though it was still hot and the open door let air move through the house a little.

Avis's dress was forest green with brown tortoise buttons and fancy stitching. The lace was on the collar and at the edges of the cuffs. It was beautiful. But it never got worn, not even once.

Idella Looks Back: The Mail Car

There was no life living down there with Dad, you know. I mean, that poor man, God bless him, but what life does a girl have? Just cooking for him and knowing there's the outside world you can go to and not be stuck there.

No matter what I done, Dad had to have somebody to take his anger out on. And he would blame me for things that I didn't do or couldn't do. So he was going to work one morning, he was going fishing, and I decided right then and there, I won't stay here any longer. I can't live this way. Why should I take all that anger? For nothing! I made up my mind right there. The mail would go down the road from Bathurst. It was an automobile. A lot of people hitched rides back up to Bathurst in the mail car. So I saw Mr. McPhee when he was going down. He had to go quite a long ways, see, and then come back.

And so when he came up, I watched for him. I told him, "When you come back around this way, I'm going with you." And I did! I had a suitcase. I don't know where I got it, but I had it. I packed whatever I owned, and he drove me to Salmon Beach. I got a job taking care of a woman's new baby, while she laid around in bed drinking tea!

I was nineteen years old. I had to get out of there. You can't stay like that! Why? Why? When you know there's a better world out there. With better people.

And when the time come that I wanted to go over to the States to work, as a cook, see, or a housekeeper, I didn't have enough money to buy my train ticket. And by God, Dad went and borrowed some money from a friend of his and gave it to me, so I could go. He understood, see.

After I bought my train ticket, I had twenty dollars. But when I crossed the line and they asked me how much money I had, I said two hundred. They never looked in my baggage or anything. That's all there was to it. And that's how I came to the States.

Part Two

The Opera

Boston
April 1929

Idella had just served the two old ladies their breakfast and had almost escaped back into the kitchen to fix her own. Her fanny was pushing against the swinging door, her hands clutching the empty silver serving tray.

"Oh, Idella!" The fluty summons stopped her in her tracks.

"Yes, Miss Lawrence?"

"I need to ask you about something, dear." Miss Lawrence, her chair pushed up close to Mrs. Brumley's, was pouring two cups of tea.

Idella stood waiting.

Miss Lawrence, Mrs. Brumley's paid "live-in companion," reminded Idella of a seagull—the way she would peer at you so steady. Her red-rimmed eyes never seemed to blink. The whole front of her looked like the stuffed chest of a bird, straining the seams of her white blouses for all they were worth. Mrs. Brumley seemed a dear little titmouse sitting there next to her. Her mind wasn't too good in the mornings, and she needed to eat as soon as the food landed on the table.

Even emptied, the silver tray was heavy. Idella gradually lowered it down her front, like a sinking ship, while Miss Lawrence spread blackberry jam for Mrs. Brumley. The toast smelled so good. Idella longed to be out in the kitchen buttering her own. She loved toast.

"Now, Idella." Miss Lawrence finally looked up at her. "Do you know what day this is?"

"It's Tuesday, Miss Lawrence." It was the day before her day off, and she was ready for it. She and Avis were going to the movies.

"Yes, and it's a full year tomorrow, my dear, since you came into our employ!" Miss Lawrence's smile broadened.

"Oh, my." Good God. A whole year.

Mrs. Brumley, nibbling busily, suddenly looked up. "Tell her, tell her!" She plucked at Miss Lawrence's cuff with two buttery fingers.

"Don't excite yourself, Abigail." Miss Lawrence gently shook her wrist free and turned back to Idella. "Mrs. Brumley thinks, dear, that you should accompany us to the opera next week, to celebrate your first year with us. She is quite set on it."

Idella clutched the empty tray. The opera!

"Mrs. Brumley maintains her late husband's two seats in a box, as you know, and I have arranged for two additional tickets."

"Two tickets?" Idella asked.

"We don't want you to sit alone."

"I could ask Avis. She'd probably come."

"Actually, my dear . . ." Miss Lawrence paused. "I thought . . . that is, Mrs. Brumley and I thought . . . that you might use the opportunity to invite some nice new acquaintance." Miss Lawrence shifted in her seat. "Perhaps there is some other young lady you might enjoy as a special guest?" Idella looked at her blankly. "Of course we understand that Avis is your *sister,* dear." Miss Lawrence paused again. "Not that your sister isn't *nice,* dear." She patted Mrs. Brumley on the wrist. "We just thought that since you visit with Avis every day off . . . a change would be nice. You do have friends here in Boston, don't you? Someone from your cooking class, perhaps?"

Idella shook her head.

"Or another domestic, maybe, from the neighborhood?"

"Not really, no."

Mrs. Brumley suddenly stopped crunching and looked up from her toast. "I think Avis will enjoy the opera!" She spoke clearly. "I like that Avis! She's a pip!"

"Drink your tea, Abigail."

"I did."

Miss Lawrence sighed. "You may go, Idella."

Idella went off into the kitchen to make her own toast and to think about, of all things, the opera.

"So what's this about the opera?" Avis was perched on Idella's narrow bed, jiggling her ankles. She could never sit still. Idella could tell that she was itching to smoke. They were in Idella's attic room, on the top floor of the old brownstone, getting ready to go to the movies.

"They go every season. They have what they call a box that they sit in high up on the wall somewheres. That's where they'll be sitting. We'll be down below." Idella was squinting into the small, round mirror over her dresser, trying to apply lipstick. "Mrs. Brumley would never give up their box after Mr. Brumley's tragic death. She goes in his memory."

"What the hell happened to him?"

"It's over twenty years ago, because that's how long Miss Lawrence has been living here. . . ." Idella turned. Her lips were all smeared.

"Are you planning to kiss somebody while I'm watching the movie?"

"Maybe." Idella puckered her mouth and smacked the air.

"Jesus, Idella. How long have you been blind?"

"The light isn't too good up here."

"Sit down. Let's aim this time." Avis took a handkerchief and started rubbing off Idella's lipstick. "Where does the tragic part come in?"

"Well he *died,* for God's sake."

"Close your mouth." Idella did. "Now open it."

"It was summer, see, and Mrs. Brumley went out walking in the field to find him. He was supposed to be doing some sort of work out there with a shovel."

Avis pulled a lip pencil from her purse. "Go on."

"Well, she found him, all right—laid out straight in the grass and dead of natural causes."

"He was probably digging his own grave and planning to jump in. Hold still." Avis expertly applied a sharp, thin line of Ruby Red around Idella's mouth.

"Mr. and Mrs. Brumley were in love, Avis. His death just about killed her. It affected her mind. That's why—"

"Stop talking. Smile. Hold it." Avis daubed Idella's Creamy Rose inside the sharp red outline. "Pucker." Idella puckered. "'That's why' what?"

"That's why—"

"Unpucker, you fool." Avis laughed.

"—she needs Miss Lawrence as a companion."

"Now blot." Avis gave Idella the handkerchief. "That Lawrence dame knows which side her bread is buttered on. It behooves her to have that old lady dim-witted."

"Is that hooves like on the end of horses?" Idella didn't know where Avis came up with words like "behooves." She tried to be so superior sometimes. Working at that beauty shop was giving her airs.

"Why, you should know about the ends of horses." Avis laughed again. "And I'm not referring to their feet."

"I don't know what you are talking about, I'm sure." Idella stood and waggled her behind.

"I wouldn't be caught dead waiting on those old biddies and letting them boss me around, wanting every little thing to be just so. They've got nothing better to do than keep an eye on you."

"It's not like you don't have to take orders and get bossed around at the shop. You say 'yes, ma'am' plenty of times in one day."

"Yes, ma'am." Avis opened her purse and reached for her cigarette pack.

"You're not supposed to smoke up here."

"Yes, ma'am." Avis clipped her bag closed. "But when I'm done work, I'm done with it. I don't answer to anyone once I leave the shop."

"Well, they asked me yesterday if I'd like to go to the opera, as a treat for my working for them one year, and to bring a special friend."

"A special friend, eh?"

"They just want to be friendly and encouraging, is all." Idella was trying to make a straight part in her hair. She did suspect that Miss Lawrence didn't like Avis. "She's your full sister? Not a relative that grew up with you?" Miss Lawrence asked after Avis's first visit. "I know that happens sometimes up in Canada. People take in children—country cousins sort of thing. It's hard to believe you two had the same mother." Idella hadn't gone into the details about their mother.

"They just want to keep you cooped up in this musty old biddy trap for the rest of your life, is all," Avis said. "Idella, let me do that. It looks like a map to the shithouse and back." She took the comb.

"Jesus, Avis, don't kill me. Leave some hair on my head."

Avis was a professional with a comb. Idella loved the way she planted herself so firmly in front of a head of hair. "They know they've got a good thing here with you. You cook, you clean, you do their bidding, and you're as green as the grass in June. I'm the only obstacle, and they're trying to get rid of me. 'Special friend.' Who in hell do they think you've got tucked away somewhere for tea and opera, the Queen of England? Let me have some hairpins."

Idella pointed to the dish on top of her dresser. "It will be fun to look at the people, you know, to see what they're wearing. And to see the two of them all gussied up. Miss Lawrence has one of them foxes she drapes around her neck, with the head and everything."

"She probably killed it herself. I'm surprised she left the head."

"They wear long white gloves, like we found in Mother's trunk that time, only fancier, with little beads sewn all over them. It's quite a sight."

"Do you think our mother ever went to the opera? Put your chin down."

"I doubt it. They don't have opera up in Canada. She wore them to church."

"Would we have to wear capes and hats and gloves and things?" Avis had stuck some hairpins into the corner of her mouth and was talking through them.

"We wear regular dresses, I guess."

"Look in the mirror. What do you think?"

Idella stood and looked in the mirror from side to side. Then she stared straight ahead and frowned. "Isn't this a little severe? You've pinned it all off my face so."

"It's more sophisticated. More sleek."

"It looks sort of hard."

"Leave it, Idella. It looks good." Avis sat back on the bed, took a cigarette from her purse, and lit it. There was no stopping her. "Get your shoes on and let's get the hell out of here before they pull up the drawbridge."

"You'll have to put that out. Couldn't you wait till we're outside?" Avis waved the cigarette wildly. "Stop that, Avis!"

"I thought it'd get your ass moving. What is the opera about anyway?"

"Oh, I don't know. People sing and dance. Mrs. Brumley said that this one was going to have bullfights. Not real ones, of course. I couldn't take that." Idella looked up from buckling her shoes. "There's one thing that I heard about it, though, that's a little off-putting."

"What's that?"

"They don't speak English."

"What the hell *do* they speak?"

"Some foreign language." Idella stood up. "There. I'm ready. Put that thing out."

"Jesus Christ, what's the point of that?"

"I don't know, Avis. I just heard them talking about it. Mrs. Brumley is very educated, you know. She knows other languages."

"How the hell are we supposed to know what's going on?"

"It's not important. You listen to the music."

"Oh, brother. If I wanted to hear a foreign language I'd have hung out with the Frenchies up in Canada."

"They won't be speaking French, I don't think. German or Italian, is my understanding. It depends on who wrote it. They might even have some in Greek or Japanese. I really don't know. We'll just have to see. Now, let's go."

"Idella! Idella, dear, do I smell smoke?" Miss Lawrence's voice came snaking up the stairwell. "You're not smoking up there, are you?"

Avis laughed and blew a puff into Idella's face.

"No, Miss Lawrence," Idella called down sweetly, kicking at Avis. "It must be coming in the window."

On the day of the opera, Miss Lawrence gave Idella two hours off in the afternoon to rest and get ready. The old ladies took an extra-long nap, so it wasn't too much of a sacrifice to let Idella spend some time alone in her room, preparing.

She stood frowning before the mirror, trying to get the wave just right across her forehead. She wished Avis were here to do it. Avis was coming with her overnight bag, but only just before it was time to leave. She wanted to get ready in her own room, she said, where the light was strong enough to make out your front from your behind in the mirror.

Idella looked with despair at her dim reflection. She'd have to wet her hair and start all over again. She took out the wave clamps and dipped her comb into the glass of water. She wouldn't get to pluck her eyebrows. That was for the best, probably. They stayed red for the longest time afterward.

Idella worried that Avis would arrive late and make them all wait. And who knew what she'd be wearing? To hear Avis tell it, she'd had great fun announcing to the other hairdressers that she was going to the opera. She'd strutted around the shop and had everyone laughing so that one customer got shampoo in her eye, and heads were coming out from under the dryers to hear what was so funny.

Avis said she was going to wear some kind of hat with bull horns on top. Idella didn't know where on earth she got some of her ideas. Avis said that it was well known that in opera some fat woman came out and sang wearing a helmet with horns sticking out the sides. Maybe that had something to do with the bullfight. Idella couldn't imagine such a thing. Even if it was all in a foreign language, it was supposed to be about people, not animals.

There. That was all she could do. It'd just have to dry in place. Idella walked carefully over to her bed, trying not to move her head, and lowered herself down flat so she could rest. She thought about what she was going to wear. Her best dress was fine for going to a movie, but she didn't know about the opera. She wondered if Avis would be upset if she wore the long white gloves that had belonged to their mother. They would make her look more dressy. She wasn't even sure Avis knew she had them. She'd taken them out of the trunk up in Canada and brought them with her to the States when she'd left home. Idella had a memory of her mother putting them on for church, of watching her slide her fingers in and smooth them all the way down to her fingertips. She remembered the soft, powdery grip of the gloved fingers when she held her mother's hand. Avis would have no memory of it. She'd been too little.

You never knew what would get to Avis. She still resented their sister Emma—for taking away their mother, she said—when poor Emma had only been a baby, for God's sake. And Avis had such a temper on her. Dad called her his loaded pistol. Avis was quick to point out that *he* was the one who was loaded. They thought that was such a great joke.

Idella shook her head. She didn't want to think about the farm, or Dad and his drinking, or even about Avis. She didn't want to have to worry, or be embarrassed or ashamed. It all made her nervous. She should have told the old ladies she wasn't interested in going.

She got a washcloth and dipped it into the basin of cool water she kept in her room. She wrung it out and laid it carefully over her closed eyes, not touching the drying wave. It felt so nice and soothing and dark. She'd just lie down here for a bit and not think about anything.

"Goosey, goosey, gander," Avis whispered, her head swinging from one side to the other as they were led down the aisle to their seats.

Idella had never seen anything like it. Just walking into the theater was a show by itself. The buzz of all the voices chatting at once was terrific. Perfumes floated at her from every direction. She had never seen so many women in long dresses and jewelry and gloves up to the elbow. Idella had taken her own gloves off before she'd left her room. She had thought them too daring and stuck them into her brown purse, which was her only purse, and which she now placed across her lap. It felt like a steamer trunk compared to all the dear little evening bags that the women in the audience, including Avis, had dangling lightly from wrists or tucked into palms.

Avis cupped her own gloved hand and whispered into her ear, "Can't you put that thing under the seat? It looks like you brought a goddamned turkey to eat."

"It's too big. There's no room for my feet." Idella could feel her cheeks flush. Who did Avis think she was anyway, Queen of the Piss Pot? She sat there in that beaded dress, with a real bracelet on and earrings and a little evening bag—her eyebrows all plucked nice as you please and a fancy wave in her hair that must have taken all afternoon to get just right—like she owned the place. She looked beautiful, and Idella felt bad—so gawky and glommy and brown.

Avis had shown up at the door dressed to the nines. She had taken the breath out of them all. One of her regular customers had decided that Avis would be the belle of the ball, lending her everything to wear, and of course she went right along with it, lapping it all up, and now she was lording it over Idella.

It was like sitting next to a whirlpool. Avis sat forward and looked over the audience. "There's more minks in this crowd than in all of Canada." She stood up to peer at the musicians. You could just see the tops of some of their instruments—those sticks the violin players used were scraping up and down, making weird noises. "They're tuning up," Avis said knowingly when Idella pulled her back down into her seat. Avis looked up at the ceiling and laughed. "Get a load of the naked babies painted up there. Their little whosie-whatsits are tinkling on us."

"Avis!" Idella held her purse closer.

Avis sat straight up and read the program. They had each gotten one, telling who was who and whatnot. Idella couldn't concentrate. Avis bounced up and down in her seat, testing the pillows. "Cushy." She ran her fingers over the velvet chair back. "Plush." Suddenly she was twisting in her seat and looking up at the fancy boxes that lined the outer edges of the balcony. "Let's find the old ladies."

"Avis, turn around and sit still."

"There they are. Like a couple of roosting pullets. I think there'll be some fresh eggs before the show's over."

"Would you sit still?" Idella hissed.

"Shhh!" Avis turned back around. "Quiet, Idella! It's about to begin." The lights had flickered and dimmed. The musicians started playing for real.

The nerve. Telling her to be still. Idella scrunched back into her seat and watched the bright light spread across the big red curtain. It looked like velvet. The music struck her as loud already. She closed her eyes and took a deep breath.

Idella was growing restless. There was too much to look at. The songs went on and on. People were running on- and offstage and singing away alone and in large groups, and the next thing she knew, they were shouting and she had no idea why.

Gypsy women came rushing onstage. One of them was Carmen. She danced around, pulling her skirts way up and swiveling her hips like there was no tomorrow. Kind of tarty. Then they started singing about cigarettes, of all things. "Cigarette" was the one English word Idella could make out. That whole scene was right up Avis's alley. She was bobbing and squirming in her seat like a buoy in a gale. Someone was going to ask her to sit still.

The Gypsies reminded Idella of the French girls up in Canada at the lobster factory. Maddie had told her how they had to clean out claws and tails, a terrible job. Idella and Avis would hide in the bushes and watch them walk up and down during their lunch break. Dad didn't allow them to go near those French girls or talk to them. He said they were from way down country, they were too rough. They were very mysterious to Idella and Avis, always speaking French. Maddie was the only one she'd ever really known.

Idella glanced at the people seated near them and wondered what their lives were like. The woman on her left wore a ring with a stone the size of a grape. It flashed and sparkled like a streetlamp. The man in front of Avis had a bald spot like a sand dollar right on top of his head. Idella was surprised Avis hadn't pointed it out with a rude remark. Idella sighed and shifted in her seat. Her fanny was starting to bore holes through the cushion. It couldn't be too much longer.

Suddenly everyone was clapping away. The lights were turned on bright all around them. "Is it over?" she whispered to Avis, who was clapping like a seal.

"No, ninny, it's intermission."

"I'm staying put." She had to pee but did not feel comfortable with these people. She'd hold it. And she'd have to carry her purse. She wished she'd left it home. There was nothing in it, really, but the gloves and a handkerchief.

"Come on, let's go mingle with the hoi polloi." Avis was on her feet, adjusting the tight-fitting dress over her rear end.

"I want to stay here, Avis. I'm perfectly comfortable."

"Well, I need a smoke. That scene in the cigarette factory had me sucking air. Get your Pony Express bag there and let's go."

People were standing in the row waiting to slide past Idella. She stood, clutching her bag, and sidled out after Avis, who hadn't even bothered to wait but plunged ahead into the crowd heading up the aisle.

"This opera is all right," Avis whispered when Idella finally wormed her way up to stand beside her. "That Carmen's a pistol."

"She seems sort of crude."

Avis smiled. "She knows how to have fun, that's for sure. Course, I wouldn't mind meeting that bullfighter some dark night myself."

Avis wasn't even looking at her. She was watching the swirl of people who filled the lobby with their smoke, their glitter, their rippling little laughs. Idella felt hemmed in.

"They drag the words out so in the songs. I don't think I'd understand them even if it was in English."

"Probably not." Avis was stylishly tapping out a cigarette, holding it between two fingertips.

"What was all that business on Carmen's leg, when the soldier came to the cigarette factory?"

"She was rolling a tobacco leaf."

"Go on. Who would smoke that?"

"Plenty of people."

"May I light that for you, miss?" A very dapper man—fortyish, maybe—in a beautiful gray suit had caught Avis's eye and offered a light. He was tall, and Avis looked right up into his face and smiled.

"Yes. Yes indeed. You may. Thanks." Avis offered him the unlit end of her cigarette like she was in a movie. "That's very kind of you." She was batting her eyes so, it was a miracle she didn't blow out the cigarette.

"My pleasure." The man said no more than that but nodded and turned to join his party. Idella watched him glide across the carpet. He was with two other men and two women, so he could be solo or not. They formed a loose circle, chatting and laughing.

Avis waggled her cigarette. "Hoo-hoo!"

Idella sighed and looked away. She felt like a broom handle standing there next to Avis, who was smoking so stylishly—blowing her smoke out in long, slow puffs that whooshed.

"Come on," Avis said, suddenly putting the cigarette out in a potted plant. "Let's get in line for the can. I need to *oui-oui,* if you understand my French." The line inside the ladies' lounge was solid, snaking out past the mirrors of the outer room where women were applying more lipstick.

"Too many cows, not enough stalls," Avis whispered. "Let's go to the upper level. Maybe the line's shorter." Before Idella could protest, Avis was walking right up the fancy curved stairway, as smooth as you please, nodding and smiling like she owned the place. Idella could barely catch up, her purse whapping against her knees as she climbed.

"Avis, we're not supposed to go up here."

"Pooh. A can's a can. Look, it's a shorter line."

It *was* shorter, and Idella suddenly was so glad to be able to pee that she didn't care if they were supposed to be using the upstairs bathroom or not. When she finished, she stepped up to the line of sinks and washed her hands. A young girl handed her a towel. "Why, thank you." The girl nodded. Idella heard the clink of coins. She noticed the little glass trays on each sink. Lord, she didn't have any change. She stood there, frozen, wanting to give the towel back, but she'd already used it.

"Here you go. That's for the both of us." Avis had come out of her stall and put a whole dollar in the girl's dish.

"Thank you, ma'am."

"Not at all." Avis smiled and took a towel from her. She turned to Idella. "I'll just powder my nose on the way out."

"Avis," Idella pleaded under her breath, "let's go back to our seats."

They walked past the remaining line, mostly old ladies, who were slow to get there. At the end, staring at them with those blinkless eyes, was Miss Lawrence. Mrs. Brumley was next to her. Idella forced herself to stop and smile.

"Why, my dears, what a treat to find you up here!" Mrs. Brumley suddenly recognized them. "Are you enjoying the show? Isn't it exciting? How sweet you look, Idella." She spoke too loudly. "And, Avis, my dear, how stunning you are. Positively. Are you enjoying it?"

"Very much, Mrs. Brumley, thank you." Avis certainly was enjoying every minute of this.

"I had a feeling the opera would find a friend in you." Mrs. Brumley nodded and smiled. "It touches your inner passions, my dear. Just wait till the climax! It's heartbreaking."

There was a sound of chimes, and the lights flickered.

"I think you two had better return to your seats." Miss Lawrence placed a protective hand on Mrs. Brumley's shoulder. "It's quite a ways back down."

All the way down the stairs and back to their seats, Avis mimicked Miss Lawrence. "'You'd better get back *down* to your *places*.' The old witch."

"Shhh!"

"I hope she pees her panties before she gets a stall."

"Avis!"

The curtain rose as their fannies hit the seats.

Idella sighed, sat back, and waited patiently for the curtain to fall.

*   *   *

It startled Idella clear out of her seat when the soldier pulled a knife and killed, actually *killed*, Carmen. She got her whole song in, though, before she let go. Then the soldier kept on singing, right over her dead body. Finally there was a roar of shouting and clapping.

Now roses were being thrown onto the stage for the singers. Idella enjoyed seeing them all lined up taking great bows and smiling, gathering up the bouquets. Carmen was back on her feet, smiling and nodding. People all around Idella were shouting "Bravo!" and standing up.

"Come on, Della!" Avis yanked on her arm till she was standing. "Bravo! Bravo!"

Idella tried to clap, but her bag was too big. She stood clutching it amid the uproar. That whole last part since intermission, Avis had been awfully still, hands folded on her lap. Now she was practically on the ceiling with her wild clapping and yelling.

They stood till the last rose was thrown and the last singer had left the stage.

"Get your things, Avis. They'll be waiting for us." Idella had put on her coat ten minutes ago.

Avis draped her coat, borrowed and stylish like everything else she was wearing, over her shoulders and walked up the aisle ahead of Idella.

"Jesus," Idella muttered when she found Avis waiting on the sidewalk. "Keep me waiting and then charge ahead, why don't you?"

"Oh, that was lovely, just wonderful." Mrs. Brumley came rushing up to them. She was lit up like one of those chandeliers, and there were tears in her eyes. She grasped Avis's hands and looked right at her. "You know now, my dear, don't you? You understand why I come here every season. You must come with us again."

Miss Lawrence loomed out of the crowd and took hold of Mrs. Brumley's elbow. "Let me give you girls money for the bus. Mrs. Brumley gets overstimulated at these operas. She needs a quiet ride home." Miss Lawrence handed Idella exact change for two bus fares. She'd had it ready. "Do be careful coming in and going up to the bedroom." She steered Mrs. Brumley toward a waiting cab.

"What the hell's the matter with you?" They were finally on their bus. Avis had gone from being all atwitter to stone quiet. Now, by God, she was sitting here on the bus crying, tears rolling down her cheeks. Idella hadn't seen Avis cry for years. "What has gotten into you?"

"Nothing, just nothing."

"Are you sick or something?" Idella whispered.

"No, I'm not sick!"

"Well, all right, then!" Idella looked out the window. Avis sat there sniveling the whole time the bus rolled along, picking up passengers and letting them off. "Two more stops," Idella whispered.

"I know, goddamn it, I'm not blind."

"Well, you don't have to bite my head off!" Idella had had enough. She wanted to be in bed and done with all this.

They got out of the bus and walked along in silence, Avis keeping a few steps ahead, as usual. It was so annoying. Suddenly Avis stopped deadbolt under a streetlight and turned around to Idella.

"Yes, I *am* sick! I'm sick, Idella!" She was yelling.

"Why, Avis!"

"I'm sick of being kept in my place. Of being told what to do and where to go and where to sit. Of being out of place and too loud and not good enough. I want to have things like other people—like the people that get to go to the opera when they want to, and take cabs, and wear beautiful dresses like this. I look good in this dress, goddamn it! I look wonderful!" She twirled about under the yellow light. "I want to feel like those singers did onstage. Carmen let herself be big and loud as she pleased. She wasn't afraid to live, Idella."

"But it got her into trouble, Avis. She got killed."

"I want to open my mouth that wide and have no one—not even you—tell me to keep it down, to turn it off, to sit on it, by God! I don't want to crawl around on my hands and knees and do for everyone else in the whole damned world for the rest of my life. Just because we came down from Canada poor as church mice doesn't mean we're not as good as anybody else. That Lawrence dame is a glorified servant. She's nobody! She wipes her ass like everybody. They all do!" Avis was yelling up to the sky, her arms flung out from her sides. People were crossing the street to avoid her. "They all shit and wipe their asses!"

"Avis, please!"

"Please what, Idella? Please, please, please, please, please! I'm tired of asking for things!" Suddenly she crumpled to the curb and sat, huddled, her knees up under her chin. The air seemed to leave her entirely.

Idella opened her purse and took out the handkerchief. "Here, take this. It floated in this trunk all night. You might as well make some use of it."

Avis reached for it. "Thanks." She started to laugh. "That's you all over, Idella."

"What?"

"A square handkerchief in a big brown purse."

"Well, that doesn't sound too interesting." Idella took Avis's hand and helped her up. "If you weren't my sister, I might hit you."

"I thought that because I *am* your sister you'd hit me." Avis was blowing her nose, thank heavens. The storm seemed to be over.

"You're right." Idella gave Avis a whack on the behind with the purse. "O-lay!"

Avis laughed and took her coat off her shoulders, swooping it around like a matador's cape. Idella came charging through it with her head down, her purse in front of her like a shield.

"O-lay! O-lay! O-lay!" They were both shouting it and charging like bulls from streetlamp to streetlamp.

"'*Toria-dorie bum* da *bum-bum bum*!' Sing, Idella, sing! We've been to the opera! Let's sing! '*Bum* dum ba *bum* dum, la la la!'"

"'To market, to market, to buy a fat ho-o-o-o-o-g!'" Idella sang out. "'Home again, home again, jiggity-joo-o-o-o-g!'"

"Oh, brother."

"'To market, to market, to buy a fat p-i-i-i-g!'" Idella let loose. "'Home again, home again, now we are d-o-o-o-o-ne!'"

"No, no, no, Idella." Avis laughed. "That's the plum-bun verse."

"Oh."

"Jesus, if you can't get Mother Goose straight, you've got no career in the opera."

"No." Idella giggled. "I guess I don't."

They jigged and jogged together until they reached the old brownstone and sneaked quietly in, giggling past the sleeping ladies, up to the attic room.

*　　　*　　　*

"Home again, home again," Idella said, thankfully pulling her blanket up to her chin.

"Now we are done." Avis sighed.

They lay side by side on Idella's narrow bed. Their bones were familiar, lined up against each other.

"What's a plum bun anyway?" Idella whispered.

"How the hell would I know?" Avis started to giggle. "A bun with a plum, I guess."

"Just asking."

"Go to sleep, Della."

"Okay."

"O-lay."

Panfried

Idella and Edward rolled over the hot sand until Idella was dizzy with him, until her hair was gritty and hopeless. Laughing and flea bitten, they rolled toward the water over broken bits of mussel shells and slimy blobs of seaweed. Sand was in her bathing suit and under her nails and between her toes. It clung all up and down her wet legs. The long fingers of a wave slapped over them. "Cold! Oh, God, it's cold!" Idella screamed. She was as happy as she had ever been.

She squirmed out from under him and ran back to their blanket, splaying herself across it. He followed. "Oh, Eddie, how will I get cleaned up enough? What'll I tell Mrs. Gray? I'm all over sand. It's in my ears, even."

He leaned over her and put the tip of his tongue in her ear. "Did you get sand under your suit?"

Idella leaned up on her elbows. "I've got to start the Grays' supper. I only have the afternoon off, not the whole day like you."

"I took the whole day. I didn't have it. I took it." His mouth was on hers, his lips soft and open and warm. "Mmm," he said. "I like eating sand like this."

"We'd better stop." She disentangled herself, then gathered up their towels and shook them out. Idella loved being with him. Even though he was a full six inches shorter, that didn't matter. He was still handsome. With Eddie she felt like she was a desirable woman. After all, she was nearly twenty-two. And . . . well, they had gone pretty far in Eddie's car—farther than she'd ever dreamed of going by choice.

She'd met him at a dance at the Grange. She was dancing with Raymond Tripp, and along came Eddie and tapped him on the shoulder and cut in. She'd been startled—and pleased. That's when he told her about selling whiskey off the pier at Old Orchard Beach. She thought he was enterprising and bold. Dad would have drunk up all the profits.

The next week Avis came up from Boston and wanted to go out to Old Orchard. It had taken some swishing around on Idella's part, but finally they got out to the pier. And there was Eddie, coming right up and taking her hand. Avis was madder than a wet hen. She went stalking off. But Idella didn't mind. They'd walked along the pier and then under it. They'd had saltwater taffy. And they'd kissed, eating that candy, all sandy and melty in their mouths. They lay there under the pier, hearing the waves and the music and the sound of footsteps up above and seeing the moonlight coming down between the boards.

Idella folded her dress and stockings and rolled them into her towel. "The tide's gone out. Let's look for sand dollars on the way back. They're good luck."

She walked ahead of him, searching for signs of the flat white shells. "They like the tide pools. We used to find them up in Canada when we were kids and make believe they were real dollars. My sister Avis would use hers to play poker with Dad. I kept mine in a cigar box. Most dollars I ever had."

"What happened to them?" Eddie was walking along behind her, watching as she searched the edges of tidal pools.

"Got thrown out probably."

Eddie stopped and poked his toe at something white. He bent down and scraped it clear. "Well, now, this isn't a whole dollar." He picked out broken bits. "I guess it's spare change."

Idella took the biggest piece from him. It had traces of a star pattern, as though etched by delicate needles. She smiled and closed her fingers around it. "You have to start somewhere. Found money. I'll take what I can get."

They walked until they came to the point of rocks that jutted out into the water. Mussels and periwinkles, exposed by the tide, were sharp to walk across. Strands of seaweed were slick underfoot. Eddie took her hand.

"Look at that man out there." Idella pointed to the smooth, steady strokes of a swimmer along the shore. "I think that's a marvel. Can you swim like that, Eddie?"

"I never learned to swim. Knight's farm had a pond where the kids would all go, but my mother wouldn't let me. Said I'd drown. Said it was full of cow dung and I'd get sick and die."

"Couldn't you just go anyway?"

Eddie laughed. "You don't know my mother. She'd of come tearing down to that pond, and I would have jumped in and hoped, by God, to drown."

"Oh, my."

"Oh, my, all right."

"I can't swim right either. The water is too cold up in Canada. None of us girls were allowed to go in. Men'd go out fishing from the cliffs. And on Sundays we'd all climb down the ladder and have picnics on the little strip of beach. But it was rocks mostly."

They had rounded the point to the bay side. Here the water was flat and calm. There were many more people. Mothers lined the scalloped edges, holding discarded plastic shovels, their eyes trained on their children.

"One time a couple of boys drowned down by the cliff shore. When I was seven. Mother was eight months along or so with my sister Emma. I remember clear as day seeing her run across that field. She lifted up her skirts, with that big belly, and ran to get to the ladder. Down over the edge she went, down to the beach to try to save those boys. But they were gone." Idella and Eddie kept walking, angling between blankets and shoes with socks stuffed in them. "Who knew that she would be dead one month later? So healthy she was. Who knew? And me just seven."

Eddie stopped. Idella was startled by the abruptness. He turned toward her. The sun was behind him, but she could still make out the lovely clear blue of his eyes, prettier than the water.

"I want you to come up to the house for supper this Saturday and meet Mother," he said. "She's been asking. You might as well meet her."

"Do you think she'll like me, Eddie?"

"No telling." Eddie smiled and shrugged. "There is no telling with her, Idella. She don't think right sometimes."

This was not reassuring.

Prescott Mills, Maine
July 1930

Eddie had come down Fletcher's Hill to meet Idella at the bus, thank God. She was nervous enough already.

"She's been sitting there since lunch, watching and waiting." Eddie helped her down and pointed at the house on top of the hill, where he lived with his parents. "It's that big gray house, see. She's on the porch. It's screened in so you can't see her, but she's watching."

"Goodness! She's been watching since lunch? Here it is almost supper."

"She's been cleaning all week. Starched the curtains. Had them things stretched out on racks all over the house."

"Oh, that's a big job. Doing curtains." Idella wondered if she should mention to Mrs. Jensen how nice the curtains looked. "You mean the sheers, Eddie? She did the sheers?"

"Hell, I don't know what you call them. The curtains. She borrows them racks from Milly Masterson with the nails all over the edges. I cut myself on them every damn time, bringing them over for her. Look here." Eddie showed her where he had been scratched as by a cat's claw across the base of his thumb.

Idella touched her fingers to her lips lightly and patted Eddie's thumb. "There."

Eddie smiled, took her arm, and started up the hill, Idella wobbling in her new shoes.

"Your mother doesn't get out much? She's not in any clubs or anything?"

"Hell no. She sits on that porch, is all. You'll like my father, though, and he'll like you."

"You mean your mother won't?"

"There's no telling, Idella. It's got nothing to do with you."

"Oh. I see," Idella said, not at all sure if she did. She felt like she was being led to market.

Eddie opened the front gate for her. It hung down off its hinges, dragging across the dirt when he pushed it. "There's another damn thing I'm supposed to fix," he muttered.

Idella could see Mrs. Jensen now, watching from the porch, from behind her glasses. She didn't move or wave or anything. As they walked up the path to the house, Idella wished she could give herself one final check and run a comb through her hair.

Eddie opened the porch door, motioning for her to go in ahead of him. Mrs. Jensen was in the act of rising up out of her rocker. A lot of bulk was involved. She had a cane lodged between her two feet, and she leaned all her weight forward and over it. She finally stood, hoisted and hovering, above that little stick of wood.

She looks like a potato, Idella thought. And the nose on her looked like one of them knobs you find on the potato that sets out growing in its own direction altogether.

But she had gone to some trouble with her appearance. She had on a nice white blouse with a lace collar that was freshly starched, anyone could see that. And she had a large oval cameo brooch right at the center of her collar, with an ivory profile, a profile that clearly did not belong to her.

"Mother, this here is Idella Hillock. That I told you about. Brought her up here to meet you." Eddie had his hat in his hand and was talking kind of formal.

"My, my, what a nice surprise." Mrs. Jensen cocked her head and smiled. "Kind of tall, ain't you?"

"Oh, just a little." Idella regretted that little bit of heel on her new shoes.

"Eddie, take her right on into the parlor."

Eddie led the way into the kitchen and through the dining room—the table was all set—and into the parlor. Mrs. Jensen hobbled along from behind with her cane, making a slow *clump-tap, clump-tap.*

"Where's Dad?" Eddie asked.

"He's gone back down to the store. We need a new piece of meat."

"We don't need an old piece, Ma." Eddie winked at Idella.

"You quit being fresh, Eddie. I sent him back down to Foley's. Too grizzly, it was. I told him to take it back. I wouldn't serve it to a dog. All over grizzly. I don't know what kind of cow that piece could have come from, but it was not a clean animal. It was not any kind of quality animal." Mrs. Jensen's breath came in spurts. "They gyp you down there at Foley's. They'll gyp you every time." She stopped and leaned on her cane. Eddie and Idella stopped, too, and waited for her to resume motion. "He'll be along any minute, and then I'll get things to cooking. He's too trusting, Jens is. He'll take whatever they give him and not see he's getting gypped."

"My, what a lovely room," Idella said as they entered the parlor. "What lovely white curtains. So fresh and stiff."

Mrs. Jensen, having reached the doorway to the parlor, smiled broadly. "Oh, well. Yes. Fresh curtains. They make a difference in a room."

"I should say." Idella smiled at Eddie.

"Now, Eddie, you help Idella get seated good there on the couch. You sit down and rest for a few minutes, Idella. Eddie has a few things to do out in the garden and with the chickens." Eddie rolled his eyes. "Eddie, you come help me now."

She turned and waddled back toward the kitchen.

"Eddie, what do I do?" Idella whispered as he started out behind his mother.

"Hold your horses while I pick the strawberries and feed the damn chickens." He bent over and gave her a kiss. "Think about that while you wait." He brushed his hand against her breast. "And this." He already acted like he had a right to her breasts, and Idella didn't mind. It seemed natural. And thrilling.

"Eddie! I need you!" Mrs. Jensen called from the kitchen. "Eddie!"

"Jesus!" he muttered.

Idella had been sitting alone in the parlor for an awful long time. This room was so stuffy and stiff and unused-feeling. Mrs. Jensen must keep it special for when company comes, like a basket of fruit all wrapped in cellophane.

Every surface had a knickknack on it with a doily underneath. Idella was not fond of knickknacks. They were so useless—glass dogs and figurines sitting around on shelves, needing to be dusted all the time. What good were they?

This was a nice big old house, though, so much nicer than what she'd grown up in. Eddie had no earthly idea of how poor they were up there in Canada. Hardscrabble. Maine seemed so friendly and civilized compared to it. Lots of big old shade trees and lawns, and flowers in the gardens along with the vegetables.

Growing up, they'd just had wildflowers. No one planted fancy flowers. The wildflowers never lasted in the house, but she and Avis kept picking them anyway and sticking them into the canning jar they used as a vase. The flowers would wizen up even before they could sit down to supper. They were such wild things, they weren't meant to be brought indoors.

That's what the men were like, too, crude men who were not brought up right. Not the farmers who lived there and had families and such. They were nice enough men. It was the strays Dad hired, who showed up sudden and left that way. They didn't even belong in a house.

Eddie was more gentlemanly. He was fresh sometimes—but a fun kind of fresh, not scary. He had those blue, blue eyes and that dark, dark hair. Idella's eyes and hair were brown as a plowed field. They were not her best features.

The front door opened and closed. Someone walked through the porch. "Jessie, here is your new piece of meat." That must be Mr. Jensen. He had a soft voice with a foreign accent. Eddie had said his father was from Denmark.

"That's too small! There won't be enough! There won't be half enough!" Mrs. Jensen's voice came out in bursts. "Why so small? Where's your head?"

"Now, my dear, that meat is more than the one I returned. I paid for the five more ounces."

"You paid too much!"

"Now, Jessie. Don't go on so."

Idella was amazed. No way would Dad have ever stood there and listened to the likes of Eddie's mother telling him to go back down to the store and get a better piece of meat. My God, my God.

"That girl will be saying things. She'll tell people I can't cook a decent meal."

Idella was glued to the couch, listening intently.

"It does you no good to upset yourself." Then his voice got too low to hear the words. She could only make out murmurs and little squeals of response, like from a . . . well, like from a pig, really.

The back door banged and brought the voices to a halt, as though a radio had been turned off.

"Scrape your feet, Eddie. Don't go walking that mud through my house."

Eddie's footsteps did not pause till he reached Idella. He was suddenly standing in the doorframe. "How you holding up?"

"Getting sort of antsy."

"Antsy, eh? Ants in your pants?" He smiled that smile of his that went from one ear to the other. "I brought you something." He reached down and took her hand and placed a large red strawberry into it. "I picked you the prettiest one. Take a bite."

"Oh, Eddie. It's got the weight of a plum to it." Idella held the dark red berry carefully by the stem and used her other hand like a saucer. She bent over and took a cautious bite. The sweet juice oozed and dribbled as soon as her teeth broke its surface.

"Now I'll have some." Eddie leaned over her and took the strawberry into his mouth and bit it off. She was left holding the little green cap. A stir went through her when he got so close—his mouth, those blue eyes.

"Ripe one, ain't it? And sweet." He leaned over her, bent down lower, and kissed her. One thumb was under her chin, pushing her head up toward him. His mouth tasted of the berry juice. It was a slow, delicious kiss.

He pulled her up to standing. When he did, the last bit of stem and berry fell from her fingertips onto the couch. A dark red smudge was left, unmistakable.

"Oh, Eddie, look!" She tried to dab at it with the hem of her dress.

"Leave it," Eddie said. "She'll never even notice."

She'll see it, all right, Idella thought as Eddie led her into the kitchen. She'll see it and she'll smell it.

"Oh, here they are, here they are." Mr. and Mrs. Jensen stood together beside the stove. "Jens, this is Eddie's friend, Miss Hillock."

"How do you do, Miss Hillock? So pleased to meet you." Eddie's father walked over to Idella and reached out his hand. He had a sweet, shy smile. He was tall and thin, with a cap on his head like workingmen wore, and trousers with suspenders. He had a dark mustache combed so nice, and light blue eyes. Even in his working clothes, there was a bit of style to him. He seemed, somehow, a gentleman.

"Jens, take your hat off." Mrs. Jensen had an apron tied around her waist. She was all smiles. "Now, Idella, can I make a glass of lemonade to refresh you?"

"Why, yes, thank you."

Mrs. Jensen already had her hands on a glass juicer. "We got real nice lemons here. We got them special." Her smile made her nose protrude even more. A bowl on the counter had four or five large yellow lemons. She set about slicing them in two. "Now, where did a name like that come from? Not from around here."

"Hillock?"

"No. Idella."

"It is an old-fashioned name, I guess." Idella watched Mrs. Jensen cut three lemons down the middle and twist them over the cut-glass juicer. "My father said it must have come from a book my mother was reading. She loved to read. He didn't have much to do with the naming of us, is my understanding. I have heard of a few Idellas up in Canada. I saw one once on a grave in the little cemetery where my mother is buried."

"You come from up in Canada?" Idella could see that large seeds were floating on top of the pooled yellow juice. The juicer was pretty full up.

"Yes. New Brunswick."

"Is your father still living?"

"Oh, yes. Very much so. He's still on the farm."

"But your mother passed on?"

"When I was seven."

"Was it sudden?" Mrs. Jensen stopped squeezing.

"Yes. In childbirth."

"It wasn't you, was it?"

"Pardon me?"

"That she was having. When she died?"

"No. I was seven."

"Oh, yes."

"It was my sister Emma. It was a great shock to all of us."

"Oh, my. Oh, my. To think of it." Mrs. Jensen shook her head in a distracted manner and poured every drop of the juice, three lemons' worth by Idella's count, into a tall glass. Then she took a spoon, with no sugar on it, and stood stirring and stirring, staring down into the glass as if in a trance. "Nothing worse than the death of a parent to a child," she finally said. "Unless it be the child dying and the poor parent left." She looked up at Idella, so sad, and handed over the glass of straight-up juice.

Two large seeds floated to the top. Idella took a sip. Her eyes watered immediately. "Delicious."

"My Albert!" Startled, Idella looked up. Mrs. Jensen was crying. Just like that. "I only had him for one month, Idella. One month."

"Christ. Here we go," Eddie muttered from behind them. He was leaning against the porch doorway.

"Now, Jessie." Mr. Jensen walked over and put his arm around her shoulders.

"Little Albert! Belly button never did heal proper. He died from it." Mrs. Jensen was all crumpled up on herself, sobbing. Mr. Jensen offered her a handkerchief. "It was nothing I did. Everyone said it was nothing I did."

"Oh, I'm sure not, Mrs. Jensen." Idella turned to Eddie. He would not look up.

The whole kitchen was filled with the sounds of Mrs. Jensen's whimpers. Idella stood mute and watched the lemon seeds floating on her drink.

Finally Mrs. Jensen pulled away from Mr. Jensen and blew her nose. She took off her glasses, all fogged up from crying, and wiped them on her apron. When she put them back to rights, she looked at Idella and smiled the most pathetic little smile. "Is your lemonade all right?"

Idella smiled brightly. "What a nice big kitchen!"

"It's old. Too old." As though jump-started by the change of subject, Mrs. Jensen set about peeling potatoes in the sink. "Just look at that stove," she said, pointing with a potato at the large black stove in the middle of the kitchen. "Burn myself on it getting them lids off. I can hardly lift them."

"Yes, they look heavy." Idella nodded.

"Will you look at how this kitchen floor sags. I've tried to get Jens to fix it. Said he would but didn't. I've heard that before. It's like walking down Fletcher's Hill to go from one side of the kitchen to the other. I'll drop right over one of these days and roll." She kept peeling and peeling.

"Well, people get so busy." Idella nodded at Mr. Jensen.

"Oh, he's busy, all right. Always out there doing something. He gives more care to those cows and horses than he does to me. Tends them animals like as if they were babies."

"You need me to pick something, Ma? For the supper? In the garden?" Eddie was restless.

"We'll be needing peas. I was waiting to get Jens to pick them so they'll be fresh off the vine, and he took too long with the meat. Always takes twice as long to do something as I would if I could. You like strawberry shortcake, Idella?"

"Oh, yes. Very much."

"It's Eddie's favorite. He eats and eats when it comes to my shortcake. I always make him an extra. Eddie's extra. You love my shortcake, don't you, Eddie?" Mrs. Jensen stopped carving the potato and looked at him over the top of her glasses.

"I'll go pick the peas." Eddie gave Idella a quick glance and started through the back room that led out to the garden.

"Take something to put them in!" Mrs. Jensen called after him. The screen door banged in reply.

"Eddie told me what a good cook you are, Mrs. Jensen. I look forward to your supper." This was not exactly true. Eddie had told her that his mother's cooking was spotty. What Idella looked forward to was the meal being over.

"I do try to lay out a nice meal for company."

"I'd be glad to help you in some way."

"I won't hear of it. You are the guest. You cook for a living, my goodness' sakes. You enjoy your lemonade. Oh! I have to start the biscuits! I'm behind on the biscuits! Jens! Now, where's my butter?"

In a waddling frenzy, Mrs. Jensen set about to make biscuits. She got out a large breadboard and took a bowl from the cupboard and a sifter from below. Mr. Jensen placed the butter next to her and then stepped back out of her working area. The potatoes, Idella couldn't help but notice, were left half done. Some were lying whole on the counter by the sink. Some, with the daylights peeled right out of them, were left sitting in a pot of water. They looked more whittled than peeled. For a flick of a second, Idella's eyes met Mr. Jensen's. And in that flick she knew that they both had decided not to mention the word "potatoes."

"You want you should meet Chocolate Milk, Miss Hillock?" Mr. Jensen spoke so softly. Like little songs, his voice was. "My horse that helps deliver the milk?"

"Oh, she don't want to go see no horse, Jens. She's seen horses. Isn't that right, Idella?"

"We had one on the farm, of course. For work in the field mostly, but he'd take us to town in the wagon. I'd like to meet Chocolate Milk. What a dear name."

"Oh, well, the children. They named her that. Used to be her name was Brownie."

"I named her that. Brownie. That was the name I give her. 'Cause she's brown." Mrs. Jensen was measuring flour and baking soda into her sifter.

"But the children, coming around the wagon when I deliver the milk, they changed it to Chocolate Milk."

"Silly name for a horse," Mrs. Jensen muttered. She was sifting flour onto the breadboard. "You love that horse more than me, the way you go on." As she turned to Mr. Jensen, flour sifted all over the floor. "Oh, oh, oh, look what you made me do! I'll have to start all over measuring or the biscuits won't be right."

Idella stood clutching her lemonade. After what seemed like forever, Eddie came in with a basket full of peas. Mrs. Jensen looked up and scowled. "Them need shelling."

"I can shell those," Idella piped up.

"Let's go sit on the porch. I'll do it." Eddie carried the basket out of the kitchen and sat on one end of an old wicker couch. Idella followed him and sat on the other end.

"Take the pot," Mrs. Jensen called. "For the peas."

"You want me to pee in the pot, Ma?" Eddie smiled at Idella.

"Eddie!" Idella whispered. She was glad he was back.

"I'll come, too," Mrs. Jensen called. "I could stand to sit a spell."

Mr. Jensen took the pot in one hand and his wife's arm in the other. He helped her onto the porch and over to her rocker. She hovered, then landed with a whoosh onto the dark green corduroy cushion. The chair set back with such a *thwop* when her weight hit it that Idella thought it might upend entirely.

"Are you comfortable, my dear?" Mr. Jensen asked as the rocking subsided.

"I'll do." Her legs were so short that only the toes of her black lace-up shoes touched the floor.

"Oh, a porch is so peaceful," Idella said.

"Yes," said Mrs. Jensen. "I sit here for a bit every day to rest my legs. Varicose veins, you know." She looked at Idella.

"Oh, no. I didn't know."

"I got them something terrible. They throb. My legs are purple all up and down. I used to be skinny as a rail, like you. Not so tall, of course. You got the height on you to stretch it all out. Short legs like mine, you get squashed come time to put on the weight. And the varicose. They are a trial. All swoled up, my legs get. I shouldn't of been on them so long today. But I had to make a special dinner."

"I hope you didn't go to too much trouble for me, Mrs. Jensen!"

"If I was younger, course, it would be no trouble. Not that it's been trouble."

Mr. Jensen sat down on a wicker chair next to his wife. "How's that lemonade, Miss Hillock?"

"Oh, fine, thank you. Fine." Idella smiled and took a sip. Her whole mouth puckered.

"We'll just set out here on the porch awhile and get acquainted while Eddie shells the peas." Mrs. Jensen took up a fan from a nearby table. She opened it, slowly waving it back and forth.

They all sat in silence, looking out the porch windows. There was just the *thud, thud, thud* of peas dropping into the bottom of the pot. Mrs. Jensen's fan kept whooshing. Idella held the tall, smooth glass tightly and took a few sips for show. Mrs. Jensen nodded whenever she did, and Idella held the glass up and smiled.

The fan stopped. "There goes Mrs. Rudolf." Mrs. Jensen leaned forward in her chair. "That's her there walking down the hill. She lives up the road. She's got no one to take care of her. Poor thing. No children, see, to look after her. All alone."

Mrs. Rudolf, a tall, skinny woman who looked to be in her sixties, was walking straight along the sidewalk, not looking to either side. She wore a little white sweater across her shoulders, the empty arms dangling beside her.

They watched until she disappeared down the swoop of Fletcher's Hill.

"Is she a widow woman?" Idella asked.

"Who?"

"Mrs. Rudolf."

"He run off on her. With Lucy DuBois—a French girl, you know—about fifteen or more years ago. Worked together down at the mill sorting stacks of paper. Usually it's the women do the sorting, but he was on some kind of disability that kept him from the big machines they got down there. They run off down to Biddeford. And not long after, that Lucy had herself a baby boy. Only 'bout four months after—five at the most."

"I see," Idella finally said. "That's sad."

"Mmmmmm. She got the house. Little green house. She still goes by the name Mrs. Rudolf. But there's no more Mister."

"Couldn't of been too bad a disability he had." Eddie stripped a pod of peas directly into his mouth.

"How about some ice in that lemonade?" Mr. Jensen asked her suddenly.

"I'll get Idella ice." Eddie shot up out of his chair. Finally, Idella thought, he was taking some notice. "I'll cool it down for you." He took her glass and went into the kitchen. They listened as he opened the icebox and got the ice pick from out of a drawer and started hacking. A dog barked across the street.

"Them Mastersons should get rid of that dog. It barks like that half the day. I hear it at night, too—barking for no reason. It's a nuisance." Mrs. Jensen flicked her fan with quick little jerks. "That dog should be done away with."

"Now, Jessie. It doesn't really bother you. Those girls love it."

"It does bother me, that dog barking all the time."

Eddie came back in. "Here you go, Idella. That should be more refreshing."

"Thank you, Eddie." Idella took the glass, now cold from chips of ice, and sipped. She glanced quickly at Eddie, who had resumed shelling peas. He smiled and nodded his head just enough for Idella to know she was right. He had also put in whiskey.

"Did the ice help cool it?" Mrs. Jensen was smiling at her.

"Oh, yes," Idella said. "Very much."

Mrs. Jensen leaned forward. "Is that the Masterson girl, out raking the grass over there? I can't see proper from this distance. Is it Susan, the older one?"

"Susan, yes." Mr. Jensen stretched his long legs out in front of him. He couldn't be very comfortable on that little wicker chair, Idella thought.

"Well, she's putting on some weight, I can tell you. Can you see how thick she's got? You see it from here. Do you know the Masterson girls, Idella? They live in that blue house there directly across."

"No, I've never met them."

"How would she know them, Ma?" Eddie reached down into his basket and took up another handful to shell. Idella longed to keep her hands busy shelling peas.

"Well, that oldest one is getting thick right through the middle. She was out there raking grass last week, too. And she was barefooted, with only a pair of shorts to cover her bare legs. The Larsen boys, they kept walking by one after the other, all four of them. They stopped and talked to her. More than one of them did."

"People talk to each other, Ma. The Larsens live next door. They have to walk by there to go anywheres."

"Eddie, don't get fresh." Mrs. Jensen turned toward Idella. "Do you own a pair of shorts, Idella"

"Well, no, I don't. My legs have always been so skinny. Bird legs. Not that I would. They don't suit me."

Mrs. Jensen leaned back and resumed her slower fanning. "Eddie tells me you are in domestic service."

"Well, yes. I'm a cook. I cook for this certain family, the Grays."

"Imagine having a separate person that you pay just to cook your meals. Do you cook fancy?"

"Oh, no. Just regular. Regular meals like anybody else."

"You went to school for it?"

"I had some lessons, is all. When I worked down in Boston, the two ladies I was working for sent me to cooking classes. It wasn't fancy, more common sense, really. But it taught me . . . oh, how to make a certain sauce for a certain cut of meat, say. Or how to roast a chicken or make biscuits. Commonsense things mostly."

"I never got schooled as a cook. I make things like my mother did." Mrs. Jensen looked sternly at Idella over the rim of her glasses. "That's been good enough for my family."

"Oh, yes, of course. Plenty good enough. More than." Idella, in her fluster, took a gulp from her glass. Dear god, the whiskey burned her throat.

"Well, I'd best get back to the kitchen and finish." Mrs. Jensen closed her fan. "Take them peas out to the kitchen, Eddie. Help me up out of this chair, Jens. Nothing fancy, mind. I don't know about sauces. Just panfried steak, is all. Potatoes and peas."

"Simple is best, I think," Idella said. "Steak cooked in a good black pan. That's the best." Idella had noticed the pan.

Mrs. Jensen smiled. "You two sit out here for a bit. You enjoy your drink, Idella. I've got things to do. Jens, come help me. You like plain mashed potatoes, Idella?"

"I love any kind of potatoes. I'm happy with potatoes only!"

It took some doing to get Mrs. Jensen up and off the porch. Idella concentrated on admiring the row of violets that edged the inside of the fence on the front lawn. "So pretty," she said out loud, as though she had been in the middle of a conversation.

"What's that?" Edward returned without the peas and slid close to her as soon as his mother had waddled out.

"The violets. So pretty."

"Not as pretty as you." He touched her knee.

"You shouldn't have put that in my drink," Idella whispered. "What am I supposed to do with it now?"

"Drink up. That's what I'd do." His eyes were so blue coming right at you.

"Eddie, I can't get tipsy."

"Who cares?"

"You had a nip while you were out picking the strawberries, didn't you?"

"What if I did?" He started slowly to crinkle up the dress on her leg.

"Eddie, you need to help me through this."

"She won't bite. She barks more than the dog across the street." Eddie's voice was right in her ear. His mouth was just an inch away. The warm puff of his breath sent tingles down her back.

She stood and walked over to the screen door. "Let's go look at the violets. I love violets."

Eddie followed her out onto the front lawn. Idella took a deep breath. "It was getting a little close in there."

"I like it close." He came up behind her.

"Show me the violets, Eddie."

"Nothing to see. Just flowers."

They walked across the lawn, newly mowed and sweet smelling, to the corner of the fence. Idella scooched down and ran her hands lightly across the cool, dark, heart-shaped leaves. "They are so lovely."

Eddie reached down and pulled a violet out of the ground.

"Don't pull out the root, Eddie."

"There's plenty." He handed her the flower, its thread of white root trailing behind it.

"Your mother don't want her flowers pulled up!" Idella plucked off the trailing root.

"You can't tell what will set her off. Gets mad over nothing. Holds grudges. People walking by, she calls them over and starts in telling things. Gossip. She makes things up, see, about people, and then believes it. They say it's the scarlet fever she had."

"You mean the fever affected her mind?"

"Christ, that was before I was born." He shrugged. "She used to try and hang herself, right in front of me and Ethel."

"No!"

"She'd get a stool and put the rope around her neck and pull up on it and say she was going to string herself up from the light. Me and Ethel were kids. Scared the hell out of us."

"What made her do that?"

"Christ knows. Ethel didn't fold the clothes. I didn't pick enough beans. Hens didn't lay eggs. Anything. I'm getting the hell out." He looked through the fence and down the hill they had walked up together.

"Where do you think you'll be going?" Idella twirled the violet stem between her fingers.

"Maybe into Portland. I'd like to sell cars. Something with a chance to make me some money. I'm not staying at the American Can Company."

"I'm glad you're not going far away."

"Now, why is that?" He smiled.

"I'd like to see more of you."

"You would, huh? Which part?" Eddie raised up his eyebrows.

"Eddie! I mean, you know, be with you more."

"Uh-huh. I know." Eddie took hold of her hand, smothering the violet in his grasp, and pulled her toward him. "Come on over here to the other side of this elm tree and kiss me."

"Eddie, stop. Not here on the front lawn! She'll see." Nervous, Idella held up her glass. "Eddie, what am I going to do with this lemonade?"

"Drink it."

"It's straight lemon juice. And the whiskey. It'll make me sick."

"Jesus, no sugar?" Eddie laughed. "I hate to waste a good swig."

"I'm going to pour it out. I have to." Idella let go of his hand. The plucked violet fell into the grass. She scooched down and slowly poured the contents of her glass out into the ground. "I feel like I'm peeing in public," she whispered, giggling.

She stood up. Eddie took her elbow, and she gave him a quick kiss, relieved to be done with the drink. They turned back toward the house. Eddie's mother was standing in the porch doorway. She was holding a second glass of lemonade and watching the two of them.

"I guess you won't be wanting another," she said directly to Idella, then turned and walked back into the kitchen.

"Shit," Eddie whispered. "Goddamn it."

Idella and Edward stood mute in the dining room and stared across the table at each other, guilty as children about to get strapped, openly listening to the conversation going on in the kitchen.

"She's uppity, that Hillock girl. Poured the lemonade all over the violets. The juice of three lemons. Not good enough, I suppose. Not good enough for her."

"Three lemons?"

"She'll be laughing at me. Making fun of me at that rich woman's house where she works. And the steak all over gristle. I can't make my biscuits now. She's been to school. She studied biscuits."

"Now, Jessie, you make the meal you planned. We'll all enjoy it."

Idella didn't know what to do. She looked down at the table. The forks were wrong. She couldn't help but notice, after all her time in service. It was her training. She saw that the dessert forks were switched with the main course.

"Should we sit?" She looked over at Edward, who was now staring out the dining-room window.

"Sit if you want to." Idella didn't know if he was angry at her or at his mother.

From the kitchen Mr. Jensen's voice was like a radio playing music low. The clamor and scrape of pans on the iron stove indicated some activity now. There was a sudden loud sizzle when the meat hit the pan. Idella knew by the sound that the pan was too hot. Way too hot.

She felt ill. All that lemon juice was seizing up down there and puckering her insides.

Mr. Jensen stood in the doorway. "Sit, Miss Hillock. Sit. Soon we will be eating." He placed a bowl of peas and a dish of pickle relish onto the middle of the table.

There was visible smoke now, coming from the kitchen. And Mrs. Jensen was calling Mr. Jensen to help turn something over. The meat must be glued to that pan.

Eddie had already set himself down across from her. He was silent, not even looking at Idella, sunk in on himself. Idella reached across the table to pat his hand. "Eddie," she whispered, "it'll be over by midnight."

Eddie smiled. It was slow coming across his face, but it finally came. "Maybe it'll just be starting," he said.

"I mean the meal, Eddie. It'll have to be over by then." She giggled. "I need to be back to the Grays' by then."

"I was thinking of dessert," he said, reaching to squeeze her outstretched hand.

"Shortcake?" she asked, smiling.

"Mmm," he said. "With cream."

"The potatoes! I forgot the potatoes!" A wail came from out of the kitchen. "Oh, there's no time for them now. No time. Everything is ruined!"

Mr. Jensen came in, carrying a platter with the steaks laid out across it. They looked as dry as last year's cow patties, Idella thought. There was no juice whatsoever under, over, or between them—just dry plate.

Mrs. Jensen came in at the very last, more composed than Idella expected, and took her seat at the head of the table. She carried a basket covered with a linen cloth and placed it on the table right up against her own plate, like she was protecting it. That must be the biscuits.

Idella praised each dish extravagantly as it was passed to her. When her plate was fully loaded, she set about to cut a piece of steak. It was challenging. Panfried, Idella thought—it's more like tanned leather. She took a small bite. A bit of gristle would have added some sweetness. "Oh, this steak is so satisfying."

"I'm sorry about the potatoes, Idella. New little potatoes, they were. So good right out of the ground."

"These things happen," Idella assured her. "We have so much good food here already."

"With fresh butter and pepper. That's how we were going to have them. Butter made right here. Jens whipped it up for them potatoes."

"Ma, I think we should stop talking about potatoes, seeing as we won't be getting any."

"Don't be rude to me, Edward."

"Why sit there and talk about what we aren't going to have?"

"Don't you go blaming me. I tried. But it's too much to do everything all by myself. It is too much!"

Mr. Jensen raised his hand up. "Eddie, Jessie, please. It don't matter about the potatoes."

"No," Idella said. "No. We have no real need of potatoes."

"If I had more help around here instead of doing it all myself, I'd of had time to remember the potatoes." Mrs. Jensen was on the point of tears again. Those damned potatoes. Idella was ready to eat them raw.

"Tell me now, Miss Hillock, have you been in this country for long?" Mr. Jensen steered to a new topic.

"Just three years. But it was just . . . you know, just Canada. Not far. Not like coming to a foreign country."

Jens smiled. "Yes, I know what that is like. When I came over, all of my papers for work were in Danish. You know—letters that people wrote about me as a worker. No one here knew what was in them. They could have said I was a lazy good-for-nothing and no one would know better."

"I'm sure they didn't say that." Idella liked him so much. It was calming just to look over at him. His eyes spoke right to you.

"Well, I should hope not," Jessie chimed in. "I hope they said something better than that."

"Of course they did, Jessie dear. *I* could read them."

"Oh, yes, o' course. I forgot." She actually smiled. "I forgot that Jens can read the Danish."

"What sort of work did you do in Denmark, Mr. Jensen?"

"Well, we had the farm, sure, we all worked the farm. But I also worked in a clothing store for men in Copenhagen. I enjoyed seeing the different people and helping them. It was a change from the loneliness of the fields."

"Oh, yes, I know what you mean. Dad talks about how lonely it gets being out in the field all day. Course, he likes it, too. Nobody to bother him. That would be the other side to it. Nobody to tell him what to do."

"Well, I tell Jens what to do." Jessie was smiling. "I tell him what needs doing and when. Don't I, Jens?"

"Well, nobody's going to tell *me* what to do." Eddie leaned forward. "I'm going to rule my own roost some day. And there won't be any damn chickens in it, I can tell you that." He laughed at his own joke.

"You'll need eggs, Eddie," Mrs. Jensen said. "You can't have eggs without the chickens to lay them."

"I know that, Ma. I know all about that."

"Why, Edward." Mrs. Jensen's face flushed red.

"I can go get me some eggs down at Foley's. I can let somebody else's chickens lay my eggs."

"This is no conversation for the supper table, Edward. Really. More peas, Miss Hillock?"

"Please!" Idella held her plate under the heaping bowl, to catch the peas.

There was too much food. Mrs. Jensen was fueled to animation by Idella's ornate compliments. She blushed with pleasure at praise of her peas and gurgled happily when Idella asked for more of that homemade pickle relish, though she didn't really think it went with the meal. The more Idella managed to eat, the chattier and happier Mrs. Jensen became.

"Look, Idella! It's that Masterson girl!" Mrs. Jensen was pointing. "See, look out the window there. Pull back the curtain, Eddie, so Idella can see. There she is sitting under that tree over there on the lawn. See her? Right out there for all the world to see." Mrs. Jensen lowered her voice. "She is in the family way. I know it. Looks high up in her, too. Could be turned wrong. They get that shape when the baby's turned wrong. That's what happened to Ethel with her first one. Breech, they call it. Almost killed her."

"Ma, let's not talk about this now."

"That doctor had to cut her right down through to get that baby out. To half an inch it was from her rectum. Half an inch, I swear, is all. I saw it. I saw."

"Ma!"

"Oh, my."

Edward was pale. "Ma, please."

"My dear, maybe we shouldn't bother Idella with these details." Mr. Jensen put his hand over his wife's. She batted him away.

"I have never seen a baby come out so hard. All turned around, he was. Facing the wrong way. Cord around his neck. It was wrapped right around it, thick as a rope. A thick rope. It's a wonder she didn't burst right open. I thought honest to God it was going to happen and we'd lose her and the baby. Half an inch to her rectum. No more than that."

"Ma, please."

"My babies come out pretty easy compared to that." Mrs. Jensen smiled and nodded toward Edward. "Eddie got the Scoullar legs like me. Ethel, too. Now, Ethel is my own daughter, and I love her, of course, but I knew when she was born, from the day she was born, that she would not be smart. Or pretty. She's a good girl, but those two features are not hers."

"Well, I haven't met her yet. Eddie's told me about her situation."

"Oh, yes. Terrible. Left alone with three boys to raise. Husband killed at the mill on Thanksgiving. Terrible shock. They had him working in an ice storm, you know. His own father sent him out that night. His own father."

"I can't even imagine," Idella whispered.

"Now, my Albert was smart. I like to think that he became a doctor. You can tell right away with babies. Albert was smart." She smiled at Idella. "Any more steak? I've saved you a nice second cut."

"Oh, no thank you, Mrs. Jensen. I'll burst. It's all so good. So delicious. I'm saving some room for the shortcake. I'm so looking forward to that. Why don't you have that extra piece yourself?"

"Yes, my dear," Mr. Jensen said. "You take that last piece."

Mrs. Jensen shook her head. "You know I always seem to make that little bit of extra. Like for another person. Enough for one more. It's Albert's portion, I tell myself. That extra portion would have been for my Albert."

"I'll take it, Ma," Eddie said, handing his plate toward his mother.

"Albert would be twenty-seven years old now. Imagine. Probably tall like Jens."

"Ma, I'll take that last piece." Eddie reached across the table and forked the last steak. He was red in the face.

"Eddie!"

"Well, what about me?" He was shouting. "Did you decide about me? Did you have me down for feeding the chickens on the day I was born? Pulling the goddamned weeds from your garden!"

"Edward!" Mrs. Jensen gasped.

"I've heard all I'm ever going to hear about Albert! He was a goddamned baby, is all!" Edward rose up out of his chair and pounded his fist on the table. "A goddamned *baby*! He wasn't anything. He died before he lived. 'If Albert had lived. If Albert had lived.' *I'm* here, goddamn it. *I* lived. You're crazy, do you know that? You are a crazy woman, and if Albert had lived, he would have hated you, too, just like I do. A goddamned crazy woman." The silver trembled against the plates. "And Ethel isn't pretty! I've heard that enough. And she's not smart. But she got out of this house. Away from your watching, watching, always watching. Always saying a mean thing. Crazy old lady sitting on the porch all day, watching."

He grabbed his dinner plate and clutched it, shaking. Idella thought it might break down the middle, he was holding it so tight. Peas rolled off onto the floor. Their soft tumbling was all that could be heard. No one moved. Then Edward threw the plate across the table toward his mother. "Here! Give this to Albert. Give him my supper!" It landed with a thump in front of her, knocking over her glass. Water pooled and spread, a darkening puddle in the white linen.

He stormed from the dining room, sending a last tremor through the dishes on the table, and out the back of the house. The screen door screeched open and slammed shut. Idella sat, stunned, staring at her plate. There was a crack in it, a faint crack like a vein that linked the dried bits of meat, disappeared under the peas, and ran off the side, right up to the gold rim.

"Well," Mrs. Jensen finally said, her voice gone all funny. "Well. Well."

Mr. Jensen righted the spilled glass and sopped the water with his napkin. He took Eddie's plate, bent down, and gathered up peas from the floor. Nothing was said. He worked gently and quietly. His long arms reached carefully across and in front of Mrs. Jensen, scraping up food.

She seemed not even to see him. The cameo brooch was heaving up and down on her blouse, like it, too, was gasping for air. She moved her head back and forth and began making whimpering sounds. She pursed and unpursed her lips, as though wanting to speak.

Idella felt so heavy—her head, her arms, her chest, all so heavy. She couldn't move. She dared not speak. She only lifted her eyes in thanks when Mr. Jensen removed the plate from in front of her.

"The shortcake. My biscuits," Mrs. Jensen simpered. The starch was all gone out of her. She peered up at Idella, so sad looking. Her thick glasses reflected the glare of the overhead light. "Do you want shortcake, Miss Hillock? Strawberry shortcake?"

"No thank you, Mrs. Jensen," Idella answered. She stood and pushed her chair in. "I'd best go find Eddie. I think he went out back."

She stepped carefully out of the dining room, past the slumped, chittering figure of Eddie's mother. Mr. Jensen was cooing her to calmness like a mourning dove, gently stroking her hand.

Idella walked through the kitchen. Such a nice big kitchen, she thought. She saw the iron skillet askew on the eye of the stove. Dried clumps and shreds of burned meat clung to its bottom in thick patches. Its surface needs priming, Idella thought. A black iron pan is no use for frying if you don't take good care of it.

The back room was taking on the evening's coolness. Its darkness was soothing. Idella walked on through it, past the jars of preserved jams. I wonder what those are like, she thought. Sour probably. Or runny. Poor old soul. She noted the nice stacked shelves along the walls, some lined with empty canning jars. This back room did make a nice summer kitchen. She reached the screen door and swung it open. The raspy, hawing sound of the rusty hinge filled the air like an old crow's call. She stood for a moment, holding the door open, looking out over the garden and field. Chickens quietly clucked in the little henhouse, their gentle pips of noise adding to the sense of quiet. A firefly blinked. Another, farther out.

And there was Eddie, over by the strawberry patch, scooched down on his haunches. He, too, was looking out at the field—a soft gray figure silhouetted in the dimming light, fuzzy around the edges as though sitting in a private fog. Mist rose up from the long field grasses and sat like puffs of smoke in the lower dips and hollows. Idella slipped gratefully out of her new shoes—she wasn't used to wearing that much heel—and stepped down onto the cool, dark grass. She walked toward Eddie, choosing to let go the screen door so it screeched and banged closed behind her. Not for the last time, she thought, as she padded toward him, smiling. Not the last time she'd hear that screen door bang.

In the Family Way

Prescott Mills, Maine
September 1931

"Idella?"

It was impossible to hear clearly over the phone. Idella put a hand over her other ear. "Ethel? Ethel, is that you?" She hated to talk too loud with the phone here in the hall, on the bottom floor of the apartment house on Haskell Street. She'd been washing her hair in the sink when she heard the three-long, two-short ring that was theirs. The towel she'd wrapped around her head kept untwisting, and she needed both hands to get it back together. "Ethel?" She was sure she'd heard Eddie's sister saying her name and then nothing, no sound. "This is Idella. Is that you?"

"It is. It's me."

She sounded terrible. "Is everything okay? You sick?" More silence. "Is Mr. Jensen okay? Ethel, what is it?"

"Idella, I'm . . . I'm . . . Oh, God help me, I'm going to have a baby!"

"A baby!" It came out of Idella like a gust of wind. Her towel fell to the floor behind her, and her wet hair flopped into her face. "You're sure about this?"

"I am. I been to Doc Russo. It's four months now."

"You been to the doctor?" Idella wasn't absorbing the information as quickly as she got it. She could feel herself a beat behind. Four months! She reached up and squeezed the back of her wet hair. Dribbles of still-soapy water went down her back and got her dress wet. What in Holy God's name was Jessie going to do? Who would tell Edward?

"I'm afraid, Idella. I'm afraid to tell."

Idella hesitated. She had to watch what she was saying out here in the hall. Old Mr. Bentley was just coming in with his daily quart of milk. He nodded to her as he shuffled by and opened the door to his apartment. He wouldn't care. But if Mrs. Rice up on the second floor got wind of this, Ethel wouldn't have to worry about who would be doing the telling.

Idella lowered her voice. "Is it? . . . Was it? You know . . . that did it, that was the source?"

"Yes. O' course. He's the only one I been out with, Idella. He said . . ." Ethel was crying. Idella could tell by the jerky gaps in her words. "He promised he loved me . . . and he said . . ." Oh, she was really going to pieces. "He said he'd been fixed. . . ."

"Fixed?" Idella didn't think she'd heard that right.

"Fixed. You know. Not like he was broke, but I thought it didn't work. He told me that. Oh, God, Idella, what am I going to do? You're the only one I dare tell. I had to tell. I'm showing!" Ethel's sobs were coming right through the wire.

It worked all right, Idella thought. That bastard. A soldier stationed down in New Hampshire. He'd seemed nice enough. He'd seemed too nice. Oily. Over Ethel. She was not the type to attract . . . well . . . attractive men. She was proud to be dating someone in a uniform who made her feel special. God knows she'd had so much trouble in her life that everybody just sort of went along with it, hoping she wouldn't get too broken up when he left. No one thought he'd leave her with something.

"I've got to talk to Eddie. He needs to help find him. He's the only one with a car." Ethel was crying so, it was hard to make out the words. "I'm afraid to tell Eddie. I can't tell Mother!"

"Someone's waiting on the phone here, Ethel. You wait there. I'll tell Eddie when he gets home. He has to be told. You go back home and wait. Rest, why don't you?" Foley's Market. That's over a mile she'd walked to make the call. People must be taking notice of her closed up in the booth crying. If she didn't get herself home, Jessie would find out by sundown.

"Get on home now, Ethel. Go on. I'm hanging up. Mrs. Tilden needs the phone." This wasn't true, but she had to get off. Mrs. Tilden was probably glued up against the other side of her apartment door taking notes. Idella'd heard the radio go off in there all of a sudden. And she smelled cigarette smoke.

She went back to the apartment and locked the door, which they normally only did before bed. She had a need to feel safe. She didn't even wash the shampoo out. She sat down at the kitchen table, with the wet towel on her lap, in her slippers, and started worrying.

Poor Ethel. Idella had felt sorry for her upon sight. She was a simple woman. Not stupid, exactly, but simple, plain in every way, and sort of wooden. Even her face didn't move much when she talked. It was a blank expanse, like a sheet of paper with a mouth and some eyes drawn onto it. And her pleasures were simple—always making afghan squares and crocheting doilies. Ethel had a toaster cover she'd made out of purple yarn that Idella thought could not be safe. But Ethel was so proud of it that she never said anything. There was a doll with a big crocheted skirt over the roll of toilet paper. That drove Eddie to distraction. He'd nearly beheaded it one time.

Her going to all that trouble to make covers for things that didn't need covering pointed out the way that Ethel's intentions were good but the thought process behind them was apt to have holes in it.

And bad things did happen to that woman. It was not Ethel's fault that her own father-in-law was a foreman down at the paper mill those ten years ago and that he sent his son out working in a big storm on Thanksgiving. Maybe it was because it was his son and he didn't want to appear to play favorites. Whatever the reason, that man sent his own son, Ethel's husband, out across the catwalk, and he slipped on the ice and fell into the machine, and that was that.

For years Ethel had to be helped through Thanksgiving. Even after Idella'd come on the scene, it was a solemn occasion.

And that father-in-law cut Ethel out! He did not help support her or offer help for those kids. And the mill itself gave her a measly six hundred dollars in payment. And for the longest time, they would not hire her. What matter if she wasn't going to be their best worker? They owed her at least that much, those damn men over there. They ruled lives in this town. Every week, for years, Ethel would walk down to the mill and ask about getting hired. The paper mill hired hundreds of workers. But they wouldn't take on Ethel until four or five years passed. It was a crime, Idella thought, an actual crime. Now, at least, Ethel was one of the clerks. She could do that, and she should have been doing it a lot sooner.

Idella sighed. Entering into a family could be such a muddle. She sat there for over an hour, till a jingle for Camel cigarettes, Eddie's brand, came on the radio and roused her. She looked at the clock and saw that it was five. He would be home inside of twenty minutes.

She quick rinsed out her hair and changed from her wet dress. There was no supper ready. She looked in the fridge and saw the eggs. She would have to do some fancy footwork, cook up some eggs, put them in front of him on a plate, and call it supper.

She was slicing bread for toast, lost in ways to tell Eddie, when she heard him pounding on the front door. She'd left it locked.

"Idella! What the hell is going on? You in there?"

"I'm coming." She ran to the door and unlocked it.

"Why've you got the goddamn door locked?" He stopped and looked at her. "Why is your hair wet?" He put his brimmed hat and car keys on the coffee table and looked around the room. "Is something going on here?"

"No. No. Nothing." Idella went into the kitchen without looking at his face directly.

"You want a beer, Eddie?"

"Beer'd be good." She got one out of the fridge and brought it to him. "You sit on the couch while I finish with supper. Put your feet up. Hard day?"

"Christ, yes. I'm so sick of watching tin cans come down the line. I'm getting out soon. Them guys think they know everything, and they don't know nothing. Franklin telling Cobb there next to me to move things along. Asshole. Cobb's doing his job. That Franklin never says anything to me, by God." Eddie sat drinking his beer. He looked around. "Why was the door locked?"

"No reason. Habit."

"You didn't want someone coming in and robbing you while you was bent over the sink washing your hair?" Eddie laughed. "Is that it?"

He came into the kitchen, stood behind her, and kissed her neck. "I'll bother you. Would that be all right?"

"It's not too good an idea just now." She stopped whisking the fork through the eggs and moved over to light the stove.

"What's for supper?" Eddie looked into the bowl. "What's this? Eggs?"

"Yes." Idella tapped a pat of butter into the frying pan.

"Eggs for supper?"

"Why not?" She kept her eyes on the butter pooling and bubbling about the pan.

"Eggs is breakfast. What's going on here, Idella? You got someone holed up in the closet?"

Idella took a deep breath and turned to face him. "Your sister called me today."

"I'll kill the bastard! I'll murder him!" Edward had been mouthing threats since they'd roared out of their driveway on Haskell Street. He gripped the steering wheel so hard that Idella feared it might come off in his hands when he made the sharp turn on Elm Street. He pulled in to the drive of Ethel's small clapboard house and was out of the car, at the front door, before Idella had her feet out.

"Ethel! Let me in! Where is he run off to?" Eddie was pounding on the door and ringing the bell at the same time. "I'll make that goddamned bastard pay for what he done!"

Ethel opened the door slowly. As soon as she saw her brother standing there, she burst into tears.

"Where is he? Where is the bastard?" Eddie charged into the house as if Ethel's boyfriend was hiding in a closet or behind the couch. Idella hurried up the wooden steps and closed the door behind her. She locked it. The whole neighborhood would be listening.

"He's run off, Eddie." Idella saw that Ethel's face was wet from crying. "He's disappeared."

"How can a soldier disappear?"

"I went there. I went down to New Hampshire to the base. So help me, Eddie. I took the bus. I tried to talk to the officers, but they wouldn't let me through." Ethel was sobbing. "They won't tell me where he's been moved to. He's gone somewhere else, and they won't tell me."

"Oh, my God." Idella went up to Ethel and led her over to the couch to sit. "You have been doing this all alone. Why didn't you tell us sooner?"

"I'm so scared. I'm ashamed. He said he loved me. I thought he'd marry me."

"There, there." Idella put her arm around Ethel's slumped body and tried to calm her. It did look like she had a little belly starting up there. Her dress was pulling some across her middle.

"He loved you, all right, that bastard! On Saturday night with a drink in him. Come Sunday he was sober. He was thinking of other things."

"Edward! Don't talk to her like that!"

"You're in a fix now, by God. We all are! Goddamned son of a bitch.

And you, acting like a whore! Bringing some soldier home like a god-damned whore! With your own kids upstairs sleeping!"

"Edward, stop this right now!"

"We can't tell Ma," Eddie said, ignoring Idella.

"I know it. I know we can't. She'll disown me."

"Oh, now, Ethel." Idella squeezed her limp hand. It was wet as a fish. "She is your mother. She loves you. She'll help as best she can."

"No. She won't help." Ethel was sobbing full out. "She'll hate me."

"She won't help, Idella." Eddie, who had been roaming the room like a penned bull, stopped and looked at her. "Ma can't know."

"This is the goddamnedest group of people I have ever married into. Are you saying she will cut out her own daughter and grandchild?"

"That's what I'm saying, Idella!" Eddie roared. "And she'll make Dad do it, too. All of us!"

"I can't believe this."

"She will," Ethel sobbed. "She won't."

"That's what we're saying!"

That night Idella lay wide awake next to Eddie. She knew that he was awake, too. They'd been lying side by side, not touching any part of each other while the clock ticked endlessly next to Eddie's pillow. Every turn or audible breath was self-conscious. Idella was not going to be the one to speak first. She was too upset.

"I don't mean to do it," Eddie mumbled into the dark.

"Do what?"

"Get so mad. It comes over me. I can't stop it."

"I know it. I guess I know it. But it doesn't help things much."

"No, it don't. But I don't know what to do."

"Ethel's in the middle of it."

"It was a goddamned fool thing to do!"

"Oh, go on. It's human. That woman has been left alone with those three boys since the day I met her. It's over ten years since the accident. My God. All alone with those kids. I know what that's like. She's homely as a post, but she's got feelings. And along comes someone who pays her some attention, after all these years of nothing. You'd do the same damn thing if you were in her shoes. I would."

"You would?"

"Yes, I would, by God. I think." Idella rolled away from him. "It is certainly possible that I might." She sighed. "Christ, I don't know what I'd do."

There was a long silence between them. Idella rolled onto her back and looked up at the ceiling. The light fixture was crooked, and she didn't suppose anyone would ever get around to straightening it out. It'd fall down on top of them first.

"She that ugly?"

"She's not pretty, let's put it that way."

"I look like her?"

"Just the legs."

"Let's see your legs."

"No." Idella smiled at the ceiling.

"Let me feel them, then." Eddie reached a hand over toward her.

Idella scrunched her legs up into a ball and turned away from him. "No."

He put his hand on her knee. "You'd date a soldier? If I was to run off?"

Idella smiled. "I wouldn't wait any ten years either."

"Is that so?"

He turned her toward him. She let her legs stretch out long. She was soft and pliable now. He took her into his arms.

"What are we going to do?" Idella whispered.

"We're going to forget about it. For now." He kissed her, and she kissed him back.

"Well, ladies, I think the October meeting of the Ladies' Townsend Club is adjourned." Abigail Wynn banged her wooden gavel lightly onto the card table. Many of the ladies, all members of the Universalist Church on Main Street, had already begun tying kerchiefs over their hairdos and pulling gloves from their coat pockets.

Idella breathed a sigh of relief. This meeting could not end soon enough. They'd all managed to get through it without incident. She'd get Jessie bundled up and back to the house in time to fix Eddie's parents some dinner, then go down to Ethel's and help do her laundry and get her kids fed, before getting home to fix something for her and Eddie to eat.

"Come on, Jessie, I'll help you with your coat. Arlene offered us a ride home." She leaned over and helped Jessie heave her coat up over her shoulders. She handed Jessie her hat. Out of the corner of her eye, Idella saw Agnes Knight approach. "Put your hat on, Jessie."

Agnes walked right up to Jessie and leaned over her, smiling. "How's Ethel getting on, Jessie?" Idella breathed in quick, as if an ice cube had been slipped down her back.

"Ethel?" Jessie looked up, her hat on but not secured.

Oh, Lord. Idella felt her stomach ball up inside of her. The meeting was almost done, she was almost out the door, and that Agnes Knight and her big mouth had just asked the question that everyone had been avoiding during the entire October meeting. Agnes's head was even thicker than Jessie's.

"Oh, Ethel's all right, I guess. I wish she'd come up to help me finish with the garden, but that's always been true. There's pumpkins that need going over, and the end of the squash."

"She's feeling all right? No complications or anything?"

"Complications? Ethel? No, that girl is as simple as mud."

"Well, I'm glad to hear that."

"Glad?" Jessie looked at Agnes. "I think I'd have preferred a little more spark. But what can you do? You get what God gives you."

"It's getting on time to head home now, Jessie. Are were finished with the business?" Idella looked pleadingly around the circle of women.

"Oh, yes." Abigail nodded at Idella. She understood. "I'm putting my gavel away till next month. We'll be discussing the church Spring Fair booths next time. And the theme for decorations. I know it seems early, with Halloween just upon us, but we all know how much time it takes to get the Spring Fair up. So keep thinking of decoration ideas."

The women took their cue and started reaching for hats and purses. Barb Jackson headed into the bathroom with her lipstick in her hand. Jessie kept talking.

"Course, I've noticed Ethel is putting on the weight lately." Jessie's voice rose up suddenly above all others. "It's the Scoullar body coming out. I was born a Scoullar." There was dead silence in the room, save for Jessie's voice scraping the air. "Eddie's got it, too. Starts in the belly and works its way down. A thickening, like pudding. It's our lot. Nice faces, every one of us. And thick bodies. At least she's not pregnant."

All movement stopped. Barb Jackson did not make it to the bathroom. Coats hung on the shoulders of some women with sleeves dangling loose.

"Time to go home now." Idella was near to panicking.

"Not like that Goyette girl up the road from me. I'm sure you all know she's in the family way. No husband anywhere from here to China. She's having a bastard baby. Walking up and down the hill out in front of our house like as if she had nothing to be ashamed of. Why, she said good morning to me the other day and waved! Imagine!"

"Jessie, it's time we were all going on home. Arlene Roberts has offered to ride us up to the house."

"Oh. Oh, yes. Well. Help me up here, Idella. Been a nice meeting."

Idella helped her to stand and balance on her two canes.

"Hand me my purse there, Idella. I'm ready. Are you?"

"Oh, yes," Idella said. "I'm ready." She waved at the stilled women as she steered Jessie out of the church meeting room. Abigail waved back, shaking her head just enough to give Idella some comfort.

"Do you mean to tell me the old bat still doesn't know?" Avis was sitting across from Idella at the kitchen table, smoking. She had arrived the night before from Boston. They had been passing one of Eddie's bottles of beer back and forth.

A huge Hubbard squash from the Jensens' garden lay between them, pale blue-gray and shaped like a sitting partridge. They were supposed to be hacking it open and scraping out seeds, but once Avis asked if anything new was happening in the burg of Prescott Mills, with little hope of reply, and Idella had said, "Well, as a matter of fact, yes," not much had gotten done, though the beer was almost finished.

"She does not know. That's what I'm telling you."

"She notice that Ethel's getting a big belly?"

"Just enough to rant that she's getting fat."

"How big is she?"

"She's getting on to the size of this squash here. By Christmas she'll be bigger."

"Jesus." Avis choked on her cigarette.

"I am beside myself with the intrigue of it. I'm pretty sure everyone in the greater Portland area knows—except Jessie." Idella upended the bottle of beer and drank the last of it. She put it down onto the table with a clunk and a sigh.

"And the father?"

"Oh, Mr. Jensen goes down to see her whenever he can. He brings her little things from the garden. And I've seen him slip her some money. But it's all on the sly, so Jessie won't find out."

"I mean of the baby, the father of the baby."

"Oh. Him. Well. He might as well be killed in action for all the army will tell us. He don't want to be found, and they're not going to make him be. It's shameful."

"Did he know about the baby?"

"Ethel told him. That was the last she saw of him, the absolute last. Eddie went down there, you know. He went storming down to New Hampshire to the army base. He caused quite a stir. You can imagine."

Avis nodded. "Only just."

"He was at fit peak! But they still wouldn't tell him anything." Idella paused. "I think he might have done more harm than good."

She reached out and put her hand on the firm curve of the Hubbard.

Avis kept smoking, watching Idella's fingers play over the squash. "Where is he in all this?"

Idella shook her head. "Oh, it's a mess. Eddie tries to help Ethel, in small ways, but he doesn't want to be involved. He's ashamed. You know. He'd like to wash his hands of the whole thing."

Avis narrowed her eyes and gave Idella one of her looks that she had seen many a time. She could feel it boring into her. Idella put her hand up. "Don't say it. Whatever you are about to throw out about Eddie, you can keep to yourself."

"I don't have to say anything. You think it yourself. Not involved, my ass. Embarrassed. Jesus."

"No more, Avis." Idella pointed a warning finger at her. "And you are to keep your mouth shut about it at all times."

"Yes, ma'am."

Avis stubbed out her cigarette and slapped her hand on top of the squash. "How are we going to get into this damn thing anyway?"

"Throw it on the floor and crack it wide open." Idella was feeling a slight trill from the beer she'd drunk. "Stand out of my way." She took up the gray squash, lifted it over her head, and threw it onto the kitchen floor. It landed with a thump and cracked into three large, jagged pieces, revealing bright orange flesh. A mass of pale white seeds spewed out onto the floor like big, slippery buttons.

Idella reached down and picked up the largest of the pieces. "Let's break it even more!"

"Jesus, Idella." Avis was laughing. "I'm getting out of your way."

"You better, by God." Idella raised the jagged hunk of squash and plunged it to the floor to splat and crack and spew more seeds. "This is just November," she said. "Imagine what state we'll all be in by Christmas."

"I'll be in Massachusetts," Avis said. "I think you might want to park your wagon in one of the Dakotas, Idella. Or maybe the North Pole."

"Where's my glass of cold cider? I asked Ethel, and nothing's come of it."

Jessie sat the middle of Ethel's couch. Her two black canes were on either side of her short legs, and she leaned back against one of those afghans Ethel was always making, this one a checkered yellowy green and orange. Jessie sat, bursting the seams of her black dress, looking for all the world like a fat spider, dead center of her garish web.

"She's got her hands full with the turkey going so slow." Idella headed into the kitchen for cider, glad to be out of the stuffed chair. She gave Mr. Jensen a pat on his knee as she passed. That he hadn't even attempted to get Jessie's drink was a sure sign he was at his limit.

Ethel's house seemed so dark and crowded. Even the little Christmas tree Eddie had managed to set up in the corner only added to the confusion and jumble. Paper stars and wallpaper chains dangled and overlapped from the tips of the branches. Ethel's boys had done the trimming without her. She was too heavy and swollen to bother.

Idella walked between the dining table and the card table, set up for Ethel's three half-grown boys. She wasn't at all hungry. This was the damnedest Christmas dinner she would ever live through—if she did live through it.

Ethel, a full seven months along now, leaned against the front of the stove, gripping the oven handle. An apron was tied around her middle, over the loose housedress she wore to hide the pregnancy from her mother.

"Your apron's kind of tight there." Idella came up behind and loosened the bow. "You go sit. Sit." Ethel nodded limply and started to shuffle out of the kitchen. "How much longer do you think it'll need?"

"I don't know, Idella." Ethel was at the end here, Idella could tell.

Eddie came lumbering into the kitchen. "Christ, Idella, will you get her that cider?"

"You get it, Eddie. I'm going to see this turkey through." All the while she spoke, Idella was getting the glass and pouring out the cider. She handed it to Eddie.

"Pour me one, too."

"Honestly!" Idella got another glass and handed it over. She motioned silently to him to help Ethel sit down.

Left alone for a minute, Idella put her hand to her forehead and took a deep breath. Mother of God. What a circus.

The smells in the kitchen were thick, unpleasant. They had a weight to them that hung in the air and pressed on her face. The turkey reeked. Ethel'd put too much sage into that bird. She must have used a child's shovel's worth. Idella opened the oven door. The bird looked like bare rock: It was bald and naked and unbasted. Whatever juices it might have had had left this earth an hour back.

She lifted the cover on the brussels sprouts. They were sogging up in the kettle, more yellow now than green. They smelled like the paper mill. She covered them. The potatoes, glopped into a serving bowl, were cold already.

At least the pies would be good. Idella'd made them—two apple, a mincemeat, and a nice little pumpkin. She'd used the canned filling to make it but did not consider that cheating in the face of all the other things she had to do.

She opened the oven again. Hell—that turkey must be done enough. She reached in and jostled a leg. It had a little give. It'd have to do. She walked into the living room. "I'd say five minutes till the turkey can come out. Ethel, you stay where you are. Me and Eddie'll get it all out on the table."

Ethel nodded. That woman was at rock bottom. She never let someone else take over hostess duties in her little house.

"Eddie, go call the boys in for dinner. They're out in the snow still."

"Bring me my plate of food, Eddie." Jessie was plumping the pillow behind her, leaning forward and beating it with her fist. "Right over here. I'm not up to sitting at the table."

"I can't be three places at once, goddamn it!"

Jens headed to the door. "I'll call the boys. They've been having fun out there throwing snow."

"Them kids are staying out as long as they can," Idella whispered to Eddie as they lugged the roasting pan to the counter and hoisted the turkey onto a platter.

Eddie stared at it. "Why isn't it brown?"

"Your next challenge is to carve it. By rights it should wait twenty minutes." Idella looked at the turkey. "For the juices to absorb." She shook her head. "But there aren't any."

Eddie carried the turkey to the table while Idella hauled out bowls of food. "I thought we'd eat buffet style," she said brightly, looking over at Jessie.

"Yes, I'm so nice and settled. Ethel, get me a little stool of some sort, will you? To put my tired feet up. And bring me a plate with extra potato."

"I'll do that, Jessie." Idella gave Ethel a direct look that planted her back into the chair she was half out of.

The three boys came bursting into the house, bringing a swoop of cold air behind them. It felt refreshing to Idella.

"Close that door!" Jessie screamed, before they were even done opening it.

Idella looked at Eddie. He had the knife and was going at the turkey like it was a tree he was cutting down. Ethel's boys got out of their boots and snow pants and coats. Jens helped line the wet mittens along the top of the radiator in the hall. They sat themselves at the card table.

"You hungry?" Idella smiled down. They were good kids. They all nodded back at her and put their elbows on the table. Arnie, the oldest, reached over and grabbed a roll. The other two protested, and he smiled and tossed one to each of them. Their cheeks were so red and full of life. Crusty bits of frozen snow still clung to their sweater cuffs. They'd been making snowballs. Idella wanted to reach out and feel the freshness of their skin, rub her hand over their impossibly round cheeks.

She didn't know just what they understood about their mother's situation. They sure knew enough not to breathe a live word of it in front of

Grammie Jensen. They talked of nothing but snowballs, sleds, and hunger.

"You kids wipe your feet?" Jessie never let up.

"Ma, they're hungry. Leave 'em be." It was unusual for Ethel to give her mother even that much lip. Idella looked over at her. She had closed her eyes and rested her head against one of the doilies she'd crocheted and pinned all over the furniture arms and backs. Ethel tried to make old furniture look good by pinning them over the bald spots and cat-torn arms, but the straight pins she used were always finding their way into the back of your neck or wrist.

"This damned thing is coming apart like shoestrings." Eddie hunched over the turkey. The knife looked so dull it wouldn't cut butter. The blood was rising up to his ears.

"Get me a leg, Eddie," Jessie called. "That don't need slicing."

Everyone watched Eddie wrestle the turkey's leg. He was starting to fume. Jens quietly stepped forward and held down the body with two firm hands. With an angry jerk, Eddie pulled the leg free. He stood frozen, the leg held aloft like a prize.

Idella brought a plate of food, featuring the leg, over to Jessie.

Jessie sat looking down at the drumstick. "That looks chewy. I'll have a slice of breast."

Eddie scraped off enough shreds of meat for everyone. Jens volunteered for the one drumstick; the other stayed firmly attached. Idella dolloped vegetables and handed out plates. Ethel took hers quietly, not eating much.

"Everyone got what they need?" Idella surveyed the plates.

"I'd like some gravy," Eddie muttered.

"There isn't any." Idella looked straight at him so that he knew not to say another word. She leaned toward him and whispered, "There's no stuffing either, so don't ask."

"Is there pie?" he muttered, his face red. "Will I get my pie?"

Idella nodded to keep him still.

They ate in strained silence. Idella didn't have the strength to comment on how good it all tasted. "Weary" was not the word. At least they were near the end here. Pie, wash and dry, then home like a bandit, that was her plan.

"You know, I hate to be the one to say it, Ethel." Jessie's voice broke the stillness. "But you're getting thick. Right down through your middle. Your body's matching up with them heavy legs of yours."

"Ma" is all Eddie could get out.

"Well, it happened to you, too, Edward. Why you two couldn't have taken after your father in body, I'll go to my grave regretting."

As long as she gets there, Idella thought. "I'll start cutting up the pies." She motioned to Eddie to come and help.

"When I was a girl, I had a trim figure. Isn't that right, Jens? I was admired. Here, take my plate. I had three young men after me at the same time. Jens was the fourth. I liked his accent, from so far off. Denmark. I didn't want a local boy."

Jens gathered up dinner plates, and Idella set about slicing the pies. She saw that Ethel's cheeks were turning bright red. Thick like pudding. Jesus. She handed Eddie a plate with three kinds of pie. "Give that to her directly."

"Now, when do I get mine?" he asked.

"When everyone else has theirs." She handed him more plates.

"Is this pumpkin from the can, Idella?"

"Yes—I think it's good."

Jessie spoke with her mouth full of pie. "You know, speaking of getting thick, I been noticing more and more lately, that little Goyette girl. . . . You know her, Idella?"

"I don't believe so." Idella loaded three triangles of pie onto Eddie's plate and handed it to him.

He smiled and took it.

"Well, that little girl is a woman now, I can tell you that. Eddie, bring me a second piece of mincemeat." Eddie, halted halfway to his chair, grabbed her plate and shoved it toward Idella.

"She is carrying a child . . . a *bastard* child!" Forks stopped. Idella, pie in her mouth, was unable to swallow. Ethel was looking down into her plate, her shoulders quivering. Idella didn't see how she could hold tight much longer.

"Have you seen her, Ethel?"

Eddie, intent on eating his pie, sat in the cushioned chair and leaned back onto one of Ethel's lace doilies. His mouth was already open for his first bite.

"Jesus H. Christ!" He lurched suddenly and slapped at the back of his neck. "Goddamn it all to hell!" The pie spewed from his plate. "I've been bit. There's a bee, goddamn it! I've been bit!" A mound of mincemeat landed on Jessie's foot. Globs of pumpkin stuck to the blowsy roses on Ethel's sad, dark wallpaper.

Idella could see the sharp glint of a straight pin sticking through the white doily it was meant to hold in place. Eddie's neck had landed on it full force.

"Now, this is like that time you lost everything in your stomach over at Aunt Sema's, Eddie." Jessie reached down and scraped the mincemeat off her foot with a finger. She held it out for inspection. "She'd made chocolate cake and strawberry shortcake for Fourth of July. It all came back up on you, as you'd had too much of both. Come out of you like a mud slide. Terrible smelling. I've never been so embarrassed in my life. Brown and red, it was. Some orange."

Idella dipped her napkin into a water glass and gave it to Eddie for his wound. She bent down and scooped up the splotches of pumpkin and smears of cream from off the floor and cushions. She licked her finger. The bit of sweet apple tasted good.

"Sema wasn't a good cook. Could have been her cooking. Course, I had food poisoning the one time. Remember, Jens? It was the fish you brought home. I had things coming from both ends at once."

Idella took a deep breath. There would be no more talk of the Goyette girl. Or thickening. Not today. She had heard this story often and long, but she had never enjoyed it till now.

Idella was alone in the kitchen up to the old house. She was standing at the table slicing cabbages for a boiled dinner. Beets and carrots and potatoes from last year's garden were piled about, waiting to be pared. On the stove the corned beef was simmering. Jens had brought it up from the cellar for her this morning. It'd been soaking in the crock of brine for two days.

There had been three dead mice on the cellar floor and signs of recent activity among the potatoes down there, so Jens and Eddie were looking for holes and nailing them over with tin or stuffing them with plaster. Every now and again, she'd hear pounding from below. These old houses were impossible, and of course there was a whole field of mice wanting to come in from the cold. Idella thought they were probably well established, making more and more babies. She sighed at the thought. Poor Ethel, making her one.

Thank God February was the shortest month and they were almost through it. There was still sloppy snow on the ground. One day it'd be sunny and melt, then it'd be cold and all turn to ice. Walking was treacherous, so they'd driven the short ways up from their apartment on Haskell Street.

Lately they'd been coming to help every Saturday, since Ethel was now in her ninth month and not up to any of it. They told Jessie she had a bad cold or one of the kids did, and she didn't question it because she didn't want to catch it. Idella didn't know how long they would get away with excuses. It was turning into a day-to-day trial of endurance.

It felt good to bang the knife hard down into the cutting board and watch the convoluted slices fall away. Even a cabbage was beautiful if you had a good look at it—such a pale green, with all those designs hidden inside.

It was nice being alone in this big kitchen. The house and garden and big field behind it were all so pleasurable in the afternoon quiet. You could even hear birds outside. There were lots of little songs going back and forth across the field and in the trees. Chickadees. Winter birds.

Jessie was attending a lunch party down at the church for Clara White, who'd been living in Florida the past year with her husband. The poor husband had died within six months from two heart attacks, and Clara hated the hot weather and moved right back to Prescott Mills as soon as she could arrange it, which was last Tuesday. Idella'd gotten all the details from Jessie before her ride had come to get her, and she was sure there'd be plenty more details after she got back.

Idella took up a beet. The earth still clung roughly to its outside, and she held it up and breathed in the raw, comforting smell before starting to peel it. It was good for Jessie to get out. She so rarely went anywhere, and she would be stoked up with gossip. That made her happy, if anything ever did.

Idella heard a car drive up and stop outside the gate. Oh, well. She'd hoped to have another hour at least. She wiped her hands on her apron and went out to the porch. Jessie would need help getting through the yard and up the steps.

Walking carefully over patches of ice and wet snow, Idella got to the car just as Jessie, helped by Abigail Wynn, emerged from the back seat. She gripped her two canes, said not a word of greeting or good-bye, and started marching stoutly toward the house.

"I'm sorry, Idella," Abigail said, getting back behind the wheel. Her motor was still running. "You'd best make sure she doesn't fall, honey." Then Abigail waved and pulled out and down the road. Idella, frozen for a moment between arrival and departure, hurried up behind Jessie. "Was it a nice lunch?" she called, trying to sound cheery.

Jessie said nothing. She placed one cane and then the other in front of her and walked with small, deliberate steps over the sloppy ground. Idella reached over to take an arm, but Jessie flinched and pulled away.

Oh, dear, Idella thought. The cat is on the roof.

She scooted in front of Jessie and held the door open. Jessie plowed past her and clumped steadily up the front steps, through the porch, and into the kitchen. Eddie and Jens were just coming up from the cellar. Eddie had a hammer and Jens a trowel covered with plaster. Both men stood still at the cellar doorway when they saw Jessie's near-to-bursting face.

She clumped over to the table and sat down. "I don't have a daughter." She lifted one of her canes and banged the floor with it. "I've got one son living and one son passed on at one month old. My Albert. But I don't have a daughter."

Her voice ricocheted around the kitchen. "It is a wonder I didn't fall over and die right there in the middle of the luncheon. 'When's that baby due?' Clara White come up to me all smiles—and evil. 'What baby might that be?' I asked her, thinking she meant that Goyette girl up the hill, the only baby being born soon that I knew about." Jessie clutched the tops of her canes like her fingers were claws. Her knuckles looked yellow. "'Why, Ethel's baby, of course! I saw her on the street.' She laughed like I was making a joke. 'She must be within one month.' I managed to nod. I'd done all the speaking I was going to till I got myself home."

No one moved. All three stood speechless, staring at Jessie's rage. Idella could feel her heart trying to get out and fly.

"So that's all the thickening in the middle that's been taking place." Jessie now turned and spoke to them accusingly. "And I thought Ethel was just getting fat like her mother. I'll never show my face outside this house again."

She leaned forward onto her canes and hoisted herself to standing. "I attended my last outing today. And I lost a daughter." She started to walk out of the kitchen. "I need to lie down." In the doorway she stopped and looked over at Jens. "That woman is never again to enter this house. She is not welcome. And neither is her bastard."

Idella looked over at Eddie, who stood pressing the hammer head against a palm and twisting it, like he was going to twist it right through his hand. He stared down at the floor. "Eddie, let's get home." He nodded.

They left the boiled dinner as it was. Idella turned off the flame under the corned beef. Jens sat slumped at the kitchen table, his hands smeared with dried plaster. "She's so stubborn," he said softly as Idella put a hand on his shoulder. "Stubborn through the bones."

Eddie and Idella left the house, got into the car, and pulled out onto Longfellow Street.

"Seems like you could have said something." Idella looked out her side window. It was clear and cold out now. The afternoon was harsh with light against the battered piles of snow. "Seems like you could have spoken up then for your sister and that poor baby."

"What am I supposed to say, Idella?"

"Seems like you could have said something. To keep that old lady quiet."

"There is no keeping her quiet, Idella."

Idella sighed. "I suppose not. Still, you could have tried."

Edward kept his eyes on the splay of cards before him. "Della, get me them nuts out of the cupboard, will you? Them mixed nuts I brought home." He didn't even look at her while he gave his orders. "I see your three, and I'll raise you two." He threw more poker chips onto the pile in the middle of the table. Idella was trying her best to carry on as though this was just a regular Saturday-night card game with the Martins from downstairs.

She went into the kitchen to find his damn nuts. She was so restless inside she was glad to get up and move around. How could he play cards and eat nuts and drink beer and carry on like nothing in the world was happening, nothing at all—when he knew perfectly well that Ethel was practically all alone, down in that little house of hers, trying to deliver a baby? His own sister! He was ashamed. He was afraid of what people might think or say—just like that goddamned mother of his. Idella wanted to let out a scream that would wake the dead.

"Get me another beer while you're at it, Della. And one for Harold." She wanted to pour the beer on top of his head and put the damn nuts down the back of his collar and under his fat ass.

"You want anything more to drink, Cora?" Idella asked.

"Oh, no thank you, Idella. Unless you've got some ginger ale. I wouldn't say no to a ginger ale."

Idella sighed and opened the fridge again. "We've got root beer left, is all, Cora. And an Orange Crush. You want one of them?"

"Oh, Orange Crush sounds good."

Idella never enjoyed these card nights all that much. Cora was kind of touchy. Finicky. And Harold took winning as seriously as Eddie did, so there was always at least one sore loser. Idella poured the nuts into a bowl. Eddie had been into the bag. Most of the cashews were missing.

She didn't want to be standing here pouring out cold drinks. She wanted to go to that house and do what she could to help that poor woman have that baby. She wanted to see a baby get born. Things could happen, delivering a baby at home like that. It had killed her own mother. At least the doctor would be there by now. Ethel had gotten Arnie to run to the store and make phone calls. Poor kid.

Idella put the bottle of soda down half poured. She stood in the kitchen doorway, still holding the cold bottle, and looked as faint and poorly as she could muster. She leaned against the frame. "You know, this is unusual for me, but I am suddenly struck with a terrible headache."

"Why, Idella, come sit down." Cora was up and over there, taking the drink from her hand.

"You left your cards up, Cora. We know what you've got." Eddie flipped her fan of cards over.

"Well, we're not staying." Cora led Idella by the hand over to her chair and sat her down. "Do you want a cool cloth, Idella?"

"I always heard ice on the back of the neck." Harold smiled at Idella.

"Eddie." Idella stared over at him until he looked her in the eye. "Eddie, I am afraid that I need to lie down. I hate to break up the party."

"Oh, shush, Idella. We've played enough already. We've lost five dollars, me and Harold. I think our luck's run out. Get your hat, Harold. It's time to go."

"How about finishing out this last hand? I got something here." Eddie was holding his cards close. He smiled at Harold and Cora. "Maybe it's not as good as I think, see, and you'll get your five dollars back."

"Next week, Eddie. Let's go, Harold. Idella needs to rest." Cora gave Idella a peck on the cheek, and Idella opened her eyes and nodded ever so slightly. She managed a wan smile, then put her hand to her forehead.

"You get her to bed, Eddie. Harold, let's go. Now."

Harold reached over and patted Idella's knee. "I hope you feel better soon, Idella. The boss is calling. I've got to move. Good night, Eddie."

"Night."

They left, closing the door softly behind them, like they were leaving a sickroom.

Eddie sat stacking the poker chips by color and slipping them back into the wooden holder. He didn't say anything. Idella sat in the chair with her eyes closed and waited until she heard the Martins all the way down the stairs.

She listened to Eddie riffling the cards, sliding them smoothly between each other again and again. Suddenly she stood. "Get your hat and keys. We're going to Ethel's, and we're leaving now. I am not going to leave her in that house to have that baby all by herself with no family present."

"I'm not going, Idella." Eddie kept moving the cards through each other. "She got herself into this." He stopped and looked up at her. "She's having a bastard."

"I am beyond angry! Beyond!"

"If I go help Ethel, Mother'll disown me, too."

"Oh, wouldn't that be too bad! Wouldn't that be a sad, sad thing! To have that goddamned mean old woman out of our lives!"

"But it's for my father! How do I cut off my father? If I don't mow the lawn and plow the field—if you don't pull the weeds from her garden—then he'll do it. And she'll be cackling at him the whole time to get it done faster."

"You can't let her run things. That woman is not right in the head. She is not capable of thinking one thing after another in a straight line. And you people let her run all over you. I've been keeping my mouth shut since joining this family. But I'll be goddamned if I'm not going to help Ethel. My God, I would help any woman in her situation. And a baby is a baby. A poor, innocent little bit of life that deserves to be welcomed into this world."

"It'll be Dad that pays."

"Why can't he stand up for himself?"

"I don't know." Edward shook his head. "He never did. He says she's sick and don't know any better."

"Imagine, her forbidding him to see his own pregnant daughter! And him obeying! Sneaking and worrying and trying to see her on the sly! What is the matter with you men? Where is your backbone?"

"I can't do it, Idella. I can't get involved."

"You *are* involved! Goddamn it, Edward, you *are* involved!" Idella reached across the table and grabbed the deck of cards from Eddie's hands. "And let me tell you another thing." They looked straight at each other. "If you treat Ethel any longer the way that you have been treating her, acting like she has committed the first and biggest sin since time began—if you don't welcome this child into the family with open arms . . . then I am not going to stay with you."

Eddie looked as though she had slapped him hard.

"You and I both know that the same thing could have happened to me as happened to Ethel." She stood above him and leaned closely toward him, her hands spread flat on the table. "We got carried away more than once before we were married. And that could have been me at Christmas dinner, seven months along with your baby. Now, you get your keys, by God, and you get me to your sister."

Edward sat for a long time, clenching his fists into tight wads and releasing them. Suddenly he crumpled forward, his head falling onto his chest, his arms like heavy ropes before him on the table. He began to sob. Idella had never heard these sounds from him. She stood before him, unable to move.

"I'm sorry, Idella." Eddie gasped. "I'm ashamed." He lifted a heavy hand and started to pound it against his chest. Idella reached over and took his hand in both of hers. He put his head up against her stomach, like a child, and sobbed.

"Come on, Eddie," Idella whispered. "Let's go get a new baby born into this family."

*   *   *

When they got to Ethel's, the doctor was still there. Mrs. Olsen from across the street had come over to help. Ethel's three kids were upstairs in their bedroom.

As soon as Idella walked in, she knew she'd missed it. Lying next to Ethel's bed was the cradle, and Idella could see right away that it was occupied. A bundle no bigger than a loaf of bread lay quietly under a flannel sheet. Ethel, pale and worn out, was asleep, one hand resting on the baby.

"She worked hard," the doctor said. "She's spent. Fine baby boy she's got. All the parts in all the right places. Let her rest. See to the kids upstairs. I expect they're curious and hungry. Mrs. Olsen here has been a great help. Maybe she can go home now."

"Oh, yes," Idella said. "You go on home. We were delayed. But we're here now."

Eddie walked over and looked down at the sleeping figures. He couldn't help but smile. "For God's sake. Look at them little fingers. He's making a fist already."

Idella came and stood next to him. She reached down and touched the top of the baby's head. It was still damp. "Oh," she said. "Oh, my."

Ethel stirred and opened her eyes. "Eddie?"

"I'm here."

"You seen him, Eddie?"

"He's fine, Ethel."

"I am shamed till the day I die!" Idella heard Jessie harping all the while she and Eddie opened the front gate and walked across the yard. She looked miserably at him as he held the screen door open. For more than four months, Jessie had refused to have anything to do with Ethel or the baby. But she never did stop talking about it. She gave them all no peace whatsoever.

Jessie had taken the picture of Ethel and Eddie as children down off the living-room shelf and cut it in two. It made Idella sick. "Look," Jessie'd said, pointing proudly, "look what I done." She'd stopped going to her women's club. She refused to leave the house. Every day she sat out on the porch, cold as it was for the end of June, all wrapped up in afghans Ethel had made for her, and watched people walking by.

"Let's get this over with," Eddie whispered to Idella as they entered the kitchen. She and Eddie continued to come up to the house every Saturday morning to help out. Then they'd go down to Ethel's and try to help her get to the store for groceries or to the doctor's or what have you. It was a strain on everyone. Jens would slip away when he could to see the baby. He had to do it on the sly and never for more than thirty minutes at a time, or she'd rake him over the coals with her questions.

When they entered the dining room, they saw Jessie leaning over her two canes in front of the big table. Her special dishes and her few pieces of silver were spread out in rows before her.

"What's all this?" Eddie asked.

"They're yours now, Idella. I don't have a daughter now, except you. I want you to have it all. I wanted to show you what you've got."

"I don't want these things," Idella said.

"Look here, these blue cups and saucers were my wedding presents. See the tiny silver spoons that go with them? I keep them wrapped special and polished. They are real silver."

Eddie shook his head. "These things are for Ethel, Ma. You always told her that. I don't want them spoons—I'd swallow one."

Jessie did not seem to hear what they were saying. She went excitedly from one treasure to another. "Here's the pink glass pitcher. From my mother. She poured eggnog from it at her own wedding. And I got it, not my sisters, because I loved eggnog more than anyone. My mother'd make it just for me. Hold that pitcher up to the light, Jens, so's she can see it. She gave me that pitcher before she died. I want you to take it home with you, Idella."

"We don't want that stuff, Ma. We don't want the pitcher or the spoons or the little teacups. I don't care about any of it!"

Jessie placed the pitcher down on the table. "You don't care about it, you say? I give you my most precious things, and you don't care about them? You don't care about me, then. That's what you're saying. You don't care about me. No one does. No one." She took her two canes, clumped on out to the porch, and huddled into her blankets. "Are you too good for them?" she called back without turning her head. She was sniveling, Idella could tell.

Jens, still holding the pink glass pitcher, slowly placed it back onto the table. His whole frame was bowed and bent and sad looking. Idella glanced over at Edward, who was shaking his head.

She spoke quietly. "Will you look at how upset and miserable that woman has made everyone? We're all of us unhappy." Eddie gazed at her helplessly. "You go get her."

"Who?"

"You go down there right now, and you get Ethel and bring her up here with that baby."

"Are you crazy?"

"This cannot go on. Everyone is miserable. And look out there and see for yourself how lonely she is. What is the point of that?"

"What if Ethel won't come?"

"You've got to make her. Go get her and walk up here."

"What if it doesn't work?"

"How can we be any worse off than we are now? Tell me."

"Okay. I'm going."

Idella paced and twittered about in the kitchen, waiting. She knew they'd have to walk up Fletcher's Hill and that Jessie would see them coming a long time before they got to the top and turned in at the gate.

Idella peeked out onto the porch. Jessie was sitting there, woolen throws pulled up all round her shoulders, like a turkey sunk into its own feathers for warmth. She wiped at her eyes and blew her nose, feeling sorry for herself. Idella glanced warily down to the bottom of the hill. There they came. She could just make out the two figures, brother and sister, Ethel pushing a baby carriage. They were walking slow, but steady and onward. Jessie was looking over at Mr. Graveline's house across the street.

"That house needs a painting."

Jens looked up from the newspaper he'd been pretending to read. "This house could do with a new coat, too, but I don't see us doing it." He yawned and stretched and looked down the hill. His arms held stiff in midair. He saw them. He watched the two approaching figures, then looked at Idella. She put her finger to her lips and shrugged. Jens nodded, got up, and stepped in from the porch to stand silently beside her in the kitchen.

"Where you going to? Bring me a glass of—" Her voice stopped in midsentence. They were more than halfway up now and easily seen.

Jessie was stilled completely. No one moved or spoke. All three watched Eddie and Ethel plodding up that hill with the baby carriage. Eddie had his hand on Ethel's elbow and was helping her along.

When they got to the front gate, Idella could see how frightened Ethel looked, staring glassily out from under her crocheted woolen hat. Jessie stared straight out the screen-porch door, watching them come up the walk. The carriage wasn't rolling too smoothly across the muddy path. Eddie had to take it from Ethel and shove.

None of them breathed for what seemed like minutes. Idella watched Jessie looking at her two children. Her features softened, and a kind of light came into them. Idella sensed that Jens noticed, too.

For a moment no one moved. Then Jessie pulled her shawl tight, planted her canes in front of her, and heaved up out of her chair. "Jens!" she called. "Jens, go help Eddie with them wheels. They'll jolt the baby."

"Yes, dear."

"And don't bang the door going out. It might be sleeping."

Jens held the porch door open. Idella rushed forward and helped Eddie lift the carriage onto the porch. Ethel came quietly up the steps. Idella motioned her to go to her mother, then took Eddie's elbow and pulled him back toward the kitchen.

Jessie leaned forward onto her canes and looked down at the sleeping baby. "He's so dolled up with clothes I can't get a good look. Let me sit back, and you get him unwrapped, and I'll hold him. He'll get held by his grandma."

Ethel reached into the carriage and removed the baby's hat and sweater with her clumsy fingers. Both were crocheted, Idella saw, smiling.

"Keep the blanket around him so his legs don't get cold." Jessie was reaching for the baby with hunger. "You just hand him over to me now. Let me get a good look at him."

He squirmed awake from all the handling, rubbing at his eyes with tiny fists. Ethel handed him to Jessie, who looked down at him, quietly, for a long time. No one moved. "Well, well," she whispered. The baby started to whimper. "Now, now," she cooed. Idella had never heard her use such a soft voice. "Now, now. He's got Albert's eyes." She nodded. "Yes. Albert's eyes." She looked up. "And your mouth, Ethel."

Ethel smiled. Jens walked over and put his hand on her shoulder.

"What about me?" Eddie said, smiling. "Don't I show up in him some-where?"

"Get my pitcher there, Idella—the pink glass—and make us up some eggnog. We'll use my silver spoons there to stir it."

Idella sighed. That was one crisis over with. She supposed there would be more. She squeezed Eddie's hand, then picked up the pink glass pitcher and set about making eggnog. She'd always liked that pitcher. And them little spoons would have been nice to have.

Part Three

Idella Looks Back:
Married Life on Longfellow Street

Now, this is how we come to live with Jessie. We had our own rent, you know, over on Haskell Street, when Jens had a heart attack. He was over there mowing around the gully, and then he was down on the ground, and some people brought him home. The doctor said it was a slight heart attack and for him to take vitamin pills and take it easy. But he shouldn't do no more mowing and all that business, you know. So Ethel was going to live up there and take care of them. She took her kids and went up there, and we just kept our fingers crossed, because we knew we'd be the ones that would have to go, in the long run. She stayed three weeks, and she packed up and went home. She couldn't stand it any longer. "All while I'm up there, I have butterflies in my stomach. Every minute I'm there in that house. Butterflies in my stomach." She had moved a few little things up there, and she moved them all back. So then we were the ones had to go.

That was in June. And in November he died, of his heart attack. And we lived with Jessie—or she lived with us—for eight years. She had her good points, but she was so hard to live with. She was impossible. You could spend the whole day making her favorite dish, say, something she'd been talking about for weeks—strawberry shortcake, maybe, from the first of the berries. You could wait and watch—I know because I did this, see—I tried to please her. I waited and watched for the berries to be just right. Real sweet. I picked just enough for her to have strawberry short-cake, and I made biscuits and whipped up the cream and got it all good and ready and surprised her with it for supper one night after she'd been feeling poorly for a spell—I brought it into the bedroom on a tray all dolled up with flowers and everything—and, by God, she sat there, had the nerve to sit there in bed leaning against the pillows that I got her, for God's sake, in the sheets I'd cleaned—and she looks at it and says, "Them biscuits look dry, Idella. You've wasted them berries on the likes of them biscuits."

Well, I wanted to kill her. They were perfect biscuits. Perfect! She couldn't stand that, see. She was jealous of my biscuits. You could not win in that house with that woman. No one could.

So I took that shortcake away from her. I didn't say a word. I wasn't going to argue. I took it, and I went out to the back step, looking out over the garden there, and I sat down, and I ate it. I ate every bit. I wasn't even hungry. I didn't enjoy it really, even though the biscuit was perfect. But I'd be damned before I let her get a second chance at it. And I would not give her the satisfaction of getting upset. Though of course I was. Plenty. The nerve! After I tried so hard to be nice to her and to give her what she wanted.

Now, the night before Barbara was born, Ethel came up to help and stayed all night. She brought her kids. And when I got up at about seven o'clock, my water broke. So I told Ethel, and she got right up. Then her kids started coming downstairs one by one. They were little boys, nine, ten years old. We were sitting around the breakfast table, and they knew something was going to happen. Eddie drove us into Portland. Ethel went with us, and all day long Eddie and Ethel came in and out of the hospital, waiting for that baby to come. Fourteen hours.

But they'd put me out. I remember, the last I knew, the nurse said, "Now, you tell me when a pain commences to get a little worse." So I said it, and then I never knew any more than that. Ethel told Eddie I was awful squeamish, but I only did what the nurse said. And when I came to, somewhere along the line, I said it again.

It was away round the clock till two in the morning, and I was alone in the bed, and I got up. I wanted to go to the bathroom—as it happened, there was a bathroom in the room. I had to pee, you see. And as I sat on that toilet, I thought, Have I had the baby? I must have had the baby. Finally I went back to bed, and pretty soon a nurse came in, and I said to the nurse, "I walked on that cold floor." Why I said "cold floor" was that Jessie always harped about someone walking on a cold floor after they had a baby, and they got consumption, and they died. So I thought, My God, I walked across that cold floor. It was linoleum. What's going to happen to me? I wondered. I've had it now.

But the nurse said, "That won't do any harm." She told me I had a little girl and what time she'd been born and so on.

Then they brought the baby in to me. She had a small scar on one side of her face. Forceps, you know. Her forehead was kind of red there, but it went away. She weighed over eight pounds. A lovely baby.

Now, Donna and Paulette and Beverly came much quicker, just a few hours. I didn't do too much suffering. When the pains got to be a little bit bad, they gave me something. And I had good, healthy babies. Four girls, all seven years apart.

Of course, when Paulette was coming, Eddie was hoping for a boy. When he found out it was a girl, he went up to Haskell Street to Mrs. Graham's, right across from the hospital, to tell her. He was so disappointed. She said, "He rang the bell, and I went to the door, and his face was long, and I thought, Oh my God, something's happened to Idella or the baby. Something awful has happened." And she said, "Mr. Jensen, what is the matter?" "Well," he said, "I got another goddamned girl." She talked him out of it, you know. She was a motherly person. She said, "Well, it's a healthy baby, isn't it? The baby is good?" and he said, "Yes, it weighs ten pounds," and she said, "Well, that's all right. Maybe the next one will be a boy." And when he saw the baby, he couldn't help but love that little girl.

It was after Paulette was born that we started the store. They were building houses all around us, and we thought, Gee, if there was a grocery store here, it might be good. So I said, "Why don't you take that old chicken house and fix it up and make it a store?"

Eddie's parents had the chickens. Eddie could not stand to clean them and feed them and do what had to be done. Who could blame him? Working all day and then come home to that mother and those chickens. And me, of course. So I did the most of it.

Well, finally we got rid of the damned chickens. It was too much. And that's when we made the store—out of the chicken house. That was my idea. Eddie took the credit, but it was my idea. We moved the chicken house over across the field and cleaned it out, of course, and remodeled and added quite a bit onto it, and we set it up on the Gorham Road and made it into Jensen's Drive-In Store. And I stood there in what was the old chicken house, behind that counter, for many years. Eddie said I stood there clucking. He thought he was so funny saying that "Idella's in the old chicken house clucking away." If he was to get any sort of joke going, he always drove it into the ground. "I suppose that makes you the rooster," I finally said. Course he liked that.

Jensen's Drive-In Store. Eddie was proud of that name. He thought it was real catchy, 'cause drive-in movies were big at the time we opened it. I saw so many people day after day, year after year. And I got to know them some, to know what was happening. If someone got a new baby or a cat or the like, they were as apt to tell me as anyone. I was a known figure! "Mrs. Jensen," I was.

I was at that store every morning to open up and every closing time. It'd be after ten at night. And many an afternoon as well, many, standing at the register in that store. Course, I had George to help. He lived across the street, and he worked for me in the afternoons. George . . . he was, well, what is the word? It's all the rage now—they have a term for it. He liked men, if you know what I mean. Though of course Eddie never knew. It went right over his head. Thank God from all of us.

George lived for years with Randall. He was my best worker. He'd wash the floors unbidden. Oh, I appreciated that so much. We laughed a lot about little things and enjoyed the customers together, their quirks—and little incidents.

There was one time I was over at the store, one morning—I was all alone, I was fiddling with something in the back there, and I happened to look out the window. And I'll be damned if I didn't see a moose run right by! A full-grown moose. Honest to God. And there was no one else there. I had no witnesses. And then in comes Jerry Masterson to get his daily pack of cigarettes—every morning like a clock—and I said, "Jerry, Jerry, a moose! I saw a moose run by the window!" And he looks at me and says, "You been drinking, Idella?" Thought I was putting on. So we run over to George's there across the street to see if he'd seen the moose, and he said, "No, no, Idella, no moose this morning. A couple of squirrels, but no moose." Well, they both thought I'd been drinking. But I insisted. I was adamant! And they come back over to the store with me, and we looked all around outside—and, by God, George found a moose print, right there behind the store. He proved that I'd seen that moose. Oh, we laughed about that over the years. "Seen any moose this morning, Idella?" Jerry would ask. "Not a one," I'd say, and we'd both start laughing. Or some mornings, just for the fun of it, I'd say, "Three."

We never did hear any more about that moose. But George found the print—unmistakable.

Good old George. I did hear stories some about parties with young men over at Randall and George's. I never knew what to believe. He was a good worker, I know that. Though Barbara said she saw him at Old Orchard Beach one night and he was holding hands with a man. I don't know if it was Randall. Life is funny. So much goes on you'd never dream about.

Well, since we didn't have chickens, we got eggs to sell at the store from the egg lady who lived up the hill. Now, what was her name? I knew her as a child growing up. We were in the one-room school together out in Scarborough that year me and Avis got to go to school. She was the prettiest little thing. Long golden hair. She'd wear a big bow on top of her head. Big bows was the fashion. My hair was too thin to maintain a bow like that. Hers was thick and luxurious, and her bow would sit proudly on top of her head all day long. Mine would droop and sidle over.

Well, for some reason the egg lady married Jimmy Forrest! They lived up the hill from us. Them Forrests were a weird bunch—from way down country somewheres. One time I heard that she and Jimmy were living in a car! Can you imagine? For a month or two, it was. People coming into the store would comment. When I saw them, they were driving around in it delivering eggs, and it looked regular enough. But I heard from more than one source that they slept in there, too, instead of beds. With a dog! I felt sorry for her. She herself was always so ladylike and genteel.

Well, when we got our new couch, me and Eddie, I offered her our old one. I can't remember her name, and I should. I felt bad offering up that old couch. That couch had a history. It used to be Eddie's parents'. It was in the living room up at the house when I met him, and it was still there years later when we moved in to help take care of things, and I don't think it had been sat upon many times in between. It was for company, which after that first visit I wasn't.

I worried more about that damn couch. Jessie watched over her things like she was a scarecrow come to life, patrolling. Anything in that living room was not supposed to be touched for fear it'd get soiled and people would say bad things about her—that she wasn't a good house-keeper or something. I mean, she really worried about useless things like that.

So I was glad to get that old couch out of the house.

Well, you'd of thought I'd offered her a bag of gold. So happy she was to get it. That old worn-out thing. Away it went.

A while after we give them the couch, we went up there, me and Eddie, to get eggs. Their car was broken down, and she couldn't deliver. So I said, "Oh, don't worry, Lilly"—Lilly! That was her name! Just come to me out of the air. I said, "Don't worry, Lilly, we'll drive up and get them eggs." So Edward agreed—it was only up the hill, for God's sake.

What a run-down excuse for a place that was! Old cars all over, of course. Every manner of junk was strewn all about the yard. "Holy Jesus," Eddie said when he pulled in. Then a couple of dogs started barking. Black, ratty creatures. We didn't dare get out. We sat there observing from inside the car—and, by God, I spy our old couch that we'd given them sitting out in front of the chicken house with chickens all over it!

I wasn't sure if Eddie'd seen it. I didn't say anything. But he saw. It took him a while, but he saw. It come over his face like a brushfire. He started making that hissing sound he made when he was mad, clenching his teeth and breathing through them—*sssssss*—and I knew the jig was up. "That's my mother's couch," he hissed. "Goddamn if that isn't my mother's couch!" Now, we had our new couch, and it was no earthly good to him—even before the chickens let loose all over it. You can imagine. It was a sight.

But Edward held his tongue, even though he was almost at a full boil—that anyone would do anything bad to something that was his, that had been his mother's. Lilly come out and called off the dogs, and we got the eggs. She was so sweet and grateful. I'm sure it was Jimmy Forrest that put the couch there. He never got it into the house proper— or was too drunk to—and put it down, and there it stayed.

Well, we got the egg boxes lined up across the back seat of the car. Then Eddie, so afraid that he'd get cheated, see, had to open each box and check every egg. He was mad, see, and he was taking it out.

When all the eggs had been checked, I paid her, and away we went. Then Edward started to fume. When he got behind the wheel, if anything was bothering him, that's how he got rid of it. So he come tearing out of their yard, and I'm saying, "Slow down, Edward! Calm down!" That made him madder, which made me mad then, and he starts on about his couch, his mother's couch, how could they let the damn chick-

ens shit all over the goddamned couch. You'd think it was the throne of
England they were sitting on!

And he never liked that couch. His mother had always been so careful
about it that we were afraid to sit on it. So it was ironic that it would meet
that end—but it wasn't tragic. It sort of tickled me, actually, to see it.
Jessie must have been spinning in her grave.

Meanwhile, Edward and me were doing some spinning of our own.
He took the corner too sharp pulling out onto Longfellow Street. And
there was George, ambling up the road, and Eddie was headed right for
him. Well, George jumped over that ditch like a stag, I tell you, and
Eddie jerked the car the other way. But the wheels on my side of the car
went in the ditch. We bumped along jerking down the ditch, Edward
cursing, me squealing, George laughing. When the car finally stopped,
we were all lopped over into the ditch. And we were stuck. And of course
those eggs in the back seat . . . The cartons weren't closed proper by the
last one handling them, if you get my meaning.

I put my head to my hands and closed my eyes before I had the
strength to turn around and look. First thing I see is yellow. Yolk yellow.
You know what that's like. Egg was oozing into every possible place—on
the inside roof, in the ashtray, and down in the crevices there behind the
seat. In the carpet. And some of them yolks hadn't broke yet. I tried to
capture them whole with pieces of shell.

Now, Eddie always wore a straw hat with a brim in summer—he was
very careful about his appearance—and he'd taken it off and set it down
when he was farting around back checking eggs. Well, he was so mad
when the car stopped that he charged around and opened the back door
and saw his hat sitting there, and he grabbed it and put it on. Then he
continued charging around and opening doors and making things ten
times worse. I was doing what I could to scrape things up, but I only had
a few Kleenexes in my purse. We were in a panic, you see, 'cause Eddie
sold cars. This was a dealer car!

So me and George were scooched in the ditch with the back door
open as far as it would go, scraping eggs out as best we could, and Eddie
is roaring, and cars are stopping now and slowing down—I was so embarrassed I felt sick—and Eddie comes around to the back—and me and
George looked up at him—and there was Edward, standing over us fum-
ing, and all the while there was broken yolk all over the front crown of

his hat. Bright yellow. Oozing down and dripping. And he had no earthly
idea. He was oblivious. He looked like a tropical bird. It was such bright
yellow. My God in heaven.

And George, who usually didn't have much to say, looked up at Eddie
and said, smooth as you please, "The yolk's on you, Eddie."

He traded that car in for another as soon as he could.

And it was all my fault, see, for giving them the couch in the first
place. It was always my fault.

I thought it would be no trouble driving the eggs down the hill and
over to the store. It was a two-minute ride. I wasn't counting on Edward
being so Edward, which of course he always was.

Avis Looks Back: The Hotel

The first cow we had, I guess, was the one Dad gave to Aunt Beth and Uncle Paul when he sent Emma with them. Emma still says she feels bad about that—taking our cow. I know it's not fair, but for the longest time I resented Emma—I was mean to her. I thought if she'd never been born, I'd still have my mother. I never said it out loud to her, but I thought about it plenty. It wasn't till years later, when she had TB and I used to go see her in the sanatorium before she got cured, that I got to like her.

Anyhow, that was the first cow I can remember, and after her we got Tater and some others, and then Bossy. But I never knew where calves came from. This is what education we had. I mean, there was no one to tell us the facts of life. What Dad always did if there was a calf born or a lamb or something else, he'd say he found something out in the straw. So we'd go out and look in the barn, and there it'd be in a heap of straw. That's what he always did.

Well, I had this little heifer, Bossy. It was a cute thing—slender legs, just like a deer. After I'd had her for a year or so, Dad said she was going to have a baby. So this one morning when Dad left, he told me to watch Bossy—and if she left the other cows, to bring her home and go get him.

I put the cows in the pasture and turned my back to put up the bars, so that she wouldn't get out into somebody's garden, and I turned around and that cow was gone. Just like that. I looked over, and there was a clump of alders, and they were quivering. She had hidden herself among them. So I got her out of there, and I brought her home.

Well, I went all around the sides of that cow looking to see where that calf would come out. Because I knew that calf was inside the cow. I looked all around to see where there was an opening. And I never found it. I was thirteen years old! I didn't know anything.

And then I saw. Here was two little toes coming out the back of her. Two toes. Her two front. I ran like hell up the road and got Dad. After that, of course, I didn't go out to the barn. We weren't supposed to. We weren't supposed to know anything about anything like that. But I saw those toes! It gave me something to chew on.

We none of us got too good an introduction to things of that nature. No one told us a damned thing. We had no mother. We used to lie there in the bed, me and Idella, and try to put the pieces together. We came up with the damnedest theories about making babies. There was a spell when we kept away from each other at night, each rolled off to a side, 'cause we knew that whatever happened, it was supposed to happen in a bed. Poor little ninnies we were.

Hell, when I got my period for the first time, I didn't know what it was. I woke up with red spots all over my nightie, and I snuck down the stairs and got a pair of scissors, and I cut the spots out so Idella wouldn't see them. I thought I'd done something wrong.

Men took advantage every chance they got. We come to know later it could happen anywhere. In the barn. In the woods. Goddamned men that Dad would get to work on the farm. One tried to grab Idella in the outhouse. They were scraped from off the bottom of the barrel.

It happened to poor Aunt May on the milking table. Aunt May was my mother's sister. She was tongue-tied. Sweet a thing as you could ask for, but kind of simple.

I wasn't any more than seven. I was poking around the farm, and I wandered into the barn. Well, right there on the milking table, up on top of it, is this big lout of a farmhand wriggling around—and under him, I can just see her shoes sticking out, is Aunt May! I didn't know what was going on.

I ran out screaming like a banshee. Grampa Smythe went running in. Aunt May was still on the table—and that poor sucker was running out like his pants were on fire. He comes across a bicycle, and it's got little wheels, see, so he starts peddling, peddling, peddling. And Grampa Smythe, who's chasing him, and Uncle John—he come running out of the woodwork—they grabbed tall-wheelers, with big, long spokes. And they start going like the wind. I remember watching them going down the road, and Grampa and Uncle John gradually gaining on him. Well, they caught up with him, and knocked him down, and beat the shit out of him.

Aunt May ended up with two children. No one knew who the fathers were or if they were the same. I think them boys of hers ended up being real good to her—a sort of blessing. No matter how they got started.

Now, Idella latched on to Eddie and settled. But I went through quite a shitload of men. And I found more shit than I ever bargained for. I had a nose for it. One of the first was Jamie. That was while I was in Boston. Poor son of a bitch. James O'Hagan. He lived with his mother—one of my regular bluehairs at the shop—and she asked me if I'd like to meet him. I had my doubts, but he had a nice car and no fleas anywhere that I could see.

Well, we went out for a couple of months, but he started to irritate me. He'd pick at every tooth after every meal with a toothpick, even in restaurants. And he was jealous. I got a prickly feeling whenever I was with him. I hated being watched. Owned. We came up to Maine one time—he wanted to meet my family—and we all went out to Old Orchard Beach. Well, Eddie had this goddamned plastic lobster, which he kept putting up my skirt. You can be sure Jamie took notice and started sulking. So I gave him what he was looking for. The more he sulked, the more I let Eddie have his fun.

All the way back to Boston, I'm hearing about Eddie and his plastic lobster. And how he was putting the claws all over, and where else did he put his claws, and how could I do that to my own sister, and on and on and on all down the road. Finally I said if he mentioned Eddie Jensen one more time, I'd never see him again—which is what I had decided was the best thing anyway.

He got all quiet after that. Stopped cold. About a week after, he asks me to go on a picnic, to celebrate my birthday. I thought he had a surprise for me, a present, so I agreed to go. Christ, I even made my special peach pie. We set out on a Sunday morning. We heard church bells ringing out there in the country, and we're going along—I had my flask, and I was drinking from it on the sly—and he turns down a dirt road. I'm thinking he's found a lake or some nice spot for our picnic. Only it's not much of a place. No lake in sight. Just scrubby trees on each side. He stopped the car. Said he had to check something in the trunk. I thought he must be getting my present. He was always buying me nice things, and I liked getting them. I was sitting there putting on lipstick, and I see out the corner of my eye that he'd walked around to the front of the car. I looked up to say where is the big surprise, and I was just in time to see him blow his brains out the back of his head with a gun he'd stuck in his mouth.

I never looked at him. No question he was dead. I sat there staring into my little mirror. Holy Christ, I was scared. My mind was going faster than my heart, which was plenty. I got out of the car and went around back, and the trunk was closed, but there was the picnic basket on the ground. He'd taken it out to get the gun, I guess. And there was my pie. I took the knife, and I'm shaking by then, and I cut a piece of the pie, and I started in eating it. I was scared shitless I'd have whiskey on my breath on a Sunday morning. I smeared peaches all over my teeth, threw down the knife, and set out to look for help. I left the pie sitting in the dirt. I followed the sound of those church bells. At one point I knelt by the road and threw up all the pie. So I had another kind of breath, but it wasn't the whiskey.

It must have been two miles I walked to that church. Cars were just pulling out, and along I come straggling in. I was barefooted by then, and I had peach-pie puke all over myself. Oh, I was pretty.

The police found everything just like I'd said. They believed me. Because Jamie had a history when they checked into him. He'd been in more than one institution. He was crazy, poor bastard.

So I kept looking for something that I never found in men. I don't even know what—excitement? love? money? Some of them were pretty tough customers. My first husband, Tommy, had me in trouble up to my armpits from day one. Handsome bugger. Flashy dresser and as smooth as a baby's ass. I'd never seen the likes of him on the farm. I met him in a rainstorm. We were in a doorway during a downpour in Boston, and I had a newspaper over my head to keep my hair dry—I was a hairdresser—and he was trying to read the sports news that I had there on top of my head, and we struck up a conversation—about statistics.

He walked me to work at the shop after the rain stopped, and he hung around. He stood by my cutting chair talking, and when I got a customer, he went and sat down in the waiting area. I could feel him watching me the whole time. I could feel his eyes like someone was pressing a hot cloth against me. My legs. The back of my neck. My crotch. I don't know what kind of cuts I gave that day.

Finally my boss, Shirley, she comes over to him and asks his intentions. I knew they'd all been eyeing him, and I didn't give a good goddamn. He said he had a great many intentions and one was to take me out to dinner. And Shirley said that those seats were reserved for clients only, and Tommy said he was a client, he would like Miss Hillock to cut his hair. They glared at each other, and then she said all right, when Miss Hillock's chair is free, she can cut your hair. The sap was running that day.

So he sits in my chair while I'm still sweeping up—and you can hear the scissors stop. The place froze. Everyone is looking at us through all the mirrors. And he asks for a trim, please. Just a trim. He didn't need a thing. Every hair on his head was perfect. But I said, "Why, yes, sir," and I took my scissors, and I went all around the back of his neck snipping the littlest bit and sort of nuzzling the tips around his ears. His hair was a pale brown, straight and thick. It looked like sawdust around my feet when I was done, I cut so little.

I could barely breathe, I was that hepped up. If he'd looked at me straight on for too long I would have spun that chair around and climbed on top of him right there in that shop. When I'm done, he sticks a fifty-dollar bill in my tip jar for all the world to see. Then he asks when I get off work. At six o'clock he is waiting outside with a car. He opens the door for me, and in I go. The girls were all lined up against the window like bowling pins, and I give a little wave to them as he pulls out into the traffic.

I thought I'd found what I was looking for, all right, dropped down from the sky. I come to find out it was just rain. Tommy always had money. He never seemed to work. He'd refer to business, but he never seemed to do any. I didn't question it. I was having too much fun just being with him. He took me out dancing and to fancy restaurants. Horse races. The works. And we drank. Everything was better with a drink in your belly. I'd heard that all my life.

Then one night—oh, about three weeks into it—he asked if I'd be interested in making some extra money. Partners, we'd be.

"What kind of partners?" I ask. "Lucrative," he says. Well, I was game. And by then I was a goner.

To this day I don't think Idella knows the extent of it. I lured men up to my room. That was the plan. Remember, now, I was a looker. And when the men got their pants down, Tommy was there to clean them out.

And we got married. Went to city hall. My brother, Dalton, was our witness. We were all three soused, but we were good at pulling things off under the influence.

One night I lured the wrong guy. Instead of a fat wallet, he was carrying a thin badge. I got two years. Tommy got four. It wasn't his first time. It's not something to be proud of. I'm sure Eddie thought I got what was coming to me. Which I suppose I did.

Idella wrote me letters. One day I got a letter. Whole pages about nothing. It was like having her there. She always asked, at the end, in little letters, how the service was in the "hotel." Those letters made me laugh. The only thing that did.

I hated being cooped up like a damned chicken. It about killed me. I lost it the one time. I was sitting at the dining table at one evening feed—all in a row, we were—and I looked down and saw those yellow and brown globs of shit they give us for food—and I started to gag. I couldn't breathe.

I looked around and saw us all lined up wearing the same thing and eating the same thing and doing the same thing and being told when to piss and when to shit and when to get up in the morning—and I stood up and started screaming that I had to get out of there, I had to get air. They didn't know whether to lock me up or tie me down.

The other women tried to quiet me. "Shut it, Hillock. Shut it fast," they said all up and down. Finally this black woman—Irene, her name was—come over to me, and she put her hands on my shoulders hard and pressed. She bore down on me with those brown eyes of hers, and we saw each other. "Shut it, Hillock. They'll put you in solitary. Now, shut it."

I heard that. That stopped me. She saved me, that Irene. "How you doin', Hillock?" she'd say after that, if we passed each other. "I'm good," I'd say. "That's good," she'd say. "Hold on. The clock's moving."

I want to tell you, having that fit scared the hell out of me. 'Cause I tried to be so tough, see, to get through it. Like nothing bothered me. Water off a duck's back. My arse.

So I was glad to get them letters about nothing. I'd picture Idella rolling along the highways with Edward on them Sunday drives and squealing about the pretty view. I wish I'd kept them letters. She's a good old girl, Idella.

It was Dad got me out of jail when the time come. I got out on probation. I never saw Tommy again. That was part of the deal. He died young—still pretty, I suppose. Bastard. It was in the "hotel" where I got an actual beautician's license. I learned about coloring and permanents and the like, working with chemicals. The learning to be a beautician part helped me out quite a bit, 'cause I was good. I was smart, see. In spite of myself. Always in spite of myself.

Barbara Hillock Jensen Looks Back:
Cherry Cider

Boston
August 1941

I don't know if it was my polka-dot dress that made it so funny, that got Mumma and Aunt Avis going so strong at the end. It had a white background with red dots the size of quarters—the size of cherries. I'd worn it only once before, and I'd had Mumma iron the skirt all over and crisp it up before I put it on again for this ride into the country with her and Aunt Avis and Aunt Avis's new boyfriend, Fred. For some reason—well, because of all the cider—Mumma and Aunt Avis and I ended up in the back seat together, me in the middle, and Fred was in the front doing the driving by himself. I mean, with no one to sit next to him.

He had a beautiful car. The seats were brushed brown leather, pale brown like beach sand on a hot, hot day. He saw me rubbing my hands across the seat and smiled. "Barbara, honey, that's what the nose of a colt feels like. You ever felt a colt's nose?" Mumma and Aunt Avis giggled. They'd lost their manners miles back. "No, sir," I'd answered solemnly up into the rearview. "I haven't ever felt a colt's nose."

Actually, I had. I'd felt the nose of a horse anyway, Chocolate Milk. Grampa Jensen used him to pull the wagon he drove delivering milk and eggs around the neighborhood. Chocolate Milk's nose certainly didn't feel as soft as those leather seats, but I wanted Fred to feel like he'd said something with weight to it.

It was stopping at the farm stand that got things going the wrong way.

Daddy didn't like the idea of me and Mumma making this visit to Boston to see Aunt Avis. He'd ranted and raved, as usual, but Mumma had insisted she had a right to take a little trip to see her own sister and her sister's new boyfriend. "If you was to go down to Boston every time that tart gets what she calls a boyfriend, you'd have to move in with her. I bet you'd like that, moving right in with her." "Oh, be quiet, Edward,"

Mumma said. That's the gist of what they said the whole time he was driving Mumma and me to the bus in Portland. We got the 9:00 A.M. express, so we'd have most of the day in Boston and much of the next. Daddy handed me a pack of Juicy Fruit as I boarded the bus and told me to be careful.

By midafternoon we were sitting on the porch of the rooming house where Avis lived, waiting for Fred to pull up in his car and take us for a ride in the country. Aunt Avis and Mumma were sitting side by side on a ratty old wicker couch, having a "little drink." I was on the porch railing in front of them, keeping my polka-dot skirt like a parachute all around me, sucking on ice cubes from out of their glasses. They fished them out and sucked off the whiskey before handing them over. Aunt Avis was telling Mumma about Fred.

She'd met Fred when he'd driven up in his new car to get his aunt from the beauty shop, where Aunt Avis gave Fred's aunt a perm once a month and a hair curl every week like clockwork.

"Hester's her name, if you can stand it. She's what a farm girl from Canada who didn't know nothing might call an old coot," Aunt Avis said.

"Why, that would be you, now, wouldn't it?" Mumma giggled.

"Or someone damn near like me." Avis laughed. "The old coot expects me to work miracles. Her hair makes a bale of hay look silky." Mumma laughed.

"And she's deaf as a post. I have to bend over like this—here, Barb, hold this glass for me, hon—and flap my arms like this, like a goddamned chicken, to get her to see me so I can get her out from under the dryer before that hair frizzles right off her head." That got them both laughing. Avis choked on her cigarette.

"Wouldn't that be something?" Mumma was wiping tears off her cheek.

Avis stood up and took her drink back from me. "Thanks, hon."

"Now, what does he do? Did you tell me?" Mumma's thoughts were easily fuzzed when she was having little drinks.

"Business of some kind. Something to do with fixtures. Plumbing, lighting, I don't know. Where else do you have fixtures? All I know is, there's money in the *damily*." That was their way of saying "damned family."

"Jesus, Avis, you'd better find out. Maybe he spends all day making toilets."

"He's flush, I do know that much." Avis held up the whiskey bottle. She kept it hidden behind a pot of geraniums in the corner of the porch. "Want another hit?"

"I'll have a sip."

Avis poured a little into each of their glasses. "Sorry, Barb, no more ice." She smiled at me and handed me the bottle. "Can you go stash that for me till we get back? No one pays any attention to that plant."

"I watered it," Mumma said sheepishly.

"You would."

"Well, is he nice?"

"He's tolerable."

"Does he have his good points?"

"A few." Avis laughed her deep, throaty laugh. Daddy called it her tart laugh. Mumma said she had a naturally throaty voice. I thought she sounded like a movie star.

Aunt Avis had real style. She'd been to beauty school. She was prettier than Mumma—if you liked flashy. Daddy said he didn't, but I was fascinated by it. She wasn't tall, like Mumma, or as thin. She had a real figure, with noticeable curves in all directions. Mumma was pretty, but in a more quiet sort of way. Mumma was like iced tea in a tall, thin glass, while Aunt Avis was more like an ice-cream sundae—big scoops sprinkled with nuts and puffs of cream and a single cherry on top. I loved them both.

"Now, where exactly are we going today?" Mumma was surprised to be leaving the city when we'd spent so long on a bus to get here. I wasn't so sure about it myself.

"Who the hell knows? I'll keep it short. He's determined to give us a ride in the country in his new car. Then we'll come back to the city and he'll bankroll us for supper. I've got a place in mind like you never saw. Anything you want on the menu, Barbie." She fluffed my skirt up. "Be sure to wipe your hands off before you get into Freddie's car. He's very particular about the leather on the seats. God Almighty, Della, I wipe my own hands before I get in."

"Well, I know Edward would drool if he was to see a car with genuine leather seats. You know what a fool he is about cars. If he could be married to one, he would be."

"Jesus, Della, Edward drools anyway. And he's a fool about more than cars. He's a fool, period." Avis finished her drink and set it on the railing.

"He's a hard worker, Avis." Mumma emptied her glass.

Avis sighed. She lit another cigarette. They neither of them spoke for a minute. Bringing up Daddy often led to taut silences between Mumma and Aunt Avis.

Suddenly a shiny red Ford turned onto the side street where Avis lived. The sun just seemed to slide along from one end of it to the other. Mumma and I sat up and watched. "Oh, Avis, could this be it?"

"The one and only." Avis glanced up, then stubbed out her cigarette and stuffed her pack into her little clutch purse. "No smoking in the vehicle."

"Why, he's not stopping," Mumma said.

"He will." Avis stood up. "Barb, honey, take these two glasses and stash them behind the plant. I'll get it all later." She adjusted her hat. "He'll drive slowly past and then turn around and come floating back. Then he'll toot the horn once. Even though we're standing here in full view. Don't you look sweet," she said to me, and tugged on my skirt.

The red car circled back to us. We all stood on the top porch step and watched. "He's going to tell one of us we look fresh as some goddamned flower." Avis whispered this out of the corner of her mouth as she smiled and waved toward the car.

There was a short beep, the driver's door popped open, and I got my first look at Fred. He was on the tall side, a lot taller than Daddy. He had on a dark brown brimmed hat and a light brown suit with very sharp creases from the shoes up. From his suit-coat pocket, he took a large white handkerchief. He grabbed at that handkerchief like he was wringing it out the whole time he was coming up the walk.

"His hands sweat," Avis whispered to Mumma. She said it without moving her lips.

"Hello, ladies. What a pleasure this is and will be." He returned the handkerchief to his pocket. "You must be Barbara." He extended his hand to me, so I grabbed it and shook it. It felt dry enough. "You are as fresh as a daisy, like your Aunt Avis informed me you would be." This was news to me, though I was glad to get it.

"Say thank you, Barbara." Mumma put her hand on my head, which I did not appreciate.

"Thank you."

He was not bad looking. Avis didn't go out with homely men. But his teeth were big, especially the two front middle ones. That was the drawback to his face. They were sort of a pale yellow. It could be that his shirt collar was so very white it gave them a dull cast.

"And you must be Avis's big sister. How nice to meet you, Idella."

"Older and wiser," Aunt Avis snickered.

"Well, I don't know about that, Avis," Mumma said. "Just two years."

"A person can learn a lot in two years," Fred said, sort of mysteriously, I thought.

"That is the truth," Mumma answered vaguely. "You're right about that, Fred."

"Well, ladies," Fred said, like a master of ceremonies, "are we ready for our little journey? I can promise you a smooth ride and cool breezes." He took my elbow, like I was his date, and led me toward the car. "Do you like going for rides, Barbara?"

I nodded. The truth is, I hadn't been all that keen on going for a ride in the country. I lived in the country. I went past farms any day I wanted to. It was being in Boston, a real city, that I liked. I wanted to go to a restaurant and walk the streets and see a movie at night, surrounded by people I'd never met or even seen before. That's why I was wearing my polka-dot dress. We were going to a restaurant where Aunt Avis said I could order whatever I wanted, including an appetizer and dessert.

"What a nice car you have, Fred," Mumma said as she walked up to it and ran her hand along the back fender. "It's so far off the ground. The seats are so high. We'll be looking down like the Queen of England." Fred had opened the door for her first. She climbed into the back. "Look, Barbara, isn't this something?" She beckoned me in. "Isn't this the limit? It's like sitting in a living room." Mumma was outdoing herself.

"You make yourself comfortable, Idella." Fred smiled broadly. Mumma was hitting her marks.

I climbed in next to her. It was grand. The seat was upholstered in soft leather, like a couch. My legs swooped up with the high curve and dangled over the edge, not even touching the carpeted floor.

"How long have you had this car?" Mumma asked as Aunt Avis and Fred settled into the front. Aunt Avis sat right up next to him.

"It's factory fresh, Idella, the '42 model," Fred proclaimed, like an advertisement come to life.

Mumma gasped. "Why, it's still only 1941."

"That's right." Fred turned around to face her, his teeth showing more and more as he talked. "It rolled off the assembly line less than a month ago. I had certain features specially ordered—the seats, the paint—it's a French red called *cerise*—and there are a few other features that are particular to the driving performance."

"Oh, yes," Mumma said, "horsepowers and all." She sat back and played aloud with the word *cerise*. It tickled her to say a foreign word, especially a French one. " 'Saareeeze.' Mmmm . . . it rhymes with 'breeeeze.' "

"It also rhymes with 'fleas.' " Avis grinned.

Fred was a natural guide. He pointed out buildings we drove past, details about their architecture. Then he pointed out historical sites—or where we were in relation to historical sites we weren't going anywhere near. He described three statues we would never see, and one cannon. "This area brims with history." Fred became so animated that Aunt Avis had to move over, to put a little space between them. "Now, if I were to take an alternate route—I wish I'd thought of it—we could go right past the Battle of Lexington, where they fired 'the shot heard 'round the world.' "

"I don't think we heard that up in Canada." Avis turned and winked at me.

"No," Mumma laughed. "I'm not too much on history. We didn't get much but the basics for schooling."

It was a relief when we hit the country. Mumma was tired, and she melted back against the seat. Now we could ride along more comfortably and watch trees roll by. Except that Fred kept it up. We were no sooner done with city architecture and historical sites than he was on to barns and grazing animals and the need for crop rotation. He was a fountain of information. Mumma was bordering on desperate. That's why she lurched forward so and called out when she saw the sign for cider.

"Oh, look!" she cried. "A farm stand's coming up—with cherry cider. Why, I haven't had that in years." A big hand-painted sign was nailed to a telephone pole with CHERRY CIDER 1 MLE AHD lettered crudely on it. I wondered at the time if a child had painted it. I could have done a better job.

"Fred, honey, let's get some cherry cider. It would be good to stretch our legs." Aunt Avis cast her eyes back toward Mumma. "Do you like cherry cider, Fred, honey?" She reached over and pulled a little curl that was peeking out from under Fred's hat. I hadn't yet seen him without the hat. It slipped down onto the tops of his ears in a way that didn't look just right.

"I don't believe I've ever had it, Avis." The car was slowing down. "I guess I'm about to find out." He reached over and patted Aunt Avis's knee the same way I pat my dog, Jigs, on top of his head.

Our arrival at the farm stand was an event. It felt like an ocean liner floating up to the dock, the way that car swooped into the moon-shaped curve of dirt road with the farm stand in the middle. People looked up.

"Oh, goody," Mumma said when it finally stopped.

Avis was already opening her door.

We all drank the first bottle of cherry cider standing around the car. Fred eased the cork loose with his thumbs. It poked out the top of the bottle like Fred Astaire's top hat, Avis said. We had little paper cups from the stand. Fred poured into them carefully, so as not to spill a drop.

"Well, my Lord," Mumma exclaimed when she took her first sip. "It's got some kick."

Avis took her own sip. "Yep." She took a longer drink. "This is hard cider. It's turned."

"Not a turn for the worse, I hope?"

"No, no, not at all." Avis held up her cup as though to toast and then drank it down.

"I thought that farm-stand man winked at me." Mumma giggled. "Could you pour me another, Fred? It sure hits the spot."

"Me, too," Avis cooed.

"Perhaps we should find something else for the little lady?" Fred was referring to me.

"Perhaps so," Mumma said.

"Oh, let her have a cup of it, Idella," Avis coaxed. "It won't do her any harm. Edward's not here. Let her have some fun."

Mumma looked at me with her head cocked to one side, the way a bird looks. "Oh, all right." She shrugged and smiled. "One cup won't do her any harm, I guess."

Fred poured some for me, a little reluctantly, I thought. The cider had fizz. It tickled my nose. Cool and sweet, it smelled earthy in a good way. I felt all grown up.

"Let's get us another," Mumma said excitedly, before we'd even finished.

"Let's get more than another. We can bring some home," Avis said. "What do you say, Freddie? I'll buy. Me and Idella will buy."

"Now, ladies. Is it wise? It tastes delightful, but perhaps we should be a bit cautious. It has turned."

"We'll bring some to your aunt," Avis said. "Would she like that? It might do her good. It's probably medicinal, don't you think, Della?"

"Well," Mumma said, "it's good for what ails ya." They both laughed.

Avis was at that curl again. "Come on, Freddie. Don't be an old stick in the mud."

"Here we are," Mumma said, sweeping her arm toward the farm stand. "We might as well. It'll never be as good."

"And here's Barbara wearing a cherry dress," Fred said unexpectedly, and Aunt Avis and Mumma stopped and looked down at my flouncing red dots. He looked into my cup and saw that it was empty. He poured a little bit more, the end of the bottle, and smiled at me like we had a secret.

Avis laughed. "Well, they could pass for cherries, Freddie," Avis said.

"Why, yes," Mumma said, holding out my skirt a little farther than I liked. "It's got a real cherry color to it."

"With no stems."

"And no pits."

"Oh, no. No pits." This sent the two of them into wild laughter.

"Come on, Idella. Fred, you stay here with Barbara." Avis reached over and grabbed Mumma's hand, and they pranced the few steps over to the farm stand, tossing their joined hands up and down.

"Very refreshing!" Avis spoke to the man first and handed him the empty bottle. "We thought you could use this again." There were no other customers at the moment.

"Just what I needed, that cider. *So* refreshing on a hot day."

"Why, thank you, ma'am. It's been a good year for cherries."

"I should say," said Mumma.

"That cider is so good, I think we'll have to buy some more. Don't you think so, Della?"

"Oh, yes." She giggled.

The farmer nodded and smiled. "How much would you like?"

"Well, now, that first bottle was *so* good—if you can promise me that it'll be as good—you know, the good stuff—why, I think we'd like ten bottles!"

"Ten!" That was Mumma, sounding more like herself.

"Yes, Della, ten. Why the hell not? As you yourself were saying, here we are, and here it is. The time is ripe."

"You mean the cider is ripe!" Mumma said. That set them off.

"Well, now, ladies," the farmer said, coming in over their giggling, "if you promise not to drink it all in one place, I believe I can round up ten more bottles." He glanced over in our direction. Fred nodded to him and touched his hat, like a detective in a movie.

"Would it be from the same batch? If you know what I mean?" Avis's voice was lower than Mumma's. They were all acting as if they were in a murder mystery.

"Yes, ma'am. I do know what you mean." He winked at Avis and Mumma both. "If you ladies will excuse me for a moment." He went out behind his stand and started bringing back bottles of the red cider. They were a lovely color, like ruby tenpins all lined up across his wooden counter. The sun shone through them as he held each bottle up to be inspected.

The way Aunt Avis ended up in the back is that we had to hold on to the bottles somehow, to keep them in place. They couldn't very well roll around in the trunk. So Avis had the idea that if she got into the back seat with us, and if we sat right up against each other, then we could put the bottles between us and our bodies would be the cushions. Avis handed three bottles in to Mumma. Then I got in.

"Sit right next to her now, Barb, leg to leg. Use your skirt as a bumper." We got three bottles snug between us. Then Aunt Avis handed in three more bottles, we lined them along my other side, and she climbed in next to me. Fred stood beside the open door, holding the four remaining bottles, not saying a thing. "Here, Fred, honey, hand them in. Della, you'll have to sit holding two of these. Barb, honey, hand these over to your mother."

"Jesus, Avis. Ten was too many." Mumma took one of the bottles and put it on the floor between her feet. "There. Try that."

Avis did the same and then glanced at me. "You doing all right there, Barbara? You look a little pale."

I nodded. I had to keep my elbows close in and my hands in my lap. I could feel the smooth curves of the bottles wedged between us. The sun coming through the back windshield was hot on my neck. I would be glad to feel the breeze through open windows again.

"I guess we're ready, Freddie." Avis smiled out at him. Fred nodded and closed her door. Then he got into the front behind the wheel and started the engine.

"I promised you ladies a ride in the country," Fred said, using the rearview to get a glimpse. "I feel like you ladies have been shortchanged."

"Oh, I've had a lovely time." Mumma spoke over his shoulder. "This has been plenty of country for me. Really."

"And we promised Barbara we'd take her to a restaurant. Didn't we, Barbie dear?" Avis reached over and squeezed my knee.

"Well, let me take you back by another route at least, rather than see the same old thing again."

"Anything she wants on the menu. Right, kid?" Avis patted my knee. "I think the direct route is best, Fred."

"Oh, yes, the direct route would be just fine," Mumma added. "Just fine."

But he had already turned off onto a different road and was picking up speed. Mumma and Avis rolled their eyes at each other. Avis shrugged. Mumma shrugged back. They started giggling. Fred's eyes filled the mirror every now and then for a quick glance back.

"We'll be coming up soon to one of my favorite barns. It's so well situated off the road. And the animals are beautifully cared for. I stopped once and introduced myself. They showed me the barn. Beautiful horses. Very nice folks."

"Why, Fred, I didn't know that you were a gentleman farmer." Avis was pointing at the bottle of cider in her hand, so we could see that the cork was loosened. Mumma slyly nodded her head.

"Oh, there's a lot you don't know about me, Avis."

"Well, I guess that could be said for most of us." Avis worked the cork from the bottle a smidge at a time. Just as she was easing it out, Mumma faked a sneeze.

"Bless you," Avis said, giggling.

"Why, thank you, Avis."

Fred's eyes flicked across the rearview and back to the road. "Is that true for you, Barbara?" I could feel Avis leaning over to the side and taking a swig. I sat up a little higher, not daring to look at her.

"Excuse me?" I stammered.

"Are there things about you that other people don't know?"

I immediately thought about the box of ice cream sitting in our freezer. I'd been opening it up and eating it from out of the bottom, so the top would look the same. Daddy must know about that by now.

"That's a hard thing for a kid to answer, Fred." Avis leaned up behind him. She slid a finger under his hat and tickled behind his ear, handing Mumma the cider bottle while she was doing it. "Is that a hawk way up there?" She leaned forward. Fred had picked up considerable speed on this more deserted road. Mumma took a sip.

"I think that's a crow, Avis. You should know that, coming from up there in Canada. You must have seen a lot of crows on your farm."

"We had a lot of bats up there." Mumma leaned in a little, passing the bottle back.

"Christ, yes." Avis laughed. "More than a few. We were all batty."

Avis and Mumma were making too much noise, talking back and forth across me, for Fred not to know there was a party going on. But he kept his eyes on the road.

"Are you ladies enjoying yourselves?" he finally said.

"Oh, yes, immensely." Mumma giggled. It was the kind of giggle I'd only heard from her in two places—at Cousin Ella's wedding reception, where everyone got tipsy from champagne, and on Saturday nights in the kitchen when she and Daddy had whiskey and water and played cards with the Martins. I looked at her now. Her cheeks and nose were as flushed as radishes.

"And you, Avis? Are you enjoying our little jaunt?" Fred stared straight ahead.

"Oh, Freddie, it takes my breath away. Truly." She wiped her brow with a hankie. "Whew. It truly does."

Her lipstick was smeared up over her top lip from the cider bottle. I pointed with a finger to my own lip, to give her a clue. She took her compact from her purse, opened it, and burst out laughing.

"I look like I've been kissing a gorilla."

"Let me see." Mumma leaned over. "Why, Avis. It looks like you've been kissing two gorillas."

"Well, one of 'em wasn't Edward."

"That's not necessary, Avis."

"And one of them sure wasn't me," Fred said.

Mumma and Avis both got quiet. They looked at each other, raised their eyebrows, and sat back. Mumma started fiddling with the cork on her bottle of cider and looked out the window. Avis wiped her mouth and reapplied her lipstick. I watched Fred's eyes in the mirror. We rode along in silence.

"This last stretch is pure country, ladies. Hold on to your hat, Avis." He jerked the car onto a gravel road. We bumped and jostled along in the back, not saying anything. A flurry of small stones flew off to the sides as the tires gouged through ruts and gravel, making tinny little spitty sounds against the hubcaps.

Suddenly there was a loud pop.

"Jesus H. Christ." Mumma held on to her bottle as the contents exploded. Cherry cider, foaming and red, shot up to the roof of the car and splashed all over the seat, the carpeting, Mumma, and me.

"Holy Mother of God!" Aunt Avis exclaimed as cider sprayed her face.

"Will you look at that." Mumma was incredulous.

Fred slowed and stopped the car. His hands were gripping the steering wheel. Finally he turned and stared at us. All my beautiful polka dots were smeared in a cherry background. The pale brushed leather of Fred's seats took on the color of blood as cherry cider seeped in. The beige carpet under my feet was red, too. Fred got out of the car.

Aunt Avis and Mumma opened their doors and got out. Mumma kept dabbing at her splotched blouse with her fingers. "We need a little seltzer water." She was flustered. I sat in the middle of the seat, using my dress to mop up cider.

Fred stuck his head right into the back and reached across my lap, feeling the stickiness of the seats and the wetness of the rug. He took his white handkerchief out of his pocket and pressed it against the cushion till it soaked through. He stood up. "Get in, both of you. Just get in."

Mumma and Avis quieted down and closed the doors. Fred got behind the wheel, turned the car around without a word, and took off. I don't know which of them was laughing first—full-out, nonstop laughing. It started with snickers between them and kept escalating. Fred and I were both silent.

"Poor Fred," Avis wheezed, but she didn't sound too upset. "Poor Barbara. Look, look at the dress. Her cherry dress." But she was laughing. "I'm going to pee, I'm going to wet my pants," Avis said, barely able to speak.

"Oh, don't, Avis, please don't." Mumma gasped for air. "We've done enough."

The whole time Fred was driving lickety-split. He drove directly to a little town we'd passed through a few miles back. When he got to the main street, he pulled up in front of a small grocery store and pointed to a sign that hung above the door. It said BUS STOP, and there was a picture of a greyhound poised mid-lope over the door.

"This, ladies, is the end of the line. I've been taken for a ride, and now the ride is over." He got out, opened the back door next to Avis, reached in, and helped her climb out of the car. "And take your cider with you."

"Why, thank you, Fred. How thoughtful," Avis said as he handed her the bottles one by one. Mumma was scurrying to get out by herself on the other side.

Fred turned and pointed across the street. "If you catch one going in that direction, it might take you all the way back up to Canada." Then he took his wallet from his pocket and selected a bill. He leaned into the car toward me, grabbed my hand to help me out, and pressed the bill into it. "That is for your supper, miss. I'm sorry I won't be joining you. Get whatever you want on the menu. And get yourself a new dress besides. You're a lovely young girl, Barbara, a flower among the few." Then he winked at me for the last time, touched his hand to his hat, and closed the door. "I hope you don't have too long a wait, but you seem to amuse yourselves nicely." Then he started up the car and sped away.

"That shithead." Avis watched him go. "Well, now I can have a cigarette." She put her bottles of cider at her feet, fished one out of her purse, and lit it.

Mumma just stood there holding two bottles in each arm, looking in the direction the car went. "Well, I'll be damned." She turned to Avis. "You do get me into the darnedest predicaments."

"But we amuse ourselves nicely."

It was a fifty-dollar bill in my hand. Mumma tried to whistle when she saw it, but she couldn't. We had to use some of it for bus tickets. Mumma and Avis had spent their cash on the cider. Avis took the bill from me and went into the grocery store. I refused to go in because of my dress. I was pretty miserable, inside and out. Mumma stood with me. In a few minutes Avis came back out with three hot dogs and the bus tickets.

"It'll be coming through in a little over an hour. We can wait right here." She pointed to a patch of grass. "At least we can sit. I got us some grub." She laughed. "Figured we already had something to drink." We sat on the grass and ate steamed hot dogs on soggy buns. Avis and Mumma passed a bottle of cider between them. Avis dropped mustard on her collar, a blob that smeared more when she wiped it with a dry napkin.

"Well, good. Now we all look right out of a slop pail," Mumma said.

"Not quite what we expected, by way of dinner." Avis stretched her legs out in front of her and lit a cigarette. "But I've had worse."

"Oh, yes," Mumma chimed in, "much worse. Some you've cooked yourself."

Avis laughed. "We could still be with Fred." The cigarette was between her teeth.

It was more fun being with just them. "Could I have some cider?" I asked, smiling for the first time in hours.

"Take it slow," Avis said, opening a bottle and handing it to me. "Don't jiggle the contents."

We sat quietly together, watching people come in and out of the grocery, and waited. Mumma said good afternoon to whoever noticed us, like we were perfectly normal, having a picnic. The bus finally came, and we straggled on board. The driver looked curious when he saw my poor dress and then alarmed when he saw the bottles Mumma and Avis were carrying. We were down to six.

"Don't worry," Avis said to him, with a sly smile. "We've had our fun for the day."

We went to the very back of the bus. It wasn't crowded. We sat in the last seat, the one that goes all the way across, so we could be together. We lined the bottles along the floor in front of us and kept them steady between our feet. I sat in the middle.

"We've certainly had our fill of buses today, Barbara," Mumma said, leaning back against the seat. "But I'm glad to get on this one."

"I'm sorry about your dress, Barb." Avis fingered the limp mass of material. "But there's plenty of money left over for a new one. Old Fred saw to it, got to give him that much. We'll go downtown tomorrow and do it up."

She reached over and put her hand on my knee. "A flower among the few," she said, smiling. "He got that right."

Mumma looked down at me. "He did," she said. "He surely did."

Of course, Avis never saw Fred again after that. And his aunt stopped coming to the beauty salon.

Aunt Avis had other boyfriends, lots. I met some, heard about others. Fred must have looked pretty good to her, in retrospect, if she ever thought about him. Avis didn't have too good a track record.

I got a new dress the next morning that was more expensive than anything I'd ever had. It was a beautiful dark blue material with a certain shine to it. Avis said it was the cat's meow. I loved that dress. Daddy never noticed that I came home wearing a different dress from the one I'd left in. He never heard a word about our ride in the country.

For years afterward, though, whenever Mumma and Aunt Avis and I were together, one of us might look up and say, "Oh, I do wish I had a nice glass of cherry cider. It would be so refreshing." And we would all three start giggling. Daddy would look up from his newspaper or his supper plate and shake his head—or even leave the room—knowing that he was being kept out of another secret between the two of them, those sisters. But this time I knew what they were laughing about. I knew. So I stayed in the room and laughed with them.

Part Four

Edward on the Road

Prescott Mills, Maine
June 1956

"Christ, I got to get back to the garage. It's after two." Edward was fastening his watch back onto his wrist. Iris had somehow gotten it off him with her teeth. There were tooth marks in the leather. How'd he explain that to Idella? He pulled on his pants, flicking off bits of twigs and pine needles. "I got a customer said he was coming by later. Lookin' for a trade-in. I hope there's no ants crawling around in these legs."

"Oh, Eddie, let's not go yet. What's the rush? People always say they'll come back to the showroom, and you never see 'em again." Iris was sitting cross-legged on the ground picking at a pinecone with those long nails of hers. She was wearing nothing but Edward's sport jacket around her shoulders. Her clothes were scattered across the ground behind her.

He and Iris never even made it into the camp today, onto one of the camp beds with the lumpy mattresses—like rolling around on cottage cheese, Iris'd said the first time he brought her up here. Today she wanted to "do it" outside, hidden by the trees, to celebrate spring. She'd made him lie down on the ground behind the picnic table, tree roots jabbing into his backside no matter where he got, and wait till she took everything off him. It drove him crazy, wanting to grab onto her bare behind and roll over on top of her and grind her into the leaves. He'd barely held on, till she finally lay down on top of him and started pushing her tits into his mouth. God. Nothing like Idella's little sacks. Nothing.

"Let's get those bathing suits out of mothballs, Eddie, and go for a swim." Iris had been through every drawer in the camp.

"I'm not going to bother them things Idella's got packed. We've moved things around in there enough." Edward carried his shoes and socks over to the picnic table and sat on a bench. Iris had wild ideas. It was damn cold on that ground, and one of them little bush things had prickles. There were scratches all up and down him.

"She'll just think it's kids breaking in, using the place in the winter. Let's get the suits and take a swim."

Iris had laughed and laughed that first day, when Edward told her the walls of the camp were knotty pine. She'd thought he'd made the joke on purpose. "We're sure being naughty," she'd said laughingly, and that's what she called the camp now, "Naughty Pine." Edward smiled thinking of it.

Iris gathered all the pieces of the pinecone she'd picked apart and threw them into the trees. "There. Scattering seeds, Eddie. Next year there'll be a tree with my name on it." She stood up.

Edward saw that his jacket came down to her knees. She looked little, with just her legs sticking out, and the jacket covering all them soft curves and them big tits. Like lobster buoys, the way they bobbed around in her sweaters and stayed firm. Iris's body had so many places you could squeeze and hold on to. Idella was all bones—bones and bird legs.

"Come on, Eddie, let's go into the water."

"Jesus, Iris, it's barely June. You see anybody else swimming?"

"Just a little dip? To say we did?"

"Iris, I got a customer coming. That bastard Murphy'll take him right out from under me if the guy shows up and I'm not there." Iris sat down next to him on the bench, pulling his jacket open a little so her tits were showing. "He sold three cars last week, and two of 'em were mine. I spend a whole morning with some guy, give him the sell—"

"Eddie, your hair's all mussed." Iris took his comb from his inside coat pocket. "Look straight ahead."

"I give them the sell. . . . They say they got to go think about it, check out another showroom. . . . What can I do?"

"Keep your head still."

"And then when they come back to the showroom and I'm not there, that Murphy guy robs me. 'Sure, Eddie,' he says with that shit-eating grin, 'take some time. Go for a test-drive in one of them new Plymouths. Can't spend your whole life sitting in here.' Mr. Friendly. The bastard."

"Eddie, we had such a nice time. Wasn't it worth it, to spend some time with little ol' me?" She was pulling bits of dried leaves out of his hair and running her fingers around the inside of his ear. "He's right, you know. You can't stay in that showroom every waking moment. You've got to have some fun."

"What's this on my collar?" Edward was buttoning his shirt. "It's on the sleeve, too. Pitch. Holy Christ, I'm covered in pitch. How am I gonna explain that to Idella?"

"Oh, Eddie, don't tell her anything. Tell her it's none of her business." Iris scraped at the streaks of pitch with her long fingernails. "You never go through *her* clothes and ask about spots and spills, do you? So why should she go through yours?"

"She goes through 'em, all right. Goes through my pockets. She don't miss a thing. So don't be slipping any more notes in them. She could of found that last one."

"What if she did? Who cares?" Iris unbuttoned the top of his shirt.

"Iris, don't start that." He brushed her hands away. "We're done here. Get your clothes on. We got to get out of here."

"Here. I'll scrape that sticky old pitch off with my teeth." Iris pushed herself up against him and started biting at the smear of pitch on his shirt collar. She slowly moved her hands down his sides and between his legs. She rubbed them gently up and down along his inner thighs. "Mmmmm. It smells so woodsy. It tastes good." He could feel his dick rising up to her hand and nodding hello. She stopped and smiled at him. "You want a taste? It's in my mouth now."

Edward grinned and pulled her over onto his lap, up against him. "That's not all that's going to be in your mouth." He stood up, stuck his knee between her legs, and rolled her down onto the cold, wet ground.

"Oh, I love a swim after making love! You shouldn't have gotten out so soon, Eddie." Iris dropped Idella's swimsuit down to her ankles and flicked it onto the ground with her foot. "I'm glad to get that off. I felt like a lamp shade with that little skirt going all around." Iris liked making fun of Idella's things. "And I'm so cold!" She laughed and hugged herself, rubbing her arms up and down her bare sides. "You never even got all the way in, Eddie. You never took your glasses off."

"I got in far enough."

"Uh-oh. You've got your hat on. I know what that means. Eddie's ready."

Edward was all dressed. He leaned against his car and watched as Iris started to pull on all her layers of clothes. She was frisky, getting things on quick, hopping around. He took his cigarettes out of his shirt pocket.

His hands were so stiff and prickly he could barely shake one out of the pack. His fingers were as white as his cigarettes. That damn water'd about killed him. His balls had shrunk up to the size of them hardball candies Idella sold at the store—"hot balls," the kids called them. He laughed. Nothing hot about his.

"You ought to learn to swim, Eddie. It's *so* refreshing." Iris was bent sideways knocking water out of her ears.

"You said I'm fresh enough already."

"And we could do it in the water." Iris pulled her dress down over her wet head and smiled at him through the neck hole. "There's ways to do it floating in the water."

"Yeah? How would you know that?" She bent her arms around her back and tugged up the zipper. He hated to think of her "doing it" with anyone else. Course she had. She'd been around. Was married to Dickie for years. Now she called herself a divorcée because it sounded French— like from France, she'd say, not Canada.

"I bet you and Idella never did it in the water." Edward watched as Iris carefully unrolled her nylons and slid them up her legs. It was like wearing a rubber, he thought, a rubber on each leg. She said she was too old for any buns in her oven, so he didn't have to bother with wearing them damn things. Pain in the ass, them rubbers. Always leaking or coming off.

Iris didn't have any kids. She'd waited and waited to get pregnant with Dickie, but nothing happened. He and Idella kept getting babies when they weren't looking. One goddamn girl after another, four of them, seven years between each. The seven-year itch, everyone said when they heard that, winking. Some Marilyn Monroe movie. If he'd a been married to Marilyn Monroe, it wouldn't be no seven years between. And it wouldn't be all girls.

"I bet you and Idella never did it anywhere but in your lumpy old bed at home. I bet she keeps her nightgown on the whole time."

"Let's get a move on." How did Iris know that? Smart woman. He looked at his watch. Christ. He ground his cigarette out in the leaves and opened his car door. "Get in."

"What'll I do with these, Eddie?" Iris picked the wet swimsuits from off the ground and dangled them in front of him. "Hang them on a tree?"

"You better give 'em to me, or Idella'll find them. She wants to come on Sunday to open the camp." Edward took the cold suits from her. He opened his glove compartment and crammed them in, slamming the door shut.

"You didn't tell me that." Iris slipped on her shoes.

"What?"

"That you were coming up here on Sunday with her to open up."

"I forgot." Edward started the motor. "I was thinking of other things." He smiled at her and patted the seat next to him. "Get in." Iris got her pocketbook and pulled her sweater tight around her and got in. She pushed herself up next to him. Her thigh felt cold against his, even through her dress.

He backed slowly down the bumpy driveway and swung carefully around onto the camp road. It was all full of potholes and oozing spring mud the color of shit. The car would sink into one of them suckers if he didn't drive right, and they'd be in it past the hubcaps. "Don't be talking to me on this road, Iris. I got to concentrate."

"You do the driving, Eddie. I'll be good." She gave his knee a pat.

Edward leaned forward to see what was coming up ahead. He'd take it slow, try to be patient, one muck hole at a time. He had to get back to the showroom. He wouldn't try to explain his long lunch. Let them bastards roll their eyes. What did he care? It was none of their business what he did.

Murphy called him "the weasel"—Irish bastard. Worse than the French, them Irish. "That Eddie, he's the weasel," Murphy would say, in front of Jones and Battier, slapping him on the back like it was a great joke. "He can sniff out a customer from behind a rock." Well, what were you supposed to do? Sit on your ass and wait for them to come running up to you? Edward Jensen was a real salesman. He'd sold more cars in his life than that Murphy had farts coming out of his ass. And that was saying something. Edward laughed, relieved, as he bumped to the end of the road and turned out onto Route 9.

"What are you laughing at?" Iris smiled over at him. She didn't like being left out of anything.

"Nothing."

"Some kind of cute nothing." She pulled at his ear as he came to a stop. They always parked her car at this rest area. It was a slate blue

Plymouth Savoy with twenty-two thousand miles on it. A good car. Edward sold it to her last October. She'd sat so close to him on the test drive, and leaned over and asked about the lights, and then the radio, and then the turn signal, sidling up closer as she moved her fingers across the dashboard. Then she'd looked in the rearview mirror and said what beautiful blue eyes he had, and such nice dark eyebrows, and that was how it got started. And then him telling her he thought she had nice tits. Or that they must be nice, the way they poked at her blouse so nice, saying hello, and she said she'd be glad to show them to him sometime, and then he'd just kept on driving and they'd ended up having quite an afternoon. And he'd made a sale, too.

Edward squeezed her knee. It was still cold. "Okay. I got to get on back."

Iris was looking at him, her hair wet and clumped around her head. "When we gonna see each other, Eddie, if Idella takes the camp away from us? Where we gonna meet if we can't use Naughty Pine?"

"I dunno." Edward hadn't thought beyond this afternoon. "Your place?"

"You know we can't meet there. My mother never goes out."

"I can't think about this now, Iris. I got to get back."

"Okay, Eddie." Iris got out and closed the door.

"We'll find someplace, Iris, don't worry."

"It's too good not to, isn't it, Eddie?" She blew him a kiss.

He pulled his car around, headed back toward Portland, and gave a little wave into the rearview mirror as he picked up speed.

Edward was hungry. He thought he'd get a burger, maybe a cup of coffee, before going back. Idella'd made one of them cream-cheese-and-green-olive things for his lunch, but he'd eaten it at a red light on his way in. He hated red lights. Couldn't stand sitting there feeling the engine throb, seeing other cars move. There was nothing worse than making a left across traffic. Those bastards coming in the other lane never let him in, never slowed up. He liked to be driving alone, no one to bother him—except dumb-assed drivers that got in front. Slow weavers were the worst. You start to pull out and pass 'em, and they weave over to the left. Nothing to do then but lay on the horn and push 'em over. Here was the

A&W. He made a sharp right. A car horn blared behind him. Some old biddy, shouldn't be on the road.

Edward looked for a good post to park next to. He liked eating in the car. He was always hungry after being with Iris. She sapped the energy right out of him. Hell of a woman. He reached out his window to push the "talk" button on his speaker. The damn post was too far over. He had to open the door and lean way out to get his finger on it. A garbled voice blared back.

"What?" he yelled at the gray box. "What?" Goddamn speaker! He pushed on both buttons. There was two of them on the damn thing. "You talking to me?" He leaned on his horn. That'll wake them up. "I want a cheeseburger!" he yelled. He felt the hotness pour down his face. "I want a cheeseburger, and I want it now, goddamn it!"

He looked around at the other cars. The people were all staring at him. Nothing better to do than stuff their faces and gawk.

"Can I help you?" A young waitress approached with a pad and pen.

"Yes, you can help me." He smiled up at her and closed his door. "Them speaker poles are all cockeyed. Giving my order to you is nicer."

She was only about seventeen, Edward thought, about the same age as Donna. Her mouth was sort of pouty, smeared all over with pink lipstick. She had on one of them skimpy uniforms the color of the root beer. Those skirts on the uniforms came way up. He'd never let Donna wear one so short. He wouldn't let her out of the house, by God. Showing over the knees like that. An invitation.

The young waitress looked at him and held up her order pad. She was pushing her knees together and pressing her arms up against her sides. It must be cold in them skimpy uniforms. "I guess I get special treatment, having you come all the way out here to help me."

"I guess so." Her eyes kept flitting back to the restaurant. Maybe she had other orders she was taking care of in there, somebody's burger getting cold. Edward smiled. His would be nice and hot.

"I'll have the afternoon special," he said, pointing up at the billboard they had painted in big brown root-beer-colored letters. "A number two." He always got the same thing.

"That's a cheeseburger, an eight-ounce mug of root beer, an apple turnover, and a cup of coffee?"

"That's right." He smiled up at her. "I don't suppose you come with it?" He couldn't help himself. It seemed like the right thing to say.

She shook her head and squinted her eyes at him. "No, sir, not in a pig's eye." She spit it out more than spoke it, the little tart, and tore the order from her pad like a goddamned queen. "Here's your copy," she said, and stuffed it through the window. "Someone will bring it out soon."

"I like my coffee black!" Edward shouted after her fat little behind as it trounced back into the restaurant.

He didn't know why he said that about the coffee. They always gave you them little packets of sugar and cream on the side. That was how he liked his coffee best, with lots of sugar and cream. One time cream squirted all over his glasses and the roof of the car when he was trying to open one of them goddamned little cups. Them little tabs they want you to pull on are no bigger than a flea's ass. He'd had to stick his thumb through the foil just to get into it. Then cream flew all over hell and back. He couldn't see clear till he got home that night and Idella cleaned his glasses with hot water. "Jesus, Edward, what did you do—pour the cream over your head? I've never seen the likes of it." She always had a remark.

Iris'd found little blobs in the car the next day and started asking about it, teasing him about the cream. He laughed. She had such a dirty mind. She was a smart one, that Iris.

"Here you are, sir." A fat, hairy bastard was standing there holding out a tray. He looked like they'd dragged him out of the men's room. He had a smart-ass grin on his face. "That'll be one dollar and forty-four cents, including tax." Edward counted out the four pennies. No tips for these bastards, not from Edward Jensen. He handed him the money, and the jerk kept standing there holding on to the tray.

"You'll have to put your window up another couple of inches, sir, or the tray won't fit."

"I knew that. I was waiting to pay you first."

"I got my hands full here, sir. If you roll up the window, I'll be glad to take your money."

"I'll bet you will." Edward rolled the window up just enough. The smart-ass hooked the tray over the top lip of the glass and held out his hand. Edward handed him the money.

The man took it and smiled. "Enjoy your special," he said, winking. He turned and hurried back into the restaurant like a hog on the trot,

Edward thought. There was no cream or sugar on the tray. Them bastards. They did that on purpose.

Edward pulled in to his parking space on the car lot. He'd been gone four hours. He checked into his rearview for signs of Iris's lipstick. A glob of apple filling was stuck to his chin. He adjusted the mirror to get a better look behind. Yes, there was Murphy, hands in his pockets like a good-for-nothing, watching him. Edward readjusted his mirror and got out of the car. Back on the job. It had been good to be out, to be moving.

"Well, well, look who's here! We thought maybe you got lost, took a wrong turn!" Murphy said, with that hale and hearty voice of his, like he was on the radio. It always meant trouble. "Where you been, Eddie?" Murphy wouldn't even let him get to his desk, following along behind him like a dog in heat. "We were just starting to get worried, weren't we, Jones?" Ralph Jones never looked up from the magazine he was reading behind his desk.

"I been with a customer. Test-drive." Edward took his jacket off and hung it over the chair. He could smell Iris's perfume in it.

"Make a sale?"

"I'm working on it." Bastard. Edward opened the drawer of his desk, like he was looking in there for something important, keeping his head down. If he looked up into Murphy's face, there'd be no turning him off. Edward lifted up a page of the manufacturer's price list that he always kept on top, over his magazines and joke books. Murphy was standing in front of his desk.

"I hope it works out, Eddie. I really do."

Edward looked up. "Well, isn't that nice of you, Murphy?"

"Yeah, well." Murphy put his hands on top of the desk and leaned over toward him. Edward could smell them Pep-O-Mints he always sucked. "See, Eddie, this customer you were out fishing for . . . well, it kept you from snagging the one you had on the hook."

"Is that so?" Christ, that Blair guy he'd spent all of yesterday buttering. He'd come back, the bastard, when he said he would.

"We kept him dangling here as best we could, Eddie, thinking you was just out for a bite, thinking you'd be rolling onto the lot any minute. We even called your wife at the store, to see if you'd surprised her with a little visit. Blair, I think that's his name?" Edward nodded. "He was gasping for air, Eddie. You could see that we had to get him off the hook or throw him back. He'd been over to Rubell Motors, and they were angling for him, they would of hooked him for sure if I'd of let him walk out of here. If I hadn't stepped in. He was losing patience."

Edward watched Murphy's tongue moving the Life Saver around while he talked. "You made the sale?"

"Couldn't throw him over to Rubell, now, could I, Eddie?" Murphy shrugged like he was sorry about something. Sorry his hairy horse's ass.

"The used Belvedere two-door that Marston woman traded in last week? That's the one I got him hot for." Edward wanted Murphy to know just who had done the real selling, that bastard, just who had done the real work. "'Cause he was a cold drop-in when I got my hands on him. He wasn't looking to buy shit till I took him around the lot."

Murphy grinned. "Oh, I don't doubt that, Eddie, not for a minute." He smiled that sickly smile of his that Edward wanted to plaster across some roadside. "Actually, Eddie, the truth is, I bumped it up a little. He ordered one from the factory. With extras. A/C. Radio. Special paint job. Four-door. Convertible, actually."

Edward could feel his face get hot. The root beer he'd drunk down so fast was trying to come up on him. He held on to the top of his desk drawer, waiting for Murphy to stop gloating and shut his trap. He needed that sale. Christ. You could sit around this place for a week and have nothing. Do a whole book of them word puzzles. Everyone had some kind of book like that in his desk. Even Murphy had them sports books. Then you go out for an hour or so, you finally get the hell out of here, and this happens.

"Did you hear me, Eddie?" Murphy again. "You seemed lost in thought there." Edward looked at him. "I say your wife wants you to call her. Hope I didn't worry her none, trying to locate you."

"I'll call her right now." Edward reached for his phone. That'd get Murphy off his desk, at least.

"You do that, Eddie." Murphy finally walked away. "Don't want to worry that nice lady." Edward watched him reach into his pocket and peel back another Pep-O-Mint.

He turned his face to the wall, where he had his calendar pinned up, some covered bridge in Vermont, and put the receiver to his ear. He dialed his own telephone, so he'd get a busy signal. He couldn't talk to

Idella now. Them bastards would listen to every word, and she'd be nothing but questions. He didn't have the strength to come up with any answers.

"Where were you?" It was the first thing out of Idella's mouth as soon as the customer was out the front door with his six-pack. She stood behind the register of Jensen's Drive-In Store, her hands resting on top of the closed cash drawer, her nylons rolled down around her ankles like little brown doughnuts. Edward barely had time to come in the side door and snag a bag of Humpty Dumpty from the potato-chip rack.

"With a customer." Edward crammed a handful of chips into his mouth.

"For four hours?"

"How do you know how long it was?"

"Because I called the showroom, finally. They said you'd just left. I never heard a word from you, did I?"

"I tried to call, but the line was busy."

"That's what Mr. Murphy said. But I been right here standing at this register all the livelong day since nine o'clock this morning, and not one call has come in on that telephone except for Mr. Murphy looking for you. The only thing that's been busy is me. Pat called in sick, George couldn't fill in for her, so I've been standing here since I woke up this morning. I'm about ready to drop. I've had three beer deliveries to put away, plus Oakhurst, Old King Cole, and Humpty Dumpty. The whole time kids kept coming in asking for candy and bringing in them damn empties. I couldn't even pee till Mrs. Rudolf come in and I asked her to keep an eye out while I went upstairs. I was ready to burst."

"Well, Jesus Christ, Idella, none of that is my fault. You blame me for everything. You'd blame me if you farted."

"Don't go getting funny."

"Who's been nagging at me since I walked in the goddamned door?"

The front door opened, and a customer walked in. "Good evening," Idella called out cheerily. "How are you this evening?"

Edward walked over behind the meat counter in the back of the store. The lights were off, and the shadows felt good. He sat on the rickety kitchen chair they had back there and stared into the display case, at the unsliced torpedoes of bologna and salami, the white cardboard containers of hamburger that Idella had carefully weighed out and wrapped, and the hot dogs from Jordan's Meats, skinny penises linked by their tails and layered into the box. They put something in them hot dogs to make them red. He didn't know why.

He could hear Idella out there making small talk. "Oh, yes, kids'll all be out of school before we know it. No, we don't take a vacation, really. We've got the camp out on Highland Lake. We're going to open it up on Sunday. But it's so hard to keep up and run the store. And renters are so hard on it. The things people'll do when it's someone else's property. You want matches, too? And kids get out there in the winter and break in and use the place for drinking and whatnot. It's terrible. Do you need a bag for that?" The high trill of Idella's voice was like water running somewhere, a leak that wouldn't shut off.

Christ, Idella'd be wanting to rent out the camp soon, or Barbara and Donna would want to use it with their friends, always wanting to go swimming. Edward reached into his shirt pocket and shook out a Lucky Strike. He and Iris had been going out there since the fall. It got cold as hell in the winter. They made their own heat, him and Iris. Edward felt around in his pants pockets for his matches. They'd walked in there in the snow one time, when the camp road wasn't plowed. Snow come up to their knees. They'd thrown snowballs. He hadn't done that since he was a kid. They'd gotten out the wool blankets Idella had in mothballs and garbage bags, and they'd made a fire from what was left stacked out on the porch. With a bottle of Crown Royal and some Italian sandwiches he'd brought from the store, they had a feast. Idella did make a good Italian sandwich, even Iris had to give her credit there.

Where were them matches? He swatted at his pockets, going around and around to the same places he'd already been—shirt, pants, jacket. Goddamned matches. Iris had stuck them in her purse, probably. She was always taking things from out of his pockets. Said she liked to keep bits of him around. He stood up, staying behind the meat counter, and waited till Idella went over to the beer cooler and slid the door open. She always restocked it right after a sale, to keep the beer cold. Edward walked over to the register and reached behind it for some matches. Idella was bent over halfway into the cooler, like a cow in a stall, with just her ass sticking out and them bony legs. She was getting them warm six-packs into the way back so the cold ones'd be up front. Edward knew he should be doing that. And he would. After he had a smoke. He got back onto his chair in the shadows and lit his Lucky Strike.

He picked stray bits of tobacco off the tip of his tongue and thought of Iris, the way her tongue got so quick. He took a long drag and felt his lungs fill up with smoke. Why anyone would smoke them filtered things, like having cotton in your mouth, he couldn't figure. You smoke or you don't. Where would they go now, him and Iris? He blew the smoke out and watched it curl up to the ceiling. Iris never stopped talking when they were "doing it," kept talking the whole time, her voice all soft and low. Christ, that was the one time Idella ever got quiet. Iris talked dirty to him. She egged him on, teased, till he'd have to stop her mouth up with his tongue and then he'd steer into her so hard and clean like he owned the road and his foot was flooring the pedal. God Almighty.

"Where the hell have you been? I thought you was upstairs going to the john or something, till I smell this cigarette. Here I been standing all the livelong day while you're out driving around—at least you get to go someplace—and when you finally get here, you sit down some more and keep me standing. Couldn't you at least help me fill up the cooler?"

"Jesus Christ, Idella, I help you plenty. What do you think I been doing all day? Driving around in the country looking at the trees? I been trying to sell some goddamned cars, that's what I've been doing while you're in here squawking with the customers." There she was, at him, at him, not even letting him have the pleasure of one cigarette.

"Did you sell any?"

"I would have, a brand-new factory convertible, if that Murphy bastard didn't steal the customer the one time I go out to get something to eat so I don't have to stare into his goddamned ugly face. I spent my whole afternoon yesterday with that customer. He said he had to go talk to his wife. His wife, my ass. He was over at Rubell's, the bastard. I offered him a good deal. Then he comes back today and gives the sale to Murphy 'cause I'm getting something to eat."

"But Murphy called here looking for you."

"Sure he did, to cover his ass. He'd made the sale already, the goddamned cheating bastard." Edward could feel that wave of heat pouring down his face. He pounded his fists against the top of his legs.

"Well, don't go bursting something over it. It's done. Sit down. I'll get you a beer." Idella was on her way to the cooler. "It's a damn hard way to make a living, I know that much." She got a cold Budweiser out, replaced it with a bottle from the back, and opened it on the soda cooler. "Here, sit down and drink this. Are you hungry? I've got some sandwiches made." Edward nodded that he was hungry. He took a swig of the beer. "Let me get you set up." Idella pulled down the wooden shelf that served as their eating area and unwrapped a long, thin sandwich from the white paper it had been rolled into. People came in from all over to get them sandwiches for their lunches, Edward thought. Jensen's Drive-In made the best Italian sandwiches. "Do you want extra oil?" Edward nodded. Idella squirted olive oil from the shaker bottle up and down the sandwich. She used real olive oil. "Extra ham?" Edward nodded again. She got some sliced ham out of the cooler and tucked it into the long roll. "Sit here. I'll get you some chips to go with it."

"Barbecue," Edward called after her, his mouth already full.

"Turn off the beer signs, Edward. Lock the front door. It's after eleven. I'm not ringing up one more customer. Jesus, what a day. I'm so tired I could drop." Idella let out a deep sigh. She stood facing the counter behind the register, preparing to tally the day's cash drawer and make out the nightly deposit. Edward would ride them down to Casco Bank on Main Street, and she'd put it into the night-deposit slot. "Ten, twenty, thirty . . ."

"Where'd we get them new flavors?" Edward had locked the door, turned off the neon beer signs, and opened the ice-cream freezer as he passed it.

"Seventy, eighty . . ." Idella stopped laying down the pile of bills. "From the ice-cream delivery, where'd you think? Jesus, Edward, I'm trying to count."

"I was just asking, for Christ's sake." He bent down closer to look at the frozen boxes before him.

"One hundred, one hundred and ten . . . Don't go getting into anything now."

"I'm just looking!"

"One hundred and thirty."

She finished counting the tens. Edward leaned into the cooler to read the flavor on the box. "Banana Rum. That sounds awful good. Do you think it's legal?"

"Course it's legal. It's just rum flavoring, is all."

"I'm going to have to try me some."

"Not now, Edward. It's so late. Haven't you had enough? I saw you with that Payday." Idella started counting the next pile. "Five, ten, fifteen, twenty . . ." He heard the soft *slap, slap, slap* of the bills as she stacked them.

"Where's a spoon?" Edward removed a half gallon of ice cream.

"Thirty, thirty-five . . . Close the freezer . . . forty . . . Out back . . . by the sink . . . fifty."

"Ow! Who left this chair here, goddamn it!"

"You did . . . seventy . . . Turn on the light . . . seventy-five . . . Do I have to do everything? . . . eighty."

"No, you don't have to do everything." He reached up and pulled on the light, careful not to grab the flypaper that hung alongside it. He'd learned that the hard way.

"Bring me a little dish, why don't you? You can't eat a whole half gallon by yourself. You *shouldn't* anyway. . . . One hundred."

"I thought it was too late for snacks." Edward was pleased that he had turned her around.

"Well, it's open, isn't it? Don't try to get my goat."

Edward tried to think of something funny to say, to make Idella laugh, something about a goat, but he couldn't. If it was Iris he was talking to, it would have just come to him and they'd be laughing already and both be eating out of the same spoon, passing cold lumps of ice cream between their mouths.

"One, t', thr', f'r, fv, sx, sev', et, ni', ten . . ." She was counting the ones. He got one of the white cardboard trays that Idella used to measure the hamburger into, and he started to scoop ice cream out for her. He was just as happy eating out of the carton.

The telephone rang.

"Holy mother of God, who could that be? Edward! Will you get that? Probably some kid asking if we have Prince Albert in a can. They think that's so funny."

It had rung three times now. Edward, thrown by the jangling noise, carried the carton and spoons in one hand and Idella's cardboard dish in his other. "All right, all right, I'm coming. Damn kids!"

"Let him out, they say. Let him out of the can." Idella was stacking quarters into piles of four. "It's so annoying. We probably shouldn't even answer it. . . . Four, five . . ."

"Jensen's Drive-In." Edward managed to put down Idella's dish and spoon and pick up the receiver. "Hello!"

"Eddie Bear?"

It was Iris. Edward felt his face flush. He pressed the box of ice cream against him and clutched the phone. "Yes," he said, using his cheerful salesman voice. "Yes," he said again, as though in answer to a second question. Idella stopped counting. She leaned over and picked up her dish of ice cream.

"Eddie, is she there?" Iris's voice was little, hard to hear, and slow coming. She'd been drinking.

"Yes, sir. Yes." Edward nodded and held the ice-cream carton closer. Idella was watching him from behind the counter, eating her ice cream.

"Eddie Bear, I miss you *so* much. I want to see you. Can you come? Please? My mother's asleep. She won't wake up. I miss you already."

"Is that so?" Edward's voice was getting louder and cheerier. The ice cream was cold, pressed against his chest.

"Eddie, where will we go without our place? Without Naughty Pine? That's our place." Iris was crying.

Jesus, what was happening here? She'd never done anything like this before. He started nodding as though he were listening to something besides this crying into the phone.

"Who is it?" Idella was mouthing at him, waving her spoon to get his attention. "Who is it?"

"Eddie, I love you. I can't go on living like this. You've got to leave her."

"Oh, now, don't you feel too bad about that." Edward motioned to Idella to keep still.

"You got t' tell her. . . . We b'long together . . . you and li'l ol' me."

"Yes, well, sure. Yes. Thanks for calling. I'll see you tomorrow." He hung up the phone. Jesus. His armpits were dripping, the ice cream was dripping. His face was burning.

"Who was that?" Edward stared back at Idella. She put down her empty dish. "Edward?"

"Murphy."

"Murphy?"

"Yeah. He wanted to apologize."

"Apologize?"

"For taking that sale. For taking my customer. Felt guilty."

"Is that so?"

"Wanted me to forgive him."

"Well, for God's sake."

"Been drinking."

"Imagine that."

"Yeah. Poor bastard."

"I guess he's got a conscience after all."

Edward watched numbly as Idella went back to counting change, sliding pennies across the counter with two fingers into groups of ten.

"Let's get out of here," he said. "Let's close up and go for a ride up in Gorham."

"That does sound good. I like a drive in the night air."

"Put the money in the bag."

"I'll be done in a minute. Go take care of that ice cream. It's dripping all down your shirt front."

Edward sat in the car waiting for Idella to make the night deposit. Christ, she acted like a criminal, looking both ways when she crossed Main Street to be sure no one was watching, holding the locked deposit bag up under her armpit. And so slow. Poking, poking. He wanted to get going.

"There," she said when she finally climbed in next to him. "That's safely done." Edward started out onto Main Street as she closed the door. "Hold your horses, Edward! Let me get in, why don't you? You trying to kill me?"

"Pretty good deposit?"

"Tolerable. We sold a lot of beer. That makes all the difference. Am I tired! I had all them deliveries at once. I thought I'd lose my mind. And in come a big troop of kids to buy penny candy. Them Forrest kids. Someone ought to do something about them. They're wild."

Edward got to the light on Main Street as it turned red. Damn! Wait, wait, wait, and wait some more! Idella was going on next to him—what customers come in and who said what. Usually he liked hearing about it, but tonight he needed to move.

There was no traffic driving through town. Everyone was in bed or

watching TV. Steve Allen would be bringing on the guests now, the
opening jokes were over. He could see the flickery gray lights of the
screens as he drove past houses on Gorham Road.

"All watching *The Tonight Show*," Idella said, "watching Steve Allen."
It was like she'd read his mind.

They got to the open country roads, the farms near where he grew up
and first learned to drive a car. He loved driving these country roads at
night. It calmed him.

"Don't that cool air feel good after being cooped up all day?" Idella
had the window down and was sticking her hand out. "Look at them
horses over there, Edward, with their heads sticking over the fence. You
can just make them out. Black horses." Edward knew that horse farm.
Gillie's Stables, they called it now. When he was a kid, it was the Bracket
place. They didn't have but two or three big old workhorses back then,
like his father's horse had been.

"Don't them horses look pretty?" Idella reached down, picked up a
can of Budweiser from the floor, and popped it open. They always passed
a beer or two between them on these evening rides, keeping the can low
so as not to get seen by the police. "Mmmmm. Nice and cold." She
reached over toward him. "You want a sip?"

Edward grabbed the can and took a swig. What was he going to do
about Iris calling like that? And getting boo-hooey—he hated that. He'd
have to talk with her. She couldn't be calling up at the store. He didn't
know where that was coming from. He wasn't in this for that kind of
trouble.

"You're awful quiet."

"Just driving."

"I know it's hard sitting in that showroom all day long. I don't know
how you do it. Waiting and waiting, never knowing if anyone's going to
come in. It's so queer, the way Mr. Murphy called like that. Late at night,
too. Do you really think he'd been drinking?"

"You know them Irish. They're worse than the French."

"My family was mostly Irish, Edward."

"And they drank anything that wasn't glued down."

"That's so." Idella sighed and took a sip from her can. "That's so."

Idella and Iris. Most men go their whole life and never even meet a
woman whose name starts with *I*. He had two of them on his hands.

Idella and Iris. Two *Is*. Christ. What a world. He kept driving, farther and farther up onto the back roads.

He hadn't meant to get involved with Iris. It just happened—she got thrown at him. It was Dickie, her ex-husband, that got her to come in. Knew she needed a good salesman. Edward had sold him two cars in the past five years, both good deals. When you give someone a good deal, they come back to you. They trust you. They tell their friends. Edward had more people come in and ask for him, by name, than Murphy'd ever have at his funeral. So Iris'd come in and asked for Edward Jensen. Heads turned plenty when she walked in. She was wearing that dress she had with all the buttons. Edward smiled, thinking of that dress. Some kind of green. Or blue.

Iris still trusted Dickie to steer her in the right direction on some things. He wasn't a bad sort. Dickie. They'd laughed about that nickname plenty, him and Iris. Poor bastard was a drinker. Couldn't hold his liquor for nothing and lost one job after another. A welder. You can't be operating a blowtorch and be drinking at the same time. He got canned one too many times, and Iris'd had enough. She left him. Collecting alimony from the poor bastard. Living with her mother, though. Christ.

Edward turned right onto Standish Road. He liked to drive by where the old house used to be. It was just a field now, nothing there. All that work Dad did to make a living. Just lying there flat, something you go by on the road.

"There's the old place," he said as he drove past. "That's where the farm was."

"Yep." Idella was rattling paper, opening up something.

"What have you got?"

"Nothing. Just one of them Ring Dings."

"You got some for me?"

"Of course. You don't think I'd take one just for myself, do you? Here, hold out your hand."

"This is a nice surprise."

"I thought we could use a little something, a treat. It's been such a day."

Edward stuffed the disk of cakey chocolate into his mouth. He liked the cream part they put in the center. Idella would eat hers with little mouse bites. She ate everything with them little bites, chewing and chewing.

Edward hadn't meant to get involved with Idella either. He sure wasn't looking for what he got when he went to that dance at the Grange hall that night out in Scarborough. Who was he with? Eva Gallant? Cora somebody? Maybe he'd come alone. There'd been quite a few willing to go out with Edward Jensen. They were all glad to be seen with him. He knew that much.

He'd been at the dance for a while before he even noticed her. She must have seen him, though. He was a good dancer. The best thing there. She was sitting alone in the corner with her ankles crossed, her foot wagging back and forth, going along with the music. And her hands were cupped together on her lap as if she was holding some little animal. "What you hiding in there?" he'd asked her. "A mouse?" "Why, nothing," she said to him, "just air." She took her hands apart to show him, and they laughed. She had a sweet smile, Idella, a real sweet smile. She was tall and skinny, he could tell that even with her sitting. Taller than him. Edward looked over at her now, in the car seat next to him. He laughed. She still sat the same way. Her ankles were crossed, and she was cupping that pocket of air.

"What are you laughing at?" Idella turned toward him.

"The way you're sitting. You were sitting like that the first time I saw you."

"Was I?" She smiled and looked out the window again at the passing fields.

Edward found out from Stanley Hillock that she'd come down from Canada on the train to find work in the States. Idella, Stan said her name was. He'd never heard that name before. He didn't know he'd be hearing it the rest of his life.

He drove on into the sweet June night. He'd cut in on Raymond Tripp when he was dancing with her. Poor Raymond. Lived with his mother all his life and still sold fish door-to-door. Idella got haddock from him and scallops when he had them. Edward knew she'd like that, being cut in on at the dance. They all did. He'd danced a few dances with her, and then he'd led her out the back door of the Grange and down the steps and out to the trees, where he kept his flask. Just one little sip won't hurt you, he'd told her. He knew he looked good. Dark hair, all slicked back, blue eyes. The girls always went for that. They always let him know. Idella had been shy, but she didn't say no. Course, she knew more about whiskey than she let on. He hadn't met her father and brother yet.

She had that job working as a cook out in Cape Elizabeth. Wealthy people. But nice. They had a little girl named Barbara. Like Shirley Temple, she was. She'd come down to the kitchen when he was visiting Idella and sit on his knee, and he'd bounce her. Pretty little thing. So when Idella was pregnant with their first child, he'd wanted to call the baby Barbara if it was a girl. Which it was. Which they all four were. 'Cause that little rich girl was so nice to him. Idella'd named the others. He'd let her choose what she wanted.

"That Ring Ding made me thirsty." Idella reached down and got the second beer from the floor and popped it open. She always brought two on these rides, just in case. "This beer is so cold it stings my fingers. You want a little sip, to wash that Ding Ring down with?" Idella giggled. "That Ring-a-Dingy? That thingy?"

"Give me that Bud." The first beer already had her feeling better. He thought he'd have some fun with her. He took the can and put it against his crotch. "I'll warm it up for you with my thingy—my ding-a-lingy."

"Why, Edward." Idella laughed. "You damn fool."

"Whenever you want a sip, see, you just reach over and grab what you can."

"You mean the can."

"I mean what you can."

"What kind of talk is that when you're driving?"

He laughed. "You want it warmer, don't you?"

"Not really. I don't want it *so* cold, is all." She laughed. "Well, give it to me. I want a sip."

"You'll have to grab it. I'm driving."

"I know you are, you damn fool." Idella reached over and put her hand around the beer can that was now wedged up between his legs. It was damn cold, all right. Idella twisted the can lightly in circles without taking it.

"What are you doing?" Edward asked. Cold or no cold, things were happening down there.

"Just stirring it," she said lightly. "This way and that."

"Well, you're giving me a hard-on."

"Is that so?"

"Mmmmmm." Edward reached over and put his hand on her knee. "Lift your skirt up."

"Why should I?" She was willing, though, Edward knew that.

"I'll make it worth your while." He slowly worked his fingers, gathering up a handful of her skirt material, pushing it up over her leg.

"Edward, look out!" A truck was suddenly bearing down with high beams, coming at them like a train. It had turned out of a side road and was barreling downhill straight at them. Edward pulled hard to the right, whumping against an embankment. The truck went charging on, blasting its horn as it passed, taking up both sides of the road. Bits of rock flew out clattering from behind it.

"Jesus God Almighty," Idella said, her hand against the dashboard.

"Goddamned son of a bitch! He come out of nowhere. The goddamned beer's all over me. My pants are soaked." Edward groped across the seat. "It's all the hell over everything. Goddamned son of a Christly bitch ought to be locked up. I'm gonna get that bastard!"

Idella started pulling Kleenexes from out of her pockets. "Here, give me your handkerchief."

"I got my pants all covered in it."

"Well, I'm not going to blot them. That's how we got into this mess." Idella was wiping the seat.

"I better check on the car." Edward pulled over, got out of the car, and walked around to the front. No scratches. He kicked a tire. It was all muddy—from the camp road, mostly. He'd take it to a car wash in the morning. He sighed. His pants were wet, clinging to him all around the insides of his legs. He needed to pee. He turned away from the car toward the field and unzipped, peeing into the darkness. It was a cow pasture. He could see a bunch of them wagging their big white heads at him. Old biddies, they looked like, wanting to know all that goes on. His mother'd been that way—sitting on the porch for hours at a time. Something to say about everyone, nothing good.

He sighed and looked up. Stars. He never bothered to look at them much. Blinking at him from way out in nowhere. It smelled good out here—spring mud had its own smell. It reminded him of picking strawberries. He'd go out in the fields and pick them little wild ones when he was a kid.

He zipped up, pulling the clammy trousers away from his legs. He felt like he'd made in his pants. What a night. What a goddamned night. Every time he thought he was in for a treat, some other goddamn thing happened. Better get on home. Idella'd been awful quiet. He walked around his open door and got behind the wheel.

"What you been doing?" he asked, smiling when he saw that she was drinking the remains of the can.

"Sitting here waiting for you, what do you think?" She was smiling, though, not mad.

"You putting on a toot?" Edward teased, reaching over and taking the can from her. There was one good swallow.

"No, not really. But I do need to pee."

"Well, there's a good ditch out there. No one to see you but the cows. I won't put the headlights on." He laughed, thinking that maybe he would.

"I wouldn't put it past you." Idella was rummaging through her pockets. "I need something to wipe with. I used up all my Kleenexes on the beer. I can't stand not having something. Don't you keep napkins somewheres?"

"Jesus, Idella, it's a car, not a restaurant."

"You might have some from A&W. You keep that place in business." She gave the glove compartment a whack with the heel of her hand. The door popped open. "What on earth have you got in here?"

Holy Christ. Edward sat with his hands frozen on the wheel.

"What in the name of God?" Idella leaned forward into the faint glow of the glove compartment's bulb. "Is that your bathing suit?" She pulled it out onto her knees. "Jesus, yes. It is." She reached in again. "And this . . . Holy Mother of God . . . this is mine. This is my bathing suit." Idella stared down at them. "Why, Edward . . ." she said finally, her voice coming out of the darkness. "They're wet." She said it so soft he could barely hear. Her thumb was going around and around in a circle, feeling his suit over and over again. The scratching sound of it was filling up the car.

Edward wished that she'd get on with it, start railing at him. He didn't know what excuse he was going to come up with. Nothing was coming to him. Then she started sniffing. She wasn't going to let loose and bawl. Oh, no. She was going to sit there sniffing, twitching her lips. She was going to snivel all the way home and make him suffer. He reached for his handkerchief. She'd used it on the beer. That's how this whole damn thing started—looking for them Christly napkins. That bastard driving the truck. If he ever found that bastard, he'd turn him in. He'd slash his goddamned tires if he got the chance.

"Take me home, Edward. I want to go home." She was all crumpled up against her door.

Edward started the engine and pulled on the lights. Them damn cows were all staring back at him, their dumb eyes glazed in the glare of lights, shaking their stupid heads. He backed straight out, swung the car around, and lurched forward onto the familiar dark road. He wished he could drive all night, keep going, leave the cows and the store and that Murphy bastard and Iris and Idella behind. Nothing stayed good. Nothing stayed easy. He'd have Iris pulling on him one way, wanting to find them a new place, calling up at the store, for Christ's sakes. That'd have to stop. And Idella'd be starting in with her questions, wanting to know every move he made. They'd both be watching him now. The two *I*s. He pushed his foot a little harder on the gas.

The Holdup

Prescott Mills, Maine
June 1963

"Now, you don't want to do that. You don't want to point a gun." Idella stood behind the counter at the store.

"Do like I say, lady. I'm not foolin'." But he hadn't told her anything yet. He hadn't expected her to say something—not before he got a chance to open his mouth. He could hardly swallow, he was so dry. "Give me all your money. Now." He croaked it out. And he should have peed before he tried to pull this.

He'd stepped out from behind the Humpty Dumpty potato-chip stand. His right cheek had a lattice grille pattern where he'd pressed against the side of the metal rack. He'd had to wait for the cigarette deliveryman to clear out. Then some kid had come in and taken ten minutes trying to decide how to spend five cents. He was hungry, too. He should have eaten something. There was never shit in the house to eat. If there was, the old man got to it first.

Idella had seen the strange young man—boy, really—enter the store and disappear behind the racks. He'd sort of skulked in. She'd never seen him before. She had been busy with the deliveryman and had lost track of him out of the corner of her eye. He had been crouched down beside the chips, she didn't know for how long. Something about him was queer, and now she knew why.

She didn't know whether she should get a really good look at him for the police or try not to see him so that she couldn't identify him. She'd read about that being safer for the victim. Her heart was beating very fast, and her cheeks felt hot from inside. Her high blood pressure was kicking up, no doubt about that.

"Now, this won't solve anything." Her belt buckle pressed into her belly as she leaned against the counter. She didn't dare step back and release it.

"I just want the money," he said, nodding toward the closed register, "and a couple of cartons of Camels—no, Winstons. Gimme all your Winstons." He made a little jab toward the cigarettes with his gun, for emphasis. He was holding it low in front of his waist.

"Well, there's not much here right now," she said, careful not to move even a finger. "I just paid the cigarette man most of the cash drawer. It's not enough to risk going to jail for."

"Who said anything about jail? I'm talking money here, not jail. And cigarettes. Get me those Winstons—and a couple of cold six-packs."

"Now, how are you going to carry all that?"

"Just let me worry about that, lady." He jabbed his gun into the air again for emphasis. It startled him, and he pulled it in close.

"Well, you can go pick out the beer—but if you want it cold, you'll have to put some more in the case. I spent all morning filling that case, and I'm just about to drop."

She could see he was ill at ease, a scared and skinny kid. His teeth were bad. Nobody took him to the dentist. "Don't tell anyone I sold it to you. I'll lose my license. You're too young to buy beer, and I don't want to have anything to do with it." No way was he eighteen. She had a good eye for it. Kids were always coming in trying to buy beer, and if they got away with it, you paid the price.

"Jesus, lady, don't worry. I'm stealing it, not buying it, so don't worry, okay?"

"You don't have to swear. Just because you have a gun, it don't mean you have to swear."

"What are you, my mother? I got two mothers all of a sudden? One's plenty."

"You don't know how lucky you are to have a mother."

"Yeah, well, you've never met mine."

Idella took a step back from the counter and let her belt buckle fall away from her belly. He was just a skinny kid, and she wasn't going to let him make her sick. She was too old for this.

"Listen, I'll get the beer, and you fix me up a bag of food. Don't try anything but what I tell you. I've got the gun right here, and I'm fast and you're old."

"It don't matter that much to me. A few six-packs and a little money. I'm not stupid." She looked right at him. "What do you want in the bag?

I'm going to reach under the counter now and get a brown paper bag and open it. I just want you to know what I'm going to do so you don't get excited."

"Who's excited?" His shoulders started rising. "I just want to get the hell out of here. Give me some of those cream rolls there." He nodded toward the pastry shelf below the potato chips. "And a couple of Devil Dogs, some Twinkies, and a couple of those beef jerkies up there by the cigarettes."

"Is this all you want? Cream rolls and Devil Dogs?" No wonder his teeth were bad. She'd like to tell him that, but it was none of her business. She didn't want to get him any more excited than he was. It's his mother that should have told him. It might even be too late for him. He won't have much of a life.

The boy's eyes darted around the overhead shelves. This was neat. He could have anything. He eyed a shelf of SpaghettiOs and pizza sauces, laundry soaps, and toilet paper. He should probably help himself to a roll of that. Buses never had anything. Just taking a whiz on a bus could make you puke.

"You should have something besides sweets. What about a sandwich? You want me to make you an Italian sandwich?"

His mouth watered at the thought. "That'd be great."

"I have to go in the back to make it. Will you watch the store?"

"What?"

"If anyone comes in, just ask them to wait."

"Right. Okay. Hurry up."

"I'm going to walk out from behind the counter now and go back to make the sandwich. You'll hear the door to the cooler back there open and close. And I'll have to use a knife to slice things."

"Enough with the blow-by-blow."

"Do you like olives? Some people don't care much for them."

"Yeah, sure." He was about to keel over with hunger. He grabbed a big bag of potato chips from the rack and yanked at the top. His hands were slippery with sweat, and he couldn't get a good grip with the gun in one hand. The bag wouldn't open. Idella stood watching him.

"Do you want me to do it?"

"No." He grabbed the side of the bag with his teeth and tore into it. Chips spewed everywhere. They flew up onto his arms and shoulders and stuck there like oily feathers. Idella stood watching as he cradled the gaping bag against his belly with the arm holding the gun and stuffed the chips into his mouth with his free hand. He eats like a mangy animal, she thought.

"Well, what are you looking at? Go make that sandwich."

Idella wasn't sure what to do with her arms and hands. She held them straight in front of her and walked from behind the counter. Potato chips crunched beneath her step, but she didn't stoop to pick them up. She walked, zombielike, into the back of the store, behind the big meat counter full of hot dogs and torpedoes of bologna and salami.

"I'm hearing everything!" he called through a wad of ground chips.

He needed a beer. He looked through the glass doors of the case. Miller High Life, "The Champagne of Bottled Beers." He slid the case open and pulled out a six-pack. "I'm watchin' you!" he called out.

"I'm just now slicing the tomato," she called. He could hear the *thump, thump, thump* of her slicing, even and efficient. "I'm using the knife now, and in a minute I'm going to be using the slicer. I won't be able to hear the door then, so keep an eye out."

He reached in and grabbed a second six-pack, then slid the door closed with his foot.

"Did you put warm ones back in?" she called. Jesus, he thought, she must be listening to every sound I make. "Take the cold ones from the back and move them up front and put warm ones in the back."

"Okay, okay, I'm doing it."

"Do you want two sandwiches? I might as well make two while I'm at it."

"Sure." He was sliding two warm six-packs into the back of the case. He had to put his gun in his pocket and get down on his hands and knees. It felt good in the cool beer case with only the purr of the motor and the cold bottles rubbing against his arms. He closed his eyes. Sometime today he'd be on a Greyhound heading south, where they had air-conditioning all over. Every room would feel as good as this beer cooler.

Idella laid strips of American cheese down the length of sliced rolls. This will make the *Prescott Mills Observer*, she thought. Certainly it'll be in the Police Blotter section, maybe even the front page. They might want a picture. It'd be good to get a picture in—might pick up business a little. People going by will want to stop in and ask about it, and then they'd feel obliged to buy something. She sighed—maybe the publicity would help make up for the money he'd take. There was always something. Last week one of the beer coolers broke down. Yesterday a Coke bottle exploded out back. Someone could have been killed. At least they weren't losing the beer license again—like when Edward sold that beer on Sunday. Jesus, she could have killed him. She was pushing the large torpedo of salami through the electric slicer. You work so hard to build up a business, try to make a little profit, day after day coming over here morning and night—and then he goes and pulls a stunt like that. Trying to be a big shot, selling beer to a group of Sunday hunters. Undercover men, every one. She sighed again and wrapped up the extra slices. There was always something. Now this.

The boy eased himself out of the cooler and slid the door closed. The meat slicer started, high-pitched and whining. It made him grind his teeth. It was like those damn paper machines at the mill. His mother had stood at them so long she didn't even hear them. He wasn't going to spend his life standing there listening to those machines and smelling cabbages. It's the smell of money in this town, his mother said. But it was somebody else's money, and it smelled like rotten cabbages. "About time you started workin' in the mill, boy. Don't you think it's time to start carrying your load?" It was bad enough the old man had to barge back into his life and make things worse for everyone. He wasn't gonna start running things. "You live in this town, you work at the mill." That's all he'd ever heard. No thanks.

He pulled out a beer, popped it open at the soda cooler, and took a long drink. It was so cold it burned his throat.

"You're not supposed to drink that here."

Two little boys stood staring up at him. He hadn't heard them enter the store.

"You work here?" the older boy asked. He was about nine. His fist was clenched into a grimy swirl.

"Yeah, what of it?" He put his beer on the cookie rack behind him.

"We got nickels!" The smaller boy opened his hand. "Can you wait on us?"

He looked toward the sound of the slicer. She was taking forever.

"Come on, mister!" The boys were already in front of the candy case.

Stepping back behind the counter, he pushed the gun down further into his front pocket. If the old man found it missing, he was in big trouble.

"Mister!"

"Okay, okay!" He bent down and reached into the large glass-fronted counter. The candy lay splendidly before him—penny stuff on the bottom and whole boxes of candy bars filling the top shelf. He grabbed a malted milk ball and popped it into his mouth.

"Do you have to pay for that?" The older boy eyed him suspiciously.

"It's part of my job. I get to take whatever I want." He popped in another. "Now, what do you kids want? Hurry up. Who's first?"

"Pete, what do you want?" The older boy gave his little brother a nudge.

"How much are those?"

"A penny. Everything down there is a penny." He'd heard the store lady answering the same question while he had crouched behind the potato chips.

"How many can I get with a nickel?"

"Five." He scooched down to look into the case. The little boy was staring through the smeared glass at him. "Hurry up and decide, or I'll decide for you."

"Get a Popsicle like me, Pete. You'll want one when you see mine. Come on." He led Pete to the ice-cream freezer, slid open the glass door, and peered in. "Do you want orange or cherry?"

"Orange."

"Here." He handed a Popsicle to his brother. "Hold on to it by the sticks."

He reached in and pulled one out for himself. "I never seen you in here before." He closed the freezer and stood looking up at the man behind the counter.

"Yeah? You live here or something? You know everything that happens?"

"Where's Mrs. Jensen?"

"That's what I'd like to know."

"Here I am. Hello, Wayne." Idella emerged from the back of the store carrying a stack of Italian sandwiches, each tightly wrapped in wax paper and secured with tape. "You kids got what you need?" She placed the sandwiches on the end of the counter in a neat pyramid. One was a little away from the others.

"Hi, Mrs. Jensen. I'm supposed to get a loaf of bread, too." Wayne placed a wadded dollar bill on the counter. He reached into the bread rack and grabbed a bag of bread.

Idella stepped behind the register. The young man stood close to her. "Get those kids outta here." She nodded and pushed the register buttons. The money drawer opened with a ping. "Don't close that thing," he whispered as she unwadded the boy's bill and placed it in the drawer.

"Here's your change. You don't need a bag for that, do you?"

"Nope." Wayne took the bread with one hand and pushed Pete through the door with an outstretched finger. Pete's gummy Popsicle wrapper dropped to the floor as the screen door banged behind them.

"Those kids," she said, shaking her head. She resisted her impulse to go pick it up.

"I want all the money in your drawer. All of it. I gotta get out of here. I've got this gun in my pocket, and I know how to use it if I have to." He was glad not to be holding it anymore. He figured she was plenty scared already.

She wanted to tell him to hold his horses, she was doing the best she could, but she thought she'd better go along with him and keep calm. Still, there was something pathetic. She collected the bills from the register, automatically counting them out as she dealt them, like giving change. "Seventy-nine, eighty, eighty-one. Eighty-one dollars."

"That's all? That's it?" He stuffed them into his front pocket.

"Do you want the change, too?"

"Everything!" He held his front pocket open. She gathered the change and poured it in.

"Gimme those rolls of nickels, too!"

"It's going to be so heavy."

"I'll worry about that. Clear it out."

"You want all those pennies?"

"Everything." He crammed the rolls of change into his back pocket. They were hard little sausages that pushed into his behind.

"You sure you want all these beer bottles?" Idella had opened up two large paper bags with a whoosh and pushed one inside the other.

"Do like I say." He had to be tough. He was getting so hot his shirt

was sticking to his back like wallpaper. That long swig of beer was the
only thing in his stomach. He could puke. "Put the sandwiches in on top.
Gimme a bunch, since you made up so damn many."

He looked over at the pile of sandwiches. The one apart from the others was marked "NO" with black crayon.

"What are those marks for?" he asked.

Idella looked at him. "That's 'no onions.' Some people don't like onions. They give some people gas."

The boy looked at the sandwich for a long moment. "Maybe I
shouldn't have any onions. I don't want to get gas on the bus."

"You never had any trouble before, did you?"

"No."

"Well, then, it's not likely. I wouldn't worry about it if I was you."

"Yeah, well, you're not me."

"You are awfully touchy." She placed three unmarked sandwiches
into his bag.

The young man shifted his weight uncomfortably. The lady was right
about all the change. He was going to have to tighten his belt. His pants
were dragging down off his waist. Jesus, this was going from bad to
worse.

"Hello, Mrs. Jensen!" The front door opened with a clang, and a
hearty voice called out.

"Well, hello there, Rickie! What can I do for you today?"

"Them sandwiches is a sight for sore eyes! Been on the road for thirteen hours." A burly customer walked past the candy and coolers and
stood in front of Idella. His muscular arms were bare, displaying a large
green anchor with a blue snake coiled around it above one elbow. "I could
eat my truck, I think."

"Oh, now, don't go eating your truck." Idella was nodding and smiling. "You'd regret it in the morning."

"Ya," he chortled. "I guess I would. Better stick to beer." He walked
heavily over to the beer case and yanked one of the sliding doors. "Nice
'n' cold, Mrs. Jensen."

"I try."

"Why, hello, young fella! Didn't see you had someone else back there.
You finally got yourself some help, Mrs. Jensen?" He stood grinning at
the young man.

"Why . . . yes, yes, I guess you could say that. For today anyway." Idella and the young man were staring at one another. "This is . . . Dalton . . . my brother's boy from down in Canada. He's just passing through for the day, helping me out a little."

"She could use you every day of the year, I bet. Mrs. Jensen works too hard."

"Oh, wouldn't that be nice!" Mrs. Jensen said, smiling at the young man. "But kids have a mind of their own."

"You don't have to tell my kids that. They know it." He reached into his pocket and pulled out a rolled wad of bills. "Gimme . . . ahhh, hell, gimme three of them sandwiches!" Idella grabbed two from the pile. Her hand hovered over the one marked "NO."

"Loaded! I hope they're loaded to the top. Everything you've got."

"Oh, yes," she said, pulling the third from the pile.

"Dalton, huh? What kinda name is that?"

"Oh, it's a family name. It was my brother's name."

"Is that so? Unusual. Well, nice to meet ya, Dalton." The boy nodded. "He's the quiet type, I can tell that. My kids are always talking."

"He talks when he wants to, don't you, Dalton?"

"Yes, ma'am."

"Polite, too. I like 'im. You oughta try to keep him on! Now, what do I owe ya?"

"That'll be three dollars and twelve cents with tax," she said, calculating in her head.

"Well, all I got is a ten." He slapped it on the counter. "Gimme some extra quarters, too, if you can. They're good for those damn toll machines."

Idella looked over at the boy and opened her eyes wide, as if to signal him. She coughed a little dry cough. He looked back at her blankly. She nodded her head toward the empty register and raised her eyebrows.

"Hold on there. Gimme a carton of those Camels. And a carton of Winstons for the old woman. That'll keep her from complainin'. Gotta keep 'em happy if you wanna keep 'em!" Rickie slapped the counter with the palm of his hand. Dalton's shoulders rose an inch. "Well, Mrs. Jensen, I bet I owe you something else now. Gimme the word."

"It comes out perfect, Rickie. Ten dollars. You don't owe me another penny."

"Now, that don't seem right somehow. It don't seem as it's enough."

"Oh, yes. Ten dollars on the money."

"If you say so. You're the boss. Take care of yourself, Mrs. Jensen." He turned to the boy and winked. "Don't you let her work you too hard, now."

"I won't."

Rickie grabbed his bag of sandwiches and cigarettes with a crunching grip. "Nice 'n' cold!" he roared as he hoisted his six-pack under an arm and marched to the front door. "Well, look who's here!" he called out. "I got the police after me, Mrs. Jensen. Officer Abbott's come to check up on me. I seen him hiding in the bushes down on the interstate, and I blew my horn at him." Rickie held the door wide open and roared. "I think I woke 'im up!"

A Prescott Mills police car had pulled up beside Rickie's semi, and a thin young officer was leaning against the front door and laughing, his arms crossed over his holstered black belt.

Idella looked over at the boy. He had turned white. "Why don't you give Officer Abbott a cold soda, Dalton? Go get a Coke out of the cooler and open it. Save him the trouble of coming in to get it."

The boy pulled out a soda and handed it to Rickie.

"Well, that sure is kind of you, Mrs. Jensen. I guess it's smart to keep the police happy."

The door closed behind him with a crash, jingling the OPEN sign that hung by a chain.

"Jesus." The boy was in a state. "Now I've got to wait till those guys have lunch. Is there a window I can climb out?"

Idella shook her head. "I have got to sit down. I have just got to sit." She sighed like the last bit of air was being pressed from a balloon and walked to the yellow chair by the candy counter. She seated herself slowly, holding on to the counter for support. "You take what you think you need or go wait upstairs, even, I don't care, but I've got to sit down. This is too much for me."

She crumpled like an old Kleenex right before his eyes. "Hey, you want a drink or something?" he said. "A ginger ale? I'll get you a cold one."

She was staring into the candy case. She suddenly looked old, with her hands crossed in front of her, one draped limply on each knee. Her head was shaking back and forth slowly, just an inch or so in each direction.

He walked over to the soda cooler and slid back the cover. The ruffled tops of the bottles stared up at him: orange, cherry, chocolate, Coke. Ginger-ale caps were dark green with white letters. His mother used to give that to him when he got sick. She'd bring him a bottle of ginger ale and let him lie in her big bed while she was at the mill. She worked the night shift then and wouldn't come home till six in the morning. She'd be so tired she'd just take her shoes off and whisper, "Move over," and lie on the bed beside him, on top of the covers, even, with no pillow. That was when it was just the two of them—before the old man came back.

He plunged his hand into the cold water around the bottles. The cooler gurgled in response. He might as well get a soda, too, to water down the beer in his stomach. It was getting to him, fogging things up. He shouldn't have chugged it like that. He had to keep a clear head. He pulled on a purple cap with one hand, grape, and a ginger ale with the other. The bottles squeaked and shifted.

"I'm gonna put two warm ones right back in," he called to her. "I'm fillin' her right back up like you had it." That should make her feel better. He reached down with one hand and pulled two bottles from a case of warm sodas. He shoved them hard into the small gaps of space, then popped the cold sodas with the opener and stepped behind the counter to hand Mrs. Jensen her drink. She still hadn't moved or said anything. She just kept staring at the penny candy.

There was a folding chair, and he sat down. He could hear cars going by. Any second, one could stop, and he'd have to act like Dalton again. The police car and the truck were out front, under a big elm tree on the side of the gravel parking area. He could hear Rickie's laugh exploding out of that belly like buckshot. They sure seemed to be enjoying themselves.

"You don't have to worry about me doing anything. I'm just gonna wait till I can get out of here. I know that stuff came to more than ten dollars. You helped me out, and I don't want you to worry no more. I'll put back some of that change."

She sighed and reached for the ginger ale, still not looking at him. "Thank you," she said, but all the starch was gone out of her. She took a baby sip of the ginger ale.

"You ought to drink up that ginger ale. I think you need liquid." She was acting so funny all of a sudden.

"We used to tell him, my sister and I, to just leave—go on and leave us and start a better life. We all wanted that, of course. There was no life on that farm. Not way down in Canada like that, with nothing else around. We offered him what little money we had from God knows who or what, not much, but we thought he was the oldest and should get out first. The only son. Dad expected too much from him on one hand—and never really seemed to like him on the other. He took a lot of things out on Dalton. I can't explain it." She took a sip from her ginger ale.

"Then one day he was gone. He'd sneaked into our room and taken our little bits of money." Her face got all red. "It must have just about killed him to do it. He'd been so proud. Somewhere he'd found a pencil and a piece of newspaper, and he printed out 'I'm sorry' in big letters and signed his name. He wasn't one to show any kind of feeling like that. It looked so sort of pitiful. I wish I'd kept it."

Idella sighed. She removed her glasses and pressed her fingers against the bridge of her nose. Her eyes were closed. He could see how wrinkly her face was. With her eyes closed like that and no glasses on, she looked old. He reached behind him and grabbed a small packet of Kleenex from the carton, one of those little packets like his mother kept in her purse. He tore it open and pulled the first one out so that it was easy to get and placed them on her knees. Outside, he could see the cop and Rickie finishing up their sandwiches.

He waited till she stopped sniffling—she had taken the Kleenex and wiped her eyes—then turned back to her. "So where'd he end up?"

Idella put her glasses back on and looked out the window, not even in the same direction as Rickie and the cop as they slammed their doors shut and called out over the roars of their engines. The cop slid out onto the road first and down the hill. Rickie gave a honk and waved at the store, then roared on up the hill toward Gorham. They were gone. The boy sat waiting for her answer.

"We didn't know where he was for a long time. Dad was madder than hell. He needed him in the potato fields and in the barn. None of us said a word about the money. Dad said he was a goddamned son of a bitch good-for-nothing. He had a wicked mouth on him when he was mad. He missed Dalton, though. We could all see he felt bad about his leaving, but he'd never say anything. We'd just see him sitting alone at the table after supper staring into the kerosene lamp. If he bit his lip, he was thinking about my mother. If he shook his head, he was thinking about Dalton. We knew to leave him be."

The boy knew that Mrs. Jensen did not see him, or the road, or the candy displayed in front of her. A car turned around in the gravel driveway, spewing tiny rocks that ground out from behind the tires. It drove away with a fading whoosh.

"All me and my sister knew is, he took the money and got a ride to town with the mailman. We figured he'd gone out west to the wheat fields to try and get a job. We were very isolated. We knew he'd never write." She paused and turned to him. "It don't matter now where he went. He had trouble with drinking all his life, and I don't know if he ever found what he was looking for."

The side door opened. A middle-aged woman with curlers in her hair and a red scarf over them came in. "Hello, Mrs. Jensen," she called. She plunked down cartons of milk and six-packs of soda and a couple of loaves of bread onto the counter. "How are you today? You look tired."

"Oh, I'm just getting a cold or something. Nothing to speak of. You heading up to camp today?" Idella got up and stepped behind the register. The boy sat quietly.

"The boys'll all be there this weekend, so I'll go up and air the place out."

"Will that be all?"

"That'll keep us alive till they catch the fish they keep saying we'll have for supper. I'll believe it when I see 'em." She reached up and grabbed two large bags of chips. "Might as well throw these in, too."

Idella laughed. The boy watched her wait on the woman—bagging her groceries, making change from the rolls he'd returned, talking about the weather. She seemed to fit behind that register. It was hard to picture her with a sister and a brother, with someone she called "Dad."

Another lady came in. Sounds echoed around him. He was tired and beyond hungry. That beer he chugged was weighing him down. Watching the woman at the end of the counter, swaying in her orange-and-white–flowered dress, was like watching a kaleidoscope. Everything seemed so far away. He could barely keep his eyes open. It was hot in here. You could really feel it when you stopped. His whole body felt like

lead. The fans of the beer coolers hummed and hummed. The *ping* of the
register opening and closing was the only sound that penetrated, like a
bell buoy in deep fog. His mouth opened a little. The soft intake of air
felt cool on his tongue. His eyes closed.

The light was different when he woke. He was still in the folding chair
beside the candy counter. Something was wadded up between his neck
and the back of the chair. He pulled out a white sweater with little flowers. The back of his neck was clammy and sweaty. The beer coolers
hummed and hummed. How could he still be here?

"I thought you might be waking up soon. Come sit in the back and
eat a sandwich." Mrs. Jensen emerged from behind the cookie rack. She
had an apron on and a mop in her hand. "Go around that way," she said,
pointing, "because the floor's all wet over here."

Her manner had changed. "Go on. I've got to open the store up again,
and I want to talk to you before I do. I closed for 'inventory' so you could
sleep in peace."

He stood behind the counter blinking at her. He felt like he'd been
scraped up by a plow. He was hungry.

"I put back those cigarettes and beer that you thought you were taking. They're right back on the shelves where they belong. I won't do it.
I won't let you walk out with those things. You're way underage." She
was swishing the old string mop in a bucket and going along behind
him with it as he walked to the back of the store. "And you won't be
finding that gun anytime soon, I can tell you that. It'll be a cold day in
hell before you lay your hands again on that." He only wanted to eat,
eat, eat.

"Just sit on that stool there and eat and listen to what I have to say. I've
done a lot of thinking. It's been nice and quiet with the lights out."

He could not get the sandwich to his mouth fast enough.

"You sit there. I'm going to tell you something. Officer Abbott drove
up while you were sleeping. He almost woke you up when he knocked,
but you were pretty deep under. It's no wonder. It must be a real strain on
the system to rob a store." The boy stopped chewing and looked at her.

"Go on with your food. I didn't say anything to him." She sat down
on a stack of piled-up beer cases. "It seems Officer Abbott got a funny
feeling driving around after he left Rickie out front. Seems Rickie de-

scribed you a little in the telling, and what he said sort of matched up with a young man who tried to rob LaRosa's out on 302 this morning. It seems the young man got scared and ran away when a car pulled up." Mrs. Jensen stopped for a moment and gave the boy a dead-on stare. Then she resumed. "Well, I had to point you out, sleeping like a baby with your mouth open to keep him happy." She stopped and watched him eat.

The boy nodded.

"Now, I'm not saying you tried to rob LaRosa's, and I don't want to know. But you're not going to rob me. I'm not going to have that on my shoulders. I'm going to take back the rest of that money and put it in the register where it belongs." He stopped eating and listened. "I'm sending you out of here with something else." She ceremoniously removed a small velvet bag from her pocket. "This was my grandfather's. He brought it over from England when he was a young man. It still works." She removed a pocketwatch from the bag. She slowly unfurled it and held it by its chain. "This watch is eighteen-karat gold. I had George, who knows about these things—he's very knowledgeable—take a look at it. That's how I happen to have it here in the store. Then I never did bring it home again. It must be very valuable. I'm going to give it to you."

The boy stared at the gold circle dangling before his eyes. He'd never seen such a beautiful watch. He wiped the oil from his fingers.

Idella took the watch into the palm of her hand and slowly ran her finger around its edge while she spoke. "I've had it for many years. Nearly forty years. I never should have had it at all. It should have been Dalton's. Dad gave it to me after Dalton left the farm. He did it to spite him. It was his way of disowning him." Her finger went slowly round and round the rim. "I've always felt bad having it. And of course we all left. None of us stayed. But Dalton was first to go. I never told my sister. It's been hidden away all these years. Dalton loved it when he was a little boy. Dad kept it hidden, we don't know where, and Dalton would ask if he could hold it and hear it tick." She shook her head. "It should have been his. I've offered it to him more than once, but he won't take it." She looked at the boy. "I'm giving it to you. You take it home with you and keep it somewhere special. Dalton ended up in Chicago, working in factories. He kicked and stumbled around, trying to get away from us. He never had something to hold on to—something from his family that said he'd come from someplace, that we loved him. Nothing passed down to him—but the drinking."

She laid the watch on the counter.

"It's yours if you take it on home and think about where you want to go. I'm putting it down here, and I'm going to leave you be. I've got to open up. You can put the money down here when you take the watch. Don't hurry your food, though. Get a bag of chips it you want them." She stepped out into the store. Lights flickered on, a key turned.

The boy sat on the stool in the dusky half-light and looked at the gold watch across the counter from him. The door opened and closed. He heard footsteps, the sound of cases sliding open and shut, chatter. It was like lying in bed, isolated for sleep, and hearing smoky drifts of adult conversation. Mrs. Jensen's voice floated back to him, riding airily above the other sounds. "Is that so?" "Oh, yes?" "Will that be all?" "Do you want a bag for that?"

The boy rolled the oily paper from his sandwich into a tight ball and threw it into the wastebasket. He went to the sink, wet a rag, and wiped all the oil from the counter. He washed his hands with the bar of soap beside the sink, then walked to the table and removed all the money from his pockets, including the sixteen dollars that he'd had of his own money. He was glad to be rid of it. He stood staring down at the gold watch. He picked it up and held it in the palm of his hand. It felt smooth and cool at first, soft and warm as it sank into his palm. He held it to his ear and heard the soft, steady tick. She had wound and set it. It was early evening. The men were coming in for their beer and cigarettes on the way home from work, just like she'd said they would. He lowered the watch into the velvet bag. He put it into his shirt pocket and pressed it with his palm, then walked out into the neon glare of the front of the store. Mrs. Jensen was standing alone behind the register, where he'd first seen her. She looked over at him.

"Maybe . . . maybe I could come work for you some Saturday. Fill up your coolers. You know, help out a little, to make up for today, to pay you back."

"Maybe," she said, watching him. "That'd be good."

"The money's where you said."

She nodded.

"I'll leave now. I'll leave you alone." He walked to the front door and stopped and looked back at her.

"It feels so good," she said, smiling shyly at him. "It feels so good in the palm of your hand. Don't it?"

His hand went back to his breast pocket. He could just hear the soft tick through the velvet bag. He nodded at her, then opened the door and walked down the creaky wooden steps.

He walked slowly, heading for home, thinking of all the different places he could hide it.

Idella stood and watched long after the young man had left. She was tired. It hadn't hit her yet, what she'd been through. She walked to the front door and turned the bolt. She turned off the lights again. It was so quiet in here with just the coolers humming. She'd close the place for a little longer—till before Edward got home from selling cars all day and began ranting and roaring and wanting to know why the hell she'd closed the store on a Saturday evening. She wasn't going to tell him. Something had happened, she wasn't even sure herself what. She'd brought something to a close, and it felt good. Maybe she'd opened something. She had to think about it a little while.

She went to the beer cooler and pulled out a cold bottle of Miller. She wasn't even going to put a warm one back. She walked to the counter and looked at the pile of Italian sandwiches that she'd made earlier. Her eyes fell on the one a little away from the stack, marked "NO." She took it into the back of the store, carrying her cold beer with her. She sighed and sat down on the stool, where the boy had eaten two sandwiches. The poor sot. She noted that he'd cleaned up after himself. "I bet he don't do that at home," she said, pleased. She unrolled the sandwich from its binding of white paper. The note lay wedged into the slit of bread between the pickles and slices of salami. The paper was translucent with oil and covered with black flecks of pepper. She removed it from the sandwich and held it out to read. The wax marking crayon had not smeared much. "HELP! HOLDUP IN PROGRESS! CALL POLICE!" She shook her head and slowly began tearing it into greasy little pieces, which fluttered heavily onto the opened wax paper, then reached into her jar of brine-soaked olives and grabbed enough to lay out the length of her sandwich. She took a swig of the beer. "Don't that taste good. Nice 'n' cold, Mrs. Jensen. Just like I like 'em."

Wake

Boston
January 1966

"Good God Almighty. We've lost the damned body." Avis stood on the North Station train platform, her small leather suitcase pressed between her knees as though it, too, might be whisked away. "Dalton, we've lost Dad. What the hell are we going to do?"

"Call Stan, I guess. He'll know."

Avis kept going through the motions of stamping snow from her feet, though it had all melted down into her boots an hour ago. They'd gotten off the train from Connecticut late last night, thinking Dad, in his coffin, had been rolling along behind them in the baggage car. The train up to Canada didn't leave till this morning, so they'd gone and gotten themselves an excuse for a room in that excuse for a hotel Dalton knew about, to try to get some sleep. But when they'd come staggering back into the station this morning, thinking to crawl up to Bathurst with Dad in tow for his own funeral, and they'd gone to make sure that the body was on board with the other baggage, there was no body to be had anywhere for love nor money.

Dalton strode helplessly back and forth in front of Avis, as though trying to determine which of the trains on either side of the platform might offer escape. His legs were so long and wiry that he could not pace without seeming to lope. He needed a wide-open field before him, not the crowded confines of this train platform filled with heavy-coated strangers who all knew exactly what they were about and how they were going to get there. None of them was missing a body all laid out in its casket.

"What exactly did the baggage man say?" Avis asked.

"There's no casket anywhere in this station. Hasn't been one since a week ago Saturday, and that one went to Toledo, and he believes it was a woman. He's going to call the Connecticut station, but it'll be a while 'cause of the snow, and schedules are off, and if we don't get on this train to Canada, we won't be going to Canada anytime soon, 'cause this is the only train connecting to New Brunswick today, and he has his doubts about tomorrow, 'cause he's heard the storm's supposed to get worse before it gets better. He says they'll be calling this the 'Blizzard of '66,' like as not. One for the books, he says. He says it's an odd thing to lose a casket like that, as they don't get that many coming through and they usually take note of it, and did we have a receipt or a claim check?" Dalton stopped pacing and stood in front of Avis. "I thought maybe you had one."

"Christ, he was ready to chat. Hadn't anyone asked him a question in the last ten years?" Avis searched through her purse for some sort of ticket or receipt or piece of paper with a number on it. "Nothing."

"Check inside your gloves. Maybe it's in a finger."

"Check inside your own damn gloves."

"I don't have any."

"I have no memory of anyone handing me anything." Avis turned her wet gloves inside out. "I never had it. It was you that talked to the man in the uniform before we got on in Cohasset, isn't it? Didn't you talk with some official? I know I never did."

"Well, if I did, I don't recall. I was awful tired."

"You were shitfaced, is what you were." Avis stuck her hands down into her coat pockets. Nothing but cigarettes in one pocket and a hole in the lining of the other. She stuck her finger down through it and opened her coat to show Dalton. "There. Maybe that's what happened to it."

"Hell, I got one of them, too." Dalton stuck his whole fist through his pocket lining and waggled his fingers at Avis. "We may have solved the problem."

"We haven't solved anything. There was no receipt. I think we got the casket with us to the station and neither one of us made sure it was on the train. That damned hearse unloaded and drove off. What did he care?"

"Do you have to buy a ticket for a dead man?"

"You've got to do something. You can't drag bodies around like it was regular luggage."

Dalton stopped pacing and flicked his fingers under his chin. "Christ, I forgot to shave."

"I guess Dwight thought we would take care of it, seeing as it's our father, not his." Avis sighed.

"He should've known better." Dalton shook his head. "Course, he married you. That shows lack of judgment."

"Shut your damn mouth."

"He should have gotten us all three onto the train." Dalton resumed his pacing.

"He was glad to get us out of the car. Poor old Dwight. He'd had his fill of Hillocks."

Dalton turned just short of an open train door. "I know one thing for damned sure."

"What might that be?" Avis reached into her coat pocket and pinched a cigarette from her pack. There were only about three more in there, by the feel of things.

"I need a drink." Dalton reached over and took the cigarette.

"You had a drink."

"It wasn't tall enough, nor wide. Not by a couple of long shots."

She slipped her fingers back into her pocket for another cigarette. Two left. "Smoke your own damned cigarettes."

"I did already."

"And quit your roaming! It's like talking to a fly in a manure pile. Stand still. We have to figure out what to do."

Dalton stopped and looked down at her. "I'm not getting on any train going up to Dad's funeral if we don't have Dad's body with us."

Avis lit her cigarette and took a long drag, blowing the smoke up past Dalton's ear. "It must not have made the switch. It must still be waiting on some platform in Connecticut."

"The man said to check back with him in fifteen minutes." Dalton lit his cigarette off of hers.

"How long has it been?"

Dalton looked up at the big round station clock. "Twenty. What if someone took it?"

"Who's going to walk off with a coffin, you damned fool?"

"Who'd walk off and leave one?" Their eyes met as they exhaled smoke into each other's faces.

"Go on," Avis said, brushing him away like a gnat. "Go find the baggage man."

Avis watched Dalton stride off through the crowds. Even slouching like he was now, with that hangdog look of his, he was a head taller than everyone else.

"Last call, last call for the Canadian to Halifax, Nova Scotia, leaving from Track Nine. Making stops at Portland, Lewiston, Augusta, Bangor, Houlton, and St. John's. Final destination, Halifax. Last call."

Avis stood smoking. That was the train they were supposed to be on. She watched as the conductor strode up and down the platform, helping people into the cars. She looked in the windows and saw passengers clogging the aisles, stowing bags onto the overhead racks. Already some were taking off gloves and scarves and settling their coats around them, slipping into their seats, and snuggling in for the long ride north. Soon they would be leafing through magazines and spreading newspapers across their laps. Some would head to the club car as soon as the train was moving, for hot coffee. Cigarettes would flicker to life, their owners leaning back into the seats, looking out at the storm.

Avis longed to be on the train with them. She wanted to be in a window seat with her toes tucked under her. Her feet were cold, her leather boots soaked through. She was beyond tired. She needed to curl up into herself and blot out everything while the world swirled around her.

It had been snowing all night—a full-out nor'easter. She and Dalton hadn't slept much. Christ, every time either one moved on that rickety bed, the springs sang the "Hallelujah Chorus." And the wind poured under the window as if it had been wide open, it was so damn cold. Then with Dalton turning on the light to go relieve himself and banging into the bed on the way back—and taking up all the space with his long Hillock legs once he got there—it was one ungodly night. They both finally said, "The hell with it," and got up and smoked most all the cigarettes till they were out of matches and drank all they had left of Dwight's whiskey.

Dad'd get a laugh out of this now, seeing his two "damned fools" wondering where they'd put his dead body. Avis didn't find it so funny. Her head pounded like someone was going at it with a sledgehammer. She couldn't absorb the shock of Dad's being gone, never to drive into town unexpected, mad or drunk or both. She'd heard his voice commenting, making jokes at someone else's expense, throughout the whole day of people coming in to view him. His voice in her was so strong it kept on going without him.

Dad's real voice had been altered for over three years, since he'd had that first stroke that left him all flaccid on the one side. He'd get so frustrated at not being able to move one whole half of himself, or talk right, or drink without dribbling all over his shirt front, that he'd kick at anything within range of his good leg. He'd kicked Avis a few times as hard as he'd kicked the furniture.

His second shock, three months ago, left him completely mute. She'd moved in with him then. Poor old Dwight just watched her pack and drove her over. She'd been living with Dad, nursing him, those last three months. He could talk with his eyes. Avis could make out his needs. She'd had him to take care of like a baby. She'd read to him by the hour the way she'd always heard Mother had read to him. Wife, mother, daughter. She'd been all three for him at the end.

"Well, sister, he's lying on the platform in Connecticut. They'll send him on here to Boston. Should be here a little before noon, no guarantee 'cause of the weather." Dalton shook a pack of Lucky Strikes at her. He'd restocked. "They can't have his funeral without him, so we're not going to miss it." He ground the stub of his current cigarette flat out on the platform with a twist of his foot. "Just like that ornery bastard, to miss his own burying."

"We'd best call Stan up in Maine," Avis said. "He'll know what to do."

"Yep. We'd best let the cat out of the bag."

"They'll blame us." Avis buttoned her coat as though preparing for battle. "Everyone will lay the blame right on us. You're prepared to start hearing about it?"

"Yep."

"We'll never hear the end of it."

"Nope."

"I'll call Stan." Avis marched down the platform and up the stairs.

She had been relying on her cousin Stanley Hillock to get her out of trouble since she was five years old. They'd emptied the well when they made him. Here she was now, fifty-five years old and married, even, to poor, meek Dwight, but Stan was the man to call.

"I hope he'll accept the charges," Dalton called after her.

Bathurst, New Brunswick

Idella stood staring uselessly down the tracks. She held her squirrel-fur coat tightly together to keep out the cold wetness. Tiny pellets of ice were biting at her eyes and hitting the tip of her nose. There weren't going to be any more trains coming down them tracks anytime soon. The one that had just pulled out was three hours late as it was, and—most important—it didn't have Dad in his casket, or Avis, or Dalton on board, as planned, as they said they'd be, as they had promised. The goddamned fools.

Frozen rain pinged and bounced off the metal rails, the wooden gates, the shingled roof of the Bathurst station. You could hear the crunch underfoot as people milled about the platform, most of them Hillocks or former Hillocks or married to a Hillock. They were all here waiting for Dad—"Wild Bill" Hillock as he was known to them and liked to call himself. The whole family lined the edge of the platform, looking futilely down the darkened stretch of track into an empty black hole, ringed with sleet.

"No guest of honor. No hallowed attendants." Her sister Emma came and stood next to Idella. She was her baby sister, but she was the biggest and tallest of the three Hillock girls.

"Now what?"

"I don't know what to do," Idella said. "I'm at a loss."

"Won't be no more trains tonight, Miss Hillock. You'd best go on inside." John Farley, stationmaster here since Christ was born, still called her Miss Hillock, even though she'd come to know herself as Mrs. Jensen, married to Edward now for over thirty years. "Sorry for the loss," he said, wiping frozen pellets from off the top of his hat.

"Oh, we'll find him, surely," Idella said, suddenly alarmed. "They've got to be someplace."

"We never should have left it to those two." Emma sighed.

"The blind leading the blind." Idella sighed.

"They're probably waiting for the storm to blow itself out," Emma said. "Probably holed up somewheres. I'm going back in the station."

"I'm going to stand here for a bit to get some air."

"Don't stay out too long." Emma patted Idella's fur shoulder. "Oh, you're so puffy, like a bear cub."

Idella took a deep breath of the cold, sharp Canada air. Good God, what a week. What a time. And it wasn't finished yet. Eddie'd gone back home to Maine with the kids, thank God. Everyone had had enough of him. Especially after that ear incident—following Avis into her cellar and falling down the whole flight of stairs, drunk, and landing with a caterwaul that would wake the dead. Everyone said it was a wonder Dad didn't jump out of the casket. And the way Eddie's glasses landed so perfect on the little shelf at the top of the stairs, like as if they'd been laid there on purpose, while Edward himself flew to the bottom. Everyone remarked on the placement of those glasses.

Eddie's ear bled like a stuck pig. There were quite a few stitches. And him being so squeamish at the sight of blood. Thank goodness the emergency was nearby. And that bandage! Idella laughed at the thought of it, wrapped up all around his head at that queer angle. He insisted on wearing his hat, perched on top of that bandage like a bird's nest. God Almighty, though, they did tease him—Avis and Dalton. Once they got going on something, they wouldn't drop it. They each tried to top the other. Eddie couldn't stand it. The more he fumed, the funnier he looked. Everyone was so giddy, and there'd been so much drinking, and it was such an odd occasion—Dad laid out in Avis's parlor like that with the chairs all around the edges of the room. People were going a little stir crazy. If Dad had been there, he would have had a field day with Edward—it was so easy to give Eddie a hard time.

What in God's name Edward thought he was going to do to help fix Avis's furnace, she'd never know. He couldn't change a lightbulb without having a fit. There was always something to get in his way. The bulbs were too delicate, breaking in his hand, or the screwing mechanism didn't work right, or something. He acted like the bulbs were purposely designed to make it hard for him, Edward Jensen.

He hadn't wanted to let her come up here, even. But there was no way he was keeping her from coming. After Dad's services in Connecticut, she was bound and determined to proceed up to Canada and see Dad get laid to rest next to Mother, these many years later. "I'm going all the way," she'd said. "All the way!" Edward had finally closed his trap.

Idella looked around her. She was the only one left on the platform. It was miserable out, and she needed to pee. She turned her coat collar up and walked into the small wooden station. "I got my air," she said as she closed the door behind her.

People were huddled in clumps with their coats and boots and hats still on. She could hear conversations hissing around her like steam from a roomful of kettles, everyone pondering what to do next.

Idella stamped the slush from her feet, adding to the dark puddles on the old wooden floor. She started to brush the pellets from off her coat before they melted and got the fur wet.

"Jesus, Della," said Uncle Sam, "I never seen so much fur except on a bear. Have you, Guy?"

"No, I ain't." Uncle Guy stretched out his long legs and winked at Idella. "Unless it was on your backside, Sam." They'd get on this bone together and gnaw it clean to help pass the time.

Uncle Sam and Uncle Guy had been teasing Idella about her fur coat ever since she got out of the car. Everyone had taken note of it and made little comments. You couldn't have anything really nice without people acting like you didn't deserve it, or had betrayed them, or were putting on airs. It was only squirrel, for God's sake, and Idella had earned it, working in that airplane factory all during the war, standing in that line assembling parts. She'd earned it.

"Looks mighty wet, Idella," Uncle Sam continued. "Give yourself a good shake."

"Well, don't shake that thing over here," Guy said, his head rising up from the group and looking over.

Idella shook her coat off by the door and headed for the ladies' room. It was empty, thank God. None of the stalls had toilet paper. It was a good thing she had some Kleenex in her purse. She stepped into a stall. The door had no lock. She sighed and pulled down her pants, bracing one elbow against her spread-out knees, holding the door shut with her other hand, and scooching over the cold toilet seat. There was no way she was going to sit down on that seat.

To get to the faucet, she had to step around pooled water on the cement floor. She slipped her hands quickly under the tap and out again. It was ice cold. The hot never worked in these places. She wiped her hands with a Kleenex and tucked the rest neatly into her pocketbook. She decided to put on lipstick. Her lips got so dry all the time, especially in the winter. She stretched her lips into two horizontal lines, spread them with color in the gray light, and smooshed them sideways over each other. There. She smacked her lips and gave herself a dim little smile in the mirror.

When she left the ladies' room, she found Emma huddled in front of the woodstove. The Hillock girls were given the best seats. She fluttered her hands in front of the fire.

"The way I see it . . ." Uncle Sam's voice rose up from behind Idella. He was speaking to the whole roomful of people, and everyone turned to listen. "Bill's just taking his own sweet time to get here, following his own route. That's his way. I say we wait over to the church and be ready to receive him. Let's make the best of it for Bill."

Idella looked over at Sam's familiar face, so like Dad's. There weren't too many teeth left in his mouth now, but the sweetness came through when he smiled. He'd been a handsome man. People down here didn't know much about caring for teeth. If you happened to get dealt a poor set, you just lived with them or pulled them out.

Mr. Farley, the stationmaster, shuffled over to the woodstove and stoked the fire. He moved from group to group, nodding and smiling. There were more people crowded into his little station today than since the war started and men headed out to go shoot the Germans. "You folks stay here as long as you want." Mr. Farley was being a real host. He was a gentleman in his way. "I won't close till the last one's out. It's an unusual time."

Mr. Farley had helped Idella onto the train the day she left here to go down to the States, to get the hell out of here, nearly forty years ago. He'd shaken her hand, as if he knew something big was taking place, and wished her well on her journey. He'd used that word, "journey." She'd been so scared and so determined, with no more than twenty dollars tucked in her shoe. Dad had gotten it from someone—Uncle Sam, probably—and given it to her right here at this station, just before she'd boarded. "Tell them you've got two hundred," he'd told her. "When you get to the border. Two hundred." Dad knew. He knew she had to go.

Now she was back, maybe for the last time. The farm'd stand empty for a while. Then someone would see a good thing and move on in. To people up here, that old house would look like a good thing. She wouldn't be surprised if some of these relatives were feeling each other out right now as to who might be taking up residence.

Course, it'd all go to Dalton, legally. He was the oldest and the male. Nothing left for the sisters but what they might scrounge from the house, which was another way of saying nothing.

"Let's head over to the church, then." Emma stood up. "No use waiting for a train that won't come."

Idella joined her. "I could call down to Maine, see if Edward has heard anything."

They stood side by side, staring into the flickering woodstove.

"Where in hell are they?" Emma asked.

Idella sighed. "The fools."

"The goddamned fools."

They pulled their coats tight about them, shaking their heads in unconscious unison.

"Where in hell are we?" Avis was squeezed into the middle of the front seat between Dalton and Stanley.

"There's the one road and we're on it," Stan answered. "We're nearly to Bangor."

"Did I fall asleep?"

"Yep. You could call it that."

"Christ. How long we been driving?"

"Going on eight hours." Stan drove steadily through the darkness, the wipers of the hearse thumping back and forth like a steadily rocked chair.

"Storming the whole time?"

"Yep."

"I feel like a puckered-up pea wedged between two stalks of corn. There's no room for my legs." Avis shifted herself around on the seat. "I'm numb. My 'dairy-aire' isn't there."

"Well, don't put it here." Dalton was slowly emerging from sleep. "Christ. My elbows is down behind my knees somewhere." He stared dully out his window. "Jesus, Mother of God. What's it doing out there?"

"Some of everything. Snowed from Boston to Portland. Rained near the coast. Few times it freezed and come down like pellets."

"What a mess." Avis stared out the windshield.

"Been that the whole time."

"I don't just mean the weather," Avis said.

"Me neither," Stan replied.

Dalton scraped his fingernail down his side window. "It's all blurry."

"Be blurred to you with the sun shining, the shape you two were in." Stan's long body was folded at sharp angles behind the wheel of the hearse. His neck was hunched over like a vulture's, trying to see through the windshield.

"I assume we got Dad in the back?" Avis tried to turn her head and peer through the little window.

"Yep. We got Bill for ballast. Took four grown men to get him in there."

"Was I one of 'em?" Dalton rubbed his eyes.

"Nope."

"He said grown men, Dalton."

"I'm grown."

"I didn't know which port you two were holed up in when I got to North Station. I thought I'd best get Bill in back so we wouldn't drive off without him."

"Were you waiting on us long?" Avis asked, looking over at Stan. The collar of his familiar flannel shirt was poking out around his neck. Avis knew he'd have suspenders on under his coat.

"Long enough to notice."

"I'm sorry, Stan. We lost track of the time."

"You lost track of everything. Do either of you remember me pulling you out of that bar at the station?"

"Not really." Avis sighed.

Dalton shook his head, slowly taking stock of his position. "Can you drive this thing all the way up? You want I should take the wheel?"

"No use showing up with four bodies." Stan glanced over at Dalton.

"Hell, they could bury us all and be done with it." Avis laughed. "Emma and Della will be ready to string us up in the barn."

Stan leaned even closer to the windshield. "I can't see but what's two inches in front of me."

"That'd be your nose." Avis snickered.

Stan laughed. "It's good to have some company. Even the likes of you two."

"Who but you, Stan, could come up with a hearse in the middle of a goddamned nor'easter?" Avis ran her hand over the front of the dashboard. MITCHELL'S FUNERAL HOME—GORHAM, MAINE was printed in gold letters across the leather.

"Promised Mitchell a well dug out back of his place come spring," Stan said. "We're counting on the Gorham population to remain steady for the next few days."

"Here's to the population of Gorham!" Avis rummaged into her purse to unearth a flask. "You want to drink to Gorham, Dalton?"

"I never liked Gorham." Dalton reached for Avis's bottle and took a drink.

"I promised Mitchell that every Hillock this side of the North Pole—and there's a lot of them—would be obliged. Said we'd all throw our business his way when the time comes."

"I'll try to remember," Dalton said, taking another drink. "When my time comes."

They rode along without talking for a long while. The sounds of the storm filled up the car—splatters and taps and whining winds. Stan kept his attention riveted on the road. Avis and Dalton stared ahead, the wipers screeching to and fro in front of them.

"The old goat is dead." Dalton's voice was clear and unexpected.

Avis looked over at him. "You sound glad."

"I can breathe. Never did when he was living."

"You get the farm, you bastard."

"That'll change my life. Lording over that pile of wind and rock."

"You inherit it all," Avis said. "Being the only male."

"The only male we know about."

"What's that supposed to mean?"

"There's more than one Hillock walking that goes by the name of bastard. And I wouldn't be surprised if some of them had French accents or Indian braids."

"You don't know that."

"Hell, he probably didn't know the half of them. Why do you think there was so many French girls come and gone so quick as housemaids?"

"They were dumb cows, is why."

"Hell, if he'd kept his hands off Mother some of the time, instead of filling her with his stinking seed, maybe she wouldn't of died birthing one."

"That's a fine way to refer to us. If they'd stopped with just you, things'd be a lot better, is that what you're saying, Dalton?"

"Before that, even," Dalton said softly.

"Seems like I was having more fun when you two were asleep. Maybe you'd best say nothing."

"Any word yet, Idella?" Uncle Sam stood up in the pew as she walked into the church.

"Nothing. Dwight don't answer. Edward don't either. Just keeps ringing." Idella had been trying to get through for almost an hour.

"The lines must be down," Uncle Guy offered.

"It's awful cackley, that's true," Idella said. "I don't know what's become of them."

"Move over." Avis elbowed Dalton.

"The only way I can move over is to open the door and fall out."

"Well, go on, then. I can't sit like this much longer."

"If you're so cramped, why don't you go lay down in the back next to Dad?"

"Maybe I will."

"I understand it wouldn't be the first time."

"What the hell is that supposed to mean?"

"You know damn well what I mean."

"I know what you think you mean, you half-assed son of a bitch, and it's not true."

"Quit yammering, the both of you. We're coming into Houlton. We'll get some coffee and try to call up there again and tell 'em we've got Bill."

"I need to piddle," Avis said.

"There's a diner up ahead, by the look of it. Don't look quite open or quite closed." Stan slowly pulled the hearse up in front of the dimly lit restaurant. "One of them signs is lit anyway, and I see someone in there behind the counter." He opened his door and climbed out. "Jesus God Almighty, that's a tight fit."

"It's pissing down like a horse," Dalton said as he stuck one long leg and then the other out of the car.

"Don't let's talk about pissing till I've done it," Avis said from inside the car. "One of you is going to have to peel me out of here."

"I preferred the snow," Stan said, tugging Avis out of the car. "At least you can see it."

*   *   *

"It's all ice out there," Idella said. "It's just terrible. I'm dripping icicles."

"Any luck, Idella?" Emma came up to her as she walked back into the church, stomping the wet off her boots.

"The lines are definitely down in Connecticut. The operator can't get through at all."

"And Edward?"

"Still no answer. But it appears to be ringing."

"The scrape of them wipers is vibrating my whole head," Avis said. They were riding on into the night with only the greeny lights of the dashboard to outline their three huddled shapes. Avis sighed and closed her eyes. She was exhausted from staring past the smeared windshield, trying to follow the wavery headlight beams as they reached out, feebly, for the road.

Dalton was pressed against her, snoring. "Nothing like bacon and eggs to set the world right" had been his last and only words after they'd left the diner. He'd been asleep since they'd pulled back onto the road.

"Don't worry, Stan," Avis whispered, "I'm not going to sleep."

"I'm into my third wind here. That coffee helped. I just wish we'd been able to get through up there. No one up to the house. They must all be waiting at the church, God love 'em."

Avis kept her eyes shut. She folded her hands and listened to the sounds around her—the steady *bump-thump* of the wipers, the slooshing of the tires as they spewed rain and snow out from under them, Dalton's raspy, smoke-heavy breath as he slept with his head pressed against the side window, his long body all curled on itself like a fiddlehead.

As cold and cramped and tired as they all were, she didn't quite want this ride to ever end. She had the only three men that she'd ever really loved, and who she knew for a fact loved her, all to herself. Della and Emma loved her, like sisters. But they weren't as forgiving. She supposed Dwight loved her, poor old soul that he was, but she couldn't return it. She was grateful to him for his kindness, for marrying her in spite of who she was instead of because of it, for putting a roof over her head. But she was beholden to him, and that brought out the worst in her.

Dalton twisted in his sleep, pushing his knee into her legs. She pushed it back. Just enough flesh on it to cover the bone. She and Dalton had never been too good at doing what they were supposed to, or what was expected of them—except now that they were expected by everyone to drink and screw things up, they did manage to do that pretty good.

Even when they bickered, which was plenty, they were still fighting a war alone against the others. They'd always been in cahoots. There was that scheme when they were about ten and fifteen—they'd worked a way to sell lobsters to the passengers on the trains going through Uncle Sam's property. The train would stop for water, and the two of them would climb aboard and sell whatever catch Dalton had managed from taking out that little boat he'd built. Avis did the talking, knowing even then that the way you asked for things, and how you looked doing it, mattered. They sold the lobsters for six cents apiece and lorded their mounting proceeds over the others at every opportunity. Dalton finally spent his getting more traps and then lost interest in the whole enterprise.

Avis had kept her money—it wasn't even five dollars total—in a variety of hiding places, each more elaborate than the last, till one day Dad ran across it when he went to empty out a seed bag in the barn. It was drunk and gone by the time Avis discovered it missing. "That's what you get for being so secretive," Idella'd said. No sympathy from her. "If you'd put it in the bedroom and left it there, this wouldn't have happened." Hiding it from Idella had been half the fun.

Avis knew she was Dad's favorite. They had found comfort in each other. She closed her eyes tighter. There were times when she'd be overcome by the need to be alone in the world with Dad, holed up in some room lying next to him, giving each other a bodily comfort that went right through them. It was like being home when she could just lie there quiet in his arms. Even Stan, dear Stan, probably thinks the worst, thinks they were being dirty. But they weren't. They were both so lonely, her and Dad, standing on earth like that godforsaken house they lived in, spindly and forlorn atop that great cliff, exposed to every wind that blew from any direction. That's how Avis had felt, as a little girl, after Mother died and there was no one to talk to about her secrets or fears. Della was, what? Too distrustful? Too scared herself to offer any real comfort.

No one who saw Dad bluster and bang, who heard him drink and yell and carry on, would ever know the agony that man went through, for years, after Mother died. He didn't let on, after the funeral and all, after that first stretch of time passed and people thought he'd gotten over it enough to keep going. But Avis knew.

It was Avis that first went down, unbidden, when she knew that Della was sleeping. She slipped out from next to her and tiptoed down the stairs and into his bedroom. Without a word she crawled in beside him, and he turned and scooped up her puny little nothing of a body and wrapped his arms around her and they went off to sleep. Dad must have woken up sometime and brought her upstairs, because she woke up the next morning curled beside her sister. That was how it began, their special closeness, that lasted right on through.

Avis knew that people wondered about her and Dad. She could feel their eyes trying to look through her. The old biddies up in Canada would make judgments about her. "She's been to prison," their eyes said when they looked at her. They'd gotten themselves through many a long afternoon discussing Avis. She could just hear them—Maisey Moore and Mrs. Doncaster—clinking their teacups and crunching their dry toast, hardly waiting to get the words out before they swallowed. "Sent away, you know, for luring men up to her room down in Boston." "Took up with a gangster of some kind." "He was handsome, I hear. He got her to do all sorts of things till they finally got caught." Avis sighed. Tommy was handsome, there was no denying.

It was Dad who drove down to Boston and got her out of that hellhole after two years of being locked up. Neither of her sisters knew the half of what she put up with, of what got done to her. All they knew is she got certified as a beautician. Like she was in some kind of finishing school.

At least Idella didn't say anything to that damn fool Edward. Poor Idella would never know the number of times he'd tried getting his big, clumsy hands up inside her skirt. Even at the wake, with Dad laid out in her parlor and the house all full of people, Edward had come lumbering after her down into the cellar to "help her fix the furnace." Damn fool. He wanted to start a fire, all right, but not in the furnace. Put more than two drinks in him and he was nothing but trouble. Avis started to laugh.

"What are you finding so funny? I sure as hell could use a laugh right about now."

Avis looked over at Stan's familiar shape, all angles and points, as Hillock as they come. He was leaned over staring hard at what little bits of road he could see. He was getting tired. The storm, by the look of it, was getting worse.

"Oh, I was laughing about Edward. He tumbled head over heels down the cellar stairs and looked so funny with that bandage all around his head. When he put that damned brimmed hat on he's always wearing, perched up on top of all that gauze, I about peed my pants."

"Poor Eddie." Stan chuckled. "If you act like a damn fool, then damn-fool things are going to happen to you."

"He brought it on himself," Avis said.

"What are you two finding to laugh about?" Dalton was coming to. "Damned if something don't ache, it hurts, if it don't hurt, it's wet. I feel like throwing Dad out of that damned box. I need it more than he does." He peered forward. "My God, it's ice now, ain't it?"

"Been more ice than rain this last half hour. I'd like to pull over to scrape some off the windshield," Stan said, "but I'm afraid if we stop, we won't get going again. The defroster in this hearse isn't up to this."

"I guess they don't want too much getting defrosted, if you know what I mean," Dalton suggested.

"Yep. Maybe that's it," Stan agreed.

"Let's change the subject," Avis said.

"What have you heard, Idella? Any news? Could you get through?" The pews were filled up. People had turned askew so as to talk better. Voices were coming at her from all directions.

She stood at the front of the little English church where the casket was supposed to be and talked loud so that everyone could hear. "I can't get through to Dwight. Those lines are down. But I *did* finally get ahold of Donna, down in Maine—she's my second-oldest. I don't know where Edward is. Donna said, 'They lost the box. Stanley has gone to get it. He's got the box.'" Idella repeated that exact quote from Donna slowly and deliberately. "That's the message she had to give us from Katherine—Stan's wife. Evidently Avis, or Dalton, or both, lost the box—the casket—with Dad in it—evidently they lost it somewhere between here and there, closer to there, and Stan's got himself a hearse and he's gone to get them. They're on the road somewheres, is my understanding."

A cheer went up through the church with shouts of "Good old Stan!" and "You can count on Stan!"

"Now, I know"—Idella put up her hands to calm things and raised her voice a little—"I know that if Stanley is involved, he'll get them here." She nodded her head, to give her speech a little ending. She'd never spoken like this before a crowd. "Thank you all for coming." She continued standing there and raised her head up. "Now I don't know what to do."

"Well, we're not leaving!" Everyone started shouting that they were sticking it out.

"Come have a drink, Idella," Uncle Sam was beckoning to her.

"We can't drink in the church!" Idella said, knowing full well that bottles were being passed up and down the pews like collection plates on Sunday morning.

"Goddamn, it's pure ice out there." Uncle Guy was at the window. "It's sticking like a new coat of paint."

Sam was on his feet now, leaning over the front of a pew. "I want to drink to Bill, to my big brother, Bill Hillock. May he rest in peace, wherever the hell he is."

Bottles were raised all up and down. Seems more had one than didn't. "To Bill" went murmuring through the little church, some voices together, some out of sync.

Then the lights went. There was a loud crack, and total darkness came down over them as if a black velvet curtain had dropped.

"Holy Mother of God," a lone voice rose up.

"Goddamn," another answered from the blackness.

"Damn it all to hell," muttered Dalton, staring down at the back wheel of the hearse as it spun in response to Avis's foot on the gas pedal.

"Take your foot off it, Avis!" Stan called in to her. "Just that back wheel we got to get up onto the road."

"Never seen ice like this." Dalton looked at the lunging shapes on either side of the road. The trees were stooped down low by the weight of ice that had been steadily falling.

"We got to get something in there for traction," Stan said. He was scooching down and feeling around the wheel.

"Where's Edward with his bag of sand when you need him?" Avis joined the two men at the end of the car. "How 'bout my hat? It's all shot to hell anyway. Being run over by a hearse could only improve it."

"If that's the case," Dalton said, "why don't I lie down there in front of the wheel. There's one thing I ought to be good for."

A sudden crack ricocheted from out of the woods behind them.

"What the hell!" Avis yelled.

"They got me," Dalton whispered, without moving.

"Tree snapped," Stan said. "That ice'll snap whole trees. Give me that hat, Avis. It'll give it something more to go on for them few inches."

A second and third crack shot out from dark woods. Dalton joined Stan behind the rear of the car and prepared to help push. Avis crawled in behind the wheel.

"Go on, Avis," Stan said. "Slow and steady. If we get her up on the road, we're not stopping." Dalton and Stanley leaned into the car with their shoulders, their fingers grabbing under the fender. "A little more!" Stan called. "Push like hell!" The two of them heaved the hearse forward, over the hat and up onto the road. It lurched forward, swerved its long behind to the left, and came to a tentative, cockeyed halt.

"There's a God in heaven!" Dalton called out into the darkness.

"Get my hat!"

Stan bent himself back down behind the wheel. "I reckon it's three more hours of slow and steady. It'll be well after midnight."

"I'm sorry we got you into this pickle." Avis pushed Stan's glasses back up his long nose.

"I'd swear them trees cracking back there was Dad firing off his last shots." Dalton pulled his door to and locked it.

"It's well after midnight," Idella said.

"The time don't matter no more," Emma said. "We're in it."

Idella settled down onto a pew. Some of the men had gotten lanterns from the back of the church and hung them all about from the rafters. Long gray shadows lurched up the walls to the ceiling. It was spooky, but it was beautiful. Everyone looked so tall, looming like giants. She pulled her squirrel coat tighter. It was cold in here, and damp. The softness of the fur was comforting and luxurious. She felt like a squirrel curling up in its hole, waiting for the storm to pass. The wind was still wrapping around and around the little church, making an eerie sound up in the bell tower. It whumped the bell back and forth, and sometimes the bell would ring out, though no one was pulling the rope. "That's Bill, now, up in heaven, ringing for room service" is what they all started saying every time it rang. "He's ordering more whiskey."

And the frozen rain kept coming. It'd let up a bit, and the tapping sound, like thousands of little chickens pecking on the floor and walls and windows trying to get in, would get so gentle you could barely hear it, and then it'd start right up again.

"Them's the ghosts of all the lobsters he took out of season," Uncle Ernest said, after a quiet spell. "Them little ones he should of thrown back are walking all over the building."

"Go on!" Maisey said. "Don't scare us."

"Then there ought to be a big deer come loping through here any-time," Uncle Guy said. "Remember that time Bill went to flush that buck out of the woods and one of you damn fools shot him? Them's Bill's words, now, not mine."

Idella didn't want to be reminded of that time, taking care of Dad after the accident.

"We had him strapped down on an old door to get him out of the woods," Uncle Sam said.

"I used my good sheets to do it. Not that I minded." Dear old Mrs. Doncaster, Idella thought, hearing her voice.

"Bill used to say he broke down your bedroom door, Elsie, and was lying between your sheets." Everyone laughed.

"It wasn't my bedroom door," Mrs. Doncaster said. "But it was my good sheets."

Uncle Sam laughed. "Bill would always fatten up a story in the telling."

Idella fuzzed out the noise around her. She tried to think of something good Dad did for them, something kind. Oranges at Christmas. Where did he get them? He always came up with an orange for each of them at Christmas, and maybe a washcloth. And there was the time he got her a new hairbrush when she promised to let her hair grow back long. Aunt Francie had bobbed her hair and Avis's, in an effort to make them stylish. Dad hated it. He liked long hair—like Mother's had been. Dad had been at such a loss when Mother died. For all his faults. That poor man, left alone with three children in the house and no idea even how to do a wash.

"Best story about Bill was the time he got hauled into court for putting a potato in some little country girl's oven." That fool Willy Smythe had to go boom that across the church. He had to go bring that story up.

"What was it Bill said to the judge?" Uncle Guy asked.

"It was the trapdoor that got him off, the one going up into the hayloft." Will Smythe was such a loudmouth, Idella thought. "She said he carried her up there, see, against her will."

"Bill stood up in court, as tall as I've ever seen 'im." Uncle Ernest jumped in. "And he looked right in the judge's eye, you know—"

"I'm telling this here, Ernest," Will Smythe cut him off. They were all over themselves to tell it. "Damned if he don't stand up and say, 'Your Honor, you see what a tall man I am. You understand what kind of small trapdoor she's referring to. Do you think that I could carry that young woman up a ladder against her will and through a trapdoor and into a hayloft with a goddamned hard-on?'"

"Had the judge laughing, right up there on the bench," Uncle Sam said. "He threw the case out then and there."

Idella hated that story. Many's the time she'd had to sit through Dad regaling everyone with it and hear him get whoops and hollers and free drinks, for God's sake, in the face of that poor girl's plight. Idella never knew what became of that girl and her baby.

Things went on when Dad was living alone on the farm. She leaned her head back. Every piece of her was tired. The tumble of raucous, familiar voices surrounded her like she was in a dream. She imagined the quiet flickers from the candles on the coffin stand gently pressing on her closed lids like warm pats of butter.

"It's a damn shame Bill's missing this," Uncle Sam said quietly, when the laughing had petered out.

That brought things to a standstill. People listened to the ice coming down.

Idella sighed. Everybody had at least one story about Dad. She had a few of her own that she would not be telling. Some stories were for keeping, hurtful ones, that she would probably never tell a soul, certainly not Edward. Good God. And there were stories Avis was keeping, but she'd never know the extent of it. She guessed she didn't want to.

Bill Hillock was no saint, that's for sure. He was a complicated man. He'd been so rough on Dalton. Beat the bejesus right out of him sometimes, like he was taking his anger at the whole world out on poor Dalton's shoulders. It affected Dalton. So much drinking and wandering. Him and Avis both got that from Dad. They'd drink to please him. Everyone always wanted to please him one way or another, and take care of him. He needed more taking care of than he'd ever let on. After Mother died, Idella had tried as best she could—cooking and cleaning and sewing. Christ, she was just a kid. And he'd taken it for granted. He'd never really thanked her, or given her any affection to speak of. He'd saved that for Avis.

Who knew the extent of it? But at least Avis had Dwight now, she'd settled down somewhat. Idella couldn't remember where they'd met. Anytime she'd seen him, he was huddled up in the corner while Avis was drinking and carrying on. But he was a sweet man, he didn't do no harm.

Idella burrowed her hands down into her coat pockets and rubbed the silky lining around and around between her thumb and forefinger.

"We're closing in on it now, Avis. Less than ten miles to Tetagouche," Stan said.

"I'm ready to be declared dead this minute," Dalton said.

"Wait till Della gets her hands on us," Avis said. "You won't know what dead is till then."

"Good thing Eddie isn't here, eh?" Emma said with her little smile, sliding in next to Idella. "He's none too good at waiting, now, is he?"

"Oh, I'm used to putting up with him," Idella said. "He's no worse than the rest. At least he don't drink to speak of."

"We've all had to put up with people," Emma said.

"And Edward's a long sight more reliable than Dad ever was. More considerate. We had to put up with an awful lot on that farm. No life at all fit for young girls, growing up with that kind of man, and no mother. You don't know the half of it. All I had was Avis, and that wasn't much."

"Well, then. I had less than no one, now, didn't I?" Emma's voice was steady and deliberate. "I was totally on my own. No mother, no father, no sisters nor brother to live with—to fight with, even. I only got to visit you all on the farm every now and again. You know, Dad scared me. I was scared of him. He was so gruff. I never got to see the soft side much, did I?"

"Why, Emma," Idella whispered, taken by surprise. Emma had tears running down her cheeks. Emma never cried. She always had a little joke or a comment to make light of things.

"I always felt, you know, that he hated the sight of me—that you all did. He never said as much, mind, but I felt it. My being there reminded him, you know. Of her dying. I always felt like it was my doing. By being born. And he couldn't get over it."

"Why, Emma." Idella reached over and took her hand. "We all thought you were lucky being taken in like you were by Aunt Beth and Uncle Paul. They wanted the baby so, we were told. You had a real home with two parents. Adopted, you know."

"There are dirty, dirty secrets." Emma wiped her cheek, not looking at Idella. "God knows we all have dirty secrets. Let's say I was glad to leave there. Let's say Dad will never know, whether he cared or not, he won't know. He wasn't so much better himself, from what I understand."

"Lord God Almighty." Idella stared into the flickering candles as she spoke. "What poor waifs we were. At the mercy of shameless men."

"Sometime, someday, when we're all drunk or sober, I don't know which, we'll ask Avis what she knows on the subject," Emma said.

"I don't think so," Idella said. "I don't believe I will. Some things are best left unsaid. I don't want to know any more than I know already."

"It's all part of growing up, is what I was told," Emma said. "If ever I was to protest or try to question. Anything anyone takes or wants from you without asking is all 'part of growing up.'"

"What's that noise, now?" Uncle Sam rose up and hushed the congregation of waiting mourners.

Idella lifted her head. She heard it, too.

"That's a car horn!" Uncle Sam said.

Everyone rushed to a window, some climbing onto pews to see. Men opened the doors and went right out into the storm. Way off, Idella could see headlights winding around the turns in the road, heading toward the long stretch of Main Street. The horn was blowing without letup.

Everyone was talking at once.

"By God, it's Bill!"

"It's Bill Hillock! He's riding down Main Street at midnight! Ain't that like him? Ain't that just the way he'd choose it?"

"By God, it's past midnight. It's two o'clock in the morning."

"It's three."

The horn got louder. Everybody scrambled together and buttoned their coats and went running out to line the street. They were making as if for a parade in the dead of night, in an ice storm, with but one vehicle in the procession. People were shouting and cheering and clapping like it was a whole troop of soldiers returning home from the war. Someone found his way to the bell rope and started clanging in earnest. That sent roars and cheers all up and down.

Idella pulled her coat around her and stepped out onto the church steps. The storm was letting up some. Emma came and stood next to her. "The damn fools made it," she whispered.

And here came the hearse. People slapped it and pounded on the roof as it passed by. The horn never stopped blowing the whole time. It was Avis, Idella could now see. Avis was leaned over practically on top of poor Stan, laying on that horn as if she were stuck there.

The two sisters stood watching from the church steps as the hearse pulled up in front of them and came to a halt. Everyone gathered around it as if movie stars were arriving at a premiere. First Stan's door opened. "Somebody get me a drink."

The other door opened, and Dalton emerged, unwinding himself with difficulty. When he got to full standing, he called out, "Bring me *two* drinks—and a cigarette!" The crowd loved it.

Finally Avis wriggled out, looking like a drowned rat. She turned to the crowd. "Bring me a whole damn *bottle* of whiskey and a *pack* of cigarettes!"

Idella watched as that Willy Smythe came and picked Avis up like she was nothing and put her up on his shoulders! Someone handed Avis a flask. Someone else passed her a lit cigarette.

"Let the funeral begin!" Uncle Sam called out.

"Hey, what about Bill! We got to get him in on this!"

Idella watched as the back of the hearse was opened, and Avis got put down, thank heaven. In this ice someone was apt to fall and break a neck. Avis would not look either sister straight in the eye.

Stan and Dalton went around to the back of the hearse. "I carried Bill this far," Stan said. "I'll get him into the church."

"He ain't been to church for a while," Dalton said, finishing his cigarette. He threw back the drink he'd been given and leaned into the hearse to take hold of the coffin. "Neither have I."

Men lined up in two rows, hauled out the coffin, and hoisted it onto their ready shoulders.

"Watch the ice!" the women called, parting on the church steps to let them through. "Step careful!"

Idella and Emma stood silent on the top step and watched the coffin pass into the church and down the aisle. It was all black shapes moving toward the gold flicker of the candles that lit the front of the church. Avis tentatively joined her sisters.

"Look what the cat dragged in." Emma smiled and held out her hand. "Jesus, Lord Almighty, you took your sweet time getting here." She started to laugh.

"Come on, you damned fool," Idella said. "Let's proceed."

The sisters stepped together into the church and down the aisle.

Sandwich wrappers and bags and paper cups with drops of whiskey still at the bottom were cleared away before the coffin could be put down proper. After much fiddling and prying with pocketknives, Stan got the lid open and propped up. Lanterns and candles were brought in close.

The four Hillock children were the first to gather round the coffin, now resting on its pedestal. The congregation lined up behind them, waiting to get a good look at Bill before the service began.

The four stood silently, looking down at their father as candlelight flickered eerily across his sunken features. Then Idella led them away in a dutiful line, to take their proper seats in the front row and wait for the ceremony to begin.

The lantern light and candles made the ceremony mysterious, Idella thought. Once there was a body in a casket laid out in the front, the solemnity of the occasion returned. Bill Hillock was dead and needed burying.

Joe Major, the minister, had gone home when he'd heard the coffin was lost. Now he'd come back from his bed, with a nice speech all prepared. And the choir, those dear old women who had waited all night long, like soldiers, sang so pure and sweet that everyone cried. Their shadows lurched around the walls when they came forward and sang. Mrs. Foster played the organ enough to get by and fill things out a little, and it was just thrilling. People Idella never would have suspected of singing knew most of the words and sang along. Uncle Ernest and Uncle Sam, especially, sang out, deep and throaty but beautiful.

Idella closed the hymnbook she'd held absently throughout the funeral and put it on the pew beside her. She'd done more watching than singing, absorbing the look of all the faces around her. They were simple faces with hard edges and lines like cracked cement across their foreheads and around their mouths and eyes. The lantern light made these crevices seem even deeper. These faces, tilted forward in song or bent down in prayer, had met storms and winds of one kind or another, head-on, all their lives. They worked fields that were best suited to brambles and wild grasses, struggling, Dad and Uncle Sam included, to unearth potatoes and carrots and turnips along with the rocks that seemed to multiply with every turn of a spade. These were the people she'd known as a little girl living up here so long ago. They hunted and fished and lived off the land and by their wits, which were more considerable and deep-rooted than their plantings, and hardier than an outsider might suspect.

Idella had left this Canada far behind and gone to find a better life. It was just being a maid, after all, and a household cook, but it had led to meeting Edward and marrying and having the children and the store and a house in Prescott Mills. She felt rich by comparison, wrapped in her squirrel coat, knowing she had a nice house to go home to down in Maine and a grocery to run. She'd set out, launched herself forward as best she could, and felt both relieved and saddened to have done so.

When the last "amen" rang all up and down the rows, Idella stood with everyone else, giving the whole ceremony an ending. She looked out the window. It wasn't quite light yet, but it was going to be soon. The storm had finally stopped. Now it was time to get Dad to the grave site. Two of Uncle Sam's sons had gone on ahead to prepare it. The hole had been dug sometime yesterday morning and covered over with canvas.

Idella watched as Dad's brothers and Dalton and Stanley all lifted the casket to their shoulders and started for the door.

"All aboard that's going aboard," Dalton muttered as he passed

Idella. He looked terrible, just terrible, but Idella figured she couldn't blame him.

"I've never seen anything close to it," Idella said as she sat in the back of Sam's car with Avis and Emma, gazing at the landscape that was revealed with the gradual coming of light. They were taking Dad on to New Bandon to be put in the ground with Mother. The sky had gone from a foggy gray shroud to yellow and pink, and then the sun showed up and brought out a morning of cold, crystal glaze that shone blindingly in every direction, the light bounced off the ice so. It was remarkable, like an entire new world had moved in overnight. Nothing seemed familiar. Every inch of anything was coated thick with ice. Little nothing shrubs and bushes and roadside weeds were transformed into delicate ice sculptures. Everything drooped, as if in prayer, or was snapped off completely, sticking up at odd angles, like farm implements—rakes and scythes and spades—tossed into the air to fall where they might when the farmers abandoned their duties.

"What'll the little birds do?" Idella asked suddenly.

"Fall on their little asses, I suppose," Avis said, laughing. "Like us."

"Jesus, Idella." Emma laughed from up front, wedged between Dalton and Uncle Sam. "Leave it to you to worry about the birds."

"I was just wondering," Idella said. "Just making conversation."

"Well, don't," Avis said.

They sat in silence, each looking out her own window, all the way to the cemetery.

Everyone stood huddled around the grave site and watched, quietly, as the men bailed out the water. They bailed and bailed. The steady slosh filled the air. There was no getting it all out.

"We're just going to have to lower him in," Uncle Sam finally said. "This here's a spigot to the bowels of the earth."

"Let's have a last drink with Dad," Dalton said, taking a new fifth of whiskey from his coat pocket with ceremony. Idella didn't know where he'd come by that.

"Hell yes," Avis said.

It did seem appropriate, Idella thought. Even it being morning would suit Dad.

"Gather round, Bill's children," Dalton called out, like he was a preacher. "Let's open him up and do it proper."

Stanley and Dalton unscrewed the clasps of the coffin and pulled back the lid. Idella looked in. Dad didn't look so good in the clear light of morning. His face was more sunken than ever, and the bits of makeup they'd used on him at the funeral parlor—he would have kicked and screamed if he'd seen that coming—well, it had gotten to looking waxy and garish.

"It doesn't look like him anymore," Avis said, staring down.

"Those are his hands," Idella said. "Those long fingers. The hands are his."

"Yep." Emma nodded.

The four of them—Avis, Idella, Emma, and Dalton—pressed up against the side of the coffin. Stan kept a hand on the open lid from down at the feet end. People stepped away a bit and let Bill's children say their last farewell.

"It still don't seem right," Emma said, "to see him in a suit. One of them red flannel shirts he wore would have been more like him."

"He could spruce himself up pretty well when he wanted," Avis said. "He was a handsome man."

"I'll start the toast," Dalton said. "Let's do it in birth order."

He lifted the whiskey bottle. "To Dad!" He swallowed a mouthful. "To the old bastard!" He handed the bottle to Idella.

"To Dad," Idella said, taking a swallow. "To Dad."

The bottle went to Avis and Emma in turn, each raising it up to toast Dad before taking a swig. Dalton took the bottle from Emma and capped it.

Avis stood pressed up against the coffin, staring down into it. Then she stepped away. "I hate sticking him in the cold water."

"Put this whiskey in with him." Dalton handed the bottle down to Stan. "Under his feet there. That way he can have a drink if he needs one when that water starts seeping in."

"There's room." Stan placed the whiskey bottle in the coffin. "Let's seal him up and set him down."

Everyone watched as the coffin got slowly lowered. There was an unmistakable splash when it hit bottom. No one commented. Uncle Sam's boys and some of the Smythes grabbed their shovels and started breaking off lumps from the mound of displaced dirt beside the grave. They had to crack down through the ice that lay on top like a hard candy coating. It'd be quite a job, but there were enough of them, they said, and they'd take turns. Everyone else should go on back to their homes.

"Well," Dalton said, helping Emma down the hill to the car, "that's that."

"Mother and Dad are together." Idella looked back once more as the men chipped and shoveled. She turned to her brother and sisters. "We're orphans now—all alone in the world."

"Oh, we've been that for a long time," Avis said.

"Christ, yes," Dalton said.

"We've been orphans all along." Avis was already lighting a cigarette.

They climbed into Uncle Sam's car and drove the two miles to the little ramshackle house on the cliff where they'd all got born.

Three Sheets to the Wind

Quinby Falls, Maine
December 1986

Avis stood in the lobby, taking it all in. "Piss Pot Palace, by the smell of it," she said. She waved her hand in front of her face.

"You get used to it," Idella said. "I've got some Evening in Paris in my purse. You want a spritz?"

"I want a cigarette. Half these people look dead, Idella."

"Well, they're just waiting. Some nod off. Because of the drugs, you know. Medications."

"What are they waiting for? Departure?"

"Social hour!" Idella said. "We hit the jackpot, Avis. It's Friday afternoon. At three o'clock the staff bring in refreshments."

"Do they haul out fire hoses, that sort of thing?"

"Look, there's Eddie. He's trying to do one of them word puzzles, and he don't see us. They got him all wheeled into place for me."

"Is that Eddie? Holy Christ, Idella. A wheelchair?"

"His legs don't go yet, since the drive-in."

"He's such a damned fool. I can't believe he got you to go there."

Idella sighed. She hadn't wanted to go, but he just had to see that movie—*Miss America Goes Down*. It was because of those pictures in *Playboy*—he thought he was going to see the real Miss America. And then, when it wasn't her, he had to go tearing out of there, pulling the damned speaker out of its post, and going straight at the screen. His foot got stuck on the gas pedal, he couldn't move it—another one of those spells he got. He shouldn't have been out driving at night in the first place. And he'd just about driven into the screen, veered left scraping those little cement posts they have, and veered left again and whacked into three or four cars before she finally reached over and turned off the key. Lord! And when the police came, his foot was still stuck on the gas pedal. They'd taken him straight to the hospital and then the nursing home.

It had been more than a month now, and all Edward talked about was going home. The first night here, he'd gotten a nurse to call Paulette at work, and he'd offered her one hundred dollars to get him out. It about killed Idella to hear that.

All this week he'd been at her to take him home. He pestered the nurses, too. They'd asked her to talk to him, explain about his walking. The doctor said he was probably here to stay, but she dreaded telling him.

They had him in his Posey, a big padded strap to keep him from falling out of the wheelchair. His feet just barely reached the pedals. He was wearing a blue sweat suit and running shoes—the soles were brand-new, no dirt.

Avis still couldn't get over the changes in him. "Even his belly is gone," she said. "A landmark disappeared."

"Let's let him be a minute." Idella held on to Avis's arm and took a breath.

Avis began to read aloud from a blackboard by the door. "'Welcome to Orchard Near the Shore.' They're near the shore, all right. 'Friday, December 5, 1986. Cloudy / Chance of Snow.' That's tricky."

"It's nice for the residents to know what day it is and the weather," Idella said.

Just then Eddie saw them. He started right in. "You was supposed to be here at noon. I was all packed—then you never showed up. They made me put everything back in my drawers."

"I said I was coming at three," Idella said. "It's not even. Eddie, look who I brought! Avis drove me over."

"Sisters teaming up on me, eh?"

Across the room an aide was setting up for social hour.

"Look," Idella said. "Everyone's rolling in. That's Gladys, in them big slippers. She's a schoolteacher—well, she don't teach anymore—and Mr. Davis, he's an accountant. Was. I'll bring us some treats."

The little bar was just across the room. While the girl loaded up a tray, Avis tried to make conversation, which for her, with Eddie, was like cleaning ashtrays with her tongue. Or so she used to say.

"So, Eddie. How you doing?"

Eddie shrugged, then opened and closed his hand. "I'm stuck in this damn chair," he said. "Soon as I can walk, see, I'll get the hell out of here. I'm going to get me a new car."

Idella could see that Avis was antsy, opening her purse and taking out a compact mirror and lipstick, starting to "refresh" herself.

Eddie piped up, "My father had a wooden car."

"I've heard you speak of it." She rolled her eyes at Idella, watching from across the room.

"You know how much he sold that car for? Five dollars! He sold that car to some crook who come around buying, for five dollars!"

"Be worth more today," Avis said.

"That car'd be worth a lot of money! I still have the bell. You stepped on it with your foot. No steering wheel on her. It had a lever. I remember driving that car through the field! Goddamned crook! He come one day when I was at work, see, some junk dealer. And my father sold it for five dollars!"

Avis was doing her best, but Idella knew what it was like. It was odd here, sitting day after day. She and Eddie didn't talk much, little dibs and dabs of nothing, usually about a meal he'd just had, was about to have, or wished he could have. Her lobster stew usually. God, didn't he love that. She'd made many a lobster stew for that man over the years and fried many a fish.

So much of the time he seemed out of it—but then he'd look up suddenly, as if he was searching, and see her, and she'd wave a little and smile, and his whole face would light up. He'd nod, a tiny nod of recognition, and she'd be glad she came. It comforts him, she thought, to see this old face he's been looking at and listening to for over fifty years. A little bit of home.

She carried over the tray, handing a plastic bowl of Tater Tots to Avis and putting one on Eddie's lap.

"If someone had told me I'd be sitting here eating Tater Tots and chatting up Eddie, I'd have asked them to shoot me point-blank," Avis said.

Eddie was still brooding about that car. He gripped his hands like he was holding a wheel. "You think I can drive home?"

"I don't know, Eddie," Idella said.

"Where would you really like to go," Avis said, "if you could drive?"

"Old Orchard Beach," he said. "To Toby's. Get me some onion rings."

"You used to go out to Old Orchard for a lot more than onion rings, eh, Eddie?" Avis said.

He smiled. "Pretty girls."

"Yeah," Avis said. "Me and Idella."

"Oh, Lord," Idella said. "That reminds me. Look, Eddie, I have a surprise for you. I come across it changing over my purse. Must have been tucked in there for years." She held up a little tattered photograph. "Here, Avis, have a look."

"I'll be damned," Avis said, laughing. "It's the three of us. Where are we?"

"Old Orchard Beach. Out on the pier. Our hair is blowing something wicked, see? And our dresses are blown back by the wind, all billowy. We're all happy, Avis."

"You look shitfaced, Idella."

"Read what's on the back. 'Three Sheets to the Wind.' That about says it."

"Let me see it," Eddie said.

Idella stared at the picture. "What are you holding up there, Eddie?"

He laughed. "That's a plastic lobster. I got it for Avis's boyfriend. We took him out to Old Orchard for a Maine lobster. He took the picture."

"Why, he was the one who *didn't* drink," Idella said. "He was peculiar."

"We was all eating lobsters," Eddie said, "and he got up all of a sudden and ran out. He was sick on the lobster over the pier. I asked if he needed help, and he tells me to keep my hands off Avis! Christ. Saying I'm after Avis." Eddie studied the picture. "He's not the gangster boyfriend, is he? That went to jail?"

"Edward!" Idella said.

"That one got you in all the papers, didn't he?"

Avis gave him a look. "No, not him."

"Well, jail was a good place for you! You caused that other guy with the lobster—"

"Edward!" Idella shouted.

Avis said, "I need a cigarette."

"No smoking here," Eddie jumped right in. "You can't smoke."

"It's smoke a cigarette or kill him," Avis said. "Which do you want, Idella?"

"I'll have to think about it."

"Well, I'm going out front—I saw a bench there. And then we're rolling, Idella. I've had enough." She picked up her coat from the chair where she'd thrown it, started to get her cigarettes, and went out.

"That Avis is always smoking in your face," Eddie said.

"I better go see about her," Idella said. "I'll be right back."

Outside, a few flakes of snow were falling. She found Avis on the bench. "Beep, beep," she said. "Can I come out?"

"No."

"I won't say a word about the smoke," she said. "You okay?"

"I've been more comfortable. I know that." Avis brushed a little snow off the bench, and Idella sat beside her.

"You two get so ugly. You hold on to grudges so. Why don't you dwell on the nice memories, for God's sake?"

"Maybe I don't have nice memories like you, Idella."

"Oh, go on! Stop feeling sorry for yourself! You had a hard life. I don't deny it. We both come from nothing and we tried to make the best of it. You had boyfriends. You had Dwight. You had a career as a hairdresser. You made rugs. You lived a life. Some parts of it didn't work out too good. Okay. But people loved you, Avis. Dad loved you! Mother did! I know she did."

"It's you with memories of her, Idella, not me."

"I've tried to share them! Little bits are all I have. Collecting eggs with her, combing her hair, using up all her cinnamon. I could have kept them private."

"Don't do me any favors."

"You make me so mad! You make it so hard to love you! You push, push, push people away."

"How would you know?"

"Because I love you!" Idella said. "I love you, goddamn it! You fool. And I'm sorry you couldn't have children. And I'm sorry you had the drinking. And I'm sorry for a lot of things. But you haven't always been so nice to me. You're so mean and hateful to Eddie."

"He makes it easy."

"It's time to stop. There isn't much time left. Make the best of it!

That's what I'm trying to do here, coming here, bringing Eddie little things to make him happy. I'm trying to make the best of what there is. That's why I brought this picture. We looked so happy, all windy and loose. 'Three Sheets to the Wind.'"

"That's us," Avis said.

"I forgot the oddness involved."

"Anyway, what have I got to show for all of it? Least you've got the girls. What've I got? Some braided rugs I made."

"Them rugs you made are beautiful."

"It was make rugs or die from cirrhosis. I didn't want to die yellow. I didn't want people lined up looking down at me and talking about how yellow I looked. So I quit the drinking and made rugs."

"Thank God you quit the drinking. It almost killed you. And you were an ugly drunk."

"I was, was I?"

"Hollering and cursing. Ugly. That's why Eddie threw you out that time."

"And he was an angel? Eddie Jensen, who had his hands up skirts like bees over honey."

"You don't have to be mean about him anymore," Idella said. "You see what he's come to. He's an old man who'll never get out of that chair. He can't go to the bathroom without two people helping him."

"You're right. I see what he's come to."

"It was Dad that got you to drinking," Idella said. "I know it. I felt bad about leaving you on the farm with him. I've always felt bad about it. But I had to get out! We all had to get out of there!"

"What did you feel so bad about?"

"Dad was so unpredictable," she said. "He had such a temper. I know the two of you . . . had a special relationship. I never should have left you there alone with him. It got you drinking. It led to things. . . . Maybe . . . I don't know. . . . It wasn't healthy."

"You don't know what you're talking about. When you rode off with the mailman, I was left to do the cooking you'd done and the cleaning you'd done and all the rest of it. And I wasn't good at it. Instead of a nice stew with biscuits waiting on the stove, Dad'd find me trying to open a can of beans. I couldn't take to it, cooking and cleaning. I didn't want to be too good at it. I saw what it was like for you—doing it all perfect and not getting a thing out of it. And Dad, down in him, hungry as he was, God help him, he understood. 'Cause we were kindred spirits."

"I know that. I know you were."

"Most nights we'd sit at that table and drink whiskey. I was what, seventeen by then? I started with a sip or two. He said it'd help get down my cooking. Or we'd get drunk and then cook something together. Some nights it was just potatoes. Then it got to be I had my own glass. He drank from the bottle. We'd sit at the table, and that's when we'd talk, with the whiskey. I was going crazy up there, see. I wanted to get out in the worst way. And I didn't want to leave him alone."

"And what about the other? The rumors?"

"And what might that be?"

"You know what I'm asking, Avis."

"All right, Idella. All right. We were alone on that godforsaken farm. It was lonely. Some nights we'd both be crying. I cried for the mother I never had. He cried for the wife he lost. He blamed himself, you know. She died having his baby. We sat at the kitchen table trying to find comfort in each other. 'Avis-Mavis,' he'd say, over and over again. 'Avis-Mavis, puddin' an' pie.' He'd stroke my hair and talk about Mother—how beautiful her hair was. How gentle she was. Sometimes he'd hold me. I'd never been held much by anyone. Never, as a kid. But he was lonely, too. He missed our mother till the day he died. 'I've had the best,' he'd say. 'There's no one better. No one half as good.' He spoiled me for others, see. 'Cause none was half as good as Dad."

"But you never . . . ?"

"I know the truth. And it wasn't ugly."

Idella paused. Then, "Thank you," she said. "For telling me that."

"I never did thank you for writing me them letters. In the 'hotel.'"

"You're welcome. I worried so about you. That never occurred to you? That someone might worry about you?"

"Can't say that it did."

"I figured. By the way—you never did say—how was the service in the 'hotel'?"

"Captivating," Avis said, and they both laughed. After that they just sat, a few flakes still falling, Avis smoking, Idella waving away the smoke. Idella was very still. Avis looked over at her, but she put a hand up for silence.

"Ssssshhh! I hear it." She began to hum. Then she began to sing, a little, very soft, "'Hush-a-bye, don't you cry, go to sleepy, little baby. . . .'"

"What the hell is wrong with you?" Avis said.

"It's that song. There was one particular song Mother would sing."

"Do you remember her voice?"

Idella closed her eyes. "I don't know. I hear a certain voice at times, in my head, that might be hers. She'd sit on the porch and sing to Dad."

"Do it again," Avis said.

She did, very delicately, and the song seemed to float in the air between them. "That's it," Idella said.

"Imagine that."

"I have," Idella said. "Many times." Then after a while, "The smoke is getting to me, Avis. I'll go see what Edwardo is up to."

"I'll finish my cigarette, and then we roll, Idella."

"Ten four. Over and out." And she went back inside.

Well, Avis thought, here's the way it is. I'm not dead yet—like some of these birds around here. What puny bits of life I've got left, I want in my trailer. I want to live alone till I'm ready and then die in my trailer—listening to the squirrels skittering over the roof. Dear God, don't let me come to a place like this. Let me die on the threshold. All them people that used to have lives. They sit and wait for the next meal or pill or piss or blood-pressure check. Sit there rotting and peeing at the same time by the smell of things. No. No thank you.

She went back inside and said, "Get your mink on, Idella. Time to roll. I want to get home before this snow gets any worse."

"Time to go?" Edward asked.

"Yes," Idella said. "Have some supper."

"You gonna make lobster stew?"

She began gathering her things. "Oh, no. Grilled cheese, prob'ly."

"I want lobster stew!" He put his hands on the arm of the chair, as though to stand. "Christ! I can't get up!"

"Oh, Eddie," she said, "you have to stay." Avis was already over by the door.

"What the hell's wrong with this chair!" he yelled. "Jesus H. Christ! Help me, Idella!"

"I can't, Eddie. I can't. You can't go home. You can't walk! The doctor says you have to stay here. Eddie, I can't bring you home, I just can't!"

And that time he heard her. He stopped struggling and just sat there staring at her for the longest time. She thought he was going to cry. But then Avis called out, "Eddie, look!"

She'd gone to the blackboard, taken the chalk, and changed the month to "April" and the weather to "Rain." Eddie saw her and smiled. Then she put a finger to her mouth, and Eddie smiled and nodded.

Idella went up to him and took his hand. "Well," she said, "me and Avis are going to get on home now."

"Be back tomorrow?"

"I don't know if I can," she said. "I'll call. Bye-bye, now. You be good."

He looked up at her. "You're my girl, Idella."

"I know that," she said. "Bye-bye." She gave him a kiss on the cheek and patted his hand.

And just then it started to thunder, a little rumble in the distance. "Well, I'll be," Idella said. "An April shower! Avis, how did you know?"

"Me and God are in constant communication."

"Put in a good word for me."

"I always do," Avis said. "Now, let's get the hell out of here."

April 1987

When Idella got to the home, Eddie was sitting with that bell in his lap, the one from the wooden car. She heard him say to himself, "Five dollars," and "Them crooks." Then he saw her, reached up, and said, "That Avis bring you?"

"Agnes Knight dropped me off. She's picking me up in an hour." She took off her coat.

"Avis too good to drive you?"

"Avis is gone, Eddie."

"Gone? Where the hell did she have to go?"

"Gone. For good. I told you. She died two months ago. You don't remember, do you?"

"She's dead?" he said.

"Yes." And she began to tell the story again. "She had an accident. She pulled out in front of a big truck. There were two trucks, see, and she waited for the first one. She didn't know there were two."

"Killed her?"

"Not right off. Not directly."

"Holy Christ."

She told him again, knowing that he didn't remember, that his mind couldn't hold things now. "She didn't seem all that hurt. One of her neighbors out that way was in the car behind. To hear him tell it, when the ambulance came and they tried to put her into it, she had some kind of fit. She wouldn't let them. She said it was all closed up in there and she couldn't breathe, and they were afraid she would hurt herself more. She was some kind of wild. So the neighbor took her in his car. He laid her out in the back. She insisted on having the cold air blow on her. He opened all the windows and drove her to the Osteopathic."

"What about the car?" Eddie said.

"Oh, it was totaled. Anyway, she had a broken rib. They released her after a day with all this medication. I think she got the pills all balled up. But she insisted on going home to her trailer. She was like Dad after he got shot—get me out of here, you know? Stan took her home, and the next morning he come to take her out to breakfast, as a treat. He found her curled up on her side like she was sleeping. There were fresh corn muffins on the counter. She must have set them to cool and gone to bed.

"I am still in shock, Eddie. It hasn't hit me yet. I keep seeing her there in her coffin, in her blue pantsuit. Something about her head wasn't right. A funny angle—too high. She didn't look comfortable."

"I sold her that car," Eddie said. "I could sell me a few cars here. That nurse, Claire, I'd give her a good deal. She gets me Pringles. I keep them in the drawer to hide them from my goddamn crazy roommate. He poured my Pringles all over his bed. Broke 'em, so they don't stack. The goddamned fool tried to get in bed with me. He pulls off the covers and puts his hand on my leg. Then he sits down next to me and says, 'Move over, Martha.' Thought I was his dead wife, crazy bastard."

"Here," she said, "let me get your hair combed. They don't pay attention here." She got out her comb and started in.

"You're like my mother, always fussing."

"Oh—go on! Your mother never waited on you hand and foot like I've done all these years. She wanted people to wait on *her*! I was among them! Now, give me your hand."

"You want to hold my hand?"

"No, I want to clip them nails. Put your hand flat here so I can get at it. You been biting your nails?"

"Gotta eat something," he said, laughing at his joke. "Say, you bring me anything?"

"Well, yes. Pringles. Of course, you need them like a hole in the head."

"How many you bring?"

"Two—plain and sour cream. They'll keep you busy for a while." She put the cans on his lap. He tried to open one but couldn't find the pull tab.

"Let me open it."

"You want one, Idella?"

"I haven't been too hungry."

She still couldn't absorb that Avis was gone. Avis wasn't an important person in this world. None of us is, Idella thought, but her being gone is a great loss, hard as she was. Things happened when Avis was around. She stirred the pudding up good for all of them.

Of course, Avis and Eddie never got along. Idella knew he probably made a pass at her, years back. Avis would allude to it. If Eddie got just one drink in him, he could be a fool. Idella herself might get foolish, have a good time, but Eddie got . . . well, she couldn't hire someone to work in the store that was too pretty or too young.

And yet he was so prudish about his own daughters. It's a wonder Barbara got married at all, or even managed to have boyfriends, the way he'd carry on. Staying up waiting for her, looking out the window, following her in his car, following her to the movies, even. Going right into the movie theater where the poor kids were trying to watch the show and charging up and down the aisles like a bull. That was so funny that one time. Barbara snuck up the other aisle and came home. Then he came home hollering, and she was upstairs in her bed, giggling, no doubt. To this day he didn't know the truth of it.

Idella was suddenly aware that the sound of Eddie munching Pringles had stopped. He'd dropped off again—all the pills he took. She sat looking at him, her Eddie. She thought of the other women, real girlfriends. She knew—she'd find little signs, things that got left behind in a pocket or in the car. Once she found her own wet bathing suit in the glove compartment. There was the one—Iris. She found letters from her. To this day she kept them in her top bureau drawer.

Iris lasted for years. All those nights he said he was working late at the showroom, coming home so late, and there she'd be, standing at the stove cooking his supper at nine and ten at night, and she never knew if he was really at the showroom or not. Some of each, she supposed. What could she do? They had the kids. The store. The house. Where would she go? She thought he'd outgrow it. Then she learned to live with it, as best she could.

But that Iris. That was hard. She'd give him things. He'd come home with shirts, and Idella knew where they came from. And she'd be expected to stand there and iron them. Well, one day she refused. She took all those shirts—one was spread out on the ironing board half done, for God's sake—and she rolled them into a ball and threw them at him. "They make me sick!" she said. "I'm damned if I'm going to stand here ironing them. I'll be damned!"

"I'm leaving, Idella," he started yelling. "I'm leaving!"

"Go on," she said. "Where you going? To Iris? You going to go have a better life with Iris? I know, see. I know all about it. I have the little cards she sends you and you leave in your pockets. You damn fool. Who the hell does all the washing and ironing? Who has to go through your pockets and find everything? Signed 'me' in little letters at the bottom. That's all—'m-e.' That bitch."

And then it came out. She'd kept it from the kids. She'd kept it from everyone. But one night all hell broke loose. Paulette—she was a teenager, and she was out on a date. It might even have been with Buzz. His first sight of his future father-in-law, that would have been. Typical. Well, Paulette and Buzz went out to the airport. People did then—Idella was no fool. They went out there, and they kissed and watched the planes. So they pulled in to a parking space, and Paulette looked over, and who was in the car right beside them but Eddie! With Iris.

Well, the cat was out of the bag then. Paulette came tearing into the house, so upset. And he came tearing in behind her. What an uproar! And he tried to deny! He tried to holler at *her* for being there! What a time! She told Paulette then, told her all about it. She wasn't going to protect him if he was going to be such a damn fool. She didn't have the strength.

So she made the best of it, went over to the store every day and raised the kids. And they had their life together. It wasn't all bad. And he came home every night. He always came home. But it was in her somewhere, the knowing. A certain sadness, always there.

The part that Avis could never understand was that she loved him. She did. She was his girl. That's what he used to say, "You're my girl." He was no prince, God knows. He'd drive any person crazy. But he wasn't scary—not like Dad.

When they first met, when they were young, well . . . they were in love. She didn't think it was possible for someone to fall in love with the likes of her. Skinny old Idella. It was Avis the men went for, with her figure and thick hair and sassy ways. Men about dropped down in front of her—and she'd step right over them and move on to the next. But when Idella found Eddie . . . well, that was all she wanted. He was very attentive then. He couldn't get enough of her. Big blue eyes and dark hair and that smile. She was quick to marry him, warts and all. Those came popping out later.

And they'd been through so much. Over fifty years. And he worked hard, all those years selling cars. And he didn't drink—not like she was used to. Avis hated him from day one. And she loved him.

When Idella looked up, Eddie was still asleep. She tried to wake him, but he was too far gone. She hated for him to miss her visit by sleeping. He got himself wheeled in hours before she could ever get there. That broke her heart. Claire told her. She was nice to Edward. He liked to be teased about his blue eyes. It made him feel like some part of him was still attractive.

She guessed eyes don't lose their color. Seemed like we lose so many things. It all gets taken away, fades away. She was surprised eyes keep hold of their color.

She heard two beeps—Agnes Knight come to pick her up. She thought she'd write something on that board for him to see. So she wrote, "Idella was here." That way he'd remember she'd come. Poor dear, she thought. I'm lucky. I can still go home and feed the birds, make my own cup of tea, fix a little dinner. I can still do for myself, as long as I don't do much. I'll be glad to get home and have a nice cup of tea.

July 1987

Eddie stirred in his chair.

Well, he thought, I guess I'll ring my bell. Claire give me this steering

wheel for my birthday. Goes with my bell, for my wheelchair here. No
gas pedal. Then there's this little car, my Cracker Jack prize. Idella left it
for me the day she died. Heart attack. Left it for me, then went home and
died.

Remember them bus trips we took, Idella? Maine Line Tours. Never
thought I'd want to go somewheres if I wasn't the driver. But them buses
had good drivers. We'd go up to the White Mountains or to Popham
Beach. You was always the last one back to the bus. "Here comes the ca-
boose," I'd say, "the end of the line." We went to nice restaurants on them
bus trips, whole busload of us. We'd get deals—all you can eat. Get your
money's worth, that's what I liked. Yokum's we'd go to a lot, down to
New Hampshire. Nice restaurant. And the Silent Woman up to Water-
ville. There's a name. The sign had a woman holding her head out in
front of her on a plate. "That's a good name," I said to Idella. I tried to
buy one of them signs in the gift shop, but she wouldn't let me. She
wanted me to be silent. She's silent now. . . . Christ . . . she's silent. But I
hear her in my head. All them years, listening, you keep hearing, like a
radio in there.

That chair there, that green one—she sat there. Her throne. Queen
Idella, she'd say. I fall asleep in this goddamned wheelchair. They drug me.
I used to wake up and look over there at that chair, and she'd be sitting in
it. She'd smile and wave to me. "I'm here, Eddie," she'd say, "I'm here."
Now when I wake up, I look over and I still see her. I talk to her. I tell her
I love her. I never said it, 'cause she was. Just was. Over fifty years.

I met her first at the Grange. They had dances out there. She was a
wallflower—shy, but pretty. Sitting in the corner with her hands on her
lap. She never knew I paid Raymond Tripp one dollar to ask her to dance
so I could cut in. I thought she'd like that, me cutting in. I arranged it,
see, made a deal.

Next time I seen her, I was selling whiskey out at Old Orchard. The
Prohibition. I'd come out on the pier to sell pints, and she was sitting
there with Avis. "Eddie Jensen," she says, "what a surprise!"

Well, we got rid of Avis. Avis was mad! I got Idella saltwater taffy. She
wanted to try it. We stood on the pier, waves coming down below. Made
me sick to my stomach, but Idella liked watching them come in under us.
Then we walked under the pier, in the shadows by the pilings. Idella
wasn't so shy there. We had ourselves some fun. Taffy kisses. We walked

along the water. I don't like getting my feet wet, but Idella was in past her knees, all wet and happy—pretty. We walked till we come to a place with no lights. Must've been Pine Point. The lights from Old Orchard was way down the beach. Like diamonds, she said. Like I give her all them diamonds to look at, them lights twinkling.

We sat in the dunes. It was nice. Real nice. Nice as it gets. Didn't need no whiskey that night. I had all I needed the whole time. That dollar to Raymond Tripp was the best deal I ever made.

ACKNOWLEDGMENTS

My deep thanks go to a number of writers and editors—true allies to Beverly and to me—who were devoted to bringing Beverly Jensen's work to the world after her death. Especially generous were Beverly's writing teacher, the novelist Jenifer Levin; the novelist Howard Frank Mosher; the editor and author Katrina Kenison; my old friend Larry Richman, founding editor of the Sow's Ear Press; Stephen Donadio, Carolyn Kuebler, and Joshua Tyree at the *New England Review;* Stephen King and Heidi Pitlor, who selected *2007 Best American Short Stories;* Michel Eckersley of Digital Design; our agent, Gail Hochman; Christopher Russell at Viking Penguin; and finally Carole DeSanti, our editor, who recognized this book's potential and guided it to publication.

Our children, Noah and Hannah, made many contributions big and small, and other friends played important roles: Sam Blackwell and Ara Watson, who encouraged Beverly to begin writing; Jennie Torres, Beverly's college roommate; Andrea Vasquez, Beverly's cousin and fellow writer; and above all Beverly's sisters, Barbara, Donna, and Paulette.

—*Jay Silverman*